~ Acclaim for Lori Whitwam ~

"Make or Break is a sexy, lyrical romance with a mystery that had me baffled. The love scenes left me panting. Wow!"

Amelia James, author of *Tell Me You Want Me*

"Seth and Abby make beautiful music together in this action-packed modern-day romance. Excellent debut novel!"

Eden Baylee, author of *Spring into Summer*

"Lori Whitwam knows how to grab you by the heart and then keep you sitting on the edge of your seat, right to the very end."

Marissa Farrar, author of the best-selling *Serenity* series

Make or Break

Lori Whitwam

etopia
press

Etopia Press
P.O. Box 66
Medford, OR 97501
http://www.etopia-press.net

MAKE OR BREAK

Edited by Annetta Ribken

Print ISBN: 978-1-937976-51-4
Digital ISBN: 978-1-936751-61-7

First Etopia Press electronic publication: September 2011

First Etopia Press print publication: July 2012

~ Dedication ~

To Virginia Lanier (October 28, 1930 – October 27, 2003), author
of the Bloodhound mystery series:

You were my friend, mentor, and inspiration. I'll never write as
well as you, but I promise to always try.

~ Acknowledgments ~

I wrote the first four chapters of Make or Break at least a half dozen times. Frustrated, I took a class through the Loft Literary Center, and the authors/instructors were Kathleen Eagle and Mary Bracho (who writes as Ana Seymour). Their talent, encouragement, and feedback finally got me on the right track. Thank you, ladies, for sharing your gifts with me, and many other aspiring writers!

My love of words is life-long and was nurtured by three exceptional teachers. Olive Watson, Mike Ferro, and Marilyn Wehrheim, thank you isn't nearly enough.

My deepest thanks to Brian Yost, who suggested Cujo (which is a real limited-edition Taylor guitar) when I needed a special instrument to sacrifice to bring Seth and Abby together. Rock on, B!

I had several wonderful, informative talks with Special Agent in Charge Bernard J. Zapor of the St. Paul Field Office of the Bureau of Alcohol, Tobacco, Firearms, and Explosives. He helped me gain a working understanding of explosives and the investigative process, and I owe him my thanks. Any errors regarding these topics are mine alone.

I had numerous pre-readers, whose feedback and encouragement were priceless. Molly Appeldoorn was my Number One Fan and Head Cheerleader, and without her I'm not certain I'd have completed the first draft. Kelli Johnson, one of the smartest and most focused women I've ever met, took on the role of chief editor of my first draft. Thanks, Kelli, and go Team Golden! Curt Rogers, Michael Grover, Jesse Gilleland, Todd Macy, Rachel Whitwam, and Jessica Levy were other stellar pre-readers. No, Jessica, I did not write Make or Break at work. I wrote the blog at work!

Further gratitude to Todd, who won my contest to compose the lyrics to the Make or Break song. He gave voice to Seth and Abby's song in a way I never could.

I'm fortunate to have the best editor in the universe, Annetta Ribken. She's one of the smartest, strongest, darkly hilarious women I know, and her talent (and occasional threats of bodily harm) kept the project moving forward, no matter how much I whined.

Saving the best for last, none of this would have happened without my wonderful husband, Tom. His love and support have been constant since we were seventeen-year-old high school sweethearts. After thirty years, we still out-rock the youngsters on our concert road trips. The bad times made us stronger, the good times made it even more worth it, and he somehow manages to tolerate life with a crazy writer who cleans and cooks even less when she's writing, though that would not seem possible. I love you, sweetie, always and always.

Chapter One

The blue Jeep Compass barreled down the forest-lined county highway, traveling considerably above the limits of both the law and common sense. Abby Delaney became aware of this fact when the right side wheels edged onto the gravel shoulder, narrowly missing an Adopt a Highway sign designating this stretch of road as the responsibility of the Emporia Elks Lodge. She realized becoming acquainted with the Jaws of Life simply because she was annoyed would do nothing to improve her day, and eased up on the gas pedal.

What the hell was Molly thinking, calling her this morning to back out of attending the concert with her *tonight*? Abby swallowed a grumble of annoyance. She understood when your friend's boyfriend surprised her with a weekend trip you weren't supposed to heap on the guilt, but Dead End Road was special. Since they rarely played this far north, she was lucky to see them once a year, and Molly's last minute change of plans left her with no time to find anyone else to go.

Abby's phone rang, and she pulled it from the console. She wasn't worried about the wisdom of talking and driving; she knew this road like the back of her hand. A glance at the display told her who was calling. "Hey, Monique. What's up?" She noticed she was drifting toward the shoulder again, and corrected the vehicle's course back into position in the eastbound lane.

"Are you on your way? The delivery guy just left." Abby heard the familiar jingle of the bells on the front door of Monique's vintage clothing shop, ReVamped, and imagined the delivery driver hadn't even made it back to his truck yet.

"I should be there in about ten minutes. Have you opened the box?"

"I'm about to. I bought it as a blind lot, but this vendor always has really good merchandise. I'm sure I'll find something in there you'll love."

Abby's toes curled just a little at the thought of getting her pick of a shipment from one of Monique's best sources. "I have the tickets, but are you sure you want to do this? I know how expensive Rosalie's stuff is."

Monique chuckled. "Oh, sweetie, I'm getting the best end of this deal. My baby sister's going to owe me big when I give her those tickets. I'm wringing my hands like a silent movie villain thinking how many hours of babysitting I'm going to get out of her!"

Abby wasn't sure it would be worth it, even to see Dead End Road. Monique's two preschoolers were utter terrors. "Maybe you should give Molly the goodies. After all, she's the reason I have two tickets for you to use to bribe Sophie into taking on the twins." Damn dumb-ass best friends with deplorable taste in men.

She heard Monique sigh, and cringed. She probably shouldn't have opened this particular can of worms.

"I know you don't like Craig, Abby, but at least Molly is out there living her life instead of letting it pass her by."

"Yeah, yeah, I know." Abby saw an approaching pickup truck, realized she might be a whisker or two over the center line, and Sammy Paulsen could be lurking with his radar gun in a break in the trees. True, he seldom gave her a speeding ticket, probably due to his longtime crush on her, but he'd be hard pressed to ignore a head-on collision. "Look, Mo, I didn't call to discuss my love life, or lack thereof. I'll see you in a few, OK?"

"Sure, honey. Now slow down and I'll see you soon."

"I'm not speeding. Much."

She could almost hear Monique rolling her eyes. "Yes, you are. Watch out for Sammy, and I'll go see what Rosalie sent."

Abby tossed the phone back into the console and concentrated on not breaking any more traffic laws.

Entering town, she was so distracted she barely took note of the 1920s-era brick storefronts or the concrete planters overflowing with pansies courtesy of the Pioneer Garden Club. She decided before she went to see Monique, she would drive by Dash's, the venue for the concert. Maybe she could get a glimpse of the band, and, if she were lucky, even Seth Caldwell, their lead singer and guitarist. But she had to hurry because Monique was expecting her.

On Buchanan Street, she spotted the tour bus parked on the left side in front of the club. She thought she could see figures moving around through the windshield and squinted, trying to determine who they might be.

Her attention focused on the bus, she suddenly caught something entering her frame of vision on the right. She only had an instant to register a man with familiar long, golden-brown hair stepping from in front of the equipment trailer she had failed to notice. An unformed expletive on her lips, she slammed on her brakes as he leaped back, narrowly escaping impact with her Jeep.

The guitar case he was carrying, however, was not so fortunate. Abby's fender caught it, ripping it from its owner's hand, and it disappeared under her right front wheel with a nauseating crunch. Stunned, Abby tried to pull to the curb behind the trailer, but after throwing the Jeep into reverse she realized the flaw in her logic. Nope, definitely not one of her smoother moves. The guitar case, once again victim to her right front tire, reappeared after another small bump and oddly lyrical grinding sound.

Holy shit. I just ran over Seth Caldwell's guitar. Twice.

Abby maneuvered the Jeep into the general vicinity of the curb and hopped out, too shocked to know whether to throw herself to the pavement in remorse or run for her life. On unsteady legs, she made her way to the scene of the crime. Seth crouched at the edge of the street, picking through the shattered remains of what had recently been an acoustic guitar.

She dropped to her knees beside him. His hair fell forward, blocking her view of his face, but he pushed it back and turned to look at her. His blue eyes might as well have been laser beams, the way they bored into her. Was it possible to be simultaneously thrilled and terrified? Apparently so.

"You killed it," Seth rasped. "You fucking killed my guitar."

There was no way she could argue. She'd never seen a deader guitar. "I'm so sorry! I was looking at the bus and didn't see you. I was irritated, and sort of distracted…"

"You were irritated? So you flew down the closest thing to a main street this town has, and ran over my 1997 Taylor Cujo, which I've had for not even three weeks?" Seth began scooping the remains of the instrument back into the mangled case, his gray T-shirt stretching across his shoulders with the effort. He somehow managed to maintain the full force of his glare the entire time.

Abby stretched out a hand to help, but Seth shifted his body to block her. "Don't. You've done enough," he snapped.

This did not strike Abby as a gracious acceptance of her apology. In fact, he was being kind of an ass. Her Irish temper began to kick in, which was something like the Hulk's, but without the green skin and purple pants. "Look, it was an accident, OK? And what the hell are you doing stepping out into traffic anyway?" She stood and scowled back at the angry musician.

"Traffic? What traffic? About three cars drove by in the last twenty minutes." Seth tried to close the lid on the case, failed, and shoved the whole thing toward the curb.

"Stop yelling at me!"

"I'm not yelling."

"You are definitely yelling." She caught a glimpse of something at his neck and did a double take. "Are those ear buds? You were listening to music? That's why you didn't hear me!" Her voice rose about three octaves.

"I could hear fine. And it doesn't have anything to do with your shitty driving." He ripped off the buds and stuffed them in his pocket. The angry lowering of his brows lessened the impact of his glare, but not by much.

Abby shook her head, walked to the open door of her Jeep and grabbed a business card from her purse. "Here. Get your guitar fixed..."

"Fixed? It's fucking mulch!"

"...or replaced, and send me the bill. And for the last time, stop yelling!"

"There are only a hundred and twenty-four of these guitars on the planet, and it took me six months to find this one. You think I can just replace it?" His voice, she noted, had a certain amount of anguish somewhere beneath the fury. Seth stood, and Abby tried not to flinch as he snatched the card from her hand.

"I said I was sorry. It was an accident. I'll pay for it or not. It's up to you. And now, I have to go."

"That's the first smart thing you've said so far. Out of my sight is a real good place to be right now," he spat.

Suppressing a shriek of frustration, Abby turned toward her Jeep and tossed back over her shoulder, "I can't believe I finally meet you, and we end up squatting in the gutter yelling at each other." She slammed the door and pulled away from the curb.

Her last glimpse of Seth as she headed down the block showed him standing by the equipment trailer, eyes wide, and a puzzled expression on his face.

Out of the Jeep again, the bell over the shop door announced her arrival as she stepped into the potpourri-scented jumble of ReVamped. The heels of her sandals echoed as she stomped across the worn plank floors. Monique appeared from the back of the shop, running her hands through her oak-brown curls. Her yellow blouse was partially untucked from her tie-dyed gauze skirt, and she was barefoot. Some people might have jumped to the conclusion her disheveled state indicated back room shenanigans, but Abby recognized it for what it was. Delivery day.

Monique's smile warmed her round face. "You got here fast. But I don't even need to unpack the rest of the shipment, because I picked out the perfect thing for you."

"I can't wait to see, but I need to get a grip first," Abby said, running a trembling hand over her mouth. Despite being only two years beyond Abby's own thirty-four, Monique had a mature, calm demeanor, which sometimes came in handy.

"You do look frazzled. Are you still mad at Molly?" Monique sorted through a basket of beaded handbags while Abby hauled herself up on a stool beside the counter.

"Well, yeah, but I just met Seth Caldwell."

"Seth Caldwell? From the concert tonight?"

Abby nodded.

"The one who makes you all drooly?"

"I do not get all drooly. But yes."

"Wow! Fantastic!"

"Not fantastic. Pretty much the opposite. I ran over his guitar." Abby shuddered at the recollection.

"Oh, no."

"Twice."

"You ran over his guitar twice?" Monique's eyebrows disappeared under the curly fringe of her bangs.

"Uh-huh. Forward. Backward. Crunch." Would she ever stop hearing the sound?

"You need tea." Monique turned from the basket to an electric kettle on a stand by the wall. She considered tea a cure for any sort of physical or emotional trauma.

"Only if you put a couple of shots of whiskey in it."

"No whiskey, but I can add some Rescue Remedy," offered Monique.

Abby doubted a holistic flower essence remedy would do much for her agitation, but she did remember one significant fact about it. "Comes in an alcohol base, right? Dump in the whole bottle. And the whiskey."

"Oh, hush. He obviously didn't beat you to death with the remains, so what's the problem?"

"He was kind of a jerk." And dammit, he wasn't supposed to be. But why did it even matter? She didn't know him, and would probably never see him again. She related the incident and subsequent snark fest, even though talking about it made a vein throb beside her right eye.

"Could've been worse, honey," Monique said as she attached a tiny cardboard price tag to a handbag with a bit of string. "Accidents happen, but nobody was hurt."

"I guess, but only because looks can't actually kill." Abby sighed. How could she explain that in one split second, every fantasy she'd had in the last five years had died a death as gruesome as the guitar's? Sure, it was only daydreaming, but knowing Seth's own fondest wish now probably involved her disappearing under the wheels of a very large truck took the spark right out of her imagination.

"Let it go, and stop being upset with Molly while you're at it," Monique advised. She poured hot water into a large blue mug, added a tea bag and a spoon, and slid it across the counter to Abby.

"Molly yelled at me, too. I'm not having a good day."

"What did you do?" Monique's skeptical squint and tone of voice reminded Abby of the time her friend's husband had shown up holding a dozen roses and a twisted steering wheel.

Abby thumped her spoon down on the counter. "Why do you assume I did something?"

"Did you?"

"Maybe," Abby admitted. "When she said she was backing out so she could go to Trail Point Lodge with Craig for the weekend, I might or might not have said something like 'I can't believe you're bailing on me to spend the weekend with that asshole.'"

Rolling her eyes, Monique placed the basket of handbags on a nearby table. "You see what the problem is, don't you?"

"Yeah. Craig's an asshole." Obviously.

"Beside the point. You know the filter, where you think things in your head, but you take out the inappropriate parts before they come out of your mouth?"

"Sure."

"Oh, honey, no you don't." The shop owner's brown curls swayed with the slow shake of her head.

"I don't? What are you talking about?" Abby sipped her tea, burned her lip, and set the mug on the counter, glaring at it.

"Yours is broken."

"Broken? That's the most ridiculous thing I've ever heard." She pushed the mug back toward Monique. Tea was obviously not the answer. Monique pulled up another stool and sat. Oh, great. It looked like this was going to become a Lifetime-movie conversation, and Abby wasn't sure she was up to it.

"I know you've had a rough time, but it's been almost six years," began Monique, and Abby's stomach fluttered. "It all locked you down somehow. You don't let anybody get close anymore. I know losing your dad was awful. And David was a total rat bastard. But you're still here, even if those two are both gone, one way or another." A note of pity crept into her friend's voice, and it made Abby want to bolt out the door, tickets and snazzy vintage clothing be damned.

She thought about the agony of watching pancreatic cancer steal her father a little at a time. And how David accused her of not loving him enough when she wouldn't move to Charlotte with him for his new job. The truth was she probably didn't love him enough, not then, because she no longer trusted him. If she hadn't been such a coward, she would have confronted him about his infidelity and the proof she knew was there.

Her suspicions were right. The divorce wasn't even final and her father not yet in the ground when Joyce D'Amico moved her slutty ass to Charlotte, straight into David's arms. It dawned on Abby then he'd been using the "follow me if you love me" ploy—knowing full well she couldn't leave—as a way to get out of a marriage that had become inconvenient.

But it was even worse than Monique knew. There were only a handful of people who knew the full scope of what she'd lost. And, for now, she planned to keep it that way.

"Mo, I've been really busy writing." David always belittled her aspirations. He never read any of her freelance magazine articles, and when she shared her plans to write mystery novels, he actually laughed. Since she was finally on her way to becoming successful, she felt she deserved the last laugh, but knew David wouldn't be impressed even if she achieved an international bestseller.

"Life's not only about books and deadlines," Monique said. "It's like you're hiding from us, and when you do come out, you're getting harder and harder to recognize."

"What are you talking about? I'm still me. Or I thought I was." She drew back and resisted an urge to march to the nearest mirror to see who looked back.

"You are, hon, mostly. But I think you've been living with your characters for so long you forget some of the stuff you say is out loud, and not just in your head or on the page. People are real, and life is real, too."

Abby didn't want to think about it, but she knew it was true. No, she didn't ask an awful lot of her friends beyond the occasional phone call or evening out, but she supposed she didn't offer very much to them, either. Not anymore.

Not wanting to see grief or recrimination in her friend's eyes, Abby refused to meet her gaze. She plucked a glittery gold handbag from the basket and played with the clasp. *Oh, great. I'm either a stark raving bitch or an antisocial nutjob. I feel tons better.*

When had she stopped participating in her own life? Could it have been six years already?

Abby returned the handbag to the basket with a sigh. "Damn. You're right, Monique. I needed that. I think." Plus, she needed to end this conversation. She was about done dealing with all this Dr. Phil shit for one day.

"Maybe, hon. Just think about it. Now, let's go in back and I'll show you what I found." Monique gathered the mugs and put them under the counter.

Abby knew whatever this miraculous article of clothing happened to be, it couldn't change her life. Only she could make a change. But there was a chance it could cheer her up. "Lead the way."

They made their way through the maze of boxes in the storeroom, until they arrived at a battered work table on which rested a lone cardboard box.

Monique's gaze was positively dancing as she reached inside. "There was a lot of gauze and patchwork stuff in here, but the second I saw this, I knew I couldn't possibly let anyone else have it." She lifted a crocheted halter top and held it out for Abby's inspection.

Drawing a deep breath, Abby reached for it. "Oh, Monique, it's gorgeous!"

"It's handmade, so there's no label, but I'm pretty sure the string is a silk-cotton blend. The lining is probably polyester and acetate."

Abby ran her fingers over the intricate, lacy crochet work. The lining was white, and the body of the halter was done in a pattern of green leaves and vines on a snowy background. The entire garment was liberally sprinkled with tiny, perfectly formed crocheted violets. She loved it. She held it up in front of herself and looked at her friend.

Monique squealed and held one hand to her chest. "I knew it! With your dark hair and fair skin, the white could wash you out, but the green does something for it. Plus it picks up the color in your eyes. I think it'll be a perfect fit, too."

"It seems like too much for a couple of concert tickets."

"Oh, hon, you don't know the whole story. Cory's decided he's afraid of the dark, and Matt thinks he's a brontosaurus. Both of them have discovered it's very hard to get them out from behind the couch, and they say they're too big for nap time. Sophie's going to have her hands full, and these tickets are going to buy me at least two nights down in the Cities sitting in a Jacuzzi." Her eyes sparkled at the prospect of toddler-free relaxation.

Abby laughed. "OK, then, we've got a deal." She rummaged in her oversize purse for the tickets and handed them over.

Monique tucked the tickets into the pocket of her skirt and gave it a pat. "So are you headed home?"

"I think so. I was going to drop off some signed copies of *Brightest Midnight* for Paige at the bookstore, but I forgot she's closed today. If I leave them with you, could you run them up there tomorrow?"

"Sure. But if you're heading home, make sure you take some lunch with you. I worry when you forget to eat."

"Mom stocked the minifridge in my office two days ago," Abby said. "She told me diet root beer and Marlboros didn't fit into any known food group, and I needed actual nutrition and fewer toxic chemicals." She had to admit the white cheddar cheese was pretty tasty, though.

Monique handed her a paper shopping bag for the halter top. Abby briefly considered changing out of her turquoise T-shirt in favor of her new acquisition. She decided against it and carefully placed her treasure in the bag. As they entered the front of the shop, she paused to admire a paisley silk blouse, and felt Monique touch her arm.

"Don't look now," Monique whispered, "but there is an extremely gorgeous man…" She aimed a quick glance over Abby's shoulder, "…wearing jeans and a gray T-shirt leaning on your Jeep and staring at the back of your head."

Abby dropped the sleeve of the blouse and sucked in her breath. Her stomach felt as if she'd swallowed a bucket full of hot rocks. "Oh, hell. What should I do? Can I sneak out through the storeroom?"

"No. No more running. What did we just talk about?" asked Monique. "You're going to go out there and see what he wants. After you introduce me, of course."

"No more hiding from the world. Right." She could do it, couldn't she? "But what if he wants to yell at me some more? Because if he yells, I'm either going to cry or smack him." Her gaze darted around the shop, evaluating potential weapons.

"Stop it. Let's go." Monique took a firm hold of Abby's elbow and steered her in the direction of the door. Abby extricated her arm and wiped her damp palms on her jeans as they stepped out onto the sidewalk.

Seth looked directly at her as the door swung shut behind her with a muffled jingle, and she gathered as much of her composure as possible. "Um…hi. This is my friend Monique, and she's going to get something out of the car and then go away. Right, Mo?"

"Yes, absolutely. Hi, Seth."

"Pleasure to meet you, Monique. Great jacket in the window." Abby thought his response was deceptively mild-mannered. But she wished he'd take his hands out of his pockets so she could be sure he wasn't clutching something sharp and potentially injury inducing.

Monique glanced at the well-worn leather motorcycle jacket Seth had complimented. "I have more from the same shipment if you'd like to stop in and take a look."

"I might do that." Abby noticed his eyes didn't look remotely laser-like at the moment. Maybe she wasn't about to be the victim of a guitar-related revenge killing after all.

"OK, Monique, books. And could you put this in back for me?" She handed her friend the shopping bag containing the halter top. Abby didn't miss Monique's appraisal of Seth's lean-muscled body, from the top of his head to the tips of his Van-clad toes, before she reached into the backseat. When she emerged with the books, Abby removed two from the box and stuck them in her purse before giving her friend a semidiscreet nudge toward the shop.

"I'm going, I'm going," Monique said, her voice pitched so low Abby could barely make out the words. "No running, but don't get carried away either." She gave Seth a wave as she went back inside.

Abby turned back to Seth and braced herself. "What do you want? I already told you I was sorry."

His eyes flared, and he straightened from where he'd been leaning against the back of the Jeep. "Save your breath. You could apologize from now till Christmas, and it wouldn't turn those splinters back into a guitar."

"Well, I don't think you're here to talk about the weather." She folded her arms across her chest. She was torn between stalking off to the Jeep, possibly running over his toes as she drove away, and arguing with him some more. Even arrogant jerks could be pleasant to look at.

He held the business card she'd given him earlier between his thumb and forefinger, as if it were somehow contaminated. "There's no address, just phone and e-mail. How am I supposed to send you anything?"

Arguing it is, then. She brought her palm to her forehead to signify sudden comprehension. "Oh, I get it now. I didn't realize you were dumb as a post. E-mail a bill? Call me and ask for the address? You certainly didn't have to track me down to make me feel worse than I already do." She was actually getting tired of looking at him now. Stalking away was imminent.

"E-mail and voice mail are easy to ignore." Nobody should look deliciously hot while scowling, but even that wasn't going to save him now. Abby felt her pressure valve hit the limit, promising explosion at any moment.

"What makes you think I was planning to ignore them? I already told you I'd cover the cost of replacing the damned guitar."

"I figured when you found out it cost four thousand dollars you might start feeling a lot less responsible."

Abby barely suppressed a growl. "Listen to me, Caldwell. I know enough about you to know the guitar wasn't some $39.95 Walmart special, so the price is no shock to me. However, you do not know me well enough to judge the extent of my feelings of personal responsibility." She was glad there were no pedestrians in the immediate area, because she was no longer using her indoor voice.

"So you're saying the cost wouldn't be a problem?" Abby couldn't decide if his single raised eyebrow made him look skeptical or condescending. It really didn't matter, because either one would piss her off.

"Would it be a problem? Do you mean, like, could I afford it? Holy shit, do you think just because I live in a small town I only shop at garage sales? Should I be pushing around a cart full of pop cans and broken umbrellas?"

"No, that's not what I thought at all. Jesus, you're a pain in the ass to talk to!" He cast his eyes skyward, as if hoping for divine intervention.

"I can't believe you just said that." Abby was so frustrated she was starting to sputter. What she wouldn't give for a broken umbrella right now. She had several ideas what she might do with it.

He swiped one hand across his face. "Will you stop talking, please?"

"Please?"

"Yes, please. I need a minute to try to stop this train wreck."

Abby made a show of pressing her lips together and tilting her head, indicating he should speak.

"Look, I'm seriously upset about the guitar..."

"Oh, really? I never would've guessed." Being quiet was going to require practice.

Seth let out a soft, exasperated-sounding groan.

"Fine." She would give him about ten seconds. Possibly.

"I'm really pissed I lost a guitar I spent six months hunting down, and I didn't expect you to actually understand what it meant to me. So, yeah, maybe I came here to twist the knife a little bit." Abby hoped the knife was just a figure of speech.

"So I guess you feel better now."

"As it turns out, I don't."

"And that's supposed to be my fault, too?" She decided trying to be quiet was no longer an option, despite the curious look from a woman biking by, towing a child in some sort of aerodynamic pod.

"No, and I get the whole thing was an accident. OK? I also realize you do have a clue about what it might mean to me, and you probably do feel bad about what happened." He paused and took a deep breath. "And I'm starting to think I'm only yelling at you because there isn't anybody else to take it out on."

"Oh? You think so?" Abby injected her words with as much sarcasm as humanly possible. It was a talent.

"Can we back up a little? I might've gone kind of insane there for a while." He scrubbed his hands across his face, as if trying to erase all the recent scowling and glowering.

"Maybe."

One corner of Seth's mouth twitched, the beginning of a smile. "Good. Let's go for a walk."

Chapter Two

Abby and Seth walked toward the park at the end of the block. Why was she going anywhere with someone who had insulted and browbeaten her twice in the space of an hour? She thought it must be because he finally started to sound like he might harbor an actual human being under all the guitar-grieving hostility.

She tried to convince her heart to stop pounding and her palms to stop sweating. To calm herself, she focused on the spring breeze and the sight of birds darting around in full nest-building mode. She breathed in the rich scent of fresh mulch in the sidewalk planters. Several of the shopkeepers were busy setting up their outdoor display tables. Emporia was a quaint little town, if you meant it in a complimentary way, which she did.

She kept sneaking looks at Seth, trying not to be too obvious. She'd seen him in person before, but never closer than from the foot of the stage. He looked different in the May sunshine, younger somehow, and she loved the way the sun brought out the gold glints in his light brown hair. It was longer than the last time she'd seen him, brushing his shoulders. She also detected a new tattoo peeking from beneath his right sleeve. But she definitely wasn't staring.

Seth cleared his throat. "Honestly, I'm not usually such a jerk, but it was a freakin' Taylor Cujo. From the Stephen King novel, you know? Did you see the amazing inlay on the neck?"

Abby stopped in her tracks. "This is you not being a jerk?"

Seth stopped, too, and to her surprise, he laughed. Damn. Who knew lurking beneath the razor stubble on those cheeks were actual dimples? Unfair.

"You're right, and I'm sorry, OK? It was an accident, it was insured, and I'm not going to send you a bill." They started walking again, and Abby's annoyance began to abate.

She considered what he said. Pursing her lips, she reluctantly admitted her own behavior hadn't exactly been above reproach. "I guess I probably let you push my buttons a little too much, too. Plus, I've recently been informed I lack a filter stopping me from saying things I should keep to myself."

"No, I had it coming." He paused for a moment as two chattering shoppers passed them. "I kept thinking about what you said, about how you finally met me and we ended up yelling at each other. It bothered me, and I felt like I should come find you and fix it. I guess I should've waited till I cooled down, though, because I made things worse. But I really wanted to talk to you again." His head dipped a fraction and he looked up at Abby, a startlingly vulnerable expression making her hesitate.

"Oh." Her equilibrium struggled to catch up with the sudden change of conversational direction. "Well…that's OK then." His voice wasn't what she'd expected, when he wasn't yelling at her. It sounded different from the way he bantered with the audience between songs, and even from interviews she'd heard. Softer, the smooth Texas drawl he'd picked up living in Austin for ten years more pronounced. And she liked it. A lot.

They arrived at the park and took a seat on a bench under dappled sunlight peeking between new leaves on the branches of a large oak tree arching overhead. They no sooner settled on the bench when Abby saw two girls lingering on the sidewalk. Wearing frayed jeans and skimpy tank tops, they had "groupie" written all over them. She didn't think much of the type, personally. All the squealing and jumping and "please sign my boobs" were more than a little nauseating. She assumed if you were on tour most of the year, being accosted every time you showed your face would get old awfully fast.

The girls stopped trying to look aloof and cool, and whispered furiously, heads together. The tall blonde one clutched the arm of her brunette friend. They seemed to have formulated their plan and advanced on the bench, a tiny tsunami of fangirl enthusiasm.

Seth saw them coming and whispered to Abby, "Hang on. I'll make this as quick as I can. Part of the job." He gave her an apologetic look and added, "Please don't leave, OK?"

Abby made shooing motions with her hands, sending him off to face his fans. She sat on the bench, watching the girls fawn all over Seth. He signed their shirts and posed for pictures, while the girls displayed their considerable feminine attributes for maximum effect.

True to his word, Seth wrapped things up quickly, and Abby heard them call, "See you at the show, Seth!" as they jiggled their way down the sidewalk. He made a visual sweep of the area, seemed to decide they were safe from further interruption, and returned to the bench.

"Doesn't it get tiresome?" Abby asked.

"Sometimes," Seth admitted. "But what success we have is from the people who come to hear us play, so it's worth it as long as they mind their manners."

He scooted a few inches closer to her, which Abby found quite interesting.

"Are you coming to the show tonight?" he asked.

"No, not this time. My friend backed out on me this morning, and I just gave the tickets to Monique for her sister.

Guess I'll go home and get back to work." The idea seemed much less appealing than it had an hour ago.

"Your card said you're a writer. Were those your books Monique was getting out of your Jeep?"

She nodded. "I promised the owner of the bookstore some more copies, but they're closed today. Mo is going to drop them off tomorrow."

"What kind of books are they?" His open, direct gaze was a little unnerving.

"It's a mystery series." It felt strange to be discussing her books with such a talented songwriter, but this day had been strange all around. "Well, it's not officially a series yet. The first book came out last year, and the second will be released in July. The third one is due to the publisher by October."

"Great. It's a special feeling to create something and know other people enjoy it."

"I guess you know all about it. It's the first thing I noticed about the band, the lyrics to your songs. Once I saw a live show, though, I was hooked." Probably best not to mention a large part of the appeal was Seth himself. She didn't want to boost his ego when she was still getting over his obnoxious behavior. It wasn't like she couldn't understand why he was upset. She just didn't want to let him off the hook too soon.

"None of what we do onstage means anything if I can't write music with meaning," Seth said. "It always makes me feel good to know it matters to other people, too."

Now that sounded like the Seth Caldwell she'd expected. Abby finally felt like they were having a conversation. "It's everything. I don't waste time on performers who don't write their own stuff. I know it's not exactly the same as plagiarism is for authors. But it feels the same to me somehow, recording music you didn't help create." Was she rambling? She didn't care. She was talking to Seth Caldwell about writing. Plus, he wasn't scary or annoying anymore, and she could look at him without wanting to kick him.

"I feel the same way." Seth tucked a stray strand of hair behind one ear. "Which is why we never buy songs. If we record something we didn't write, it comes from a friend of ours. Paying for music feels too much like paying for sex...I imagine." He quirked an eyebrow at the risqué analogy, and Abby laughed. He was clearly playing with her, which beat the hell out of wanting to strangle her.

"I never thought of it like that," she said. "But I see your point. It's the easy way, for somebody who can't or won't create something themselves."

"Exactly." Seth casually draped his arm across the back of the bench, not quite touching her shoulders. "So, tell me about your books."

"Oh, they're just mysteries," she answered. She never knew how to respond to that particular question without boring people or sounding as if she were bragging.

He turned toward her and leaned in close. "Don't say that. I'm sure they're not 'just' anything. Whatever they are, you spent a long time working on them, creating a whole world and the people in it. Your readers must enjoy them or you wouldn't be working on your third one, right?"

"I know, I know." She fought the temptation to reach out and touch his face, which was so much closer to her than before. "But here I am, talking to you, being kind of an idiot, and all I can think is you can't really be interested."

Now it was Seth's turn to laugh. "*You're* being an idiot? Sorry, I didn't notice, because I was too busy being one myself, as you pointed out."

Abby gave her head a little shake. "Should one of us say 'takes one to know one' and get it over with?"

"There you go! And I am interested. Books, poems, songs, art, any kind of creativity is what makes us who we are."

Abby took a moment to absorb his last statement. "Well, like I said, they're mysteries. The main character trains service dogs in a town sort of like this one. People seem to have a tendency to turn up dead, quite unlike here. The dogs are a key part of the story because she's so tuned into their behavior and reactions. Dogs always notice things people overlook."

Seth nodded. "I'm going to have to stop by the bookstore and get a copy. I read a lot of mysteries, and I love dogs."

"Maybe I can save you a trip." She reached into her bag and withdrew a midnight blue book. "If you're sure you really want one, and weren't just being polite."

"No, I'd love it, under one condition."

"OK, shoot." She wouldn't have used the expression a half hour ago.

"Sign it for me."

Abby's hand shook slightly as she found a pen and wondered what to write when signing a book to a guy about whom she'd had countless steamy fantasies and whose guitar she'd recently reduced to kindling. There probably wasn't much of a precedent. After a moment she wrote, "To Seth, who totally made my day. Don't ever pay for it. Abby Delaney. PS Thanks for not killing me about the guitar."

Seth smiled at the inscription, and she watched him study her photo on the back cover for a few moments before setting it on the bench beside him. "So, Abby Delaney, can I convince you to come to the show tonight?" Abby froze, and almost sustained a concussion from the mental whiplash. Oh, she wanted to go, but it was most likely a spectacularly bad idea. Should she try to get out of this gracefully?

"It's probably too late. Dash sold the place out weeks ago, and I just gave my ticket away." Which, right now, she could kick herself for doing. She might have to murder Molly after all. But then again, if Molly hadn't dumped her, she would never have run over Seth's guitar. Wait. Would it be a good thing or a bad thing? She wondered if her brain was swelling.

Seth interrupted her jumbled thoughts. "Don't forget who you're talking to. It's my band. I'd like you to come as my guest."

Abby's heart skipped a beat. His guest? But wasn't it what she wanted? She'd have to talk to Monique. This "participating in your life again" was exciting, but also seriously scary. At exactly what point did it become "getting carried away"? She probably should have asked for specifics. Not to mention the Universe was not being subtle. She tried to appear more confident than she felt. "One of the perks of being self-employed—as long as I don't blow off my deadlines by too much, I can rearrange my schedule."

Seth grinned. There were those damned, adorable dimples again.

"Great," he said. "How about if you meet me at the bus around seven thirty? We usually hang out there before the show." Hang out with Seth and the band? And *Seth*? On the bus? *With Seth*?

When she spoke, she suspected her voice might be slightly too loud, but it was hard to tell over the roaring noise of all the blood rushing out of her head. "Sounds good. I'd better get moving so I can take care of some things at home." Like find her favorite jeans, see if she still owned any makeup, and call Monique.

They stood, and Seth reached for her hand and stepped closer, until Abby could feel his heat through their shirts. At five six and wearing three-inch heels, she only had to look up an inch or two to meet his eyes. She repressed an urge to place her other hand on the tempting plane of his chest to feel his heartbeat.

He said softly, "Don't forget to come back."

Giving his hand a gentle squeeze, she said simply, "I won't."

He didn't let go. "You said you'd been to some of our shows before?"

"Yeah, I have."

"Why didn't you ever come talk to me? I mean, I'm not pulling an ego thing here, but you said you wanted to."

She swallowed, her throat suddenly dry. "Because I didn't want to be one of those girls."

Seth looked at her a second. "I don't think you ever could be."

* * *

Seth watched Abby walk down the sidewalk, unable to tear his eyes away until she slammed the door of the Jeep. Sure, he appreciated the view, but this woman was a puzzle, and an intriguing one. She had gone from ditzy driver to morally outraged spitfire in the blink of an eye, then managed to work in smart, sensitive, and vulnerable on top of it. He wondered how many more facets of her personality remained to be discovered. Shaking his head, he ducked into the bus to put her book with his things. He dragged the guitar case and its contents from under the trailer where he had stashed it earlier. In some sick way, it was like carrying the grisly remains of a beloved pet from the roadside, only with no blood and way more splinters.

Seth stepped into the cool darkness of the backstage hallway and made his way to their staging room, placing his precious cargo on the battered table. He wondered what he was supposed to do with it. This morning it had been a beautiful, expensive classic guitar. Now it was roadkill.

"Whoa! What the hell happened, man?"

Seth looked up from his somber contemplation to see Marshall Rogerson, his rhythm guitarist, standing in the doorway.

"Traffic fatality," Seth said, looking at Cujo and wishing he didn't have to have this conversation.

Marshall approached the table with the reverence of a fellow guitar lover. He removed his backward-facing baseball cap from his shaved head in a show of respect, sincere rather than sarcastic. Replacing the hat, he sat at the table and rested his dark-goateed chin on his fist. "So, in what creative ways are we going to torture the asshole who did this?"

Seth leaned against the door frame. "It was an accident. But she did give me hell when I lost it and yelled at her." He found he was rather impressed, and his blood began to warm at the thought of seeing her again in a few hours.

"A chick did this? Looks like she used an ax."

"Jeep."

"Shit."

"Yeah."

Marshall reached into a cooler beside the table and located a beer, paying no attention to the icy condensation dripping onto his sleeveless red T-shirt. He twisted off the cap and took a deep swallow, followed by something that might have been a belch or a sigh. "Still, man, major crime. Cujo was sweet. What're you gonna do about it?"

"Nothing. I invited her to the show tonight." Seth knew what was coming, and braced himself.

"No fuckin' way! Really?" Marshall's dark eyes widened in surprise, but this was soon replaced with his I'm-totally-going-to-mess-with-you expression. "Oh, wait. I get it now. This chick is seriously hot, isn't she?"

"If you like the type."

"And that type would be...?"

"Gorgeous, smart, feisty, a whole mess of long, dark hair... Shit, I don't know. I just met her." This was not the sort of conversation he could have with Marshall, who had long held the undisputed title of biggest hound in the band. Joey Garvin, their drummer, and Pete Carroll, their bass player, were both married. Maybe they'd understand his confusion, but Marshall wouldn't.

"Marsh, I can't talk about it, OK?" Seth knew he was interrupting his buddy's fun before he got to his best material, but he wasn't in the mood. "Don't we have things we need to do? And can you have somebody take care of that?" He pointed to the wreckage on the table, unable to bear the thought of consigning the remains to a trash bin himself.

"Yeah, sure, it's cool." Marshall rose and started toward the door with one last look back over his shoulder at Cujo. "Mouse has the soundboard set, but I think Danny needs you onstage."

Seth never had to worry about their sound setup. Mouse Thibaudeau was the best in the business. "I bet Danny has the lights pretty close to done. He's picked everything up way faster than I expected." They headed across the hall and toward the rear entrance to the stage.

"Yeah, and Andy's the best all-around hand we've had in a while. Always seems to know what I need before I do. Kinda spooky sometimes. Usually at this point I still have to kick ass on a regular basis."

"Pretty sharp kids." Kids? Did he just call two members of his crew, who were in their midtwenties "kids"?

Seth stepped onto the stage and accepted his guitar from Roberto Acevedo, their seasoned guitar technician. Marshall's assessment of the setup was accurate. Mouse was making some adjustments to the soundboard with Andy Hicks, who was in the early stages of learning this important skill. Danny adjusted the lights overhead, his wiry frame scrambling among the supports like an escaped lab monkey. Joey and Pete sat on the edge of the stage. It sounded like they were finalizing plans for some time in Gulf Shores, Alabama with their wives during the break before they all headed back to the practice studio.

Seth looked up, cupped his hands to his mouth, and called, "Hey, Dawkins! What do you need?"

Perched behind a bank of small spotlights, Danny replied, "Not much. But if you can get behind the mike for a minute, then right up at the edge of the stage, I'll make a few adjustments."

Seth complied, moving from place to place as Danny fine-tuned the positions of the spotlights. The tasks were exacting, but routine, and Seth had trouble keeping his mind on the job. It had been a hell of a day. More than once he looked at the guitars waiting on their stands, and remembered Cujo had gone to the great music store in the sky. Which reminded him of Abby and invited a whole new level of distraction.

An authoritative voice finally called a halt. "OK, guys, stop screwing around. Everything's fine. Head back to the bus, get something to eat, and rest up. Gonna be a busy night."

"Yeah, yeah, don't get your jimmies in a jingle," quipped Marshall.

Trent Singleton lifted his chin and took a half step toward the smart-mouthed guitarist, but Seth grabbed his friend and gave him a shove toward the door. "Dude, you know better. Trent can pound you into a puddle. Never question The Man," he said, grinning back over his shoulder at the burly road manager. With the show preparation behind him, Seth's thoughts immediately returned to Abby. He regretted how things had started this afternoon, and wouldn't blame her if she didn't come back for the show. What if she changed her mind? And why did it matter to him so goddamned much?

Back on the bus, they tore into the takeout Andy brought from a nearby deli, and coolers were ransacked in search of favorite drinks. Bags rustled, ice cubes clinked into glasses, and the smell of melted cheese and toasted bread drifted through the air. Seth listened to the light conversation around him but didn't participate. Should he dig out her business card and call Abby? No, he decided. He didn't want to be pushy. Or a loser.

Danny stopped on his way to the cooler. "Hey, Seth, I wanted to tell you I took care of Cujo for you…"

Seth cut him off. "I appreciate it, Danny, but I can't talk about it right now, OK?"

"Sure, man, I understand. I wouldn't want to talk about it either." He gave Seth a nudge in the shoulder, and went to dredge a Mountain Dew from the overloaded cooler.

To pass some time and avoid any more conversation about Cujo, Seth retreated to his bunk and fished Abby's book out of his duffel bag. He looked at her picture and smiled again at the inscription before settling down to read. By the time he finished the first chapter, he was impressed. She had a snappy, clever writing style and strong characters. He found himself very curious about what would happen to Jill and her dogs, and he allowed himself a few minutes to reflect on the woman who had crafted the story.

Seth pulled out his cell phone and checked the time. Again. He didn't want to be sacked out when Abby arrived, so he made his way out to the main lounge area and took a seat, the fingers of one hand tapping restlessly on the arm of the couch.

Pete emerged from the bus's tiny bathroom, vigorously applying a towel to his short, sandy hair. "Yo, Seth, you need a drink?" He tossed the towel on the counter and took two beers from the cooler.

"Yeah, sure."

"Or maybe you want me to get your bottle of JD?" Pete's eyes took on a mischievous shine.

"Think I'm still off the bourbon, bro."

"Getting old, huh?" Pete handed Seth the beer and dropped onto the couch beside him. "Never thought I'd see the day a couple of drinks put you under the table."

"It wasn't the Jack, man. I was just tired or coming down with something, that's all." Though he kept his words light, the incident disturbed him. He downed most of his beer in several deep swallows. Two nights ago, in Cincinnati, he had a couple of Jack and Cokes after the show. He stepped out to do a quick interview with a reporter from a local college radio station, and by the end of the interview he felt like he'd had the whole bottle instead of two drinks. There was something seriously off about the whole thing.

"Well, 'coming down with something' looked exactly like 'shitfaced' to me," teased Pete. "You were slurring and couldn't have walked a straight line to save your life. You're never the first one down for the count."

"He ain't lyin', Seth," added Marshall. "I had to tuck you in and thought I was gonna have to call your mama."

"Y'all are real fuckin' funny. Now shut up and toss me another beer." Seth pitched his empty bottle, aimed to narrowly miss Marshall's head, and the tall man caught it effortlessly. "It was something besides the booze, because the day two shots make me throw up stuff I ate in high school is the day I get on the wagon for good."

Marshall delivered a fresh beer. "I'm just glad we were staying at the hotel, because I purely hate it when somebody pukes in the bus."

"Can't argue with that," Seth conceded. He would've liked to say more to defend his so-called reputation, but he honestly couldn't remember much more about the night. Maybe it was something he ate. Whatever it was, it had put him down hard. It took him the whole next day to feel somewhat human, and he didn't think he'd given his best performance last night in Chicago.

Pete went back to his bunk, and Marshall nagged Mouse about some feedback from one of the speakers. Mouse told him, in no uncertain terms, the problem was his own ears and not the speakers. Seth ignored them and looked out the window and across the parking lot. How long would it be until Abby arrived?

If she showed up at all. His mental solitude was interrupted when someone perched on the arm of the couch.

"Marsh told us about Cujo, man." Joey's voice was pitched low. "Said you didn't want to talk about it, but if you need to talk without getting hassled, I won't jerk you around." Seth knew it was true. Joey Garvin might look like a slightly rough-around-the-edges cherub, but he was the smartest, and deep down, the toughest of the bunch. That, combined with his calm determination, saw them through the early days when they were playing for gas money.

"I know, Joey, and thanks. I'm trying not to think about it." He picked at the ring around the neck of the beer bottle. "I was still getting used to it, you know? Hadn't even gotten the tune just right yet."

"Sucks."

"Undoubtedly."

Sliding from the arm to the seat of the couch, Joey asked, "So, what's up with the girl?"

"Marsh told you about her, too, huh?"

"Yeah. He about broke his neck running to give me the news." The drummer's eyes crinkled with amusement. "But this girl, she's coming here?"

"Any minute now, I figure. I hope." Seth looked across the parking lot again, in case she'd arrived while he wasn't looking.

"You hope?" Joey's voice held a definite note of disbelief. "Excuse me for being totally fucking clueless, but this girl..."

"Her name's Abby," Seth said, his focus still on the parking lot.

"OK, Abby runs over your guitar, you yell at her, she yells back, then you kiss and make up and invite her to the show. This does not compute. I'd expect you to be waiting for your bail hearing, not making a date."

"Yeah, me, too." Seth looked into his friend's curious eyes. "It's just..." His voice trailed off. He had no idea what to say.

"Oh, no. Dude. I can't believe Marsh actually picked up on this. But this is monumental, because you don't do this. Ever. Not since things went balls-up with Stacy." Joey's expression shifted from curious to concerned, and Seth could see why.

What Joey said was true. He never dated women he met on the road, or he hadn't for the past year and a half. That's when he and Stacy Ballantyne had broken up. Or, to be more precise, when he caught her in bed with a crack pipe and the bass player from their opening act.

"Seriously, man, I don't know what's going on. Once I pulled my head out of my ass and stopped screaming about the guitar and really looked at her, and listened to her..." Seth launched his empty bottle toward the trash can and it fell in, rattling the bottles already there. As if jolted free by the sharp sound, a thought occurred to him. "OK, you know what it's like when we've been working on a piece for hours, trying to figure out what doesn't work? Then we find the exact beat or the perfect bridge to bring it all together?"

"Yeah, it's the best, man."

"And, you know how you can't see why we hadn't tried it hours ago, and you don't even remember how we used to play it, because this way makes perfect sense?" Why hadn't he thought to sort this out in musical terms before? It was usually how his brain worked best.

"Yeah, and now I don't know whether to be happy or worried." Joey slapped his palm onto Seth's shoulder.

Seth didn't think he liked the sound of that. "What're you talking about?"

"Because I've known you forever, I heard what you just said, and I'm pretty goddamned sure I know what it means. Man, your bad-boy, hard-partying days are officially over. You're hooked."

"No way." But, truthfully, "hard-partying" had checked out right around his thirtieth birthday. "Really? You think so? Me and Abby?" Why didn't the idea upset him nearly as much as he might have expected?

A red-haired Kewpie doll of a woman appeared beside them and smiled, a mischievous gleam in her eye. "So, did you talk to him, Joey? What's the story?"

Joey rose and put his arms around his petite wife, giving her a kiss on top of her head. "Yes, Caroline, I did, and you were one hundred percent right, as if there were ever any doubt."

"Did he use a music analogy?" she asked, lifting an eyebrow in Seth's direction.

"Yep."

Sitting beside Seth and throwing an arm around him, she said, "That's it then. When do we get to meet her?"

Seth sat there, stunned, until Joey hauled him to his feet and gave him a shove in the direction of the bunks. "Grab your shit and get ready. I'll yell if Abby shows up before you're done." Seth swore he felt his friend's smug grin follow him down the hall.

Seth changed clothes and made sure he had plenty of guitar picks in his pocket. The entire time he tried to sort through what Joey said. It couldn't be simple. Nothing ever was. Certainly not anything involving women.

He remembered the spark in Abby's eyes when she felt he was questioning her personal integrity. He thought about watching her walk back up the street after their time in the park. How would those long legs feel wrapped...? He shoved the thought straight back in the can. He'd think about the leg wrapping in great detail later, as well as the fact she fascinated him far too much for his own good, but now was not the time.

He came out of the bathroom and was stowing his gear under his bunk when Joey called, "Seth, hot chick approaching, two o'clock! Haul your ass up here."

Chapter Three

Abby's drive into town that evening was much less eventful than the one earlier in the day. There were no near collisions, and she didn't run over a single guitar.

She'd tried to quell her nervousness with a walk along the lakeshore in front of her house. This almost never failed to calm her, but her stomach was still full of butterflies.

She attempted to rally some confidence. At least she had the perfect thing to wear, thanks to Monique. With the crocheted-violet halter top, she wore dark boot-cut jeans and purple leather sandals. She had a jacket in the backseat in case it got chilly before the evening ended.

The bus had been moved off the street, and Abby parked nearby and walked toward it. She chastised herself for the way nervousness tightened her neck and shoulders.

The door to the bus swung open, and Abby breathed a sigh of relief as Seth came down the steps and walked toward her.

He looked different. He was in full concert mode now, which included the ever-present jeans, but his shirt was now a faded black, with the logo of an outdoor music festival on it. He'd added more jewelry, too, including a heavy-linked bracelet and some leather wristbands. There were several charms on cords or silver chains around his neck and small, heavy hoops in his pierced ears.

He looked fabulous, and she had a sudden uncharacteristic urge to lick his tattoos — not only the ones she had already seen on his arms, but any others he might have which were not visible to the general public.

"Hey," he said, his head slightly down, almost like a bashful schoolboy. "Glad you made it back."

"I said I would," she replied. "And it was nice of you to ask, considering."

"Well, let's go in and meet the guys. They're kind of obnoxious, but they won't bite. If they do, it's OK to bite 'em back."

Taking her arm, Seth escorted her on board the luxury bus. It took a moment for her eyes to adjust to the dim, recessed lighting, and she'd just become accustomed to the deep blue-and-gray cave-like atmosphere when Seth started the introductions. The band members she recognized, of course, and she waved at Joey where he sat perched on the counter of the kitchenette, his wife leaning against his knees. Pete and his wife sat at a small banquette, and some of the crew members emerged from a hallway leading past bunks to a rear seating area to say hello.

Abby was glad when the introductions were over. She hated being the center of attention. She always felt awkward in new situations, but managed to make some small talk without too much trouble. Since Monique broke the news about her malfunctioning brain filter, she found herself a little paranoid about what came out of her mouth. She felt less self-conscious when Seth guided her to one of the upholstered benches.

In response to her drink request, Abby received a gin and tonic, which tasted like it contained turpentine instead of actual gin. She must have made a face when she took her first sip, because Seth said, "Shit. I should've warned you to stick with something straight out of the bottle." He turned to Andy. "Hey, Hicks, she's barely in the door and you're trying to chase her off? Man, you suck as a bartender."

"It's the chance you take, unless you want to stop being a lazy ass and make it yourself." She thought with his lank, sandy hair and wide brown eyes, he looked barely old enough to drink and probably a poor choice for a bartender. He flashed an apologetic grin at Abby. "Don't worry. They get better after the first one."

"If I have any enamel left on my teeth when I finish this, I'll give it a try."

Seth snorted. "Don't believe him. It won't be any better, but your tongue will be numb, so you won't be able to tell."

As they sipped their drinks, Abby was intensely aware of Seth. Since taking her arm outside, he'd never fully released her. His hand had moved from her arm to her waist while he was introducing everybody. Now, as they sat side by side, his arm was across the back of the seat, his fingertips barely touching her right shoulder. While she certainly had no objections, it made her wonder. She didn't think it was exactly possessive behavior, so the only reason she could think of was uncertainty. Did he think she was going to get up and walk out? Or simply disappear? Was Seth Caldwell ever insecure? She didn't have enough information on which to base a hypothesis, so she forced the thought aside.

"Hey, Joey," Seth said. "What time are y'all taking off for the airport?"

"Soon as we're done here. Flight's at 7:00 a.m., which is totally brutal."

"But the sooner we go, the more time we have on the beach," Caroline reminded him. "And if I don't get some beach time, I will be forced to leave you for a mariachi in Puerto Vallarta."

"Don't make me forbid you to ever set foot in Mexico," Joey said, brandishing what Abby guessed was an imaginary sword.

Caroline laughed and gave him a swat on the butt. "Don't worry. I'll let you go home and set up the practice studio as soon as you're sufficiently relaxed and tan."

"Make sure you do," Seth said. "He needs the practice. If he doesn't nail the bit in 'Crimes and Misdemeanors,' his next trip to the beach will be as shark bait."

"That's harsh," Joey said, hanging his head in mock sorrow. "And mariachis know nothing about percussion. They're all about guitars and trumpets." He still had his hand pressed to his heart as he led Caroline toward the lounge in the rear of the bus.

Seth edged a bit closer. His thigh now pressed along the length of hers, and his hand rested more firmly on her shoulder, which tingled at his touch. Would it hold true wherever he touched her? She repressed a small shiver of anticipation.

"Hey, Seth, you ready for another beer?" called Pete. He and Marshall snorted and elbowed each other, indicating they found this innocent question utterly hilarious.

"Fuck you, man," said Seth. "I don't know what bit me the other night, but it sure as shit wasn't beer."

"If you say so, but I'd stay off the hard stuff tonight if I was you," said Marshall.

Abby quirked a questioning eyebrow at Seth.

"They're just being asshats," he replied with a shrug. "They think I had a drinking malfunction in Cincinnati the other night. Which I totally did not. There was something wrong, that's a fact, but I can't figure out what."

Heads turned as a giant of a man climbed aboard the bus. The man waited as Seth introduced him as Trent, their road manager, and gave a friendly nod before turning to face the group.

"OK, boys and girls, time to rock the house. Let's go." Everyone moved to comply, and Abby thought it would be a bad idea to disobey a guy who could probably bench-press a Buick.

Pete and his model-pretty wife, Jackie, were the last to leave, and he turned back to Seth. "Hey, man, you comin'? I figure you have a little more time, if you want it."

"Yeah, I'll be there in a minute."

"Sure, take your time. Don't do anything I wouldn't do." Pete winked and headed toward the club.

"Which eliminates absolutely nothing," Seth grumbled, but Abby was charmed by the easy, locker-room-style banter. They really were like brothers.

She felt her heart race at the thought of being alone with Seth. He now held her more firmly, his arm warm across her shoulders. She leaned into him, getting used to the sensation. Nice.

Something had been on her mind since their earlier conversation, and she decided to bring it up, even if it did sound like something people probably said to him all the time. "Do you remember when we were talking about your songs, and how they matter to people?"

"Sure."

His hand traced back and forth across her shoulder. This made it very difficult for her to concentrate, but she forged ahead. "There's one song that's always been my favorite."

"Really? Which one?"

"'Make or Break.' When I first heard it, I was really lost." She glanced up at him and saw he was paying close attention, despite the fact his hand was now skimming across her bare back. "I felt like I didn't have any direction or focus, and I couldn't write worth a damn. I considered giving it all up. Then I heard 'Make or Break,' and it felt like it was about me. It said to get past worrying about what anybody thought and do what I needed to do. I know it sounds cliché, but if it weren't for that song, I don't think any of my books would've ever been written."

Seth looked at her for a long moment after her admission, his hand still sliding across her back. Her skin came alive at his touch, and the back of her mind was whispering "more."

"That means a lot to me," Seth said softly. "It's where I was, too, when I wrote it. We'd been listening to too many 'executives' trying to change us. But we wouldn't have been us anymore, those guys from the wrong side of the tracks. We'd be another cheap copy, and I could never do that." He picked up his beer bottle and drained it. "I couldn't write for months. When I stopped trying to please other people instead of listening to what was coming from inside, it all came back, and we've been rolling ever since."

"My favorite part is the second verse. It was determined, sad, and defiant all at the same time. It was exactly how I felt." In her mind, she heard the echo of the lyrics.

Better stay true to your vision
Ignore how they tell you to roll
If you don't listen to your own voice
It's the hook that will rip out your soul

"Maybe I need to sit down and play it a few dozen times," Seth confessed, "because I've been stuck again. Maybe worse. I wonder if I've said all I have to say."

"That can't be true."

"I sure hope not. Can't play the same songs for the rest of my life, so I've gotta find it again."

Shifting to face her, Seth said, "I started your book."

"When did you have time to read?"

"I made time. I couldn't wait to see what it was like. You have an amazing style."

Abby searched his face. He seemed sincere, but she struggled with the reality of Seth reading something she wrote.

He took her hand and gave it a gentle squeeze. "What, don't you believe me?"

"Just a little overwhelmed."

"Don't be. It's really good. I already like Jill and her dog, and the director of the service dog group." He tilted his head and appeared to take a moment to form a thought. "I think writing a song is like building a room. And the finished album is a house. But writing a book seems more like building a whole city."

Abby found herself nodding. "Maybe. At least it's like building a small town. If you do it right."

"I'd say you do it right," Seth said. "You learn a lot about people when you read what they write. And I'm thinking I want to learn all about you." His voice had lowered to a husky, seductive rumble, and for a moment Abby didn't think there was enough air in the bus. Seth leaned toward her, one hand at her waist. The space between them pulsed, heavy with energy, like two powerful magnets whose polarity had not yet been determined. Would the force coalesce and push them away from each other...or would it be an attraction neither of them could resist?

Abby realized Seth was very near, very warm, and watching her intently. "Something's happening here, isn't it?" he murmured.

"I think so." Her head spun and her hormones cheered at the thought.

He raised his hand to cup her jaw. "Good. Like a first verse or a first chapter..." His voice trailed off and the space between them diminished. He paused, his face just inches from hers. His eyes asked the same questions she knew must be reflected in her own, and gave the same answers. At first, his lips barely touched hers, a mere promise of a kiss. It intensified, and her lips parted.

They were tentative at first, testing, seeking, before they found their ease.

He tasted of smoke and barley, and she felt as if her spine were dissolving at the base of her skull. The softness of his lips contrasted in the most sensual way with the rasp of razor stubble against her chin and the sensitive skin around her mouth. She lifted her hand to touch his hair, something she had dreamed of doing more times than she would ever admit. His thumb traced her lower lip, before he slowly drew back.

"I've never been less happy to leave this bus in my life," Seth said.

"The show must go on, as they say." Damned show.

"Well, 'they' wouldn't say it if they were here with you." His hands continued to skim up and down her body, and he peppered her neck with tiny, nerve-tingling kisses.

Abby knew she was becoming way more excited than was wise, but she allowed herself to savor his kisses for a few more minutes. She placed her hands on his chest and slowly eased herself back, even though she wanted nothing more than to stay exactly where she was. She glanced out the window and noticed the people who had been lingering on the sidewalk were gone. "We'd better go, but don't forget where we were."

"I couldn't forget, because I don't plan to stop thinking about it." The look in his fathomless blue eyes made Abby want to barricade the door and dare anybody to try to drag them out.

They stepped into the evening air, which felt improbably frigid without the warmth of Seth's embrace. A group of about a dozen fans waited near the stage door, and Abby stood off to one side while Seth signed autographs and posed for pictures.

She wasn't really listening to the pleasantries he exchanged with the fans or the buzz of voices from inside, but her ears perked up when she heard him begin to tell a story she'd read in several interviews. She couldn't imagine many of the fans hadn't already heard the story of how Dead End Road was named, but maybe they wanted to hear Seth tell it, just as she did.

"So, we were sixteen, right? Playin' fairs and rodeos and shit back home in Montana, because we were too young to play the bars. Too young to play 'em, but somebody always had a brother or a cousin who'd buy us a couple cases of beer." The fans nodded knowingly. "We were good at drinking, but really bad at not getting caught, and about the third time this one deputy nailed us, he decided we needed to have a talk. Gilbert, his name was, or Gilbertson, I forget now."

"Where were you that night?" asked a girl wearing short-shorts and cowboy boots. Abby recognized her as the tall blonde girl from the park. She was still wearing the autographed tank top. Her friend was also nearby, with a husband or boyfriend.

"Out behind the 4-H barn, after we played some dance. Anyway, Deputy Gilbert or Gilbertson was this tall, skinny guy, maybe in his fifties, and he was trying to be all wise. He goes, 'Boys, I know you think this is hot stuff right now, but you gotta grow up. You think you're gonna be big rock stars or something? Well, you ain't. You need to put your mind to school and finding real jobs, 'cause if you keep this up, you're just heading down a dead end road.'" Seth waited for the fans' chuckles and comments to die down. "And that was it. Right then we named ourselves Dead End Road to remind ourselves there were a lot of people who didn't believe we'd ever amount to anything. Every time we release a CD, I have my mom send him one."

His story complete, he collected Abby, one arm around her waist. She received a few curious looks and a couple of dirty ones, particularly from Blondie McTank-Top. Seth thanked the fans for coming to the show, and they slipped inside.

* * *

They made their way through the narrow, dimly lit hall leading to the backstage area, Abby's heels echoing on the ancient, abused hardwood. She suspected her face was still flushed from his kiss as Seth went to join the rest of the band to make a final check of the setup.

She heard heavy footsteps and looked up to see Dash Hendricks, the club's owner, lumbering in her direction. "Hey, Abby, good to see ya. Thinking about being a groupie?" The not-funny comment and the accompanying guffaw were Dash's idea of humor.

"Well, a girl likes to explore all her options before she's too old."

"Sugar, you ain't never too old. Just in a few more years you might be hangin' out here for Thursday night karaoke and followin' around the fella in the black sequined jacket, does all them Neil Diamond songs." Dash found this idea hilarious and wheezed himself halfway to an asthma attack, his gut undulating gelatinously over his saucer-sized pewter belt buckle.

"Guess I'd better start shopping for spandex pedal pushers, then, huh? Maybe zebra print?" Abby pretended to look for something in her purse, hoping to signal an end to this conversation.

"And you'd look right fine in them too, sugar." Dash patted her ass for emphasis.

Ew. Ew. Ewwww. She'd graduated from high school with his daughter. Thoroughly infested with both the heebies and the jeebies, she turned on her heel and hurried off in search of the restroom.

Moments later, she stood at a small mirror with its backing showing through at its chipped edges, touching up her lipstick in the barely adequate light. *Hmm. Wonder how that got so smudgy?* She smiled at the recollection. She turned at the sound of the door opening, and recognized Joey's wife, Caroline.

Abby wondered if someone could "perk" into a room, because Caroline was probably the perkiest person she'd ever encountered. "Good, I found you," the petite redhead said. "It's always crazy after the show, and I wanted to talk to you before we leave."

Abby remembered Pete, Joey, and their wives were heading out as soon as the concert ended to start a short vacation. "I ran in here to escape Dash's lecherous clutches," she said, grimacing.

"He's a piece of work, isn't he?"

"If there's such a thing as a north woods lounge lizard, he's it. If he touches me again, I swear we're going to find out exactly which body parts a lizard can grow back."

"He's an old friend of Joey's dad, which is why they always play here when they're up this way." Caroline took a brush from her handbag and fluffed her short hair.

"I figured there had to be some reason. This isn't exactly the Hard Rock."

"The guys like it up here. Except for the time Dash took them fishing. He never shut up, and they all had massive hangovers. Not pretty," she said with a knowing shake of her head.

Abby smiled, thinking that had definitely been one ill-fated excursion. "Why were you looking for me? Please don't ask about the guitar thing. I'm trying to pretend it never happened."

"We've been forbidden to mention Cujo. It's like in some cultures where they're not allowed to speak the names of the dead."

"It's dead all right."

"No, I wanted to talk to you about Seth."

"OK." Abby wondered where this was headed. Caroline seemed friendly enough, but Dead End Road was a close-knit bunch. Maybe she planned to warn her away. If that were the case, this conversation was guaranteed not to turn out well.

"Oh, no, you look worried! It's nothing bad, I promise. Well, it's bad, but not about him." Caroline tucked her brush into her purse, fidgeting with the straps. Returning her attention to Abby, she said, "Look, I know this is all going to sound weird coming from someone you just met, but I think it's important."

Abby's palms dampened as her anxiety spiked. What kind of information could follow an introduction like that? "OK, go ahead. I'm listening."

Caroline hoisted her tiny frame onto the narrow counter surrounding the sink. Apparently this wasn't the world's shortest story. "A while back, about a year and a half ago, I guess, Seth went through a really bad time."

"Bad how?" Abby asked.

"He'd been seeing this girl. Stacy Ballantyne. One afternoon she borrowed his phone and forgot to give it back. He noticed about an hour before the show, and went to find her." Her jaw was noticeably tighter as she continued. "He found her in bed with some guy from the opening band, sharing a pipe. Crack, I think, or maybe it was something else."

Abby felt her jaw drop in disbelief. "Oh, hell, no."

"Yeah. Anyway, we all knew her drug use was getting bad, but she was pretty good at keeping it away from us. I wasn't there, but Joey said Seth slammed out of the room and shut himself in the bus. She went ballistic, beating on the door, screaming and crying, but he wouldn't come out."

"Her own damned fault."

"You got that right. The cops came, Joey told them what was going on, and she left. No way she wanted to deal with the cops as messed up as she was." Caroline took out a tissue and dabbed at her eyeliner. "Seth had to change his cell number, and Trent made sure security at the next few shows knew she wasn't allowed in. But, thank goodness, none of us ever saw her again."

Abby felt a strong need for a road trip to find her. She'd thank Stacy for staying gone, and then rip her hair out by the roots for putting Seth through such an ugly scene. She realized, belatedly, her filter was on the fritz again. "Uh-oh. That was out loud, wasn't it?" she asked.

Caroline laughed. "Yeah, but it's OK. I like that about you." She leaned against the rust-stained sink. "Well, I wanted to tell you. Seth's kind of the same way."

"Really?" Somehow Abby couldn't imagine Seth blurting out random vigilante thoughts.

"Well, not exactly. I mean he's the real deal, and he speaks his mind. He's not a player, not anymore. The situation with Stacy bugged him, made him think about what was important." She ran her hand through her hair, undoing her earlier tidying job. "But the problem is he's been closed off ever since. I just wanted to tell you if Seth says something, he means it from deep down, and if he's feeling something, you can tell a mile away."

Abby thought a moment. "I think I know what you mean."

"Seth's like a big brother to me. I saw how he looked when he talked about you, and how he was with you tonight. Joey noticed it right away. He has a spark we haven't seen in a long time. I thought you needed to know why he might act confused, and I couldn't leave without telling you."

"I appreciate it, Caroline, I really do."

"We love Seth, and want him to be happy. Tonight, he looked like he could be happy again."

"He's lucky to have friends like all of you." She opened the bathroom door, but turned back to Caroline. "Look, I don't know what's happening yet, but I can tell you I'm nothing like Stacy. You don't have to worry about that, I promise." Abby gave a little wave as the bathroom door closed behind her, a bit unsettled by the emotional, intimate information just dropped on her out of the blue.

She found Seth off by himself in the backstage area. He appeared to be deep in concentration, but a smile softened his features when he saw her. He reached out and took her hand, seating himself on a tall equipment crate and positioned her, facing him, between his knees. "I was wondering where you were."

"I bumped into Dash and felt a sudden need to escape. The only place I thought he might not follow me was the ladies' room. I had a chat with Caroline."

"Caroline? I hope she talked me up a little," he said with a wink.

"Mmmm hmmm." Abby figured if Caroline was right in her assessment of Seth, that was fine with her.

"Almost show time," Seth said. He slid his arms around her waist, and she leaned against his chest, her head tucked under his chin. She could get very used to this. She was a little afraid she already had.

Their privacy was interrupted when the rest of the band began gathering. Roberto bustled around, fussing over "his" guitars, strumming a few notes to make sure they were properly tuned, and carefully placing the instruments on their stands. Abby felt the adrenaline zinging through the air around them. The crowd, impatient for the show to start, could be heard over the music playing on the club's PA system.

"Don't forget the change in the set list, guys," said Trent.

"Already printed and posted," Joey assured him. "We're good to go."

Seth slid off the crate and said to Abby, "I thought you could sit over at the sound board with Mouse. It's above floor level, stage right." He indicated the position of the board with a nod of his head.

"Uh-uh. No can do," Abby replied.

"What do you mean, 'no can do?'"

"Sit? Are you out of your mind? I mean, maybe you are, but you're so cute most people don't point it out."

"Where do you think would be appropriate, then, and not involve any sitting?"

Rats. He was even cuter when he was amused. "Front and center at the stage, of course."

"In the crowd?"

"Yeah. That's half the fun."

"Let's go, then."

Seth led Abby around the black backdrop curtains and down the side of the stage. The crowd murmured and parted, not daring to complain when the headliner edged them out of their carefully guarded positions, especially with Trent's imposing form shadowing him. Seth brushed his lips along her jaw, and whispered, "This is going to be the longest damned concert of my life."

"Better get to it then," Abby whispered back, using his proximity to bestow a nibble on his earlobe, giving his earring a flirtatious flick with her tongue.

"For future reference, that is not a good way to get me to leave."

"Noted. Now, go." She still couldn't believe she'd just behaved so wantonly. In public.

"Going." Seth hopped onto the stage and disappeared.

Abby kicked off her sandals and pushed them and her handbag between her and the stage. This was typical preconcert preparation, so she could dance without the risk of snapping an ankle or perforating the feet of anybody nearby with her heels. She looked around and was surprised to find the blonde fangirl elbowing her way through the crowd. She came to a stop right beside Abby, glaring furiously.

Abby gave her a faint nod of recognition and started to turn away when the girl grabbed her arm and demanded, "Who are you, anyway? I saw you with Seth in the park and getting off his bus. Are you his girlfriend?"

Abby jerked her arm from the girl's grasp and sputtered, "No. I don't know. Maybe." Could you be somebody's girlfriend the same day you met him?

"Hey, don't act like you're anybody special. You're nowhere near good enough for Seth."

Oh, so that's how it was going to be? Great. Abby was ready for it now. "You don't know me, and you sure as hell don't know Seth."

"I've been to twenty-nine concerts in seven states. I'm his most loyal fan, and he knows it. He sings to me all the time." The girl's face became flushed, and it dawned on Abby this girl wasn't even in the same time zone as reality.

"Oh, really?" Abby made a show of studying the autograph on the girl's shirt. "Well, listen—Pam, is it? I bet you wish your name was longer, huh?—go away and keep your little button nose out of my business." Abby stepped aside and refused to be further engaged. Pam opened her mouth as if she might be inclined to escalate things, but just then the lights dimmed and the band took the stage.

Dead End Road, in all its energy-intensive glory, launched into a fast-paced fan favorite "Should Have Known Better." The crowd was swept into the show, and Abby put the surly fan from her mind.

By the time they were three songs into the set, she experienced a serious bout of cognitive dissonance. On one hand, she was enjoying a fantastic concert, loving every minute. On the other hand, it felt surreal. Had she really been kissing Seth in the bus a while ago? Taking inventory, she found her lips were still tingly, and a faint taste of him remained on her tongue. OK, she hadn't completely lost her mind. What a relief.

She couldn't take her eyes off Seth, which was par for the course when she saw him perform. His presence enveloped the crowd, and he poured everything he had into the music. The hair around his face was soon damp with perspiration, and a dark patch formed around the neck of his shirt. From time to time their eyes met, accompanied by a quirk of his mouth, but he seemed to be making a serious effort to give the entire crowd the show they were expecting.

The band reached about the two-thirds mark in the set list by Abby's calculation, and played "Every Man's Darkest Night." In the haunting piece, each band member played an extended solo. During the solos, the rest of the band disappeared from the stage for a quick break, before returning for their segments. This time, though, Seth deviated from the routine.

He introduced Pete, and as the bass player laid into his solo, Seth approached the front of the stage. He shook a few hands, and seated himself directly in front of Abby, his elbows on his knees. "I thought I could get through the whole show, but it turns out I can't."

"I hope you're not waiting for an argument."

"Nope. Waiting for a kiss." Abby stepped closer, and he enfolded her in his arms and kissed her as if they were the only ones in the room.

"Wow," Abby had to almost shout to be heard over Pete's guitar. "If you'd do more of that, your attendance would go through the roof."

Grinning, Seth said, "Only for you, darlin'."

"You're going to get me beaten to a pulp, you know." Abby glanced around, noting her earlier nemesis seemed about to reach the boiling point. Pam's face was flushed again, and her jaw hung open. If she exploded and spewed gory groupie bits all over her, Abby was going to be extremely pissed.

"Nah, Trent's watching, and so is Dash's staff."

"Good thing."

Seth placed his forehead against hers. "Time to get back to work. Another half hour, OK?"

"Go do your thing," she said, giving him a light pat on the thigh.

The set finally wound toward its conclusion. As the band came out for their encore, she heard the opening bars of "Make or Break." She felt a fluttering in the pit of her stomach, and her entire focus narrowed until all she could see was Seth. He closed his eyes for a moment. Then, his fingers playing over the strings of his guitar, he said to the crowd, "This has always been a real special song for me, and now more than ever. She knows why."

Abby had a lump in her throat as Pete and Marshall faded to the back of the stage. Joey's percussion was light and nonintrusive while Seth played the song that had first captured Abby's attention.

The blank page bleeds, the words won't come
You've been left high and dry by your muse
Time to burn it all down and throw it away
Tell yourself you've got nothing to lose

As he sang, his smooth, smoky voice filled the room. He glanced frequently in her direction, but he mostly let his focus linger somewhere beyond the rear of the hall. She'd been anticipating the end of the show, but as she watched him standing in the wash of a blue spotlight subtly shifting to purple, flowing into the chorus of the song, she almost wished it would never end.

Sometime in life you're gonna make or break
And which one is all up to you
But if you should find you can't make it alone
Darlin', I'll always be there for you

The song had changed her life once, and now it seemed to be changing it again.

After a second encore, the lights came up. People shuffled toward the exits, but Abby stayed put since she wasn't sure if Seth expected her to come find him or to wait where she was.

Seth and Marshall appeared and made their way to the front of the stage opposite Abby's position. They signed a few autographs before Seth came to her side. He flung a hand towel over his shoulder and slipped his arm around her, and they headed out of the club.

In the bustling parking lot, the intermittent illumination of headlights cast flickering shadows. Pete, Joey and their wives threw things in the back of an SUV so they could make their early flight. The crew, with the assistance of some of Dash's in-house hands, was already loading equipment into the trailer. Outside the bus, they found Marshall and Trent, as well as Roberto, their guitar technician. Marshall carried a guitar and boarded the bus, but Roberto turned to Seth, a pained expression on his face.

"Man, I heard about Cujo, and I..."

Seth held up a hand. "Stop. Can't talk about it." He shot a glance at Abby and added, "Not helping. Could you grab the Gibson for me? Everything else can go in the trailer."

"Sure, no problem. My heart is breaking, but I'll survive." He went off in search of Seth's guitar with a sad shake of his head.

Abby frowned.

"Don't worry, he's fine," Seth assured her. "He's just messing with me."

"I'm going to be the guitar killer forever, I just know it," she said with a groan.

"No, only till the next time Marsh beats the crap out of the amps with some guitar 'Berto especially likes."

"Does he do that often?"

"Not so much, but I'll ask him to step up the schedule, take the pressure off."

"Appreciate it."

Trent looked around the lot. "I think we're a man or two short in the house crew. Guess I'd better go make sure everything's getting packed up." Looking fully prepared to kick as many asses as it took to keep everybody on schedule, he strode off toward the stage door.

Seth took Abby's hand and led her onto the bus. Marshall was rummaging in one of the bins above the couch. "Hey, Marsh. I want to talk to Abby, so could you give us a few minutes?"

A knot tightened in Abby's stomach. Was this the part where he said good-bye and promised to call her soon?

Marshall closed the bin with a thud. "Sure, no sweat. The bar's inside, anyway. I figure you have at least an hour before I come back and crash, regardless of what's going on in here." He tied a fresh bandanna on his head. "But you might want to throw the privacy lock in case 'Berto comes back." Abby thought it sounded like an excellent idea.

"Jesus, Marsh," Seth said. "Can you be semimature for a few minutes once in a while?"

"Why would I do that when it's so much fun bustin' your chops?" He laughed and left the bus, giving them a wave as he crossed the parking lot toward the club.

"Now, what I wanted to talk to you about..." He leaned in for a soft kiss before continuing. "I've been thinking about this all afternoon. We have three weeks off after tonight. We're all planning about a week on our own to take care of personal business before we get together again to work on some new arrangements."

"You're probably anxious to be home after so long away." She tried to sound calm, but the knot in her stomach had grown, and possibly sprouted thorns.

"I love it on the road, but it's good to have some downtime once in a while. The thing is, I don't really want to go home right now."

"Oh?" A bit of hopeful anticipation bloomed somewhere in the middle of her chest. Or possibly lower. Or both.

"I was thinking maybe I'd stay up here for a while, spend some more time with you."

She tried to compose some profound yet lighthearted reply, but gave up and simply said, "I'd like that, Seth." She silently congratulated herself that her malfunctioning filter had prevented things like an ear-ripping squeal and *ohmygodohmygodohmygod* from escaping.

Seth let out a breath suggesting he hadn't been at all sure of her response and said, "Great. Um, I'll go tell Trent to check me into a room across the street, if there are still any left."

The time for pretense had passed. After all, he'd just made it clear he wanted to get to know her better, and she was hardly a maiden playing at virtue. If Seth Caldwell wasn't worth taking a risk, she couldn't imagine who would be. She gathered her courage and prepared to be daring. "That doesn't make any sense. I live outside of town, and you'd have to rent a car or wait for me to drive you back and forth. Why don't you stay with me?" She started to second-guess herself as soon as the words were spoken. Oh, hell. Had she gone too far? Maybe he only meant he'd like to go out to dinner. Risk taking was way trickier than hiding out at home. "I mean, I have a spare room if you want your own space, or…damn. I'm making a mess of this." She slapped a hand to her forehead and groaned quietly in dismay.

The corners of his mouth twitched. "No, you're not. And I'd love to stay with you."

Dropping her head onto his shoulder, she said, "I'm such a goof."

"Yeah, darlin', join the club. Aren't we too old for this?"

"I'm pretty sure I am, but I have a couple of years on you."

"Not so's you'd notice."

Abby heaved a small, internal sigh of relief and snuggled into the curve of his arm. "Well, we agree we're both huge goofs..."

"Hey! I didn't say huge goofs!" Seth interrupted.

"...huge goofs, but we're going to let it slide for now, and pack your stuff so we can go."

"In a minute."

He took her hands and brought her to her feet, putting his hands at her waist and pulling her close. Their bodies pressed together from chest to thighs. Her arms looped up around his neck in a way that felt wonderfully natural, her fingers sifting through his hair. He shifted his hands lower on her back, over the swell of her bottom, molding her to him. He bent to kiss her, and Abby felt a flare of energy between them unlike anything she had ever experienced. The kiss deepened, and her response intensified. His hair smelled like warm sandalwood, and their mutual heat wrapped around her as surely as his arms.

She knew despite the swell of her breasts between them, he had to be able to feel her racing heartbeat. Her nipples begged for more direct attention, but she suspected if either of them went a single step further, stopping might become a bit of a problem.

She was highly aware of the activity in the front of his jeans, and ached to reach down and touch him in a promise of future exploration. She had numerous ideas, none of which were at all unappealing.

This kiss trailed off after a series of nibbles directed in the general vicinity of her collarbone. What were they supposed to be doing? Oh, right. Stopping.

Seth grabbed a bottle of water while Abby examined some crayon drawings taped to the cabinet over the sink. He took a few steps down the narrow passageway, pulling back the dark blue curtain of the first bottom bunk on the right side. From a storage compartment beneath the bunk he withdrew a large army-style duffel bag. He took a quick look inside. "Looks like I'm ready. Everything I need is in there pretty much all the time, so I'll jump in the shower, then we can take off."

"OK, I'll wait outside."

"I'll hurry."

"You'd better," she said, smiling, and went outside.

She moved toward the back of the bus, away from the activity around the equipment trailer, and lit a cigarette. She needed to think, and not about Seth in the shower, presumably naked and covered in fragrant, slippery lather. While it definitely merited thought, too much had happened today, and it wasn't over yet.

She understood all the points Monique made earlier. She knew she had to come out of her shell and be part of the world if she ever wanted a real life with real relationships. But, seriously, zero to warp speed all in one day? This whole thing was crazy. Seth Caldwell and her? How could she expect that to work out? She shouldn't be thinking of anything beyond tonight. And she probably shouldn't even be thinking that far.

Any time with him would be on the road, assuming he didn't ride off into the sunset in a day or two with an "I'll call you," which never happened. As a musician, leaving was literally in his job description. Did she really think she could handle it? And if she couldn't, what was the point in even taking the time or the risk of getting to know him any better?

She'd refused to leave her tranquil small town before, and that was with someone who was her husband. True, he was a selfish, cheating bastard, though she mainly had suspicions and little proof at the time. It was true, too, she stayed here to be with her dad, and to help her mom through her grief when the cancer finally took him. But she'd never seriously considered leaving, before or since.

And there was the fact she'd known Seth for — she paused to do a quick calculation — approximately eleven hours, and was about to take him home with her.

Underneath it all, though, she knew herself. She had to take the chance, even if it scared her. It was bizarre this encounter occurred so promptly after she finally saw what her life was in danger of becoming. But she knew if she said, "Gee, this risk is too scary, I'll wait for the next one," there wouldn't be a next one. Once she made one excuse, it would be far too easy to keep making excuses.

And, she couldn't forget — this was Seth Caldwell. She couldn't count the number of nights she'd fallen asleep, alone, listening to his music. Maybe this was impulsive, even reckless, but she knew now there was no way she was going to change her mind.

She tossed her extinguished cigarette in a trash can as Seth stepped off the bus. He changed into a dark blue T-shirt under an open denim work shirt with the sleeves rolled up. His hair was damp, and he carried the duffel bag. Before he reached her, he looked toward the side door. "Great, here's Roberto with the Gibson." He jogged over to meet the technician. He said something and nodded in Abby's direction, took the guitar, and hurried to Abby's side.

He flashed a full-blown smile, complete with dimples under the razor stubble, which she still found way too sexy for words. "So, change your mind about taking me home?"

"Unless you're going to confess this is all an elaborate plot to get me alone for revenge purposes, I'm definitely taking you home."

"Getting you alone may be part of the plot, but I'm pretty sure there's nothing in there about revenge."

"Check the fine print before we get in the car."

His hands were full, but it didn't stop him from stepping close to her and nuzzling her neck. Her entire body erupted in delicious goose bumps as his lips grazed the edge of her jaw. "So, where'd you leave the car?"

As soon as Abby remembered, they were on their way.

Chapter Four

Seth placed his things in the back of Abby's Jeep, glancing at the right front tire to confirm it was still fully inflated before he climbed in. When Abby clambered in beside him and fastened her seatbelt, it was all he could do not to lean over and kiss her again.

What was wrong with him, anyway? She'd really gotten to him, and that simply did not happen. Out of the blue, he wanted her in ways he couldn't begin to identify. He wondered what it meant not all of those ways, or even most of them, involved nibbling the flowers from her lacy halter.

"Oh, damn," Abby said. "I forgot to turn on my phone. Could you find? It should be in the console."

Seth located it and hit the power button. The phone rang just as he was about to put it back in the console. He couldn't repress a smile and sideways glance at Abby when he heard the ring tone was the melody from "Make or Break."

Abby took the phone from his hand and made a small, dismayed sound. "Yeah, shut up. Totally not embarrassing."

"No, I love it. If it had been anything else, I'd have been crushed."

"Well, we wouldn't want that." She swiped the screen to answer the call. "Hey, Molly."

The rest of her side of the conversation consisted of things like "yeah," "uh-huh," "shut up," "no way," and "is everything OK?" His attention had wandered when he heard her say, "No, he's right here. He's going to stay at my place for a while." She winced and held the phone from her ear for a few seconds, and he could hear the high-pitched sound of her friend's response from where he sat. He breathed a sigh of relief when she concluded the conversation and put a percentage of her attention back on the road.

"It was the friend who bailed on me this morning. Apparently, she had a voice mail from Monique telling her you'd invited me to the concert, and she had to call and do the girl-squeal thing."

"You didn't squeal back, I noticed."

"I'm not much of a squealer." Seth made a mental note to test the theory. "Plus, I could tell her heart wasn't in it. Something's up."

"Did she tell you what it was?"

"Just that Craig was down in the bar, she was sitting alone in the room, and they'd had some kind of argument. I'll get to the bottom of it tomorrow." Despite her casual assessment of her friend's predicament, Seth thought the crease between her eyebrows indicated more concern than she wanted to show.

Abby pointed out a few landmarks as they drove. These mainly consisted of small lakes, creeks, bridges, and where things used to be before they burned down. "I saw Joey and Pete leaving, but what was everybody else doing tonight?"

Seth thought for a second. "Marsh, Mouse, and Trent were staying in the bus, I think. Mouse mentioned sleeping in tomorrow, since we don't have another show we have to make, and they'll take turns driving home."

"Is that how you usually do it?"

"Yeah, except Pete, Joey, and I are usually there, too. But there's no rush, and they can take an extra day if they want." He ran down the rest of the crew list. "Danny was going to leave as soon as they loaded up everything. He had a buddy coming up from St. Cloud to get him. Andy and Roberto are going to stay with the van and trailer and head out as soon as it gets light."

He explained the band planned to gather at Joey's place in Austin in a week or so, as it was the biggest and had a good practice setup downstairs. The rest of the guys didn't have to show up till a couple of days before they headed out on their next string of dates on the West Coast.

Abby turned off on a narrow, paved road, and again onto a gravel one. A little further on the road forked, and Seth could see the shimmer of moonlight through the trees, suggesting a lake just beyond. Abby took the right fork, and the Jeep soon pulled into a gravel driveway and stopped between a single-car garage and a neat brown house with lighter trim.

"It's small, but living alone, I don't need much space." Abby rummaged in her purse and pulled out her key as they reached the side porch. "Between some insurance from my dad, and my divorce settlement, I had just enough to build it."

They stepped inside, passed through a laundry room and into a hallway, and turned left. Set against the same wall as the side door through which they'd entered, Seth saw a walk-through kitchen with a breakfast bar. Straight ahead and facing the lake was a large living area, with floor-to-ceiling windows and a pair of French doors leading onto a wide deck. Seth liked the room's colors, rich reds and golds, with gleaming hardwood floors. A golden-tan sectional sofa sat on a jewel-colored area rug, and a loft rail was visible on either side of the fireplace in the right wall.

He placed his bag on the floor and the guitar case against the breakfast bar, and walked toward the French doors. "You must have an awesome view of the lake." He saw a grassy area, and a wide dirt path led through the trees and toward the moonlit sheen of the water beyond.

"I love it," Abby replied. "The water makes me feel peaceful. All the houses here are backward. The back faces the road, because the front needs to face the lake."

"Not much point in living on a lake if you can't see it."

"Right. Well, let me give you the tour."

She started down the hall in the opposite direction. Seth saw the stairs leading to what looked like the loft, and two doors that proved to be a bedroom and a bathroom. A short, perpendicular hallway led to a larger bedroom that was clearly Abby's. It had pale green walls and white trim, and an inviting-looking bed adorned with a blue, green, and white comforter and a tempting mound of pillows.

"OK," Abby said. "This has been the *Better Homes and Gardens* portion of the tour. Now are you ready to see where I really live?" Her tone was a blend of humor and B-grade horror movie foreshadowing.

"Sure. If you want to show me." He slipped his arms around her waist.

"I'm glad you're here. I just can't remember when anybody's been here, other than my mom. I'm trying to think what sort of embarrassing things we're likely to trip over."

"I live on a bus with a bunch of overgrown teenagers. I'm pretty hard to embarrass."

"You're kind of sweet when you're clueless. Let's go then." She kicked her sandals in the direction of the side door and led the way up the stairs. This arrangement suited Seth perfectly, as it gave him a spectacular view as they ascended.

He had to work to control his surprise as they arrived in Abby's loft. While the rest of the house was neat, though lived-in, the loft looked like a family of badgers had recently vacated it. A computer sat on a desk situated in a dormer alcove facing the lake, but the desk itself was virtually buried in piles of papers, folders, books, empty pop cans, food wrappers, and an overflowing ashtray. A printer perched on a shelf to the right of the alcove, above a minirefrigerator. The rest of the space was filled with bookshelves, and two well-worn armchairs on either side of an end table. He had just noticed a doorway on the interior wall appearing to lead to a half bath when his eyes were drawn back to a whiteboard hanging above the printer shelf.

His surprise must have shown, because Abby laughed. "Don't pay any attention to that. It's just my murder board."

"Uh, yeah, guess no home's complete without one." The board said things like "Ways to kill Jenny: transdermal poison, ice pick between vertebrae C2/C3, fall down stairs?" The part that said "fall down stairs" was crossed out with "too uncertain" written below it.

"No mystery writer's home, at any rate." She sat in one of the armchairs, still grinning at him. "The pieces of the book show up in my head whenever they feel like it, and I need a place to write them down. I tried a notebook, but it works better if they're visible all the time. Parts of my brain are constantly working through the details instead of only when I go looking for them."

"I get it, but if I see my name on there, I'm going to be concerned."

"No worries. You promised not to kill me, so I won't kill you back." She plucked a sandwich wrapper from the end table, wadded it up, and tossed it toward an already-full wastebasket. She missed, but didn't give it a second glance. "Are you hungry? I think I have some chicken in the fridge."

Seth agreed a snack wouldn't be unwelcome, and they headed back downstairs. She pulled chicken and potato salad from the refrigerator, added some biscuits, poured a glass of white wine from a half-full bottle, and presented him with a fresh beer.

"Mom brought this by yesterday. She believes I'll waste away if she doesn't feed me."

"Why would she think that?"

"Because I tend to forget to eat when I'm writing, and after the divorce, she watched me lose thirty pounds. I told her I needed to lose it. I'd gained at least that much in those three years."

They took their plates to the breakfast bar. Seth decided to ask about her marriage. He was burning with curiosity about what kind of man Abby had married, and what happened. She already mentioned being divorced twice, so it must not be a forbidden topic.

In response to his question, Abby told him about the period of time in which she'd lost both her father and her marriage, and his heart went out to her. He also had a strong urge to pummel her ex-husband. At one point he noticed a haunted expression flicker across her face and felt there was even more to the story, but she wasn't yet ready to talk about it.

"No wonder you felt like your life was falling apart." He wished he could do something to take those bad memories away from her.

"It was rough. Dad gave me this property before he died, like he knew how much I needed it. He and Mom planned to build here someday, but she didn't want to be out here alone after he was gone. I always loved it more than my sister did, so he gave it to me and gave her his boat and camper. She lives in Kentucky. She and her husband and kids get a lot of use out of them."

"This place means a lot to you," Seth ventured, hoping she'd tell him more.

"You bet it does. It's the only thing I've ever had that's really mine, and I don't know how I'd have survived those first few years without it."

"I envy you. I have a place in Austin, but I'm not there enough for it to feel like more than a rest stop." Seth wasn't sure he'd ever had a "home" since he left Montana. Why hadn't he realized that before?

"People have started pointing out I've become a bit of a hermit, but this is a tough place to leave." She emptied her plate in the trash and placed it in the dishwasher. Leaning against the sink, she sipped her wine.

When Seth's plate was empty, Abby led him to the living room. While she tuned a satellite radio, keeping the volume low, he admired the long column of her spine framed by the open back of the halter top, and imagined tracing it top to bottom with his tongue. Or bottom to top. Either way.

Abby flipped a switch on the wall, and the fireplace added a warm glow to the room. "Go ahead and relax," she told him. "I want to go change."

Abby departed for her bedroom, and Seth took his duffel bag into the bathroom. He tucked his denim shirt and shoes into the bag. He dragged his comb through his hair, before putting the comb and his shaving kit on the shelf over the sink. Back on the sofa, he considered his conflicting desires and emotions. He knew bringing him home indicated a very good chance they'd end up in bed, but he cautioned himself not to assume it would be tonight. He was definitely voting for tonight, but he sensed this was too important, and everything had to be right. He wasn't used to thinking this way, and it was getting on his nerves.

Abby returned, wearing gray yoga shorts and a thin, pale pink tank top clinging to her breasts in a most delightful way. She retrieved her wine glass from the coffee table, and curled against his side.

With her legs tucked up beside her, he noticed a vivid peacock quill tattoo on her calf, poised above the scripted words I Write. He wouldn't have guessed Abby had a tattoo. Further evidence he was going to enjoy unpuzzling this particularly enticing puzzle.

He wanted nothing more than to spend the entire night uncovering and exploring every bit of her, savoring each delicious second. Yet he didn't want to push her. Somehow, he had to show her while her body was driving him to distraction, she was already more than that to him.

Abby's hand on his arm jolted him back into the moment. She looked up at him, the firelight's soft shadows playing across her face. "You look like you're thinking about something important," she said.

"Us." It was the only word currently on his mind.

"You know, it's crazy," she said, shaking her head slowly in wonder. "When I was sitting right here this morning having my coffee, there was no 'us,' but here we are."

"And at the same time, I was trying to sleep on the bus from Chicago, listening to Marsh snore." It was kind of mind-boggling.

She stretched her legs out alongside his, and turned more fully into his embrace. "I don't pretend to know why the Universe does stuff, but everything so far since Molly called this morning led us right here. So, no overanalyzing or worrying. Not tonight." He thought she was talking to herself as much as to him.

He brushed her hair from the side of her face, his hand lingering under its silken sable weight. Her lips looked so full and inviting, and he brought her face to his. He deepened the kiss, losing himself in the tang of wine and sugared vanilla, a taste uniquely hers.

She reached under his shirt, her fingers warm across his stomach and moving up to his chest, leaving a trail of surging nerve endings in their wake. She returned his kisses hungrily, and he was already as hard as he ever remembered being.

He lifted his hand to explore her breasts through the thin fabric of her top, and found her nipples already straining for his touch. He shifted to angle her hips more tightly against him, while he redirected his explorations under her shirt, feeling her breast swell in response. He cupped its weight in his palm and played his thumb over her nipple, eliciting a throaty sigh. He loved the way she felt as she clung to him, and her responses excited him almost more than he could bear.

Her hands were once again under his shirt, gliding over his chest, teasing the scattering of hair she found there. She seemed to reach some sort of decision, broke their kiss, and pulled herself up on her elbow. She tugged upward on the hem of his shirt. He took this to mean he should make it disappear, so he did. He must have been right, because her shirt chased his to the floor, and she guided him onto his back and stretched out over him. Her hand brushed over his unshaven cheek as she looked into his eyes before returning to their kiss.

This was so much more than Seth felt he had any right to hope for, but he couldn't help wanting more. He burned for her, for everything she was willing to give. The feel of her breasts pressed against him was making him crazy. The weight of her lower body was resting on his pelvis, which wasn't helping. Well, it was helping a lot, but not in terms of retaining any scrap of self-control. He was so close to losing it altogether, sending their remaining clothes to join the shirts on the floor and rolling her beneath him, that he shifted her upward, straddling his waist.

This had the benefit of raising her breasts into the perfect position for maximum enjoyment. He made the most of it, kneading gently at first, then more firmly as she responded, arching her back to present them more fully for his ministrations. Her nipples were dark coral in the firelight, contracted to tight buds. He drew her down and took one in his mouth, swirling his tongue around the taut flesh before trapping the tip between his tongue and the roof of his mouth. She made a small, desperate whimpering sound, her fingers twining through his hair. He switched his attention to the other breast, and felt her heart pounding under his hands.

He needed to touch more of her, all of her, and rolled until they were side by side, facing each other. He paused to catch his breath and caressed the smooth skin of her back, taking in her tousled hair and flushed cheeks. Her eyes had a half-lidded, dreamy glaze, telling him she was as caught up in this as he was. She was the most gorgeous thing he'd ever seen.

Still, some gentlemanly trait he had not previously been aware of possessing compelled him to say, "Abby, darlin', this can be as much or as little as you're ready for, OK? I want you so much I have to think really hard just to blink. But like you said, this morning you didn't even know me."

"Oh, you really are insane, aren't you?" She slid her hand across his zipper, causing his erection to strain even harder against the confining denim.

"Probably. Yeah, I'm pretty sure. I need to make sure you know this is your call." He had to think frigid thoughts to get the words out. This was next to impossible with her hand where it was.

"I know that. Now, less talking, more touching."

Seth had absolutely no argument. He buried his face in her neck, and breathed in her warm, floral scent, before returning to plunder her willing, kiss-swollen lips. Touching was something he could definitely manage. He skimmed his hand along her waist and over her hip and dipped under the waistband of her shorts.

She had foregone wearing anything under the shorts, and he thought his body temperature spiked about four degrees at the discovery. He encountered a small patch of coarse curls, but everything else in the region was slick and smooth. This woman was going to drive him out of his mind.

She shifted her position to give him better access, a sure sign of encouragement if he'd ever seen one. He slid his finger along her cleft, teasing his way through the slick inner folds. She made a sound deep in her throat, and he felt her opening to him. He eased one finger inside her, then two, astounded at the flood of wet heat welcoming him. He moved his fingers, and her hips moved to match his pace. His thumb brushed the swollen bud at her nexus with each stroke.

Her breath quickened, and he almost gasped out loud himself when she unfastened his jeans and began caressing him in a matching rhythm. But were they moving too fast? Could there be any such thing when he wanted her so fiercely?

With strength of will he didn't believe he possessed, he removed his lips from hers, though he did leave his hand in her shorts. Seth figured you could only expect so much from a guy, after all.

As if reading his mind, Abby whispered, "I don't want this to be over yet."

"I know. I mean, I do and I don't."

"Exactly."

"Time for a breather."

"Yeah," she said, "I don't think I've breathed in at least twenty minutes."

Seth reluctantly withdrew, and she sat up and retrieved their drinks from the table. He noted with great pleasure she didn't reach for her discarded shirt. As she handed his drink to him, he saw a bright shimmer in her eyes, and realized she, too, was experiencing everything between them on an emotional level as much as a sexual one. While it complicated everything for both of them, he was sure it was better. Yes, definitely better. Unless you asked a certain part of his anatomy, which raged with displeasure.

They were curled on the couch and sharing a cigarette when Abby traced the tattoo of the band's logo on his back.

"Don't laugh, but I actually thought about getting the logo, too."

"I don't know if that would have been really profound or really creepy right now."

"Me, either, so I'm glad I didn't get it." She snubbed the cigarette out and returned the ashtray to the table.

Seth chuckled and kissed her, still enjoying the feel of her bare breasts against his side. His erection was finally subsiding, and he hadn't felt this at ease with anybody for far too long. He finished his beer, then noticed Abby's glass was empty, too, and her eyes were threatening to drift shut. He took the glass and placed it on the table and took her hand.

"C'mon, let's get you to bed." She became completely still, and made no move to leave the sofa. "No darlin'. Just sleep, OK?"

"OK," she murmured drowsily. She walked with him to her bedroom, leaving the discarded tank top under the coffee table. He turned down the blankets, and she slid into bed with a sigh.

He made a quick trip to the living room to put the bottle and glass in the kitchen. He turned off the fireplace and radio before returning to Abby's bedside. He paused, unsure whether he should join her or make his way to the other bedroom, possibly by way of an icy shower. Abby must have sensed his hesitation, because she reached for him and said, "No, stay."

Seth slipped off his jeans and slipped into bed beside her, gathering her in his arms. "I'll stay as long as you let me," he said softly. But she was already asleep. As he held her, the single word thundering through his mind and resonating in every cell of his body was "mine." He wondered what that meant, but suspected he already knew.

Chapter Five

Abby opened her eyes to the first blush of dawn peeking in her bedroom window. While it was unusual for her to wake this early, the arm draped over her waist was completely unprecedented. She rolled over, careful not to disturb the arm and the person connected to it. She saw Seth sleeping beside her, and took a moment to savor this spectacular sight.

Seth was here. In her bed.

She placed her head on the pillow beside his and studied the way her own dark hair contrasted with his golden-brown strands in the early morning light. She could really get used to this, but her problem remained the same as it had been the night before. Seth lived everywhere or nowhere. She lived here. No matter what her feelings for him might be—and she was still afraid to think about it too much—would she be able to uproot herself from this place if it came to that? Was it what she wanted? Perhaps more importantly, would it be what he wanted? The whole situation screamed "cart before the horse," and she understood she'd had a head start in getting to know Seth through his music over the years. She reminded herself he'd literally just met her, and she shouldn't assume he was experiencing the same wild, exhilarating rush of feelings she was. It was way too soon to make any assumptions. But she was a woman, so she wondered.

Beside her, Seth stirred and his eyes slowly opened. They focused, and his mouth curved in a sleepy smile. "Mornin', beautiful." His voice was still husky with waking.

"If you call this morning. We couldn't have been asleep for more than a few hours."

Seth stretched and rolled to face her. "I'm pretty used to short sleep, but if you want to rest a while longer, I can go out and make some coffee."

"Nope, wide-awake now. And don't you budge. I'll go start the coffee and be back in about thirty seconds."

Seth ran his hand from her shoulder and down her arm, coming to rest on her hip. "Make sure you hurry back then."

"You'll hardly know I'm gone." She bounded out of bed and scampered — topless, she realized — toward the kitchen, with a brief stop at the bathroom. She considered retrieving her shirt from the living room, but decided against it. No point, when she had every intention of removing it again almost immediately.

She hit the switch on the coffeemaker and heard the bathroom door close. She took a deep breath and headed back to her room, where she slipped into bed, the sheets still warm from their bodies. She fluffed the pillows and arranged the blankets to emphasize her cleavage and hide her softening, thirty-four-year-old belly. Best if he not see her in all her glory, in daylight, until he was so blinded by lust — she hoped — he wouldn't notice certain problem areas.

Seth wore only boxers as he joined her under the covers. She suspected it wouldn't be long before those boxers were on the floor, and she hoped she hadn't chewed holes in them first.

He slid his arm under her, and she snuggled her head in the curve of his neck and shoulder. "Sorry I conked out on you last night. I'm not used to being up so late."

"Wasn't anything wrong with last night." He tucked one finger under her chin and kissed her.

She wouldn't have believed it, but he looked even more incredible now, in the slowly brightening light of morning, than he had in the firelight.

He glided under the sheet and moved over her, capturing her hands and extending her arms over her head, holding them against the pillow as his lips brushed along her cheek. He kissed her, and the sandy rasp of whiskers thrilled the delicate skin of her face. The feel of the whole length of his body stretched over her, his elbows bearing enough weight to keep her comfortable, held a note of possession she was surprised to find very appealing.

He released her hands, and she put her arms-around his shoulders. Her lips found the soft, delicate spot just below his ear, and she breathed in his scent, imprinting it in her mind. She couldn't resist the urge to steal a quick taste, adding his flavor to the memory. The flick of her tongue brought a hoarse sound from his throat.

He moved down her body, and she couldn't decide whether to urge him to move faster or to take his sweet time. From her throat to her shoulder, his mouth left a burning trail, cooling slowly with his passing. He cupped the globes of her breasts, and he brushed them with his cheek as he tasted his way across their fullness to the peaks of her nipples, one after the other.

The weight of his lower chest was on her pelvis, and she squirmed, helpless to control the need for more pressure there. Her shorts felt confining, and they were getting wetter by the second. The hair on Seth's chest teased at her midriff as he slid lower, arousing every inch of her flesh along the way. She almost cried out when he nibbled his way along her hip and to her thigh rather than go directly to the center of her need. She closed her eyes for a few seconds and reminded herself to breathe. His teeth nipped at her inner thigh, and only his grip on her hips stopped them from arching from the mattress.

Seth's hand skimmed inside the leg of her shorts, and he caressed her with his thumb. She felt a rush of moisture, and she dropped her hand to his, urging him further. Finally, he relented and eased her shorts down her legs and onto the floor. He parted her, his fingers tracing along her crease from bottom to top as she shivered with pleasure.

He retraced his fingers' path with his tongue, focusing his attention on the swollen bud, which Abby was certain could no longer take "wait" for an answer. He slid his finger into her while his mouth worked its magic, and Abby brought her hands to her breasts, adding to the swirl of sensation. She felt him zero in on the pulsing spot within her, and knew she wasn't going to last much longer. She tangled her fingers in his hair, urging him on, as her hips began to move in time with his caresses.

A strangled cry escaped her, and her muscles contracted around his fingers as the wave crested higher and higher, until she was sure it was impossible to survive the coming crash. Then it broke and roared over her, singing through her blood and stealing her breath. Seth's rhythm slowed, encouraging the last shudder from her body, as he drank her in.

He licked his way up her abdomen until he was once again positioned directly above her. His lips found hers again, and she encountered her own salty sweetness. She reached between their bodies and tugged at his waistband until he disposed of the boxers. Abby's manual investigation of the night before had been woefully brief, given her exhaustion, and she planned to correct that mistake right now.

Fingers barely encircling his girth, she stroked him from base to tip, and let her thumb swirl around the dampness she found there. She marveled at the way he filled her hand. "Mmmmm," she murmured. "I thought so."

"Thought what?"

"Nothing. That wasn't out loud."

"Yeah, it was."

"Well, let's just go on record as saying I'm pleased." She wrapped her legs around Seth's hips, making it very clear she was done talking for the moment.

Positioned at her entrance, Seth moved into her, a smooth, steady penetration, and she opened to receive him. She was still soaked and quivering from her climax, and the sensation of stretching around him brought her close to another peak.

He kissed her deeply as her hands played across the firm, taut muscles of his back and down to his hips, pulling him tightly inside her. He began moving, withdrawing almost completely before plunging again, and Abby had to interrupt their kiss to get enough air into her lungs. He balanced above her, looking into her eyes, his hair tenting their faces, and his pace increased. Every bit of her was straining to be a part of him, needing him. She shifted her legs higher around his waist, seeking any way to accommodate more of him. A second and more intense orgasm claimed her, surging through every nerve ending in her body.

Her legs tightened around his waist, a long, satisfied moan vibrating from her throat as her head fell back. Seth buried his face in her neck, and with a final thrust he tensed and stilled. His release flooded her, his groan blending with her own.

Still tangled together, they collapsed on the mound of pillows, as Abby's breathing and pulse slowly returned to normal. Seth's touch skimmed over her, and her entire body hummed with pleasure. She caught his hand and brought it to her lips, letting the delicate skin of her mouth map the strong fingers with their calloused tips.

Her body was languid and satiated, but her mind was chugging away, concerned about things she was too nervous to bring up. They'd had sex now. Toe-curling, nerve-flaming, these-sheets-are-never-going-to-be-the-same sex. But was that all it was? She had no reason to expect more, wasn't even sure if it was a good idea, but the alternative would ultimately be demeaning. For both of them.

Seth curled a finger under her chin and tilted it up so she met his eyes. "Darlin'…"

Her stomach bottomed out. This must be where he'd tell her it was nice and all, but he had to be going.

"Darlin', this is not just a hookup." His sunlit hair framed his face, which bore the most intense, holding-nothing-back expression Abby had ever seen. "At least, it's not for me."

Maybe she should've been insulted, if he were implying she brought strange musicians home and screwed their brains out on a regular basis, but she knew it wasn't what he meant. "I hoped not. It's not for me, either."

He closed his eyes, and when he opened them, the relief she saw there was nearly overwhelming. Had he really thought she didn't care about him? He said, "If that's all I wanted, I wouldn't have come here. Not with you, not like this. I wouldn't do that to you." His thumb stroked along her jaw. "You couldn't know it, but I don't live my life that way. Never have."

On some level, she thought she did know. But it was still nice to hear. "So, this is…?"

"More." His lips brushed hers. "A lot more."

Her heart stuttered. Enough heavy stuff. She gave herself over to kissing Seth for a while, and they lay there, warm and content.

"I'm not sure I can move," she sighed.

"Well, when you're able, let's have some of the coffee I smell. We can rendezvous back here as soon as possible, because I think we'll both be due for a nap. Or something."

"Excellent idea."

With the motivation of caffeine, Abby eventually forced her legs to comply and made it out of bed. Seth retrieved his boxers while Abby rummaged in her closet for a robe, following the aroma of coffee to the kitchen.

Abby just filled their cups when Seth said, "Hey, I think your dog wants in."

"I don't have a dog," she said, handing Seth his coffee.

"There's one on your deck."

"Oh. Dilbert. But he's not my dog."

She went to the French doors and opened them, letting the medium-sized black dog into the room. She filled a bowl with an assortment of leftovers and dry dog food from a container under the sink. Dilbert licked the bowl clean in under twenty seconds.

"He kind of looks like your dog."

Abby shrugged and stooped to retrieve the bowl. "He showed up about six weeks ago. People dump dogs around here a lot, with the asinine notion they'll 'find a home in the country.' I've been feeding him." She took her coffee and went to the couch, picking up last night's discarded shirt and throwing it toward the hallway. Dilbert promptly fetched it, so she stuck it between the sofa cushions.

Seth sat beside her. "What happened to his eye?"

Abby looked at the angry pink scar tissue bisecting where the dog's left eye should have been. "Your guess is as good as mine. A branch, maybe, or barbed wire. Maybe even a scratch from a coyote or something. It was a mess when I first saw him, but I took him to the vet clinic where Molly works, and they patched him up. We think the fur will cover most of the scar eventually."

"But he's not your dog." A dimple appeared on his right cheek, as the corner of his mouth quirked.

"No. My neighbors on the west side of the lake, the Nygaards, feed him, too. They're the ones who named him. He spends a lot of time here, though, because I let him inside more often than they do."

"I love dogs, but I've never had one," Seth said. "My dad didn't have any interest in them, and being on the road so much isn't exactly ideal for a dog. I tried once, a Boston terrier named Herschel, but things were wilder then and I knew it wasn't fair to him. I ended up giving him to my sister."

"David took my dog in the divorce," Abby said, thinking if the asshole had let her keep the gentle collie, she wouldn't have gone after quite so much of his money.

"How'd he get away with that?"

"Because Duffy was his dog before we were married, so technically he owned him. But I worked at home, and for three years I was with him 24-7. I loved him. David didn't. He only took him because he could." Her throat tightened with the memory of yet another loss.

"Not to be nasty or anything, but he sounds like a real bastard."

"No doubt about it." Had David cheated on Joyce the way he'd cheated on her—with Joyce? If the day ever came, Abby knew she'd spend a great deal of time tracking down the perfect greeting card for the occasion. She might even make one herself.

The attention shifted to Dilbert, and Abby immersed herself in the sweet dog's joyful affection. A few minutes later, her robe liberally dusted in dog hair, she stood and said, "Let's go outside and let Dilbert show you around."

"Sounds great, but can I throw a few things in your washer first?"

The extended road trip had probably left him with a whole bagful of stuff needing some freshening, and Abby went to the laundry room to make sure she didn't have a forgotten load incubating mold before telling him to go ahead. Seth grabbed last night's shirt then took his duffel bag to the spare room and sorted through it, throwing an armful of items into the wash.

They took their coffee and some bagels out onto the deck, though Abby thought the clothes they'd put on were taking her further from the bed than she'd prefer. The morning sun glinted on the water, and a family of ducks paddled along close to shore. The forest around her smelled of new growth, and birds flitted from branch to branch as they called to each other. When he figured out he wasn't getting any bagels, Dilbert bounded off through the underbrush in search of something small and furry.

Seth's arms encircled her from behind, so she put her coffee cup on the railing and leaned back against his chest.

"How much of this is yours?" he asked, as one hand played languidly over her ribs.

"Just six acres, over that way," Abby said, indicating off to her right. "The Nygaards own most of it, but there's a cabin between us on the north side, a guy from Rochester who's only up here some weekends and about two weeks during the summer. Usually it's pretty quiet. Let's get Dilbert and we'll take a walk around."

Abby called the dog, and he returned immediately, tail waving and his single eye fixed on her, awaiting instruction.

He led them to the shore, and Seth held Abby's hand as they turned up a narrow path angling back into the woods. They walked through the cool, shady acreage, and she showed him some of her favorite spots. There was a tiny brook trickling its way toward the lake over moss-covered rocks, a leafy patch of thimbleberries, and a hollow tree that was home to a plump, entertaining squirrel.

As they wandered, she wasn't surprised to find herself paying more attention to him than the familiar landscape around them. She loved seeing him in her world, and had to give herself a few mental shakes to believe he truly was here with her.

They finally reached the far side of her property. "That's all of it. It's not huge, but without a bunch of other houses around, I can go for days without seeing anybody. It can be annoying when the cabin people are up here, but they make up for it by doing fascinating things like getting drunk and falling out of rowboats."

Seth chuckled. "But don't you worry about being so isolated up here? What if something went wrong?"

Abby had certainly heard this particular statement before. "I have my phone, and the Nygaards are retired, so they're usually around if I need them. If we have really bad weather in the winter, I go stay at Mom's house in town till I can make it back out here."

Seth nodded, but a slight tightness at the corners of his mouth indicated her explanation didn't completely eliminate his concern. They followed Dilbert back toward the lake, where he ran along the shore, barking at the ducks.

"He never gives up," Abby said. "He chases them, but they can outswim him or fly if he gets too close. He thinks it's important to keep trying, though." She had to admit she admired his good-natured determination.

She led the way to an Adirondack-style bench situated slightly back from the water. The sun drew the chill from her skin, and she was warmed further by her proximity to Seth. She pointed out the Nygaards' house, and the cabin on the north side of the lake. "You should see it in October." Despite trying not to think too far ahead, she wondered how many times she'd see him between now and then. Thinking about it made her head hurt, so she stopped.

The ducks abandoned Dilbert, and he retreated to the edge of the trees to crunch with obvious pleasure on a stick. Though she was enjoying the tranquil moment, Abby said, "We should probably head back up to the house, don't you think?" She definitely wanted to spend some more time with him in her bed. Or on the couch, the floor, the deck, or the breakfast bar. She wasn't inclined to be picky right now. This morning might not have been the first orgasms for which he'd been at least partially responsible, but they were the first for which he was actually present. She didn't intend for them to be the last.

Instead of starting back up the path, Seth gathered her to him for another spine-melting kiss. Plans for immediate departure evaporated. Just as she was reaching the seriously hot and bothered stage and adding "lakeshore" to her list of acceptable locations, Seth pulled back. His eyes mirrored the lake as he looked off into the distance, and he seemed to be struggling to find words for something he wanted to say.

"What is it?" she asked.

He brushed his fingers along her cheek before taking her hand. "This is going to sound crazy, and I'm sure it's going to come out wrong, but let me try, OK?" She nodded her agreement, though tendrils of apprehension curled upward from her stomach. "In the past, I've made a lot of stupid decisions. For a long time now, I've avoided making any at all."

"I've done that, too."

"I guess, for me, nothing mattered enough to bother. But now, all of a sudden, it does matter, and it happened when I met you." He held nothing back in his direct gaze.

Abby couldn't believe he was saying something like this, let alone so soon after they met. It was wonderful, yet disconcerting, and she attempted to lighten the tone of the conversation. Or possibly derail it. "You mean when I ran over Cujo?"

"Yeah. And when I managed to resist the urge to strangle you right there, I knew there was something going on. I had to find you, talk to you again, and everything since then…well, it's been *right*. I don't know how to explain it, but I've never been so sure of anything."

So much for tone lightening. While it was amazing to hear, it was also making the vein by her right eye throb again. "Sure? What are you sure of?" Maybe she didn't want to know. Not when her mind was still so chaotic. He took a deep, shaky breath and squeezed her hand. "When I have to leave Minnesota, I can't go without you."

Abby's "tendrils of apprehension" morphed into pythons and squeezed the air from her lungs. She knew she shouldn't say anything yet, but she couldn't stop herself. "Whoa. Back the truck up. Aren't I, in the role of the girl, supposed to be the one saying stuff like that? And don't guys usually run screaming for the horizon when we start talking about the future?" Her voice trembled, but she was fighting down the rising tide of panic.

Apparently this was not an acceptable response, because his spine stiffened and he dropped her hand. Abby's throat tightened, realizing she'd managed to hurt him.

He stood and walked to the edge of the water, facing away from her. Dilbert trotted over, bringing his splintery stick, hoping Seth would throw it into the water for him to retrieve. He reached down and stroked the dog's head but declined to accept the stick, so Dilbert returned to the shade to continue his gnawing.

Seth turned, still not facing her directly, and scuffed one toe on the rocky ground. His jaw flexed, as if biting back words he didn't dare allow to escape. His voice, when it came, was ragged. "Abby, this is not a joke. It's not some stupid fucking line. And I believe you know that."

"Is this what they call being swept off your feet? Because if it is, it's not at all like I imagined." Damn! Why couldn't she shut up? It was like her mouth was falling down the stairs.

"Call it whatever you want," he said, looking at her again. "I know it's nuts. I sure never expected this." His voice was choked with emotion, clear evidence of how much it was costing him to be so open about how he felt. "Hell, I don't even know what 'this' is. But I do know it feels like a turning point, maybe the biggest one of my life, and it's all about you. I can't figure it out—we can't figure it out—if we're not together."

The constriction in her chest eased the tiniest bit and she went to him. She placed her hands lightly at his waist, needing to touch him. She would not cry. While it was a reasonable response to her turbulent emotions, she didn't want to make this any worse than she already had.

"You know what you're asking, right?" She hoped he really did understand what giving up the emotional anchor of her home would mean, if she agreed to do this, because she wasn't sure she could find the words.

"I do, darlin', and I hate putting you in this position. But I'm not the kind of guy who can feel something like this and not let it show." He put one hand at the small of her back, not quite an embrace. "We have to find a way. I need to be in Austin next week. I have to go back out on the road, and the thought of leaving you behind, seeing you for a day or two here and there, damn near kills me."

"I'm scared," she whispered.

Seth drew in a long, deep breath. "I know. I am too." His lips brushed her hair. "Look, I'm staying for a while, right? So let's take some time and work this out, OK?"

"I'll try."

Seth hugged her tightly. "That's all I can ask, darlin', that's all I can ask."

They returned to the house, with Dilbert trotting along in front of them, and stepped onto the deck. Abby filled a stainless steel water bowl from the outdoor faucet and gathered their empty coffee cups from the railing. Dilbert took a noisy, sloppy drink, and ambled off to lie in the impressive hole he had dug beside the deck.

They were about to go inside when a colossal roar shook the house. The blast rattled the doors, and forced Abby back a step, the deck rumbling underfoot. She dropped the coffee cups, and they clattered at her feet as her shriek was reduced to a strangled cry lodged in her throat. Seth grabbed her arm and pulled her back from the French door and raced in ahead of her. Abby was right on his heels, desperate to find out what had happened inside her precious house.

On the other side of the living room, smoke billowed from the hallway. Seth led the way toward the back of the house, and it was soon evident the blast had occurred in the spare bedroom. There was a jagged, refrigerator-sized hole where the window and part of the wall had been, and the smoke was already beginning to dissipate in the cross breeze. A few tongues of flames licked around the edges, and plaster from the ceiling littered the splintered and blackened floor.

Seth grabbed a towel from the bathroom and batted at the small fires until they merely smoldered. Fine black ash drifted down, adding to the mess. Abby stared in shock at the splinters of her grandmother's table, which had been beneath the window. Her stomach roiled at the nauseating sweet-scorched scent of burned marshmallows stinging her nostrils.

"What the fuck just happened here?" asked Seth, as Dilbert's face appeared on the other side of the gaping hole, the same question echoed in his single eye.

Abby stomped out a flaming scrap of olive green duffel bag. "Well, I'd say your luggage just blew a hole in my house."

Chapter Six

Seth pulled his cell phone from his pocket and discovered he didn't have a signal. He stared at it, trying to generate one by force of will.

"No signal?" asked Abby. "No, you probably wouldn't have one. There's only one company with consistent coverage out here." She dashed out the door and quickly returned with her own phone. Seth listened as she called 911 and reported the explosion. "It'll probably take about ten or fifteen minutes for the fire department to get here."

"I think we should wait outside, in case…well, just in case," Seth said. They probably shouldn't have gone inside to begin with.

"Guess we'll have to postpone the nap, huh?"

"Looks that way." Damn.

Standing out in the driveway, Seth's head was spinning. He rubbed his temples in a futile attempt to focus his thoughts. Had his duffel bag blown up? Really? Or was the source of the blast something related to the house itself?

"Good thing you had some of your things in the washer, or you'd be down to the proverbial clothes on your back," said Abby, sagging against her Jeep.

Stated out loud, Seth felt startled. He hadn't yet thought very far into it. "I don't guess there's much left of the rest. My shaving kit's in the bathroom, and I left my favorite boots on the other side of the bed when I was digging through the clothes, so maybe they survived. That's about it." A thought occurred to him. "Oh, shit, your book was in there."

"I'll give you another one. At least your guitar is still out by the breakfast bar," Abby said.

"Yeah, good thing. I don't think I could stand losing two guitars in twenty-four hours. Especially not the Gibson. It hasn't been out of my sight a single day in ten years." He'd written most of his songs, including "Make or Break," on it.

Abby called Dilbert away from the damaged side of the house. "Hey, guess what. You'll get to meet my mom."

That bit of information seemed oddly out of context. "I will?"

"Yeah, in about fifteen minutes."

"And you know this, how?"

"As soon as the call went out on the scanner, someone would definitely call Mom. I bet she gets here about five minutes after the fire truck."

"Well, this should be interesting."

"Yep. I'm thinking about it rather than the fact there's a gigantic hole in my house, and it could still theoretically blow up some more and burn to the ground." Her voice, while light, had the tightness of a person trying to avoid hysteria, and Seth noticed her legs were shaking.

A few minutes later, a fire truck pulled into the yard, followed by a battered SUV. Two suited-up firemen emerged from the truck and went directly to where a few wisps of smoke still drifted from the broken wall, dragging a hose attached to their pumper truck. A short, stocky man in jeans and a plaid shirt stepped out of the SUV and approached Seth and Abby.

"Hi, Frank. Thanks for getting here so fast," she said.

"Abby, what the hell happened?" Frank pulled a filthy baseball cap from his head, revealing a large bald spot surrounded by short, ginger-colored fuzz. After giving the fuzz a good scratching, he replaced the cap.

"You got me. We were on the deck, and *boom*. Lots of smoke and a great big hole where the wall used to be." The pinched lines of barely controlled panic around her mouth belied her casual tone.

"Sammy and Karl should be here any minute. They had a kid who ran his car off the road tryin' to miss a deer, but nobody's hurt. They were about done when we received your call."

"Mom'll probably be here pretty soon, too," she said.

"Then we don't need nobody else. Marilyn most likely has you a new set of curtains all ready to hang. By tonight, it'll be like nothing ever happened."

Abby laughed, the sound brittle. "She's not quite that good, but almost." She nodded toward Seth. "Frank, this is Seth Caldwell. Most of his stuff was blown up along with the wall. Seth, this is Frank Paulsen, our fire chief."

Frank extended his hand, and Seth shook it. "Pleasure to meet you, son, though we generally like to meet folks without involving emergency vehicles."

"My first choice, too," Seth said. "I'm just glad Abby wasn't inside when it happened." He put an arm around her waist, feeling they could both benefit from the contact.

Their conversation was interrupted by the arrival of a police car. Seth watched as the occupants stepped out and looked at the house, and started toward where the three of them were standing. The two young officers were of average height, but one had a head of shaggy blond hair, and the other had close-cropped hair the same color as Frank Paulsen's.

Hands were shaken all around. Abby introduced the blond as Karl Briggs, and the one with red hair and a sharp chin as Frank's son, Sammy. Sammy's pale eyes narrowed a bit when he noticed Seth's hand resting on Abby's hip, giving Seth the impression there was some history there, at least in the mind of the hometown cop. Everybody had run out of comments to make about the circumstances when the two volunteer firemen joined them.

Taking off his helmet, a young-looking man with a face full of freckles said, "I don't think you have to worry about fire, Abby. Looks like once the blast went, the fire was extinguished in the vacuum it left behind. Happens like that." His eyes darted toward his fire chief, who gave him a nod. "Thing is, we don't want to pour a bunch of water on it if we don't have to. We're going to have to call in the ATF guys. We don't have resources to investigate a bombing, and there's all these new Homeland Security laws."

Abby looked shocked. Her mouth opened and closed several times before she said, "Bombing?" She rolled her eyes. "Well, of course it was a bomb. I just didn't want to think about someone doing this on purpose."

Neither did Seth. But as big a kick to the gut as it was, he knew he'd have to do a lot of thinking about it in the immediate future.

Frank said to Sammy, "You'd best call your chief, son, and have him contact the ATF." Sammy hurried off to make the call, casting a worried look over his shoulder at Abby.

They were still standing off to the side of the driveway when a bright red Volkswagen Beetle skidded to a halt at the edge of the yard. This previously quiet little homestead was getting awfully crowded.

A sixtyish woman bounded from the car and power walked toward them, her stark white athletic shoes churning the gravel. Salt-and-pepper hair fluffed around her face, and she wore teal track pants and a sweatshirt covered in pictures of birds. Abby took a few steps toward her, but whether to meet her or head her off, Seth wasn't entirely sure.

"Abby, sweetie!" the woman cried, flinging her arms around her daughter. "Thank goodness you're OK!"

Abby disentangled herself, returned to Seth's side, and said, "Mom, you knew I was fine. I called the fire department, remember?"

"I couldn't believe it till I saw you with my own eyes. Do you know what happened?" She was talking to Abby, but kept shooting appraising looks in Seth's direction.

"No, we're waiting for the ATF to get here."

Sammy rejoined the group, and nodded to Abby's mother. "Chief said ATF will be here in about an hour. They had a few teams up north of the Cities for a training seminar, else it would've taken a lot longer." He directed a pointed look at his father, the fire chief. "They said to stay away from the scene till they get here. Lots of times there's a second bomb set to explode when investigators start poking around."

Frank bristled. "Damn Feds think we're stupid? We don't have the sense to stay away from something liable to blow up in our faces?" Even as he spoke, he was casting disappointed looks in the general direction of the house. He, Sammy, and Karl moved as close to the house as they dared, muttering among themselves.

"Let's get out of the sun," Abby said. Though she seemed to be passing it off as a comfort issue, Seth could see she had paled and seemed unsteady on her feet. She walked to the shady side of the garage and pressed her back against it. Seth followed, and Abby leaned against his shoulder. Dilbert plopped beside them and placed his head on Seth's foot.

Abby's mother looked toward Frank and the two police officers, but turned and approached the garage. "I know you've had a terrible shock, Abby, but shouldn't you introduce us?"

"I didn't imagine I needed to. I'm sure you already know who he is." Though Abby's words were somewhat direct, her tone was affectionate, and the color began to return to her face.

"Now, sweetie, how would I know?" The older woman tried to look innocent, but failed spectacularly.

"Monique called Molly, so it's a sure thing she called Paige, too. You probably had two calls about Seth last night, and three this morning." She massaged her temples, as if afraid to consider the full extent of her mother's inquiries.

Her mother looked smug. "For your information, it was three last night and two this morning, not counting Paige calling to tell me about your emergency or the calls I made myself." Abby's mother was not at all the mild-mannered widow Seth had for some reason expected after seeing some photos of her in Abby's living room. This could be fun.

Abby sighed. "At some point we're going to discuss the exact nature of your phone calls, but right now I prefer to remain oblivious. Mom, this is Seth Caldwell. Seth, my mom, Marilyn Delaney."

He clasped the offered hand. "Nice to meet you, Mrs. Delaney."

"Now, now, none of that 'Mrs. Delaney' nonsense. It's Marilyn. And it's nice to meet you, too." She turned to her daughter. "Sweetie, do you think you should go ask Frank if there's anything he needs you to do?"

"Forget it."

"Why?"

Abby folded her arms. "I'm not leaving you alone with Seth. He's not yet been fully briefed on how to deal with you. We haven't even had time to work out a hand signal meaning 'run, run for your life.'"

"Ridiculous. What could I possibly do?" She looked at Seth, and he swore he saw her eyelashes flutter.

"You'll ask him completely inappropriate questions."

"I most certainly will not," Marilyn said, trying for indignation but missing the mark by a mile. "Besides, you're my daughter. What could be inappropriate about wanting to chat with someone who happened to be here very early in the morning when your guest room blew up?"

"He didn't blow up my guest room, Mother."

"I'm sure he didn't. Not on purpose." She smiled in Seth's direction, conveying he didn't look the least little bit like a crazed guest-room bomber.

Abby clenched her jaw and fumed, moving on to grinding her teeth. Seth covered his mouth with one hand to conceal a grin. Marilyn Delaney was a pistol, but he sensed only curiosity, not hostility, in her determination to talk to him. He knew the type well, since he was raised by someone with similar tendencies.

Abby clutched his hand and attempted to postpone her mother's interrogation. "Can't this wait till we can go inside and sit down? And have eight or ten beers? Right now I want to try to get my head together, not dodge land mines with you."

Marilyn patted Abby's cheek. "Of course, sweetie. I'm sure I'll have plenty of time to get to know Seth." An electronic sound crackled from where the rest of their patiently waiting little band was gathered, and Frank pulled his radio from his belt. "I believe I'll go see what's going on. We'll find time to chat later, though, won't we, Seth?"

"Absolutely. I'm looking forward to it." And he was.

Marilyn went to pester Frank, and Abby's shoulders relaxed. "Don't worry. I'm sure your mom and I will get along fine."

"That's not what I'm worried about."

"What, then?"

Abby's eyes rolled. "Believe me, you'll find out. Come on. Let's go sit by the lake. The bugs aren't bad this morning. Mom will come find us when they need us."

It sounded like an outstanding idea, and they walked down the path to the bench. He draped an arm around her shoulder. "Alone at last."

Abby looked toward the top of the path, where her mother wandered in and out of view while talking nonstop into her cell phone, complete with hand gestures. "Relatively. Dammit, Seth, this is not what I had planned for the rest of our morning."

"No, me either." What he wanted more than anything was to be back in that big bed with her, and for the world to leave them alone for at least three days. "We'll be swamped with even more people in a few minutes, but I need to know if you're doing OK."

"I'm fine."

"Abby, stop. Look at me." She tilted her chin and he saw the distress in her eyes. "You're not fine. This is your Fortress of Solitude, and something just happened to upset it. Don't cut me out."

"I know. I won't. But right now I don't know whether to be mad, scared, sad, or just sit here and scream."

"Those are all part of it. You think I don't feel that way, too? All I can think about right now is who the hell would want to..."

She interrupted him, gently placing her fingers on his lips, which he appreciated. He really didn't want to complete the thought. "No. Don't talk about it. Not yet. If someone wanted to hurt you, I can't deal with it right now. Let's wait until the bomb experts get here. Maybe it was just some freak accident."

Seth knew he didn't have anything in his bag with the potential to blow a hole in a house. Someone had put something in it, with the intent of leaving him in the same condition as the wall in Abby's guest room. But he was willing to keep the thought to himself for now.

"Fine by me. I have a better idea, anyway." Seth wrapped his other arm around her and zeroed in on her lips.

He was amazed. Overwhelmed. Confused. He'd never felt this way before, and didn't know how to balance all these different emotional and—had to be honest, here—physical issues. He tried to convey his feelings in the depth of his kiss, and the gentle but insistent touch of his hand as he refamiliarized himself with her tantalizing curves. He cradled her in his arms, hearing her very appreciative sounds, when footsteps approached. *Damn.* "Company coming."

"Naturally." Abby sat up with a disgruntled sigh and flushed cheeks.

"The sooner everybody gets here, the sooner they'll get gone."

"One can only hope."

They watched the approach of a tall, lanky man with dark hair displaying a serious case of bed head. Abby introduced him as the Emporia police chief, Bob LeFevre.

"Guess you've had a pretty interesting morning, Mr. Caldwell," he said, shaking Seth's hand. Saying Minnesota men tended to be a little stoic was like saying Lake Superior tended to be a little damp.

"Yes sir, you could say that."

"What can you tell me about what happened?" He pulled a notebook from the pocket of his dark gray uniform pants and extracted a pen from his breast pocket.

"Near as we can tell, my duffel bag exploded."

"You don't think it was a gas line or something in the structure of the house?" the chief asked, glancing up from his notebook.

"I doubt it," Abby said. "There aren't any gas lines along that wall. Plus, there were flaming bits of duffel bag and jeans all over the room. The table the bag was on is gone, and there's an enormous hole in the wall."

"I saw the hole when I came by. Impressive. From what you're saying, I'd guess you're right. We'll find out." A furrow appeared between his eyebrows. "Son, who knew you'd be up here?"

"Nobody, really. I didn't even know till after the show last night. The bag and I should've both been in our tour bus this morning, far as anybody knew, right up until I left." Which meant the bomb was all about him, and had nothing to do with Abby or her house till be brought it right to her doorstep. The thought was like an icy fist squeezing his heart.

The chief's furrow deepened. "Where's the bus now, and who's on it?"

"They planned to leave town an hour or two ago, so probably headed south on Highway 169. Our road manager, sound engineer, and rhythm guitarist are onboard."

"I need their names and a cell phone number."

Seth provided the information, and wondered what was so urgent. Whatever it was, it couldn't be good.

Chief LeFevre keyed his radio. "Paulsen, get down here. Pronto." He tore the page out of the notebook as Sammy came running.

He skidded to a stop at the bottom of the path, his face flushed and his narrow chest heaving. "What do you need, Chief?"

"The ATF is gonna need the bus, and everybody in it. If that's where the bomb was supposed to be, they need to make sure there's not a second one, and question everybody who's been around the bus in the time the bomb—or bombs—could have been placed there." He indicated the page from his notebook. "Give them this information, tell them it's where the device was intended to be. They'll try to call the bus, tell 'em to pull off the road. You don't have to call the Troopers. ATF will do that. Now get moving, before we have more trouble."

Sammy ran.

"Holy shit," Abby said. She looked stunned by the chief's reaction to what Seth told him. "Bob, what's going on?"

Chief LeFevre's steady gaze took in both of them. "Did anybody but the two of you have access to the duffel bag at any time after it was taken off the bus?"

"No," Seth said.

"Then the bomb was in the bag when you left, which makes the bus a crime scene." He flipped the notebook to a fresh page and started writing. "Since it's not likely somebody was lurking in Abby's yard waiting for the right time to blow the thing, it was probably on a timer. Where would you have been at that time, if you'd been on the bus?"

"It's damned near certain I'd have been asleep in my bunk, with the duffel bag right underneath me." He suppressed a shudder as a vision of his blast-dismembered body flashed through his mind.

Abby's gasp caught in her throat, and Seth silently cursed himself for blurting it out in front of her.

"But you were here instead," Abby said, clutching his arm. "Thank goodness."

"Mr. Caldwell..." said Chief LeFevre.

"Seth."

"OK, Seth. I'm sure the ATF agents are going to need to talk to everybody who could have been on the bus recently. Everybody." Seth opened his mouth to protest, but was silenced with a stern look. "Sure, it's possible somebody watched and waited for an opportunity, but the fact is the person responsible is almost certainly somebody who knows your schedule extremely well and has access to the bus and your belongings."

"No way. Those guys are my family. It has to be somebody else." Seth stood and began pacing along the rocky shore, Dilbert prancing around him. His thoughts churned as he sought any explanation that didn't involve his closest friends.

"Well, could be, could be. But it's still somebody who was on the bus yesterday. They wouldn't want to plant it too soon and take a risk you'd find it. If they wanted it to blow this morning, I'd guess it was set up last night."

"During the show," Abby said. "Seth, it had to be then."

He considered. "Maybe. People were in and out of the bus all day, but once the show started, it'd be pretty unusual for anybody to be out there. We were all working, and some of us aren't real good about locking up when we go inside."

Chief LeFevre asked for the names and contact information for the band and crew who weren't on the bus this morning. He noted the equipment van would also have to be stopped and searched. After he gave the information, Seth sat down beside Abby to think. "It can't be any of them. Can't be."

"Nobody's going to jump to conclusions, son. Stranger things have happened. But don't be so sure about it that you put yourself—or Abby—in danger, you hear?" He stuck the notebook in his pocket and turned to go. "We'll talk some more after the team gets here and checks things out."

"OK, Bob. Thanks. I think," Abby said. When the chief had gone, she turned to Seth. "Well, that was disturbing."

"Little bit." Honestly, he felt like he'd been punched in the diaphragm.

"I wish we could just disappear."

"We can't?"

"Not yet." Abby stood, and a tiny smile softened the corners of her mouth. Seth's heart lightened at the sight. "But I'll show you where I go when I want to relax."

She led him around a fallen, weathered log and a few steps into the trees, and pointed. He saw a rope hammock, sheltered but not concealed. He was surprised he hadn't noticed it earlier, but he'd had a lot on his mind.

It took some maneuvering and coordination, but they tumbled into the hammock and lay together, swaying gently, facing the lake. With Abby in his arms and no one else in sight, he did feel calmer.

He traced the outline of her lips with one finger. "Trying to peel you out of those jeans in a hammock is probably a bad idea, huh?"

"I think it sounds brilliant, despite the risk of landing on my head in the dirt. But I don't imagine we'll be alone very long."

"Maybe if we started right away?"

Abby laughed. While it wasn't exactly the reaction he'd been hoping for, it still pleased him. "Nope. When you get me out of my jeans, I most definitely don't want any interruptions. Possibly till August."

He liked the sound of that.

Abby was on her back, semireclining in the lazy curve of the hammock, and Seth pulled himself up on one elbow beside her. With his hand on her opposite hip, he gazed down at her. A whisper of breeze fluttered a few layered strands of hair around her face, and the sunlight filtered through the leaves overhead, giving her skin a subtle glow. She wore almost no makeup, and her eyes, framed by thick, dark lashes met his without reservation.

He hoped to have many such opportunities to study the angle of her cheekbones, and the faint pink blush across her nose from standing too long in the morning sun. But this moment was priceless. He experienced a tightening in his chest and groin, evidence of how much he wanted her, in so many ways. He was most amazed, however, at the expansive sensation deep within him. It was as if previously unexplored regions were opening for the single purpose of accommodating the feelings awakened by the woman lying beside him.

Abby reached up and tucked his hair behind one ear, allowing her fingers to linger at the edge of his jaw. "See? It's peaceful here. It won't last, but I needed a few minutes away from the disaster area."

"It's perfect. And I totally could've had your jeans off by now."

"I don't doubt it for a second. But listen."

Seth heard the sound of feet disturbing the rocks along the shoreline. A moment later, Abby's mother appeared around the screen of trees.

"Sorry to interrupt," she said. "But the ATF agents are here, and as soon as they make sure it's safe, they want to talk to both of you."

Seth reluctantly rolled from the hammock and offered his hand to help Abby regain her feet. With her mother already on the way back up the path, he placed his lips near Abby's ear and whispered, "Next time, you're wearing sweat pants."

"Only if you do, too," Abby said. And then she pinched his ass.

Chapter Seven

They crested the slope from the lake, and the first thing Abby saw was a Chevy Suburban bearing the emblem of the US Bureau of Alcohol, Tobacco, Firearms, and Explosives. This was not a sight she'd ever expected to encounter in her own driveway. Three men wearing protective vests led a yellow Labrador retriever around the yard near the damaged wall. Her home was officially a crime scene.

One of the agents, a weathered-looking man in his forties, noted their arrival and approached them. "Miss Delaney?"

Abby nodded to indicate she was. "This is Seth Caldwell."

The man shook their hands. "I'm Special Agent Roger Kincaid. Before we discuss what happened, I'm going to have our explosives canine, Roxie, check the house and yard. Once we're sure there aren't going to be any surprises, we can go inside and talk. Sound OK?"

What was she supposed to say? "Sure." Special Agent Kincaid returned to his team, while Abby, Seth, and her mother waited in the shade of the trees along the driveway. Dilbert bounded from the woods. He froze when he saw Roxie working back and forth through the debris-littered yard. His tail waved wildly, and he leaned forward in preparation to greet his guest. Seth reached down and snagged the dog's collar, foiling his plans.

"Dilbert, now's not the time to visit," Abby said. "Seth, could you put him in the garage till they're done?"

He opened the side door of the garage and coaxed the reluctant dog inside. "Sorry, buddy. I know she's cute, but she's working."

Frank, Chief LeFevre, and his two officers stood by Frank's SUV, looking somewhat perturbed to be left out of this stage of the investigation. "I'm surprised Sammy and Karl are still here. Where are the firemen, though?" Abby wondered aloud.

"A call came in about a grass fire out by the Ford dealership," her mother answered. "But unless we have a crime wave, Sammy and Karl won't leave till the food arrives."

"Food?" More people were going to invade her home?

"Yes. I called my craft-club ladies, and Grace will make sure we have enough sandwiches to keep everybody from starvation. Goodness knows we can't count on what's in your refrigerator."

"Feeding a battalion isn't something I have to do on a regular basis."

Marilyn patted her on the arm. "I know, sweetie. It was an observation, not criticism." Abby thought the two were too closely related to merit distinction. "And Grace's husband, Butch, will be by later with plywood and things to do some temporary repairs, until you can get Clancy out here. You missed the gas company. They came while you were down by the lake and shut off the gas to the house. You won't be able to use your fireplace for a day or two, until they come back to do a full inspection."

Abby blew out an exasperated breath. "I don't imagine I need the furnace or the fireplace right now, so it's fine." Good thing she had an electric water heater. She was annoyed at having so little control over what was happening with her own house, but grateful her mom was handling the details.

The ATF team disappeared inside the house with Roxie and emerged several minutes later. Dilbert could be heard scratching at the inside of the garage door.

Special Agent Kincaid said, "Which vehicle were you driving last night, Miss Delaney?"

Abby indicated her Jeep.

"We'll need to go over it, too, just to be thorough. Would you open it for us, please?"

Abby complied, and Roxie circled the vehicle several times, sniffing in each open door and under the wheel wells, and climbing through the interior. When she reached the rear hatch, she sat and looked expectantly at her handler. The special agent, who resembled a Hell's Angel more than a federal officer, praised her and rewarded her with a treat from his pocket.

"Roxie's given us the all clear, so we can go inside and talk about what we know so far, and how we're going to proceed," Kincaid said.

The group assembled in Abby's living room. She, Seth, and her mother sat on the couch, but Special Agent Kincaid remained standing. His men, whom he called explosives enforcement officers, went to the bedroom carrying bags and various containers for the collection of evidence. Chief LeFevre hovered nearby, but Frank, Sammy, and Karl waited out on the deck. Roxie had been placed in her kennel in the Suburban, a fact Dilbert deeply resented. He sulked under the coffee table.

In response to Kincaid's questions, Seth repeated what he had told the police chief regarding his change of plans, and the typical comings and goings of the bus's occupants. When he got to the part about the probability he would have been in his bunk if he hadn't stayed with Abby, she clutched his hand.

"We were able to reach your friends on the bus, Mr. Caldwell, and they pulled off the road this side of Mille Lacs. Troopers are on the scene, and there's a team checking out the bus."

"What about the van?" Seth asked.

"They left later than they planned, so they're only about ten miles farther down the road than the bus. I imagine you'll be talking to them shortly."

Abby was having a hard time sitting still. There were federal agents in her house, someone had tried to hurt—she couldn't even think the word "kill"—Seth, her mother itched to interrogate the man she'd had sex with that morning, and a herd of sandwich-bearing craft ladies were due to descend on the whole circus at any moment. Where was the positive part of all this? "But everybody's safe."

"Yes, they're safe, other people on the highway are safe, and we'll be able to identify and question everybody." He turned his attention once again to Seth. "If you could, tell me everywhere your bag was from the time you left the bus last night."

"Well, it was in the back of Abby's Jeep. We brought it in, and it sat at the breakfast bar for a while. I took it in the bathroom, and it was on the floor in there till this morning, when I took it in the other bedroom."

"Anyplace else?"

Seth paused and shook his head. "No, sir. That's it."

"It fits all the hits by Roxie. The Jeep, the breakfast bar, and the bathroom. The other room, of course, was a given." He gave a wry smile. "OK, then, Mr. Caldwell, let's take a look at what's left of your belongings and see if we can come up with some useful information."

Seth rose and went with Kincaid, and Abby felt brittle and vulnerable with him out of her sight. The magnitude of the situation started sinking in. Frank and the other men congregated in the kitchen, raiding her meager store of pop and snacks while they waited for lunch to arrive.

"Come on, sweetie," her mother said. "Let's go outside and get a little distance from all this testosterone."

Seated in the deck chairs, her mother silenced her phone. "Abby, isn't your phone ringing like crazy?"

"Nope. I turned it off. There's nobody I need to talk to right now." The thought of dealing with twenty calls from people asking what happened and gushing sentiments about how happy they were she was OK was more than she could handle. And the fact they'd also be fishing for details about her houseguest had not escaped her. "I think I'm still numb."

"Well of course you are. Nobody expects something like this." Marilyn scooted her chair closer to her daughter's.

"The last twenty-four hours have been all over the place." Abby's voice caught, and she realized she was going to cry. It kind of snuck up on her, but there was nothing she could do about it now.

"I heard your introduction to Seth didn't go well."

"It was awful. He was so furious and was being such a jackass, but we started talking..." Abby tried to swallow a sob, failed, and gave up, allowing the tears to flow. Her mother stroked her hair, patted her back, and eventually handed her a tissue from her well-stocked purse.

As soon as she was able, Abby poured out the whole story, from Cujo's accident, to the talk in the park, the concert, and arriving here last night. She even told her about the conversation down by the lake this morning. She glossed over the juicy bits, but her mother was no fool. She knew exactly what had transpired, and had undoubtedly noted the rumpled condition of Abby's bed.

When she was finished and had mopped the tears and snot from her face, she discovered a new emotion was taking hold. It was anger, and it was directed at her mother. It was unexpected and unwarranted, but she had opened the emotional floodgates, and there was no holding it back.

"And what the hell did you mean earlier when you said 'calls I made myself'? Calling half the town—and I don't even want to know who else—about Seth? What am I, fifteen years old?"

"I don't know why you're upset. I'd think you'd be happy I don't have any objections to your relationship with Seth." Marilyn leaned back and looked as if she might be building up a head of steam of her own.

Abby leaped to her feet and began pacing. "Relationship? You don't have any idea what you're doing. Do you know what it means if I'm with Seth? Do you? I leave. I leave you, my friends, this house, Emporia, everything. Seth can't stay here. He makes his living on the road. I'd have to…" Her throat closed up again. She clenched her fists and silently cursed herself for not being strong enough to get it all out.

"Do you love him?"

Abby's head snapped up. "How can I love him? I just met him. That would be insane."

"It doesn't mean it's not possible."

"I know, but…"

Her mother set her shoulders and looked at her with hazel eyes hard as granite. "Abigail Kathleen Delaney, you listen to me."

Abby knew the tone. Out of years of conditioning, she gathered the tattered remains of her composure and listened.

"Sit yourself back down there, and don't you budge till I'm finished."

Abby sat.

"You ought to know I'm not a dim-witted old woman who likes her daughter's boyfriend because he's handsome and polite. When I received the first call last night, I had a feeling, and, yes, I've been talking to people. I woke Dash and Nancy out of a sound sleep before dawn—and he didn't appreciate it, let me tell you—so I could ask about Seth. Nobody had a bad thing to say about him, including people who usually find something bad to say about everybody."

"The Emporia grapevine at work, huh?" Abby almost choked on the bitterness in her tone.

"Emporia and elsewhere. Believe me, you truly don't want to know," Marilyn said with a dismissive wave of her hand. "From everything I learned, he works hard, couldn't tell a lie to save his life, and would do absolutely anything for people close to him. He doesn't lose his temper often, but if somebody wrongs him, he never forgets. I can't really fault him. Your father was the same way.

"Like I said, I had a feeling, but I had to be sure. Once I was here, all I had to do was watch him. He never took his eyes off you, and I could see it was driving him crazy he couldn't somehow fix this." Her mother reached over and gripped Abby's hand. "And you, you leaned on him for support, which is not something you do. You're too independent and hardheaded and much too cautious, which is why I might have gone slightly overboard." A small wince hinted maybe she did understand she'd crossed a very definite line. "This was so out of character for you, rushing into something with somebody you just met. But there you were, letting this man take care of you." She tipped her index finger under Abby's chin, angling her face so she couldn't avoid meeting her eyes. "If you're too stubborn or frightened to trust your own instincts, you're a fool, Abigail."

"You couldn't know all that from talking to a few people and watching him hold my hand." Abby said the words, but she suspected it was altogether possible.

"I could, and I do." Marilyn rose and began pacing, eerily mimicking her daughter's earlier movements. "Then, of course, there's Dilbert."

"Dilbert?" Abby thought her brain might have skipped a track or two.

"Yes. Haven't you noticed how Dilbert is with him? He follows Seth around, goes to him for reassurance, and he just met him, too. I always say trust your dog. Bingo never liked David, you know."

Abby couldn't believe her potential future could be decided based on a cantankerous old cocker spaniel's instant dislike of her ex-husband. "He's not mine."

"Dilbert or Seth?"

"Both. Neither. I don't know, and stop confusing me! Besides, it's one day, Mom. How can I trust anything I feel this strongly, so quickly?" Her anger was fading, but unfortunately the tears threatened to return. *Holy mood swings, Batman.* She swallowed and took a few calming breaths.

"Just because I'm your mother, and a widow, doesn't mean I was never young and in love. When I met your father forty years ago, he told me before he took me home the first evening I'd be his wife. Of course I lived with your grandparents, so he didn't end up in my bed, but still..."

"I didn't know that," Abby said quietly. "But how did you know he was right?"

"I didn't at first. I was like you. I didn't think it could happen that way, and it scared the daylights out of me. But he didn't give up, I got over being afraid, and it was the best thing I ever did." Marilyn's eyes misted with cherished memories.

"People say things like that all the time, and they still end up going from one disaster to another. I don't want any more disasters." Abby felt so broken up after everything that happened, so damaged. She feared she was one last disaster away from shattering altogether.

"What people, sweetie? The ones going from disaster to disaster aren't thinking about anything, aren't feeling anything. They're just reacting. They're so desperate for somebody, anybody, and that's all that matters. But when is the last time you even thought about letting somebody share your life?" Marilyn plowed ahead, not waiting for an answer. "I'll tell you when. Never. Not since David left. But Seth found you, and if you stop protesting everything you think you'd lose and think about what you'd gain, you'll see I'm right."

Abby was stunned. "It's a lot to think about."

"I know it is."

"Just yesterday, my life was rolling along, and I wasn't unhappy with it. Now everything's changed." How was she supposed to make room for all this in her head?

"You weren't unhappy, sweetie, but were you happy?"

Abby's mind flashed back over the last few years. They were kind of...empty. "Probably not."

"Well, you think about it, but don't let something special pass you by because you're afraid. It's the best advice I can give you." Having said her piece, Marilyn rose, patted her daughter's shoulder, and walked toward the road, flipping open her cell phone. She never was one to linger and deal with the aftermath.

For a moment, Abby sat, dazed, wondering what storm had just blown through. She went inside and found Seth on the couch. He took one look at her and was instantly at her side, holding her, and she breathed in his now-familiar scent. "You've been crying," he said, stroking her hair.

"Yeah, a little bit, but I'll try not to booger up your shirt if you promise not to let go." His arms tightened, and she stood there for a few minutes, absorbing his strength.

"What can I do, darlin'?"

Abby took a breath and looked up at him. "This is good." She was surprised to find she could muster a small smile. "How'd it go in there?"

"They're bagging a bunch of stuff, but I have my boots, and we found some jewelry blown clear. Gotta love cheap, heavy sterling, I guess."

"Were they able to tell anything about what happened?"

"Not a lot. It'll take a few days in the lab. But they said it was some kind of pipe bomb with a timer, like Chief LeFevre suspected. We can talk more about this stuff in a while, OK? I'm still processing it all." He kept his arm around her and guided them both back to the couch. "Ready to make a run for it yet? We could lock ourselves in your room."

"It wouldn't stop Mom. Wouldn't even slow her down."

"She is kind of a force of nature."

"So's an avalanche."

The avalanche in question returned, still talking into her cell phone. "Don't mind me. I want to see if Grace can bring ice. She's down at the Readi-Mart getting some things." She turned her attention back to the phone pressed to her ear. "No, Grace, no ice. You'll need to bring some. See you soon." She looked at the men who had edged from the kitchen to the dining area when faced with her purposeful approach. "You boys scoot. Grace will be here shortly, and she'll need help bringing things in."

Knowing better than to argue, they scooted.

Abby wished her mother would go back outside too, and leave her alone with Seth, but Marilyn had her own agenda. She sat on the other side of the sectional sofa and beamed at them. She beamed. Abby didn't think that boded well.

"So, Seth, how long do you plan to stay in Minnesota?"

Gee, Mom, totally subtle.

"We haven't really had a chance to talk about it yet," he said. Abby pinched the bridge of her nose. She wanted to warn him to look out for traps, but she had a sinking feeling her mother's snares were laid for her, not the man sitting beside her.

Seth continued, "I have to be back in Austin in a week, week and a half. Assuming nobody manages to blow me up before then."

Marilyn's smile faltered, but only for an instant. "I'm sure they'll figure out what this was all about. Awful. Just awful business."

"It's a mess, that's for sure. I keep thinking there'll turn out to be some sort of mistake. But I guess it's not likely." Abby heard the pain lurking beneath the surface of his words. It was tearing him apart to consider the possibility one of his closest friends felt they had a reason to want him dead.

"We'll simply have to have faith things will work out. What I'm wondering, though, is what your plans are regarding Abby."

"Mother!" For the love of all sacred things, what was her insane parent doing? Did she think it was 1845, when a suitor was required to state his intentions to the family? She realized she'd lurched to her feet, and sat down again, rolling her eyes in Seth's direction. "You do not have to answer."

"Actually, darlin', I don't mind." He took her hand and addressed Marilyn. "My plan is to convince her we belong together."

Abby squeezed his hand. Hard. By the way the corner of his eye twitched, she thought she might have squeezed it almost hard enough. She hadn't heard any crunching. How had Seth and her mother figured each other out and joined forces so quickly?

Marilyn put one hand to her bird-bedecked chest and said, "Oh, sweetie, that's wonderful."

Sweetie? Seth was "sweetie" already? This was worse than she thought. Not that she was opposed to the whole Abby-plus-Seth scenario, but she still had some thinking to do and felt as if she were being railroaded.

"How does Abby feel?" Marilyn asked, continuing her clever tactics.

"Well, Marilyn, it appears she has some reservations about it."

It must have been the cue her mother was waiting for, because she launched into a speech sounding as if she'd prepared it well in advance. "Don't you dare let her get away with that. She's had some setbacks in her life, and she's afraid of doing anything to upset the balance she's found. But if you don't push her too hard, she'll realize some things are worth the risk."

She folded her arms and smiled at him, before shifting her gaze to her daughter.

Abby tried to make her eyes as laser-like as Seth's had been when she ran over his guitar. Since her mother didn't burst into flames, she guessed she'd fallen short. She had to marvel at the woman's talent. She'd found a way to clue him in on Abby's personality and fears, make sure he knew he had the Marilyn Delaney Seal of Approval, and to deliver another lecture to Abby at the same time. Manipulative, well-meaning, and efficient. The Maternal Trifecta.

"Don't worry. We'll work it out," Seth said.

"I'm sure you will. But if she gets stubborn, you let me know."

"Mother! I am sitting right here," Abby sputtered.

"Yes, sweetie, I know. Oh, and you might want to do something with this." She reached between the sofa cushions and plucked a scrap of pink fabric from its depths. Abby immediately recognized the skimpy top she'd been wearing the night before, and stuck in the couch this morning. Her mother had probably spotted it right away, and saved it for her grand finale. Beside her, Seth burst out laughing, which she was certain had been her mother's intention.

Abby lunged across the couch and snatched the shirt from her mother's hand. Her face burning, she stomped off to her room and stuffed it in the hamper with an exasperated grunt. Once again on the couch — beside Seth, though she sort of wanted to kick him in the knee — she squinted and glared. Was she being childish? She considered it, and decided she didn't care.

"Abby, honestly," said her mother. "Don't be so sensitive. I'm sure Seth and I are going to get along fine."

"Darlin', really, it's OK. I grew up with a mom, a grandma, a whole passel of aunts, and an older sister. I know how it works." Damn if he wasn't still smiling.

"Fine, fine, fine. But I must point out we have other things to worry about today. So can the two of you stop negotiating my dowry? Please?"

"Of course, sweetie. Far be it from me to tell you what to do."

Abby knew this was as much of a concession as she would receive and prepared to change the subject. Weather. Weather was always an acceptable topic of conversation in Minnesota.

Abby was spared a discussion of relative humidity when the door opened and Sammy entered, lugging an oversize cooler. More coolers followed, toted by Karl and Frank. Finally, Grace and Marnie, two of her mother's friends, came in with some bags. Everything was soon arranged on the kitchen counters, and the three men began piling plates with sandwiches and cookies. Chief LeFevre came in a moment later, but went directly to the spare bedroom, mumbling about checking on the progress being made.

She and Seth nabbed sandwiches and sat on the deck steps. She could only nibble, and fed the majority of her sandwich to the very persuasive Dilbert. He'd learned how to do the "sad puppy dog eyes" trick with only one eye, so she felt he deserved the treats.

The fire chief and local police officers departed, leaving only the ATF agents behind. Butch arrived with some plywood and other supplies, which he unloaded before heading into the kitchen for lunch.

Abby made introductions and small talk as people came and went, but her mind was busy mulling over the bizarre nature of the day. Parts of it had been, quite literally, a dream come true. The rest had been a nightmare, with bits of darkly comic relief. She couldn't write a day this strange if she tried.

After Grace whisked away their plates, Seth dug his phone from his pocket and turned it on.

"Probably no point in that," Abby said.

"Probably not. But a couple of years ago, when Dash took us fishing, every once in a while our phones would pick up a signal." He waited for it to power up.

"Caroline mentioned the fishing trip. Sounds like a memorable day."

"It was so memorable I've spent two years trying to forget it. Imagine four exhausted, hungover guys on a boat with Dash, who drank, belched, and spit tobacco juice all over the place. Pete got seasick, and it went downhill from there." His smirk implied while it might not have been an especially enjoyable excursion, it had become an often-told story.

Seth's phone chirped, announcing new messages. "Great. It's probably twenty messages from the guys wanting to talk about what happened, but there's a text message, too." He began tapping at the phone, and Abby saw he was accessing the text in-box.

She decided to give him some privacy, and sat on the deck steps and scratched Dilbert under the chin. When she hit the right spot, his tail thumped on the ground, and his eye rolled back in his head.

"What the fuck?" Seth exclaimed.

Abby stood too quickly, tried to turn, and rapped her shin on the top step. She hobbled to Seth's side, rubbing at her injured limb. All the color had drained from his face, and he stared at the screen on his phone.

He turned it so she could see the display. When she finished, it took her a few minutes to puzzle out what it meant. She remembered a conversation, which previously seemed insignificant, and her stomach lurched. "Seth, you have to get that to Kincaid. Now."

She didn't think the day could get worse, but it just had.

Chapter Eight

Seth stalked into the house, rage and fear battling for position as his most prevalent emotion. He found Special Agent Kincaid in the hallway. "I have something you need to see."

Kincaid directed him through the laundry room and onto the side porch. Abby followed, one hand clutching the back of his shirt like a lifeline.

"My cell phone hasn't had a signal up here most of the day, but it came in a few minutes ago. I have a bunch of voice mails, but the first thing I saw was this." He handed the phone to Kincaid and waited as he read it.

The agent's eyebrows drew together, and he took a deep breath, which he held for a moment before speaking. "It's clear this isn't good, but I'm going to need you to explain the details."

Seth disentangled Abby's fingers from his shirt and reached for her hand, only then noticing his own hand was shaking. He didn't have to ask to see the message again. Every word was burned in his mind, he suspected, forever.

Hear u got lucky in more ways than 1. But I know how 2 hurt u now b4 u pay. 3rd time's a charm.

Seth closed his eyes and swallowed, getting his heart out of his throat so he could speak. "They know I was with Abby and not on the bus, obviously." He rather resented the "got lucky" remark, though he certainly felt lucky.

"So we need to think again about who knew you were coming here." Kincaid arrowed through the message again and shook his head.

"Pretty soon after I left, they'd all have known. And I'd guess some of the people who work at Dash's, and maybe even some fans who hung around last night, saw me leave. I mean, we made the plans at the last minute, but didn't exactly keep it a secret. We walked right across the parking lot with all my stuff."

"What about the rest of the message?"

"That's the part I really don't like. If they didn't know how to hurt me before, the only thing that's changed is I met Abby. And if it's a threat against her, I swear I'll find this asshole and feed him his own fucking heart." His right hand clenched as he momentarily envisioned the very satisfying, very bloody removal of said heart.

Kincaid raised his eyebrows. "I understand how you feel, Mr. Caldwell, but it's probably not something you want to go around saying, especially to a federal agent. You know, just in case." Kincaid looked back at the phone. "What about this other part, about the third time being a charm?"

"It took me a few seconds to figure out, but it's important. You have to tell the agents at the bus there's a bottle of Jack Daniel's under my bunk. They need to get it and have it tested."

"Tested? Why?"

"Because three nights ago in Cincinnati, he had two drinks from the bottle and was really sick. Right Seth?" she asked, clutching his upper arm. "That's what you guys were talking about on the bus last night, when they were teasing you."

Seth nodded. "I bought the bottle straight from the club's bar, and I'm the only one who drank from it. I drink bourbon, or at least I did, but the rest of the guys drink beer and tequila, except Mouse. He likes vodka." He explained the bartender had cracked the seal when he served it, but they'd all milled around, finishing a late dinner, before any of them started into the liquor. "Anybody could've put something in it, and been sure I'd be the only one who drank it."

"But you only had two drinks?" Kincaid appeared to be finished with the phone for now, but didn't offer to return it.

"Yeah. I had to go down to the office for an interview with a guy from the radio station. Took about twenty minutes. By the time I was done there, I was sicker'n a dog. Normally, though, I would've stayed in the bar and had at least a few more before we called it a night."

"Which means this bomb was actually somebody's second attempt to kill you."

That was the part bothering him now. "The bastard's not getting another shot. No fucking way. I'll figure out who it is." He raked his fingers through the crown of his hair in frustration. "I've been telling you it can't be one of my band or crew, but I guess I have to consider it. If this started in Cincinnati, it seems like it has to be somebody on the road with us, but I still want you to look into the people I told you about. They could be trailing us, or maybe hired somebody. I just don't know why. Make me pay for what?"

Kincaid put one hand on Seth's shoulder. "I understand how unsettling this is. I really do. I'll call the team deployed to the bus right now, have them get the bottle. I'll be meeting with them in town later, to discuss what they found, and they'll help me interview the club staff. Hopefully, we'll get some solid information and resolve everything before this person can make any more plans."

"I appreciate all you're doing. Please, let me know anything you need. This became a whole lot worse for me when that message came through." He looked at Abby and tried to appear reassuring, but didn't think he pulled it off very successfully. She still looked shell-shocked.

"We'll be in touch soon. If we find the bottle right away and get it to the lab, I'll put a rush on it and we might have preliminary results by late this afternoon. Since there's an ongoing threat, it'll get priority." He wagged the hand holding Seth's phone. "I'm going to hang onto this for a while, if that's OK. I want to forward the message to our tech department, see what we can find out. Did you recognize the number?"

"No. I noticed it was a local area code, though. All my guys have out-of-state numbers."

"We'll look into it. When can I get this back to you?"

"The guys are coming back to Emporia, right?"

"I'll find out in a minute, but probably."

"I guess I'll go into town. I need to look 'em all in the face, see if I can tell anything, though it makes me sick to think about it." He tried to picture what hidden malice looked like. "Can I catch up to you at Dash's?"

"That'd work. Before you go, listen to your other messages in case there's anything else we need to know about."

Seth had been so upset about the text message he'd forgotten all about the voice mails. He accepted the phone and accessed his mailbox. Eight messages, all but one from band and crew members. He listened to each only briefly, determining they were of the "holy shit, are you all right?" variety, before deleting them. "Uh oh."

Abby's eyes widened. "What? Not another threat?"

"No, no, nothing like that. My mom. Guess I should've called her right away, huh?"

"You can use my phone before we go into town. Guess moms in Montana aren't so different from the ones in Minnesota."

"Not even enough to notice. Stupid of me not to call her, though."

"This isn't a situation you exactly had an action plan for."

Seth handed the phone back to Kincaid. "All right, then. I'll see you at Dash's later."

Kincaid headed back inside, already pulling out his own phone to call the team searching the bus.

Seth and Abby walked around the house toward the deck. Dilbert was lying in his crater and thumped his tail as they climbed the steps. Abby's mother sat in one of the Adirondack chairs, working her way down a list in a small notebook.

"Hey, Mom," Abby said. "Anything else I need to know about?" She sat on the top step and leaned against the rail.

"No, everything's going fine for now. Butch will board up the hole in the wall and the other window soon as they tell him he can. Grace and Marnie and I will get everything tidied up for you." She crossed something off her list and stuck the notebook in her purse.

"You don't have to do that. I can clean it up."

"Sweetie, you have more important things to think about than sweeping up glass and plaster dust," Marilyn said, glancing pointedly in Seth's direction. Looking at Abby sitting there, the sun bringing out auburn glints in her long, dark hair, he imagined her hair brushing across his chest, and had to agree.

"OK. I really appreciate it. We're going into town as soon as Seth calls his mom." She leaned toward him and handed him her phone. "The guys will be coming back after they're done with the bus and the van, and he needs to see them."

"I understand. Just be careful, please."

"Of course we will."

Seth left them there and walked to the far side of the deck to call his mother. He couldn't believe he hadn't done so already. He normally spoke to her at least every other day, though his father seldom came to the phone. James had always been a distant father, which Seth knew had led to the exceptional bond he and his sister had with their mother. To compensate for her husband's lack of involvement, Rebecca Caldwell filled the roles of both parents, and then some. Seth not only adored her, he respected her more than anyone he'd ever known.

She answered on the first ring, and he spent several minutes assuring her he was fine and wasn't in any danger. He didn't know if it was completely true, but it wouldn't do any good to worry her even more. There was nothing she could do from Montana. Then she said something perking his attention.

"Are you going to tell me about this woman you've met?" She sounded curious, but there was a hint of chastisement there, too.

"Sure I am, Mom. I haven't exactly had a lot of time to make any announcements." Not to mention he didn't know what to tell anyone. Abby hadn't yet come out and said where their relationship was headed.

"I talked to Dianne this morning."

"Joey's mom called you? Before or after the whole explosion thing?"

"Both, actually. She called the first time because she and Joe Senior received a call from your friend's mother. Seems she woke Dash up awful early wanting to know about you. She talked Dianne's number out of him." Seth heard the humor dancing around the edges of her voice, which made him chuckle. That was his mom. She always got a kick from anybody outtalking Dash.

"We knew Marilyn made some calls, but we didn't know how many or who. Did she call you, too?" The very idea should make him apprehensive, but he found himself thinking his spunky but soft-spoken mother would hit it off with Marilyn just fine. Whether it was a good thing or a bad thing, he wasn't sure.

"No, not yet. But after Dianne called back to tell me about the explosion, I asked her to call Marilyn and tell her we'd talk tomorrow, after things have settled down a bit."

"I don't think I'm going to tell Abby that."

His mother laughed, a melodious sound reminding Seth where he'd come by his singing voice. "Tell her not to worry. It's just a phone call."

"You'll like Marilyn. I do. She reminds me of Aunt Gwen."

"I'm sure it'll be fine, hon. But what about Abby?"

Seth let his head fall back and looked up through the trees. What was he supposed to say? "All I can tell you is she's special, Mom. First thing she did was run over my new guitar, accidentally, and we yelled at each other for a while. Real romantic."

"And then what?"

"After I was done being completely nuts, we talked, and I invited her to the show. I can't explain it. I just know. She's special. And the fact my being here put her in danger makes me want to kill somebody."

"I'd like to meet the girl who could crack through that tough shell of yours." The lilt to her voice was both amused and affectionate.

"I hope you will, soon. I want her to come with me when I leave, but she's really attached to this place. She's a writer, works at home, and kind of made this her haven after her dad died." He didn't think he needed to mention the divorce right now. "I don't know if she's ready to be away from it much, and she'd be gone a lot if she's with me."

"You'll sort it out, hon. If you don't make it an ultimatum, let her work things through, I'm sure it will be fine." He heard the screen door slam, and he pictured his mother stepping out of her kitchen onto the wide, covered porch. He wondered if the apple trees at the edge of the yard were blooming yet.

"I hope so, Mom. This completely snuck up on me, but now I've found her, I don't want to mess it up."

"I always knew that's how it'd be with you."

"How what would be?"

"Well, you've had girlfriends, but you never had long-term plans. You never gave them any reason to expect anything from you, because you didn't even expect anything from yourself." Seth thought he heard a small sigh during her brief pause. He'd always wondered if he'd disappointed her on some level with his lack of interest in pursuing a real relationship. He hoped not. She was one of only a handful of people whose opinion he cared about. "I knew when somebody mattered enough, you'd want to do something, be something more. And once you expect something from yourself, that's all she wrote."

"Right now I'm just trying to convince her I'm serious, and get her to think about a future."

"Bring her here when you can. You might live on a bus now, but you come from somewhere. She needs to see that."

"You're probably right. I will."

They talked a few more minutes, and his mother agreed with his belief the guys in the band couldn't possibly have anything to do with the attempt on his life. He told her he was headed into town to see everybody but Joey and Pete, and she said to give them all her love.

He went back to Abby. "Where'd your mom go?"

"Not sure. Around front somewhere with Grace and Marnie. She had a tape measure." She stood up and Seth handed back her phone.

"Ready to go?"

"Let me go splash some water on my face and I'll be all set."

A few minutes later, Abby came out of the bathroom, her face fresh and free of evidence of her earlier tears. She made sure Dilbert's water bowl was full, and they headed toward the driveway.

Seth drove. No way was he going to ride all the way to town with Abby behind the wheel after the day she'd had. She ran over guitars when she was "irritated." There was no telling what sort of calamity would occur if she tried to drive after recently having part of her house explode. She argued at first, but eventually settled in the passenger seat without any outward signs of resentment.

For the first few minutes Abby sat slumped forward, her head in her hands. She leaned back and said, "I'm not sure I want to know, but I think I have to. What else did the ATF guys say?"

Seth thought about the discussion, which made him feel helpless and defensive. Those were not emotions he'd often experienced, and he didn't like it. "I told you they think it was some sort of pipe bomb with a timer." She nodded. "After I told them what was in the bag, some clothes, another pair of shoes, my iPod, a bunch of other junk, they figured the bomb was inside the case for my pool cue."

"You carry around a pool cue?"

"Sure. We play a lot of bars, and pool is a good way to pass the time when we're not working. I had a custom cue in a wooden case, and it fit right in the bottom of the bag, so I usually left it there. They looked at burn marks and a bunch of other stuff I didn't bother to try to understand, they think it was the cue case." He hated somebody he knew and trusted might have dug through his personal things, determining which item would best conceal an explosive device meant to kill him.

"Could they tell how bad it would have been, I mean, if you…" She couldn't complete the thought, but Seth knew what she was asking.

"Bad. The bag was on the table by the window, a more or less open space. But if it'd been in the compartment under the bunk, the weak point would be the mattress. The force would've mainly gone up, and… It could have been bad." He was glad he was still busy being confused and angry, because if he let himself think about what almost happened to him, he'd be scared shitless.

"Guess it's a good thing I'm so shameless and brought you home with me, then, huh?" She was trying to smile as she said it.

"Coming home with you was the best thing I thing I've ever done, darlin', even without the 'avoiding getting blown up' part. And I happen to like 'shameless' when it's you." He gave her thigh a reassuring rub. "Thing is, Mouse was scheduled to drive, and Trent and Marsh usually sleep the first shift. Marsh's bunk is on the other side toward the back, and Trent likes to crash in the rear lounge, so it might not have killed them, but it definitely would've messed them up."

"Which means whoever it was didn't care if somebody else was hurt."

"Nope."

"If it was one of the guys on the bus, they could've planned to be up front or in the bathroom or something when the bomb went off."

"They could, but deep down I just can't believe it was one of them. Shit, Marsh is my brother in every way that counts. Trent's been with us for seven years, and his number one job is taking care of us. Mouse joined up ten years ago. He was the first guy we hired when we moved to Austin." Seth shook his head. No. No way could he accept any one of those guys wanted him dead.

Abby leaned across the low center console and brushed her lips across his cheek. "I know you can't stand to think about this, but I'm really scared. If we don't find out who it was, they'll try again."

"I know. The cops are almost willing to rule out the guys in the band, because they were onstage the whole night. And they're the last guys I'd ever suspect. I was Joey's best man when he married Caroline. He's been my best friend since we were eight years old and I whacked him in the head for using pencils to drum on the back of my seat on the school bus." Despite the current situation, he had to smile at the recollection. He wondered if he and Joey would've still ended up friends if Seth hadn't had his lunch box in his gym bag when he hit the annoying drummer-to-be. The blow opened a cut on Joey's forehead, and eight-year-old boys always bonded better if there was a little blood involved. Seth redirected his thoughts and returned to the subject at hand. "I'm a godparent to Pete's little girl, and Marsh and I have been through everything together. No way in hell it was one of them."

Abby nodded. "Not to mention if you were gone, so is the band."

"Right. None of us could be replaced. If anything happened to one of us, or somebody decided to quit the road, that'd be the end of it." He knew they could all find work with other bands, but it would never be the same. If he had to, he could play some solo gigs to pay the bills, but imagined he'd spend most of his time writing songs.

"So, who does that leave?" Her fingers were fidgeting in her lap, making Seth think she really wished she had a notebook handy.

"Danny Dawkins, our light guy, and Andy Hicks, our gofer and apprentice sound tech." Seth replied, cracking the window to let some of the fragrant May breeze into the vehicle. He hoped it would help stave off the headache threatening. "They were hired right before Christmas. They hung around one of the clubs in Austin, doing odd jobs. When they heard we were looking for a couple of new guys, everything just connected. They're doing great work, and fit right in. They're both from outside Texas, but a lot of guys come to Austin if they want to get into the music business."

"And Roberto?" Abby asked. She'd stopped fidgeting, and pulled a lip balm from the glove box. She applied a quick coat, which she immediately began gnawing off.

"Been with us about five years, give or take. Couldn't be him. I had my Paul Reed Smith electric guitar under the bunk. Even if 'Berto decided he needed to get rid of me, he'd never risk a guitar. He'd just bust me in the head with a rock or something."

"Seth! Don't joke about this!"

"Darlin', if I don't crack a couple of jokes, I'll go nuts."

Abby sighed. "I know. I wish we could be alone back at the house right now, instead of walking into the middle of whatever this is."

"Me, too. I feel like I'm on the world's worst reality show." One he definitely did not like the consequences of losing. "But how about you? Are you doing any better?" He knew it was a stupid question the second the words were out of his mouth.

"Not even close." The tiny sound escaping was somewhere between a hiccup and a humorless laugh. "I'm kind of over worrying about the house, though. It can be fixed. I'm way more worried about keeping you in one piece."

"Sounds like maybe you're planning on having me around for a while."

She ran her hand down his forearm. "Look, I can't say for sure yet how I'm going to handle this 'we're together, and that's the way it is' thing, but I'm working on it. I don't want to promise you something if I can't follow through. But no matter what, wherever you are, I'd definitely rather have you be alive."

"I'm way more fun that way." His weak attempt at banter failed to draw Abby in. She seemed focused on potential suspects, and he wondered if this was her mystery-writer brain at work.

"Who are the 'other people' you mentioned to Kincaid?"

"I had a hell of a time thinking of anybody, but when he started asking questions a few things came to mind. He wanted to know who the guys were Danny and Andy replaced." One of them left when he got married and didn't want to spend so much time away from his new wife. The other was fired after less than a year for being too drunk to do his job once too often.

"They don't sound very likely," Abby said. The tilt to her head suggested she was trying to figure out a scenario in which the two former crew members could be involved. It would be preferable to focusing suspicion on his closest friends.

"I didn't think so, either. But since they both know my habits pretty well, they want to talk to them." Seth lit a cigarette as he drove. He hoped to achieve the right antiheadache ratio of fresh air to nicotine. "There's the ever-popular 'crazed fan' angle. I couldn't think of anybody who stood out, but they're going to ask the other guys if they noticed anybody unusual lately."

"If it was Pammy Short-Shorts, I'll kill her myself." Abby glowered, and Seth had to smile.

"Was that the girl who was giving you grief last night?"

"Yeah, and she's one of the ones from the park, too. She's of the very firm opinion I have no business being with you."

"Good thing what she thinks doesn't matter."

Abby gifted him with a brief smile. "Sure doesn't matter to me. So, anybody else?"

Seth saved the most likely two "suspects" for last. "There's this guy, Drew Purcell. He lost a court case against us last year. He accused us of stealing two songs he wrote. We never read or listen to songs people send, so we don't get in to any kind of mess." He opened the window a bit more, still seeking a balance to clear his head. "He claimed we must've heard it somewhere. Our stuff didn't sound anything like what he wrote, so we won."

"Go ahead and say it. His stuff sucked."

"His stuff sucked. Pure country-pop crap." Seth was glad to hear Abby give a short laugh.

The last name was going to be tricky. He wasn't sure what, if anything, Abby knew about the situation. He stubbed out the cigarette in the ashtray and said, "Stacy Ballantyne."

"Your ex."

"Yeah. You know about her?" Caroline. It had to be. While he didn't necessarily like having other people give Abby his life story, in this case he was glad she already knew.

"Caroline told me."

"I figured." His hand tightened on the wheel. He did not like thinking about Stacy, and he liked discussing her with Abby even less. "Well, Stacy was plenty pissed after we broke up. But once she was gone, we realized she was poison, and everything was better without her."

"Do you know where she is now?" Her voice was gentle, and her fingertips brushing his cheek, ostensibly to tuck a strand of hair away from his face, though Seth knew it was to reassure him it was all right for him to talk about this difficult topic.

"Not a clue," he said with a small shrug. "Last I heard, a few months after she left, she'd hooked up with some West Coast band with a real reputation. She's left me alone, and I'm more than happy to return the favor."

"Why is she on your list?"

"Because of her drug issues, and from what she was saying to people after we split. She'd twisted it all up in her head I'd somehow ruined her life, instead of owning up to her own lousy behavior." He cringed at the bitterness creeping into his voice. He moderated his tone and continued, "Unless she's really gotten her shit together, I could imagine her holding a grudge. She'd be capable of coming up with something like this and convincing somebody to do it."

Abby nodded. Seth guessed it fit with what she'd been told. "I accidentally told Caroline last night I wanted to find Stacy, thank her for not being with you anymore, then seriously mess her up for putting you through what she did."

"You 'accidentally' told her?" Seth smiled. Abby's tendency to let whatever was on her mind come leaking out was kind of endearing. Or at least entertaining.

Abby snorted. "Filter malfunction. Fixed now. Well, probably not, but I'm usually the last to know."

"I think it's cute," Seth said, reaching for her hand.

"It's not boring, I'll say that."

"Never." Seth slowed as they entered town, and guided the Jeep to the parking lot at Dash's club.

Two Emporia police cars and a county sheriff's cruiser occupied the parking spaces closest to the building. The fun never ended. They climbed out, and Seth mentally prepared himself.

"My mom called Dash this morning. About you," she said.

"Yeah, I know. My mom told me."

"Your mom told you? What the hell?"

"Let's see. Marilyn called Dash, talked him out of Joey's mom's number, and called her. Joey's mom called my mom…well, you get the picture. Bottom line is our mothers plan to talk tomorrow."

Abby stopped in her tracks. "You have got to be kidding me."

"Nope. They're totally going to be best friends," he said, grabbing her hand.

"That's what I'm afraid of."

He kissed her on the forehead. "Darlin', you worry too much about stuff doesn't need worrying about. Let's go talk to Dash and find a place to meet the guys. Maybe by then everybody'll be out of your house."

"None of you play fair," Abby said, shaking her head. "You or the mom squad."

"All's fair in love and war."

She made a decidedly unladylike comment and pulled open the side door.

Chapter Nine

They walked through the back hall and found the door to Dash's office open. When they entered, Abby saw the club owner seated behind his dented metal desk, and a Sheriff's Deputy in the old wooden chair, the only available guest seating. Dash hauled his bulk from his chair and stood, leaning forward with both hands on the desk.

"Well, looky who's here. Guess you two had an exciting morning, didn't you? Though I reckon things were plenty exciting before that, too." His laugh was like the braying of a mule dying of asphyxiation. Though she knew his crass behavior was due to a perpetual adolescence rather than any perverted or malicious intent, Abby wasn't amused. Since Seth didn't allow himself to be drawn into an exchange of adolescent banter, she surmised he wasn't, either.

"Guess this is the place to be today, huh, Dash?" Abby asked.

"Looks like it," Dash said. He turned worried eyes toward Seth. "I'm damned upset about what happened. You know you boys are like kin to me, and I'm sick any part of this mess might've had anything to do with my club." He lowered himself back into his seat, smoothing his tent-sized green golf shirt over his belly. "And Abby, shame about your house. I'm sure you'll get it fixed up right quick, though."

"Mom's already on it," Abby said. "I'm sorry about her calling you so early this morning. When she's on a mission, basic manners go straight out the window."

"Don't worry about it, sugar. I figure me and Nancy'd be doin' the same thing if our Courtney was shackin' up with some crazy musician." He shot an apologetic look at Seth, letting him know he didn't consider him a "crazy musician." "I told her you couldn't hardly do better than Seth, here. I think the world of all four of 'em."

"I appreciate it, Dash," Seth said. "Made for a real interesting conversation when Marilyn showed up this morning."

"I bet it did," the club owner wheezed. "Now, this here's Deputy Bledsoe from the county. Your bus is going to be spending some time in his garage till the federal boys are done with it."

The deputy, a man in his late forties, unfolded his stork-like frame from the chair and shook Seth's hand. He waved to Abby, suggesting she take his seat, but she shook her head and declined. He sat back down. "Dash's staff is gathering in the restaurant, and I'll be helping the Emporia department keep things running for the interviews with the ATF."

"Anything you need from me, just let me know," Seth said. "Any idea how long they'll be holding the bus?"

"Not my call, but I'd guess at least a few days, maybe a week."

A rap on the door frame announced the arrival of Special Agent Kincaid. He stepped into the room and introduced himself to Dash and Deputy Bledsoe before turning to Abby. "My men will be finishing up at your place soon, Miss Delaney." He looked at Seth and held out his cell phone. "Here you go, Mr. Caldwell. Turned out to be very interesting."

"Really, how so?" Seth leaned forward and reclaimed his phone. His voice was tense, as if not entirely sure he'd like the answer.

Kincaid looked at Dash. "The phone used to send Mr. Caldwell a text message this morning belongs to one of your employees."

Dash's brow furrowed. "Who would that be?"

"Kevin Merinar."

"Kevin? He sent Seth a text?" Dash's eyes squinted in confusion.

"Someone using his phone did. Have you been able to reach him today? Is he coming in for the interview?"

Dash shook his head. "I've been tryin' to call him all morning, and it goes straight to voice mail. I asked one of the other boys to stop by his apartment, but it don't look like he's there." He took a noisy slurp from a supersized soft drink cup and dribbled a wet patch onto his shirt. "Not unusual, though. After we have an event, he likes to find a party somewhere. Might not even be home yet, sleeping it off in somebody's living room."

Kincaid frowned. "Any ideas how we might find him? The message was sent locally, but the phone isn't active right now, so we can't track it. It's crucial we talk to him."

Rubbing his chin — or chins — Dash said, "I expect him here tomorrow morning, around ten. He's scheduled to do setup for a retirement party. Boy might drink some when he's not working, but he's reliable. I figure he'll show up then."

Kincaid didn't look pleased by this bit of news. He scrubbed blunt fingers through the graying hair at his temple. "If you hear from him, please let me know right away."

Dash said he would, and accepted the business card Kincaid offered.

Turning his attention once again to Seth, Kincaid said, "After we were done checking out the source of the message, we kept the phone off. I'd like you to check it now, see if you've gotten any more messages."

Abby took a step closer to Seth, prepared to be supportive if he heard something he didn't like.

He accessed his voice mail and listened. He hit Delete a few times and turned to Kincaid. "Nothing important. Just a couple more calls from people wondering what happened, and another call from Joey." He looked at Abby. "I need to call him back while I have a signal."

"Let me know if you hear anything," said Kincaid. "In the meantime, I talked to the other response team right before I arrived here. Your friends should be back by now. They mentioned going to the bar down the street. Something about needing 'several dozen drinks.'"

Seth blew out an amused breath. "I know how they feel." He stuck his phone in his pocket and put a hand on Abby's back. "Should we go on down there?"

She knew they had to, but part of her was deeply apprehensive at the thought. Seth needed to see his friends, but knowing one of them might be involved in the attempt to blast him to bits was sure to introduce a certain amount of tension. "Yeah, we should. I want to give Mom a call first, though, and see if she can call the insurance agent for me."

"We'll call Miss Delaney's number if we learn anything," Kincaid said. "We might have preliminary results on the liquor bottle later today."

"Fine," Abby said as she and Seth moved toward the door. She was eager to get out of the cramped office.

They walked through the club, slowing as they passed the restaurant. Abby glanced through the open double doors and saw about a dozen people scattered among the tables. Sammy and Karl moved from group to group with notebooks in their hands. Three ATF Special Agents conferred with Chief LeFevre, and Abby surmised the questioning would soon get underway.

Shortly before they reached the door leading to the alley and parking lot beyond, Seth pulled her into a shallow alcove, which once held a pair of pay phones. He slid his arms around her, and she leaned into his chest.

"I need to see Marsh and everybody," he said, "but I wish I didn't."

She could feel the tension in his arms, and brushed her hands lightly up and down his back, hoping to soothe him. "I know. I don't want to think of any of them being mixed up in this. I'm voting for the songwriter guy. What was his name?"

"Drew Purcell."

"Yeah, him. If this were one of my books, I could make it work." She put her arms around his neck. Since she was wearing flat, beaded sandals, she had to look up several inches to meet his eyes.

"I wish it worked that way," he said. "But Purcell is as good a bet as any right now. He's definitely mad enough."

"Have you seen him since the court thing?"

Seth nodded. "A few times. He likes to come to shows and make a scene, holding signs calling us thieves. We have a restraining order, though, so he can't get inside. But there's one interesting fact."

"What?"

"He's from Owensboro, Kentucky."

Abby leaned back a smidge, in order to get a better view of Seth's face. "Why is that interesting?"

"Owensboro is right across the Ohio River from Cincinnati."

Cincinnati. Where Seth was so sick a few nights ago. "And you didn't mention this before...why?"

He shrugged. "Didn't put it all together till a few minutes ago. I didn't even know the bottle had been messed with till I got the text. Still processing, I guess."

Abby took a moment to do a little processing of her own. "OK, but it totally puts him at the top of my suspect list."

"Mine, too, I think. I need to see the guys, but first I want to talk to Joey. He's giving me shit for not calling him back."

"And I'll talk to Mom. I've had my phone off, and she might've called with questions or something."

"I hope she's as efficient as everybody keeps saying." His hands glided low on her hips, holding her body to his. It didn't seem especially appropriate when she was about to call her mother, but Abby couldn't object. Not when it felt so wonderful. "The sooner she gets done there, the sooner we'll have the house to ourselves."

"My thoughts exactly," Abby replied.

Seth nuzzled her hair. "When we get back, we're going to pick up right there. We'll forget about all this other stuff for the rest of the day, and let the people in charge deal with the whole mess."

"Can you really do that?" She wanted it to be true. She craved time to simply absorb the sensation of being together, to try on the fit of being a couple. His intensity had knocked her for a loop, and the mere sight of him still stole her breath. Caroline was right about him. He wore his heart on his sleeve, and having his raw, unfiltered emotion directed at her made her heart ache with the need to know just what was this thing between them.

"You better believe it. I'm not dumb enough not to take it seriously, but what's happening between us is the most important thing in the world right now." His lips brushed hers as if to emphasize his point. "I want it to be just us, watching Dilbert chase ducks, then sharing a blanket on the couch, watching a movie we don't even care about." The tense lines that had bracketed his eyes all day softened. "No cops." Kiss. "No bombs." Kiss. "No friends, relatives, neighbors, or random guests." Kiss. "Just us, and a world full of possibilities."

If he kept it up, Abby was going to have a moment right there. "That's sweet, even if it's completely unrealistic." But was it?

"How is it unrealistic? Sure, I'm mad as hell, but we have the city, the county, and the feds on the situation. But us, what's going on, where we go from here…we're the only ones who can sort it out."

Damned internal conflict. How could she be so optimistic about a lasting relationship with someone who was — literally — the man of her dreams, yet so scared? As she absorbed his warmth and strength, she hoped they'd have even a little bit of time, because there were things they both needed to know before either of them could make any decisions.

"You're right," she said. "It's all snarled up together, but only the two of us can deal with this part."

"Exactly."

He kissed her, turning so her back was pressed to the wall. She considered tightening her arms around his neck and hoisting her legs around his waist, but thought it would send the wrong signal for a not very private alcove in a building full of law-enforcement personnel. Instead, she put her hands on his hips and pulled him against her. Her heart and her hormones merged and ignited, a biochemical detonation of the sweetest kind, flowing through her veins like warm honey. He upped the ante by sneaking one hand under her shirt to fondle her through her bra. His thumb began doing tantalizing things, and her knees weakened at his gentle but intimate touch.

Abby heard voices near the intersection of the hallway and reluctantly broke the kiss. Seth's hand fell away from her breast, and he stroked her cheek before bestowing a final kiss on her forehead. A mental sigh reminded her to take a physical breath. "Hey. Let's make those calls and get going." The hitch in her voice suggested she should have taken two or three more breaths before attempting to speak.

Seth took a half step back, accompanied by a small groan of displeasure. "Guess this isn't the place, is it?"

"Sadly, no. Call Joey, I'll call Mom, then we'll go down to the bar. Afterward, we'll get to 'the place.'"

"Few too many steps involved, but I guess that's the way it is." A wry smile produced a dimple, which nearly made Abby reconsider her previous statement.

"Afraid so." Abby reluctantly moved several yards down the hall and checked her phone.

As expected, there was a voice mail from her mother, as well as a text from Molly, which said only, "What the hell??? Call me!" She texted Molly back she was fine and would talk to her tomorrow and dialed her mom.

Once again, Mom had exceeded all expectations. She said the ATF team had left, and they'd let Butch board up the wall and other window even before they were completely done, since rain was expected. She already called the insurance agent and he came out to view the damage. The contractor was expected on Monday.

"Mom, I don't know what to say. You've taken care of everything."

"You're my daughter." This was her answer to lots of things, but this time Abby didn't mind.

"I'm also thirty-four years old. You didn't have to do all this."

"Of course I did. You have Seth to worry about. Cleaning up a little household disaster is nothing compared to that."

Abby laughed. "Yeah, I guess you're right."

"Don't worry about dinner. Your fridge is full of, well, it's full."

"I love you, Mom."

"Love you, too, Abigail. The ladies and I will be out of here in about an hour and a half, maybe sooner. When will you be home?"

"We're going to the Shamrock to meet up with his band. I don't know, a few drinks probably, then we'll head home."

"Call me tomorrow?"

"Sure. And thanks again."

"You don't need to call early, though," Marilyn said, when Abby thought the conversation already over. "I imagine you and Seth might need to sleep in." She had an innocent trill to her voice, which Abby knew was anything but. Way to ruin a moment.

"Crap on a cracker, Mom," she huffed, resisting the urge to drop her phone and stomp on it. "Could we talk a little less about my sex life? Please?"

Mrs. Innocent did a spectacular job of sounding both confused and offended. "Who mentioned any such thing? That would be extremely inappropriate." As if it'd ever stop her. "I just meant you've been through so much today you'll probably need your rest."

Abby swallowed a frustrated groan. "Yes, Mother, I'm sure we'll be quite exhausted. I'm very tired of a lot of things right now. But I'll call you when I can lift my weary, shell-shocked head and locate the phone."

Abby hung up, sure she heard her mother chuckle as she did so, and saw Seth still talking to Joey. He noticed her watching him, and held up a finger to indicate he'd be done in a minute. Abby pointed toward the back door, and he nodded his understanding.

She stepped into the alley under the darkening sky. As she walked across the alley and into the parking lot, rounding the corner of one of the ATF vehicles, she caught sight of her Jeep and was startled to find a figure crouched near the driver's side door. It took her a moment to recognize Pam the Groupie, who was busy keying her car.

"Oh, this is the last fucking straw," Abby said to herself with a growl. Intent on her task, Pam didn't see her coming, and in half a dozen swift steps Abby reached her and gave her a solid hip-check. The vandal sprawled to her knees, and Abby quickly knelt on her and pinned her arms. Looking over her shoulder at her beloved Jeep, she saw a jagged "B" carved into the door. She dug her knee into Pam's back. "A 'B'? As in 'bitch'? You were scraping 'bitch' into my car?"

"Get…off…me," Pam grunted.

Abby wished she could let go of one of her prisoner's arms long enough to grab a fistful of blonde hair and rap her head against the pavement a few times. "Enormous mistake," she said through clenched teeth.

Pam arched her back in an attempt to throw Abby off, but failed and sagged back to the ground. "You *are* a bitch, and you don't deserve Seth!" She twisted her head back and forth, trying to look at Abby or possibly bite her. "Stay away from him! You need to disappear just like the other one did!"

For an instant, Abby almost lost her grip on Pam's arms. What she'd just said sounded threatening, elevating the girl from slightly obsessive fan to flat-out psychotic. Fortunately, she had an idea what to do with her.

"Oh, Christ, what now?"

Abby turned her head at the sound of the exasperated question to find Seth standing by the ATF Suburban.

"Darlin', is this going to keep us from getting home any time soon?" he asked.

"Nope. Would you run inside and get Sammy, please? Miss Pam here was vandalizing my car and seems to have threatened me. And you should probably hurry, because she's going to lose feeling in her arms soon, and I have the urge to do unpleasant things to her hair." Abby tightened her grip.

"You whore! You attacked me!"

"Seth? Sammy. Now. Please?"

Seth rushed to get Sammy, while Abby kept the squirming Pam pinned firmly to the ground. She was hissing and spitting like a cat, and Abby had never much cared for cats.

Sammy arrived a few minutes later and looked more amused than concerned. If he could read all the vengeful thoughts in Abby's mind, he might have felt differently. She explained what she'd witnessed, but did not yet release Pam.

"She attacked me!" Pam wailed. "I didn't do anything!"

"Yeah, like I carved that 'B' into my own car, and those aren't your keys right there on the ground. Not to mention the part about me 'disappearing.' Kinda sounds like a threat to me, Pammy. Not smart." She couldn't resist digging her short — but sharp — fingernails into the girl's upper arm, but only a little. She congratulated herself on her restraint. "But there's more to the story, Sammy."

"Oh, really? Do tell." He unhitched his handcuffs from his utility belt, a fact of which Abby highly approved.

"You might recall one of the potential suspects Special Agent Kincaid mentioned regarding the bomb was the 'crazed fan.' And it would seem we have one of those right here. She approached Seth in the park yesterday, was waiting outside the club door last night, harassed me during the show because I was with Seth, and now she's vandalizing my Jeep and threatening me. Seems to me she needs to have a chat with Kincaid's men."

Sammy smiled, and for a moment Abby thought he almost looked dangerous. "I think you're exactly right." He approached, and Abby reluctantly relinquished her grip on Pam's arms so Sammy could apply the handcuffs.

"Bomb? What bomb? What are you people talking about?" Pam screamed.

There were crumbs of asphalt sticking to the girl's cheek, which made Abby happier than it probably should have. Seth leaned on the Jeep, smirking. She couldn't resist smirking back. Sammy disappeared inside, hustling the protesting groupie along beside him.

Abby stared at the gouge in her door. She ran her fingers over it, wincing at how deep it was. When she looked at her hand, she saw flecks of royal blue paint clinging to her fingertips. "I cannot believe this."

Seth laughed. "Oh, man, you took her down and I missed it!"

"It was her third strike. At least. I have a pretty high rage threshold, but she crossed it."

"You did kind of assault her."

"Do you see Sammy arresting me? He won't even give me a ticket." She paused to consider. "Usually."

"But do you really think she had anything to do with the bomb? Did you have to turn her over to the ATF?"

"No, I don't think she had anything to do with the bomb. But I do think she needs to learn some manners."

"That'll do the trick."

Abby wiped her hands on her jeans and picked up her purse from where she'd dropped it before charging Pam. She took Seth's arm and they started down the sidewalk toward the Shamrock. "What did Joey have to say?"

"Pretty much what you'd expect. Keep my head down, watch my back, and stay out of trouble. And don't mess things up with you." He gave her hip a little bump with his own.

Abby grinned. "Think you can handle all that?"

"Absolutely. He also said Caroline wants you to call her."

"I'll call later. If I'm not distracted."

"You'll definitely be distracted, darlin'."

"I'll call her tomorrow."

"Better plan. I might be tired by then."

Yippee Skippee.

Through the window of the bar Abby spotted Mouse, Marshall, and Trent. They had dragged two tables into the alcove along the back wall, where a folk singer sometimes put a portable stage for Wednesday night happy hour. The manager wouldn't like it, but one look at Trent and he probably decided to make an exception. She noticed an abundance of plates and glasses already spread out. She nudged Seth. "You ready?"

"As I'll ever be."

Chapter Ten

Seth tried to gather his thoughts before going into the bar. He looked at the green neon sign in the plate glass window to the left of the door. "The Pickled Shamrock?" He'd seen some unusual bar names, but this one was near the top of the list.

"We usually just call it the Shamrock." she said. "It used to be the End Zone, but the guy who owned it got married and moved to Minneapolis. The new owner wanted something original. It's still a sports bar, though, heavy on the hockey and football."

"I might need a T-shirt."

"They have them. But you're stalling, aren't you?"

"Uh-huh."

"Do you want to get out of here any time today or stand outside and discuss whimsical bar names?"

"You're right. Let's go." He reached for the door and held it open as Abby stepped inside.

Being Saturday afternoon, the bar was crowded with groups of people watching a Twins game on the flat-screen televisions positioned strategically around the room. The home team was playing the hated Chicago White Sox, and the cacophony of cheers, jeers, and barstool commentating made it hard to hear normal conversation. The morning round of local league games was over, and the team from Molson's Honda-Isuzu was already half-sloshed and loudly recapping every pitch of their win over Olssen's Nursery. While there were several women, the customers were mostly male, young, and boisterous. There were plenty of Twins caps and University of Minnesota T-shirts in evidence and pitchers of beer on nearly every table. Framed jerseys and sports memorabilia adorned the walls. A pool table in one corner made Seth's stomach clench at the thought of his custom cue, and the case that had probably held the bomb meant to kill him.

They wound their way toward the tables his friends had set up. Marshall saw them coming and stood, intercepting Seth before he reached the table. "Man, what the hell took you so long?"

Before he could answer, he was dragged into a back-pounding guy hug, which was repeated with Mouse and Trent. He thought Trent might have bruised a few of his ribs. "We'd have been here fifteen minutes ago, but Abby had to apprehend a vandal." He slid into a chair along the wall, and Abby sat beside him.

Marshall took the space on Seth's other side, while Trent and Mouse sat across from them.

"Abby did what?" Marshall asked, adjusting the black bandanna covering his shaved head.

Seth told them what had transpired in Dash's parking lot, and soon had them nearly falling out of their seats with laughter.

"Whoa!" Marsh exclaimed. "Wise move, man, staying out of the line of fire of a chick fight. Good way to get your balls racked."

"Wasn't much fighting involved. By the time I got there, Abby had her pinned and was threatening to remove most of her hair." He grinned. "Actually, it was kind of hot."

"I'd had about all I could handle for one day," Abby said, blushing.

"Well, I sure don't blame you," Trent said. He turned to Seth. "And we, my man, have a lot to talk about. But before we start, you need a drink." He indicated the dozen or so full-to-the-brim shot glasses clustered in the center of the table. Everyone took a shot, downed it, then focused on Seth, waiting for him to fill them in.

Seth shook off the sharp bite of tequila. "Guys, I don't know what to say. But the first thing is if y'all start cracking jokes about a 'big bang,' or anything 'going off prematurely,' I will smoke you where you're standin', got it?"

Marshall's dark eyes widened in feigned innocence. "Would we do that?" He licked some hot wing sauce from his fingers. "Besides, we've been shooting those cracks back and forth all day, and we're getting kind of tired of 'em."

"Good to know," Seth said. All the humor left his voice as he continued. "It's so fucked up, somebody hating me so much, and I have no idea why. I got this text message, sent from Kevin Merinar's phone. He works for Dash, but nobody's seen him today. It said I got lucky, they knew how to hurt me now before they make me pay, and third time's a charm."

"Third time's a charm? What's that shit mean?" asked Mouse. He grabbed a gob of cheese-dripping nachos from the centrally located platter and dropped it on the plate in front of him.

"Took me a minute, but it looks like I was right about there being something wrong with how sick I was on Wednesday night." Seth waved to catch the server's attention, and received a nod of acknowledgment.

Marshall slapped the table, rattling the glasses and drawing curious glances from several people nearby. "No wonder they nabbed the bottle under your bunk. You think somebody messed with it."

"I'm sure of it," Seth said. "Nothing else makes sense. When whatever shit they gave me didn't do the trick, they moved on to

Plan B. They figured the bomb would blow up the bottle, too, and there'd be no evidence of it."

Trent took another shot from the middle of the table and gulped it. "But you screwed it up, because you took the bag off the bus."

"Got it in one."

Their conversation was interrupted by the server, whose nametag identified her as Chanda. They consulted briefly, and a few minutes later a tray arrived bearing two pitchers of beer and five frosty glasses, as well as a replenishment of the tequila. Chanda departed, blonde ponytail bouncing.

Mouse did the honors, filling all five glasses with ice-cold beer. He tossed his long, graying dark hair behind his shoulders and gave Seth a pointed look. "So, what are they saying, Caldwell? They think it was one of us, don't they?" He didn't sound happy.

Seth took a long swallow from his glass. "Yeah, they do. I told 'em y'all are my brothers, my family, but they're set on the idea it had to be somebody on the inside." He tried not to allow any trace of suspicion to cross his face. He'd sooner die than hurt these guys, and had to believe the same was true of them.

Trent's huge hand tightened on his glass, and Seth hoped he didn't crush it. "Bullshit, man, total bullshit."

"I know, Trent. I don't believe it, either. They're saying the bomb was planted in my bag sometime during the show, though, and whoever did it knew an awful lot about our schedules and how we run things."

"Gotta be another answer," Marshall said.

"They're looking at some other options, too," Seth said. "Including the girl Abby assaulted in the parking lot, though she says it was mostly to teach her some manners." He wrapped his arm around Abby's shoulders and kissed her cheek.

"She keeps popping up everywhere," Abby said. "At least I know she'll be busy for the next couple of hours." She wiped a bit of melted cheese from the corner of her mouth, and Seth wished he'd noticed it first, because he was in the mood to lick it off.

"They're also going to talk to the guys who left the crew last year, and they want to check out Stacy and Purcell. They all know enough about us to plan something. A couple of 'em might hold a big enough grudge to want to try."

Trent leaned forward, setting his still-intact glass on the table. "Purcell, huh?"

"Yeah. Why? You know something?" Seth asked.

"Maybe," Trent answered. "Hadn't given it any thought, since it never came to anything, but security told me before the Cincinnati show he was outside and had to be escorted off the premises."

Pretty damned interesting. Had anybody seen the disgruntled songwriter in Chicago or here in Emporia? Seth made a mental note to ask Kincaid when he talked to him again.

"What about Stacy?" Marsh asked. He cut a look in Abby's direction, then looked at Seth, one eyebrow raised inquisitively.

Seth correctly interpreted the expression and said, "It's OK. She knows about Stacy." Abby's eyes narrowed, but she remained silent. "She doesn't seem inclined to like her much."

Marsh snorted. "Nobody does. The chick is bugfuck crazy. I couldn't see her pulling it off herself, but she'd sure be able to twist some guy into doing it for her."

"I told Kincaid the same thing." Seth refilled his glass, looking at Abby to see how she was holding up. Her posture seemed tense, and he rubbed her thigh soothingly. The knot in his stomach loosened when she smiled at him in return.

Trent's phone vibrated on the table, and he looked at the display. "It's Cassie," he said, referring to his fifteen-year-old daughter. "I best go outside and take this. She has a softball tournament on Monday, and final practice was today." He rose and headed out the back door to the bar's patio.

When the big man had gone, Marshall and Mouse exchanged glances. Marshall turned to Seth and said, "Look, man, we need to talk. Just us."

Seth drained his beer, certain he wouldn't enjoy the conversation, but recognizing its necessity.

Marshall lowered his eyes for a moment, before directing his gaze around the table. "Mouse and I were talking."

"Yeah? About what, exactly?" Seth noticed the tension in his friend's shoulders mirrored his own, and forced himself to relax. He looked around the room just as the Twins' pitcher threw a strike and ended the inning, bringing a deafening round of cheers from the fans. Given their location and the fact the other patrons were paying exclusive attention to the game and ingesting as much beer as possible, he decided they could speak with relative privacy, as long as they kept it brief.

Marshall hesitated, and Mouse stepped in. "Look, Seth, I know you don't want to think it was one of our guys. Shit, I don't, either." He put down his shot of tequila, untouched. "But it's possible, you know?"

"I know." The thought sickened him, but he'd be a fool not to consider it.

"They're pretty sure the bomb was put in your bag during the show, right?" Marsh asked, as he reached for Mouse's untouched drink.

"That's what they tell me. The person wouldn't want to give me time to find it, and knew I'd be asleep in the bunk in the morning." He felt Abby clutch his hand under the table.

"That makes it easier, then," Mouse said, nodding.

"How?" Abby asked. Seth wondered the same thing. He doubted anything about this mess could be called "easy."

Marshall counted out four fingers. "You, me, Pete, and Joey were onstage the whole time." He extended his thumb, bringing the total count to five. "And Mouse never leaves the sound board during a show. That'd be against the Malcolm Thibaudeau creed."

Seth cracked a smile at the use of Mouse's given name, and Mouse reached over to bend Marshall's thumb back, until the bandanna-wearing band member yanked his hand away. "I'd say you're right."

"So that leaves Danny, Andy, 'Berto, and Trent," Marsh clarified. "Trent was standing off stage left almost the whole show, but not every minute. 'Berto was backstage during the instrument changes, but other than that, he could've been anywhere. Andy's all over the place, being the gofer. Danny's usually in the light booth, but he turns it over to the house technician for a break or two, since we do such long sets."

Seth knew all this, but hadn't thought about it in much detail. They were silent for a few minutes as Seth sorted through the information.

"I get what you're saying, guys. I hate it like all hell, but I get it. We need to know who left the building, when, and why. And we need to find out where this Merinar guy is, too, and what happened to his phone. Dash says he might be sleeping it off somewhere, but thinks he'll show up to work tomorrow morning."

Marshall pulled off his bandana and dragged it across his face before he repositioned it on his head. "Man, I know you want to beat feet out of here and get back to Abby's. I sure would. But let's find out what we need to know first, OK?"

Seth nodded. Marshall might be a clown most of the time, but when the chips were down you could always count on him. "OK. It's making me fucking insane to even think this way, but if we can't rule 'em out a hundred percent, we can't be so blind we miss something big."

Abby's fingers twined tightly through his, and he was grateful for this reminder he had more reason than ever to stay alive. He hated the time which should have been spent with her, figuring out this powerful thing springing up between them—and where it would lead—was being taken up trying to determine if one of his closest friends wanted to kill him.

Abby took a sip from a sweating glass of ice water. A Twins batter got a hit, and she had to wait for the din to subside before she could speak. "When everybody gets here, we need to walk through the evening. Without making it like an interrogation, let everyone talk about where they were, who they were with, what they saw, stuff like that."

Seth agreed. "We know all these guys, which is part of why this sucks so much ass," he said. "But if stories don't fit with what we know, or if one of them says something making somebody else act nervous, we might learn something."

"Exactly," Mouse said, as Trent came in the back door from the patio. "But don't sweat it, man. We're just covering all our bases."

Seth nodded, and Trent reached the table and dropped into his seat.

"Cassie says she gets to start on third base Monday," Trent said, smiling. He didn't smile often, but always had one to spare when it came to his daughter.

"Didn't get her athletic skills from her old man," Marshall said, ducking a fist-delivered reprimand from the road manager.

Seth had just tossed back another shot when Roberto and Andy made their way through the maze of tables. Chairs were shuffled, and they took their seats, with Andy at the end of the table by Abby, and Roberto to his right, next to Trent.

"What a fucked up day," Andy said, brushing long, sandy bangs out of his eyes.

"It seems to be the general opinion," Seth said.

The next several minutes were spent catching Andy and Roberto up on what they discussed, keeping the investigation and suspicions focused solely on non-Dead End Road members. Seth let the conversation flow around him, except when his direct input was required. Instead, he held Abby's hand and watched everybody's expressions and reactions. Stroking his thumb across her palm, he worried she'd been pulled into this clusterfuck. He probably wasn't even good enough for her in the first place, multiple attempted murders aside. He found it hard to believe he deserved someone like her, and it might be wrong for him to even try. But, damn. He'd never felt anything like this before, and he was slightly ashamed to admit he was selfish enough to try to convince her they could work.

"You know what almost happened, don't you?" asked Roberto, slamming his shot glass down on the table, causing Seth to realize his attention had wandered.

Seth blinked and focused on the outspoken guitar technician. "Um, yeah. I was almost blown up."

"Well, sure, that. But if the bomb had gone off under the bunk, it would've wiped out your Paul Reed Smith." The potential horror was significant enough to make his voice tremble.

Seth nudged Abby and said, "See, I told you. 'Berto's all about the guitars."

Roberto gave a short laugh. "Screw you, man. You can take care of yourself, but the guitars are helpless. Somebody's gotta look out for them."

"I told Abby the same thing. If you ever wanted to do me in, it'd be over a guitar and I'd totally see it coming."

"You better believe it. And the next time you fuck up a twelve-string, I'm taking your head off with a brick."

Seth held his hands up in surrender. "Fair enough. I'll take it easy on the twelve-strings."

Trent's phone signaled a new message. He picked it up to check the display just as Chanda arrived with fresh pitchers, glasses, and a platter of stuffed potato skins.

Trent swiped his finger across his phone, blacking out the screen. "That was a text from Danny. He'll be here in a few minutes."

Seth was glad to hear it. The sooner he saw and talked to everybody and put his mind at ease, the sooner he could devote all his attention to Abby.

"Hey, guys," Seth said. "I'm not the only one who's had a tough day. Must've been a big surprise to see the state troopers this morning."

"You got that right," said Andy. "Then the ATF guys showed up and went over every inch of the van and the trailer."

Marshall reached for the fresh beer pitcher. "It ain't the first time we've been pulled over. Cops always figure they'll find something on a tour bus. Woke me out of a sound sleep, and I'd only been down about two hours when Mouse pulled over."

"What happened on the bus?" Abby asked. "Did the dog find anything?"

"Just the bunk and the countertop beside it," Marshall said. "They took the bottle and other stuff under the bunk, including the guitar." He cast a cautious glance in 'Berto's direction. "They hooked up the bus to be towed, and drove us back here."

"They think we might get the bus back by the end of the week," Trent said, picking a bit of tortilla chip off his black T-shirt.

"I guess everybody's going to have to figure out how to get back to Texas now, huh? And when?" Abby's eyes met Seth's and he got the distinct impression she was warning him not to invite any of them to stay with them at her house. She didn't need to worry. He had no such intention. He just wanted to know where everybody was going to be during the next few days.

"Yeah," Trent said. "They said we can leave tomorrow if we need to. Unless something points to somebody in particular, they won't have anything else to go on till they get stuff back from the lab, and it could be a couple of weeks. They can't keep everybody here that long without any evidence." He looked at Mouse, who nodded. "We have some ideas, but we'll work out the details here shortly. I have to fly out tomorrow for sure, because if I'm not home for the softball tournament on Monday, my ex-wife's gonna skin me alive."

Seth found it amusing Trent, who was one of the most formidable-looking guys he'd ever met, was so easily cowed by his pint-size ex-wife. He suspected it had more to do with not wanting to disappoint Cassie.

Andy glanced at Abby, then at Seth. "What about you, Seth? This whole thing going to change your plans?"

"Nope. I'm just keeping my head down and letting the professionals handle it. I have more important things on my mind." He put his arm lightly across Abby's shoulder, and she shifted against his side. How much longer did they have to stay here in the Pickled Shamrock?

"We'll be OK," Abby said. "I live kind of out there, but it also means it's hard for anybody to get near the house without my knowing about it."

"Must be nice living in the country," Andy said. "I grew up in Atlanta, lived in Chicago for a while. Austin's small compared to that, but I always wanted a place on a lake."

"I live on a small lake off Gleason Road, and you're right. It's really peaceful. When stuff isn't blowing up, at least."

Roberto's face lit up and he opened his mouth to speak, but Seth suspected where he was going and cut him off. "'Berto, I already warned these guys. If there are any jokes involving banging, blowing, or exploding, ass will be kicked."

Roberto closed his mouth and his head sunk in disappointment. "Bummer. I had some good ones."

"You can share them with the class after I leave."

Finally, the last member of the group arrived. Danny dropped into the chair at the far end of the table. The young man displayed the slumped but careful posture signifying an effort to keep nausea at bay. Even as short as Danny's blond hair was, it managed to look as if he'd recently had an encounter with a fork and a faulty toaster. His eyes were bloodshot, and his eyelids sagged.

"Little hair of the dog, Danny?" teased Roberto.

"Need a whole lot of hairs, man," Danny muttered.

"Well, try to get it together, Dan my man," said Trent. His no-nonsense tone conveyed they were going to take care of business and not whine about the inconvenience. "We wanted to get everybody together, compare notes, and decide how to get all our stuff back to Texas once the cops are done with it."

"No problem, Trent. I have a couple of ideas," Danny said, widening his eyes in a futile attempt to appear alert.

"Good. Get some food in you, and we'll get it sorted out. You have a room?"

"Yeah, across the street. That's where y'all are staying, right?"

Trent nodded. "Except for Seth, the lucky bastard."

Seth rolled his eyes, but couldn't argue. He was a lucky bastard.

Abby picked her purse off the floor and poked around inside. "I thought so. Out of cigarettes. I'm going to scoot over to the bar and buy some, and stop off at the bathroom. Back in a few."

Seth watched her cross the room, exchanging hellos with several customers along the way. He noticed the appreciative looks she received from the largely male clientele, and wondered if she'd ever dated any of them. He needed to know who to hate. As he forked up a stuffed potato skin and began cutting it into pieces, he thought he had a way to steer the conversation to everybody's whereabouts the night before. But he needed to set it up just right.

As soon as he could work it into the discussion, he said, "I've been thinking. A big key to the whole thing is finding Kevin Merinar and figuring out where he was last night. He'd be stupid to send me a threatening text from his own phone. So where was he, and did somebody else get their hands on his phone?"

Trent rubbed his chin thoughtfully. "Kevin and another guy, Josh somebody, were helping with security most of the night. I sent both of 'em off on a couple of errands, messages, stuff like that." He paused and his eyes sharpened as if he'd just remembered something. "I did send Kevin out to the bus once. My radio died, and I sent him for the spare battery."

OK, very interesting. "Anybody else see him?"

Andy chimed in. "I did. I was up in the lighting booth with Danny, remember?"

"Yeah. I went out for a smoke and grabbed a bottle of water from the fridge on the bus, about halfway through the show, maybe a little before. When I came back, I remembered I left my phone on the counter, and sent Andy after it." Danny tossed back a shot and grimaced. Seth hoped he didn't barf under the table. He still looked pretty rough. Tequila was probably not a great idea.

"When I went out," Andy said, "it took me a few minutes to find the phone. It fell behind the cooler. I passed Kevin in the parking lot on my way out."

"Kevin came back in and gave me the battery, worked the floor with me and Josh for a while, then he took off. Said he had to go see somebody. I didn't see him again, but it was after the solos. Maybe a half hour before we finished up."

Seth knew by the last twenty minutes of every show, the crew and the house staff were moving around, getting ready to wrap things up. It was a lot harder to pinpoint where everybody was. Still, it was interesting nobody saw Kevin after the solos. And now he had a decent idea where all his own guys were. He didn't know what it meant yet, but he'd work it all out sooner or later.

Abby returned to the table and grabbed his arm. "Look, Sammy just came in. Maybe he has some news."

Chapter Eleven

Sammy crossed the room and pulled up a chair, which he wedged in beside Trent, directly across from Seth and Abby. He looked serious, but Seth thought he detected a glint in his eye suggesting he was looking forward to being the one to impart significant information.

"Well, Sammy, don't keep us in suspense," Abby said. "Did you beat a confession out of somebody?"

The police officer cast a sidelong look at the pitchers of beer. He probably needed one. "Things are clearing out at Dash's. They're about done talking to the employees, but nobody really had any useful information."

"What about Kevin? Has he turned up?" Seth asked.

"No. They haven't found Purcell yet, either."

"Tell Kincaid Purcell was at Gatsby's in Cincinnati on Wednesday. I didn't see him because security made him leave before he came inside, but they told me he was there," Trent said.

"Good to know. We'll get a picture if we can, have somebody show it around the club in Chicago in case he was there, too." Sammy looked at Seth. "Kincaid's team did talk to those former crew members of yours, though, and they're both clear, far as they can tell. And the guys who left for Alabama last night gave their statements to the police down there."

Seth sighed. "That's all good, but not exactly helpful."

Abby studied Sammy for several seconds. "There's more, I can tell. Spill it, Sam."

"Oh, there's more. For starters, the 'crazed fan' is a lot more interesting than we expected."

"In what way?" Abby asked.

"She's been in some trouble in the past."

"If I have to drag this out of you one sentence at a time, none of us will ever get out of here," Abby said. Though she tried to sound threatening, Seth thought she mostly sounded tired.

"OK, OK," Sammy said. "The girl's not wound too tight, that's for sure. She was arrested a couple of years ago in Iowa for breaking into some actor's hotel room. He was in town for a press event, and found her hiding in his shower."

"Yeah, creepy," Seth said.

"She was also arrested for assault. She went out with a guy a few times, no big deal, but she thought it was. He started seeing somebody else, and Pam cut his tires. He caught her in the act, and she went after him with the box cutter she was using. Just a scratch, lucky for him. By the time her lawyer was done, she received sixty days in a mental health facility instead of jail time."

Seth was glad she hadn't had anything more dangerous than a key ring in her hand when Abby jumped her. The girl was obviously unbalanced, but was she crazy — or clever — enough to orchestrate an attempted poisoning and bombing? "Where is she now?"

"Headed back to Iowa, I guess," Sammy said. "There's no evidence to tie her to the bomb, but they'll keep an eye on her. She was in Cincinnati and Chicago this week, so they'll keep digging, see if there's anything there."

"Any news on the bourbon bottle?" A lot of Seth's thought process hinged on the results of those tests.

"No, but Kincaid was going to call the lab as soon as they move the last of the club staff out of there." Sammy suddenly looked uncomfortable. He licked his lips and began turning an empty shot glass. He looked down at his hands, saw what he was doing, and pushed the glass aside. "There's one more thing, and I'm not sure how to say this."

"Just spit it out," Abby said.

Sammy drew a shaky breath. "There's one person we can rule out for sure."

"Who?" Seth asked.

"Stacy Ballantyne."

"Why? Where is she?" Seth didn't doubt Stacy's ability to fuck with him, even from the other side of the world.

"She was found dead in a hotel room in Vancouver last November."

Their table became an island of silence in the otherwise bustling bar. Shocked expressions froze on faces before everyone's attention turned to Seth. He felt like he had picked up a live electrical wire, his body coursing with sickening numbness. "Dead? How?"

"Bad combination of pills and alcohol, according to the report."

"Accidental? Or did she...?" Seth couldn't complete the thought. Abby clutched his hand under the table.

"Inconclusive. She didn't leave a note, but the investigators felt there were indications it might not have been an accident."

"Fuck," Seth said. "I can't believe this." The idea Stacy was dead was too much to comprehend.

"When's the last time you heard from her?" Sammy asked.

"None of us saw her after the night we broke up. She tried calling for a while, until I changed my number. She was involved with a band out west, Darknoise, I think."

"She was running around with a different band when she died. Cold Apathy or some stupid-ass name, but I hear they're bad news," Sammy said. "The guy she was with passed out in somebody else's room that night, and found her the next morning."

"Are they sure of his whereabouts?" Seth would find it easier to believe someone else was responsible for Stacy's death. She'd always seemed so determined and indestructible.

"Yeah, they're sure," Sammy said. "Security video shows him entering a room with Stacy, but she left and went back to her room. He didn't come out of the first room till about ten o'clock the next morning."

Trent shook his head. "Rotten news. Not surprising, though. She was a lot worse, more reckless, the last couple of months before she left. I hoped she'd get her shit together before it was too late."

Sammy stood and returned his chair to the neighboring table. "I have to get back to the club, but we thought you needed to know about some of this."

"I appreciate it," Seth said, shaking Sammy's hand. "It sure isn't what I expected to hear, though."

"I'm sorry," Sammy said. "No easy way to break news like that."

"I guess not."

They all sat in silence for a few moments after Sammy departed. Mouse said, "Last November? How come we never heard anything before now?"

Seth took a deep breath, trying to clear the dull feeling in the middle of his chest. "No clue. She was out west and died in Canada, but you'd think somebody would've said something." He looked around the table. Everyone looked shell-shocked, even Andy and Danny, who had joined the crew long after Stacy left.

"I'll call Joey," Marshall said. "Caroline needs to know. She didn't like her, but they did spend a lot of time together."

"Thanks, man," Seth said. It was a conversation he didn't want to have, and he was relieved to have it taken off his hands.

Abby's hand tightened on his thigh. At first he thought she was sending a signal they should get the hell out of there, but he noticed she was looking toward the door. He saw her friend, Monique, scanning the room. Abby caught her eye and waved, and Monique made her way in their direction, her loose-fitting Indian print dress billowing around her.

"I saw your Jeep out behind Dash's. I hoped I'd find you here."

"Seth wanted to touch base with everybody after what happened this morning. We're heading home pretty soon, though."

"I saw Paige when I took her your books, and she told me what happened." She tucked a loose curl behind her ear. "But I need to talk to you about something else."

"Sure, Mo. I want to go outside for a cigarette before it rains, anyway."

Seth introduced Monique to the guys, mentioning she owned ReVamped, and had some nice vintage leather jackets if they felt like doing any shopping. He watched the two women go out the door to the back patio, greatly enjoying the enticing sway of Abby's hips as she walked. Despite all the shocks and traumas of the day, his number one priority was still to get back to her house, wrap his arms around her, and ignore the rest of the world for as long as they could.

"Seth, did you really think that Stacy chick had anything to do with what's happening?" Andy asked. "I mean, she'd been gone a long time."

"I don't know. Maybe. She was so intense. If something happened to get her thinking about us again, I could see her getting worked up enough to consider it." Though, to be honest, Stacy struck him more like the ice-pick-through-the-heart type than a calculating mastermind.

"Plus, it's a lot easier to think about it being Stacy or Purcell or somebody else, rather than one of us," Marshall added.

Trent snorted. "One of us. Like I said before, bullshit."

"I know, man, I know," Seth said. He hoped they would locate Drew Purcell soon, preferably carrying a little bottle with a skull and crossbones on it, and a suitcase full of bomb-making supplies. It sure would be good to have everything all tied up in a nice, neat package.

He looked up and saw Abby standing inside the back door. Monique's figure was retreating toward the front entrance. Abby crooked her finger at Seth in a "come here" gesture, her lips pressed into a hard line. He told the guys he needed to talk to Abby, and followed her out onto the patio. There were several wrought iron tables and chairs, and a few of the tables had bright green umbrellas.

"Hey, darlin', what's the matter?" He wrapped his arms around her waist, and she lowered her head to his chest with a deep sigh.

"After I told Monique about our eventful day, she had some news for me. And it was the last thing I needed to hear."

He leaned back, his fingertips under her chin, and tipped her face up so he could see her eyes. "What did she say?"

"My rat bastard ex-husband, David Higgins, is in town. He was just in her shop fifteen minutes ago."

* * *

Abby dropped into one of the chairs and lit another cigarette. She couldn't remember if it would raise or lower her spiking blood pressure, but she needed something to do with her hands. "I can't believe he's here. I haven't seen him since the divorce, and didn't plan on ever seeing him again. But they're in town for Joyce's sister's baby shower, and he was just in ReVamped picking up some stupid antique baptism set." If he was walking around Emporia's small downtown area, he would be drawn to the Shamrock for sure.

Seth plucked the cigarette from her fingers, took a drag, and set it in the ashtray on the table, exhaling a thin plume of smoke. He took her hand and pulled her onto his lap. "Very handy. Saves me the trouble of looking him up next time we play in Charlotte. I have to meet the man who was too stupid to hang onto you."

Abby rolled her eyes. "Believe me, you do not want to meet David. He's a grade-A asshole."

They shared the cigarette until it was gone, and Abby was annoyed to notice that her hand trembled. Seth took her hand and brought it to his lips, kissing each finger before holding her palm to his cheek. She stroked her thumb over the stubble. An instant later she was lost in the comforting softness of his lips, her fingers sliding through his thick hair. Then her phone rang. Shifting on his lap with a disgruntled huff, she listened to several bars of Make or Break before she reached for her purse and retrieved the phone. "I've really gotta change that," she muttered.

"Don't. Please?"

She smiled at him, checking the display as the song continued to play. "It's Mom. I'll let it go to voice mail." This bought her another minute or two for Seth-kissing before the phone interrupted with the beep indicating a message. She listened to it, and said, "Mom says they're leaving the house now."

"Good. The coast is clear."

"She left a note, but she had other very clear instructions."

"Which were...?"

"Call her if anything seems strange, make sure to check the board-up job for leaks when it starts raining, and don't let you go."

"Do I look like I'm going anywhere?"

"I think she's afraid I'll chase you away."

"Will you?"

"Don't plan to."

"OK."

"I know she's serious, because she used my middle name for the second time today. She saves that for times she really needs to make a point." She ran her hands across his firm shoulders and thought they probably had time for some more kissing.

"What's your middle name?"

"Kathleen."

"Abigail Kathleen?"

"Uh-huh."

His dimples reappeared, and one eyebrow lifted. "Abby-Kat?"

"What?"

"Abigail Kathleen. Abby-Kat. That's what I'm going to call you." He looked delighted at the idea.

"No. No you are not."

"Am."

"I will not be pleased if you start calling me Abby-Kat."

"How about just sometimes?"

Abby considered. "Maybe. But I reserve the right to smack you."

"Deal."

"What's your middle name?"

His eyes twinkled. "I'm not saying."

"Not fair. I told you mine. Now, what is it?"

"I am not telling you."

"Why not? Is it horrible? Like Euripides or something?"

"Worse."

Abby feigned acceptance. "Fine. I will find out, you know."

"I don't doubt it."

Seth gathered her against him and kissed her neck. Goose bumps erupted on both arms, but their chill was offset by the heat gathering in her nether regions. Yes, it was time to leave. Any minute now. But first she had a mission. She kissed him again, and while his hands were busy working their way toward her bra strap, she targeted his back pocket. She could just reach the edge of his wallet. He was sitting on most of it, but a firm tug dislodged it, and she leaped to her feet and darted to the other side of the table.

"Hey!" Seth laughed as he jumped up and grabbed for her.

She zipped in and out of tables, staying just beyond his reach as she tried to flip open the wallet and see his driver's license. They were both laughing so hard, it was a wonder they were able to run at all. He drew close and his hand brushed her hip, almost catching her belt loop, but with a twist and a yelp, she evaded him. She rounded a table in the middle of the patio and caught her foot on one of the heavy chairs. This slowed her down, and Seth caught her around the waist.

"Gotcha!"

"Rats. So close, too."

"Know what we do to pickpockets in Texas?" He stuffed his wallet back into his pocket.

"No. What?"

"This," He backed her against the wall of the bar and delivered the hottest kiss in the history of the world. At least, her world. Part of her mind reflected she had been kissed more in the past twenty-four hours than she had in the last six years. She wasn't complaining. In fact, she was so pleased by the entire situation she did what she'd been thinking of doing back at Dash's. She locked her arms tightly around his neck to support her weight while she lifted her legs and wrapped them around his waist.

"Nice touch. Most pickpockets don't do that."

"I'm not most pickpockets."

"So I noticed."

The only problem with her current position was she didn't have any leverage to press her pelvis any more tightly to him, which was a crying shame. Happily, he anticipated her need and shifted his weight, pinning her more firmly to the wall and giving her the intense contact she craved. From the feel of things, he was enjoying it, too. The breeze wafted across her exposed lower back, spiriting away the perspiration from her short-lived attempt to evade capture.

The bar's back door creaked, but she chose to ignore it. The subsequent throat clearing, however, demanded attention. With a muffled groan, Abby lowered her feet to the ground and detached her lips from Seth's. Looking over his shoulder at the intruder, she was glad she still had her arms around his neck, because she wasn't sure her knees would have held her up.

Standing there, his lip curled in a sneer of distaste, was her ex-husband.

He'd changed a bit since she last saw him loading suitcases — and Duffy — in the back of his car. He was still about six feet tall, of course, and still had medium brown hair in an unimaginative investment-advisor-approved style. His brown eyes were still mocking. He had a goatee now, and while his shoulders were broad in an artificial, gym-induced way, his stomach had expanded. Too many rich client lunches, she surmised. He wore razor-pressed khakis with a royal blue golf shirt meticulously tucked and belted into submission. He looked at them as if they were something he would have to scrape off his loafers at the first opportunity.

She got her legs firmly under her and straightened her posture. She removed her arms from around Seth's neck, and he turned. As she stepped up beside him, he put an arm around her waist, and she could almost hear the wheels turning in his head as he assessed the situation. He gave David a slow head to toe evaluation, then squeezed her waist, letting her take the lead in this unwelcome encounter.

"David," she said through gritted teeth.

"Abby. I heard, but I had to see for myself."

Damn small towns. And Joyce's mother was right up there at the top of the gossip food chain. Like a barracuda. "What did you have to see?"

"That you'd hooked up with some singer and were making a fool of yourself."

"What I do is none of your fucking business."

"Oh, my, and language, too. Joyce's mother told us you met this lowlife, took him home, and he's already brought you a bunch of trouble."

Abby lifted her chin and glared. "Why are you here? You didn't care when you left, so I sure as hell don't believe you care now. You're just here to piss me off."

"Abby, you sound so bitter. I thought we put all that behind us." He shook his head, its slow, steady motion like the pendulum in a dusty old grandfather clock in a maiden aunt's sitting room. "I'm here to meet with Martin Sundegaard. He handles real estate now, and I'm selling the property my uncle had on Shedd Lake. But when I heard about you, of course I was concerned. I came to see how you were and found you here in public, attached to this person like a barnacle." He stood there with his hands on his hips, a smug, superior smirk on his face.

How had she ever thought he was attractive? The contrast between his rigidly maintained pomposity and Seth's natural grace was mind-boggling. She must have suffered a head injury shortly after she met David that temporarily caused her to confuse "ass" with "class."

"Yes, and if you'd go away, I could get back to it," she growled.

"Aren't you going to introduce me to your boyfriend? Or have manners gone by the wayside along with your good judgment?"

"Manners? Don't you fucking dare talk to me about manners, you chickenshit, dog-stealing asshole!" She felt Seth tense beside her and took a deep breath. She touched a hand to his chest to let him know he could relax. She would maintain control. She hoped.

"Dog stealing? How can I steal something which was mine to begin with?" Abby opened her mouth to tell him exactly what she thought of the question, prepared to invent several new swear words to convey the depth of her disgust, when she observed a cruel glint in his eyes. Before she could figure out what that meant and prepare for more verbal assault, David said, "He's gone now, you know."

No, she hadn't known. Duffy would have been eleven years old. Not a puppy, certainly, but not an unheard-of age.

"How?" Even as she choked out the word, she hated having to ask, hated needing anything from David Higgins.

One corner of his mouth twitched, and Abby knew she definitely would not like what he had to say. "We put him down a few weeks ago. We found out Joyce is pregnant, and we didn't want an incontinent animal around the baby."

Abby was so busy figuring out the most violent, bloody, horrific way to dismember her ex-husband she literally could not speak. Beautiful Duffy, gone, merely because he was an inconvenience. Just like she had been.

"Oh, that was probably insensitive of me, mentioning the baby. It might be for the best you lost ours, though. You're not exactly the maternal type." He shook his head in mock sorrow. "I wouldn't have had any trouble getting full custody now, though, with you rolling around in the gutter."

A red haze descended to cloud her vision. Maybe by letting him upset her so badly she'd already lost, but at the moment she didn't care. All she wanted to do was claw the bastard's eyes right out of his head. She took a step toward him, but Seth's arm tightened around her, halting her forward momentum.

"Abby," he said softly. "Look at me."

The instant she met his clear blue eyes, she was able to distance herself from David and his calculated insults. Seth smoothed a tendril of hair back from her face.

"Let me see if I have this straight." His voice was utterly calm, and his eyes never left her face, as if David weren't even worthy of his recognition.

"Go ahead," she replied, surprised her voice sounded so steady.

"This piece of shit is, I'm assuming, your ex-husband."

"Correct."

"The one who cheated and left you. Showing spectacularly bad judgment."

Abby nodded.

"In the last couple of minutes, he has called me a lowlife and you a bitter, vulgar barnacle."

"Right again."

"And while standing there looking like he just stepped out of some tight-assed board meeting, he told you he killed your dog, he's glad you lost a baby, you would have made a terrible mother, and are now a piece of gutter trash."

"I'd say you just summed it up." It sounded ridiculous when Seth spelled it out that way.

"That's what I thought. I just needed to be sure, first."

"First?"

"Uh-huh." He gently guided Abby back a step. As he turned toward David he shifted his balance, drew back his right arm, and unleashed a very impressive punch, catching David right on the jaw. David reeled and stumbled against the table and fell with a meaty thud into one of the chairs. Too bad, actually. She would have liked to see him bounce on the patio a few times. It would have been easier to kick him that way.

"Kick him?" Seth asked.

"Whoops. Filter malfunction again. I'd been doing so well, too."

"Nothing to worry about. I wouldn't have minded seeing some kicking, but we have better things to do."

David lurched to his feet, sputtering furiously about sucker punches and assault charges. He took a step toward the door to the bar, but Seth intercepted him.

"No," he said, his voice devoid of all inflection. "You need to be somewhere else right now."

David stared at him, clearly unable to believe anyone would dare tell him what to do. He adopted a posture that might have intimidated an underling at work, but wasn't going to work on Seth. "I have. A meeting," he said through clenched teeth. Abby suspected his jaw might not be working so well.

Seth held his ground. "Pay attention, dickwad. That was not a suggestion." He took a step forward, right in David's face. "If you're still here in sixty seconds, my little love tap is gonna feel like a kiss from your sweet old granny."

Abby put a hand on Seth's arm. Any kind of violence or conflict usually made her very uncomfortable, Pam the Fangirl being the notable exception, and she didn't want to see this go any further. "David, how about you go down the street to the Fontaine. Totally upscale, much more your style." She didn't even try to keep the sarcasm from her voice. Luckily, David seized on her suggestion, recognizing an exit line allowing him to escape further ass kicking and pretend to retain some dignity.

"But, Martin…"

Abby cut him off. "Johnny's behind the bar. I'll tell him to send Martin your way when he shows up."

David straightened his belt and tried to pretend this was all his idea. "You do that. If this is the kind of clientele this place attracts, it's clearly gone downhill." He stomped off the patio and down the alley.

Feeling drained and a little dizzy, Abby leaned against Seth. His fingers stroked at her nape until she took a deep breath and looked up at him. She knew what was coming.

"Abby, about the baby…"

"No."

"But, I…"

She straightened and put as much strength into her voice as she could. "No, I am not letting David do this."

"Do what?"

Her fingernails dug into her palms, and she hoped he'd understand what she had to say. "David is not going to force us to have this conversation here, on a bar patio, with all your friends waiting for us inside." She made herself unclench her fists and softened her tone. "We will talk about it, but this isn't the time or the place, OK?"

Seth still had a worry line between his brows, but he nodded. "We'll talk when you're ready. Soon?"

"As soon as I can."

They stopped by the bar to deliver the message to Johnny, who gave them a questioning look before shrugging and making a note on a cocktail napkin. When they arrived at the table, Trent immediately noticed Seth's reddened knuckles. "What the hell were you doing out there?"

Seth glanced around the table. "No big deal, y'all. Just met Abby's ex-husband." He examined his right hand and flexed his fingers. "I gotta learn not to go for the face. Hurts like a bitch every time."

Marshall laughed and gave him a playful punch in the shoulder. "Nice job. You're out of practice, though. You're supposed to use a bar stool. Can't play guitar with a busted hand." He picked up one of the last shot glasses remaining in the center of the table. "I assume the asshole had it coming."

"For sure. He's just lucky I didn't let Abby at him. She was planning to kick his head in."

"Now, that I'd have paid to see." Marsh said.

Chuckles and nods of approval came from around the table, except for Trent. He was frowning.

"Look, guys, not to piss on your Cheerios or anything, because I understand about blowing off steam. But should we really be laughing about bar fights considering the news about Stacy?" Most of his stern expression was aimed at Seth and Marshall. Abby felt like slumping under the table herself. Mouse and Roberto didn't completely escape chastisement, but Andy and Danny, perhaps because they hadn't been part of the gang when Stacy was around, seemed immune. They looked like they didn't dare open their mouths, though.

Seth and Marshall exchanged a long look, and Seth spoke. "I'm going to say this, and it's the last time I want to have this conversation."

Trent nodded. "Fair enough. Go ahead."

Seth's jaw clenched a few times as he fidgeted with a ring on his left hand. He looked up and made eye contact with each man around the table. "I brought Stacy into this group, and maybe it was the wrong thing to do. I knew she had some problems, but we were all hanging just shy of being out of control back then. Only we moved one way, and she got closer and closer to the danger zone. I probably should've done something, found some way to stop her from being so reckless, but I didn't. I never felt like I had any ground to stand on, telling somebody else to get their shit together. Probably still don't." He grabbed the open bottle of water in front of Trent and took a long swallow.

"Man, I didn't mean..." Trent began.

"No, Trent. I'm not done." He returned the bottle and cleared his throat. "She's been out of my life for a long time, and I've never been sorry she left. There wasn't enough holding us together, and the last stunt she pulled made the decision for us. I wasn't going to live that way. No other way it could've worked out.

"But when I say I haven't been sorry she's gone, it doesn't mean I don't care she's dead. I do. She meant something to me once. It makes me sick she was so messed up or felt so bad, whichever way it went down, and she was alone." His voice choked off and he had to pause to collect himself before going on. "I feel like shit because I wanted to think she was involved with whatever's happening, and we didn't even know she was dead. I'm sorry she's not out there having the time of her life, maybe straightening out, being happy. Maybe most of it was her own fault, but knowing me didn't ever do her one bit of good."

Abby looked around the table. She was surprised to see Marshall had tears in his eyes. Seth looked like he was hanging on by a thread, and she realized her own cheeks were wet. Maybe it wasn't her place, but she'd had enough. She stood. "Well, gentlemen, I think everything's been said that needs to be said. Got anything else to add?" Her gaze swept the table, and nobody seemed eager to meet her eyes. She guessed she'd learned something from her mother after all.

Trent stood, too, and extended a hand to Seth. "No. Just... I'm sorry, bro, OK?"

Seth clasped his hand. "Yeah."

"Excellent," Abby said. "Today's been the roller coaster from hell, and believe me when I say seeing Seth clock David was the biggest bright spot since my guest room exploded. I'm not going to apologize for finding it amusing." She scooped her purse from the bench beside her. "That's it. I'm done, and as soon as you boys wrap this up, Seth and I are going home." She was a little winded after her speech, but felt better for saying it.

Seth rose, wiped her still-wet cheeks with a napkin, and kissed her. He looked at his friends. "So, what did y'all decide about the trip home?" He was trying hard to act as if nothing dramatic had happened.

Trent emptied the last pitcher of beer. "Like I said, I'm flying out in the morning. Danny and Jake will go to St. Cloud till the van is released, probably a few days, and drive it home."

"You all right with that, Danny?"

"Sure. I've done my share of driving and towing the trailer. It's all good." Mouse spoke up. "I hate to fly, and I ain't waiting around for the bus, so me and Roberto are going to rent a car and head out tomorrow. He wants to stop at a custom music shop in Kansas City and look at some equipment he's been e-mailing them about."

Marshall appeared to have regained his composure. "I think I'll hang around here until they let us have the bus back. Won't hurt to be nearby in case you get your ass in more trouble."

Seth snorted. "You're more likely to cause trouble than patch it up."

"You'd think so, wouldn't you? I'm starting to see a change in the trend, though." He scooted his empty glass toward the center of the table. "I'll hire somebody local to help me with the drive, so I don't have to take any extra time."

"I'm going to rent a car, too, and drive to Chicago to see my aunt," Andy said. "As fucked up as this is, makes me feel like I should see her. She practically raised me. I'll fly back to Austin from there in a few days."

Abby did a mental roll call. "That's everybody then, isn't it?"

Seth nodded. "Yep. This would've been a disaster if we had gigs this week, but I guess if your bus is a crime scene, this is the best time for it to happen."

Abby pinched his ribs. "Not funny."

"I think my mood is turning around, so it's almost funny," Seth said, digging some cash from his wallet and tossing it on the table. "So, guys, we good?"

"We're good. Get out of here," Trent said.

Seth took Abby's hand. "We're gone. C'mon, Abby-Kat."

She would have smacked him for the "Abby-Kat" thing, but she found the idea of going home with him — again — was putting her in a very good mood, too.

Chapter Twelve

Abby and Seth were almost back to Dash's when the wind picked up, a sure sign rain was imminent. She pulled back the hair blowing around her face, and folded her arms against the slight chill. "We'd better hurry if we don't want to get soaked."

Seth stepped up the pace after a quick look at the threatening sky. They rounded the corner of the club, and met an unwelcome sight. Two news vans were parked near the building, and a reporter and cameraman were keeping watch on the back door.

Abby moaned. "Oh, shit. Why didn't it occur to me reporters would show up?"

Seth pulled her out of sight behind a pickup truck. "I should've thought of it, but I didn't think the media up here would pay me much attention. I forgot you're a local celebrity."

"Must be a slow news day," she said, rolling her eyes. "Let's go in the side door."

The side door was still unlocked, and they retreated into the building's dim interior, where they encountered Special Agent Kincaid.

"I was about to call you," he said. "We lucked out on the lab testing your whiskey bottle."

Abby wondered if finding evidence of drugs in the bottle would be considered lucky or unlucky in this case.

"Lucked out how?" Seth asked.

"Bad word choice," Kincaid admitted. "But it was fortunate the toxicology expert was really on the ball. He had a hunch based on the symptoms you described, and ran a test he might not have otherwise."

"Really? What did he test for?" Seth's shoulders tensed, as if he didn't believe he'd enjoy the answer.

"Rohypnol and GHB, commonly known as 'date rape' drugs. The sample tested positive with a high concentration of GHB, or gamma hydroxybutyrate."

"What made him think of it?" Abby asked.

"Let's get out of the hallway," Kincaid said, steering them toward a staff break room. As they sat around a chipped Formica table, he pulled out a single faxed page and perched reading glasses on his nose. "He thought of Rohypnol, GHB, and a couple of other possibilities, because of the rapid appearance of being intoxicated, as well as the fact you don't have much memory of what happened after you finished your interview."

"That's for sure," Seth said. "I couldn't tell you the last time one of the guys had to make sure I got to my room in one piece. And the few times they did, it was after a real balls-out bender, not two drinks."

"Right. And this is exactly why it's effective. The victim doesn't remember much, and is so compliant the perpetrator has total control."

Abby searched her memory for information on GHB and came up dry. She hadn't even researched it for one of her books. "Where would somebody get it?"

Kincaid placed the fax on the table and leaned back. "You used to be able to buy it in health food stores, as an additive body builders used to supposedly increase the production of growth hormone. It was banned in 1990, but people can still buy the components and cook it up at home." He shook his head. "Which makes it even more dangerous. You never know how strong a batch is going to be."

"So was somebody trying to poison me or put me out of commission so they could finish me off some other way?"

"Could be either," Kincaid said. "It can take thirty to forty minutes to peak in your bloodstream, and alcohol intensifies the effect. So if you had a few drinks of a really potent sample in a short amount of time, you could have a lethal dose before you even knew you were in trouble. It's a clear liquid, and other than a slightly salty taste you wouldn't notice it, especially if it's masked by alcohol or another strong flavor. The victim would appear very drunk, but could sink into deep unconsciousness or even a coma. Respiration might stop, or they could vomit and aspirate."

Abby tried to envision this scenario as if she were considering it for one of her books. It helped keep the freak-out at bay if she processed it in a fictional context. "But they couldn't be sure about the dose, especially not if they made it themselves, right? Plus, Seth blew the plan because he stopped drinking to go do his interview."

Kincaid nodded. "I'd say so. It means the perpetrator probably intended to take advantage of the other effect of GHB, which is the victim being defenseless, maybe incapacitated."

Seth leaned his elbows on the table and put his face in his hands. "This is fucking unreal." Lifting his head, he shoved his hair back in frustration. "But you know what? Marsh probably saved my life, because he stayed in my room all night. He's gotten a kick out of riding me about it ever since, but he really thought something was wrong."

"Remind me to thank him," Abby said.

"Thing is," Kincaid said, his voice deepening in a deliberate manner, "they'd have probably gotten away with it. Think about it. People drink too much, vomit, and choke to death a lot more often than most people realize. If they found a high blood alcohol level, they'd say, 'Damn shame, guy drank himself to death,' and never look any farther. Plus, GHB occurs naturally in the body, so even if they did find it in your bloodstream, they'd almost certainly write it off unless there were other reasons to be suspicious and do more tests."

"Guess all my lucky stars must be in alignment," Seth said. Despite the attempt to shrug it off, his voice had the flat tone of someone who had heard all he could handle.

"I'd say so," Kincaid said. "Now, listen, I can't imagine anybody having three separate plans in the pipeline or being crazy enough to try anything else with investigators all over the place. But it doesn't mean you shouldn't be careful. We arranged for one of the Emporia officers to make some passes out your road tonight, and as many nights as you're in town."

"We're grateful," Abby said, rubbing Seth's forearm. She needed to draw some of his attention away from the dark facts she knew were bouncing around in his head. "It's pretty hard to get near my house without someone hearing, but at this point I appreciate any extra security we can get."

"I'll be talking with you both again tomorrow." Kincaid rose and shook Seth's hand. "Now, if you want, I'll go see if I can get those reporters to focus on me for a minute, give you a chance to get past them."

"Much appreciated," Seth said. "But I should write out a statement for you to give them. Otherwise, they're liable to show up out at the lake later."

"Good thinking," Kincaid said, handing Seth a small spiral notebook from his pocket.

"I'm saying the entire band is shocked by these events. We have no idea what it's all about. We're grateful nobody has been hurt, and we have full confidence in the officials conducting the investigation. Sound OK?"

"Perfect," Kincaid said, accepting the return of the notebook. "Now let's get you on your way."

* * *

As they drove home, the rain intensified, spilling across the road, filling ditches, and leaving deep puddles in the low spots in Abby's gravel road. There had been some conversation regarding who would drive, but Abby prevailed. Seth argued she'd allowed him to drive that morning, but she said it was a moment of weakness and shouldn't be considered a precedent. She also pointed out the "B" for Bitch monogrammed on the door.

"I'm not letting you drive the Bitchmobile, especially when you've had more to drink than I have."

"You call your car the Bitchmobile?"

"As of about three seconds ago."

So Abby drove, and only had to ask Seth to stop trying to put his foot through the passenger-side floorboard twice. They hurried from the driveway to the side porch, and as Abby unlocked the door she thought she'd never been so happy to be home in her entire life.

"I guess the first order of business is a tour of the crime scene or the disaster area or whatever it is." She tossed her keys and purse on the kitchen counter, not yet looking toward the guest room.

"That's your first order of business? Because I kind of hoped you had one or two more…urgent ideas."

She turned and saw him leaning against the wall, arms folded, and looking completely edible. "Down, boy. As a matter of fact, I have numerous ideas. But first I have to confirm there aren't any unpleasant surprises or stray federal agents lurking." She passed where Seth stood, and he fell into step behind her.

They entered the spare room, and Abby switched on a lamp and gasped. "Well, would you look at that?"

"Impressive."

"I didn't get a good look from outside because of the rain, but if you ignore the wrecked ceiling you'd almost never know anything happened." She assessed the amazing feat her mother had accomplished. The wall hole and other window were both securely boarded, and someone had even stapled a blue sheet, fan folded to resemble drapery pleats, over the plywood. Another piece of plywood covered the splintered area on the floor beneath a bright throw rug, the whole room had been cleared of debris, and the bed was neatly remade. There was still an underlying scent of charred wood and drywall, but it was almost completely masked by Lemon Pledge and Pine Sol. Not her favorite scents, but definitely preferable to scorched house.

"Let's check the fridge," Seth suggested. "She said they were leaving food, right?"

"You can't possibly be hungry already. You ate almost a whole platter of potato skins all by yourself." A finger poked at his stomach emphasized her point.

"I'm planning on working up an appetite."

She was, too, but couldn't concentrate until she'd finished her inspection.

The refrigerator's contents included not only sandwiches, soft drinks, and potato salad, but several covered baking dishes.

"Ooh! Chicken and noodle hot dish with potato chips on top. Mom knows that's my favorite. But look at these others. I'll have to freeze some of them."

Seth peered around her and into the lighted interior of the refrigerator. "Is that barbecued chicken? When did she bring barbecued chicken? I missed it."

"Hard to tell. I don't think she made it here. The propane tank for my grill hasn't been filled yet. She probably contracted it out. She has her sources."

Seth plucked a piece of paper from the breakfast bar. "Here's her note."

Abby took it, but didn't immediately read it. "One more thing. My room."

"Now you're getting to the right part of the agenda," Seth said, reaching for her.

"No, we need to see what she did in there."

"What's she going to do to your room?"

"One never knows. That's what has me so concerned." Abby pictured several dozen strategically placed candles and a bottle of champagne, given her mother's obvious determination to present an over-the-top endorsement of her relationship with Seth.

They crossed the hallway to her room, and she flipped on the light against the rainy gloom.

"Tulips on the bed table. Scary," Seth teased.

"Nice touch, even though I have no idea where she got them. It's my vase, though. Subtle." Her quick visual inventory noticed several things. "First, your guitar is over there leaning against the dresser. She didn't leave it in a neutral area like the living or dining room. She put it in the bedroom."

"Don't you think you're reading too much into this?"

"Excuse me, didn't you meet Mom this morning?"

"I..."

"Shush, I'm looking."

Seth shushed.

"I'm not surprised she dried and folded your clothes. She's incapable of leaving laundry more than five minutes after it's done. But she did put your T-shirts, socks..." She took a step closer to verify her suspicion. "...and boxers on my dresser. Less subtle, but effective." Her next stop was the closet. "And here we have your jeans, two button-down shirts, and a denim jacket. Don't be surprised if she ironed your jeans. At least she didn't overdo it. Much." Though she had to admit there could be other discoveries yet to be made. "OK, I'm done. Do you want something to drink?"

"I don't think so. I'm not sure why I had tequila at the Shamrock. Should've stuck to beer."

"What about coffee? Tea?"

"Coffee'd be good."

Abby set the coffee brewing, and put a mug of water in the microwave with a lemon teabag. After the day she'd had, she didn't think excessive amounts of caffeine jangling her nerves would be wise. And she didn't think she'd need any extra assistance to stay awake tonight. Not considering how hot Seth looked stretched out on her couch, flipping channels on the television.

While she waited for the coffee, she read her mother's note. It included specific instructions for reheating the chicken and noodles in the oven, but Abby mentally disregarded them. Why would she waste time on the oven when she had a perfectly good microwave? The note also included information about Dilbert's whereabouts, which was helpful. With the rain pelting the French doors, she'd begun to worry about him.

"Mom says Dilbert's over at Walt and Trudy Nygaards'."

"Inside, I hope," he said, thumb still on the remote control.

"Yeah. Trudy called and told her he was on their screen porch with a fresh bone. He'll most likely stay the night." She poured the coffee, remembering from the morning—had it really only been this morning?—Seth took his with cream and no sugar. She added honey to her tea and joined him in the living room. She was pleased to see the movie where he either stopped flipping or the batteries died was a comedy she'd seen many times. She didn't need any more horror or drama in her day. After a sip from her Deadlines Amuse Me mug, she sat it down and sank back onto the couch.

"This is where I've wanted to be all day," she sighed.

"Me, too. This morning we thought we'd have the whole day to ourselves." He brushed her hair aside and kissed her neck.

Abby glanced out the French doors and assessed the level of sunlight still detectable through the rain-laden clouds. "It's not quite over yet, thankfully."

"No. And you're forgetting the best part."

"Which is?"

"We also have all night."

The mere thought made her stomach surge in the best possible way. She melted into his kiss and let all the stresses of the day melt right along with her. It was surprisingly easy. The cloud-shrouded light and the steady hiss of the rainfall, combined with the barely audible sound track from the television created a soothing sense of total isolation.

The jeans she wore were far less convenient than her yoga shorts, but Abby didn't want to waste time changing. Seth deftly unhooked her bra, and she used her favorite trick to slide the straps down her shoulders and pull the undergarment off through her sleeve. She dropped it to the floor, then had a thought. "Hey, make sure I pick that up," she mumbled against his lips. "You know. In case Mom comes by tomorrow."

"She'll probably make a point to check the couch cushions after this morning."

"I'm not letting her in unless she brings croissants."

Seth laughed softly and pulled her closer, his hands performing wondrous acts beneath her shirt. She unfastened the button on his jeans, tugged down the zipper and dipped her hand inside. She readjusted him into what she hoped was a more comfortable—and definitely more accessible—position, and was delighted to feel him become even thicker and harder in her hand.

"Darlin', one thing about tonight," he murmured.

"What's that?"

"Tonight, we linger."

"I'm a big fan of lingering." She knew exactly where she wanted to start. She drew her fingers lightly up his ribs, catching his shirt and taking it off over his head. Allowing her lips to drift slowly across his cheek, she kissed the warm, musky spot just below his ear, and spent a moment letting her lips and tongue toy with his earring. It was so entertaining she moved to his other ear and repeated the process.

She trailed kisses down his neck, past the prickly rasp of razor stubble, and tasted the hollow of his throat above his silver chain. She delighted at the vibration of his hungry growl on her tongue.

As she moved further down his body, she discovered he'd grasped the hem of her shirt, and her progress was causing it to ride up her back. She straightened her arms and allowed him to whisk the shirt off to join the growing laundry pile. She pressed her skin to his, reveling in the sensation, and kissed her way to the center of his chest.

There was a lot to be said for lingering, but there was also a lot to be said for moving along. On that note, she meandered from the light covering of hair on his chest toward the thinning line guiding her downward. She had purposely kept her hands on his torso following her earlier detour to assist him with his jeans. Now, though, she needed to make further, more significant, adjustments.

Before she totally committed herself, she glanced up at his face. The intensity of his gaze sparked. She wondered if he was beginning to think lingering was overrated. He looked as if he'd like to throw her over his shoulder, toss her on the bed, and forget all about taking their time. Not that she'd object, but she really, really wanted to finish what she'd started.

She'd see how long he'd let her linger.

She slithered to the floor, and an instant later he kicked his shoes under the coffee table. His socks followed suit, and she prodded him to lift his hips so she could edge his jeans and boxers out of the way. The laundry pile was reaching Everest-like proportions. As were other things. Excellent.

Now she had him naked — at long last — and allowed her eyes to make a quick but incredibly scenic tour up his body. The flat, firm planes of his abdomen stretched before her, but in the immediate foreground was a rigid, tongue-tempting form demanding her prompt attention.

His hands clenched, his blunt fingernails making a scratching sound on the sofa upholstery. "I can't reach you."

"Reach me later. I'm occupied."

"Oh. Yeah. Lingering." He managed to inject a note of wonder into his hoarse comment.

Abby brushed her hands up his thighs and over his hips as she leaned toward him. Her proximity brought her breasts in contact with his thighs, and they tingled at the sensation of the light, coarse hair they encountered. She applied a feathery brush of her fingertips up his length and saw his stomach muscles contract. Whether it was taking pity or showing no mercy, she finally allowed him the touch of her tongue, but she started at the juncture of his legs, savoring the velvety skin. Only then did she work her way upward.

He watched her every move, and she knew it. She wanted him to. She needed him to. She loved knowing he couldn't take his eyes off her. Her tongue swept up him from base to tip, and she marveled at the sensation of soft, hot flesh over the powerful hardness beneath.

She swirled her tongue around the ridge below his apex, allowing him to see the moist tip of her tongue and the glistening trail it left in its wake. She licked her lips, and swept them across his crest, gathering the creamy droplets beaded there. He shuddered and cautiously brought his fingertips up to comb through her hair. She took note of his reaction every time she touched or tasted him in a new way, filing the information away so she'd always be able to recall exactly what he liked best.

Her lips parted, and she drew him in as slowly as she could bear. Her own arousal was reaching critical mass, and the need to abandon her jeans was almost maddening. She took more of him into the wet heat of her mouth, swirling her tongue firmly over the sensitive glans. A little more deeply, a little more pressure, a little more moisture, a little more stroking of her hand, until he was fully seated at the back of her throat. Her lips wrapped around the girth of his base, brushing the wiry thatch of hair surrounding it.

His fingers gripped her hair more tightly, but she didn't mind. She withdrew, almost allowing him to glide free of her mouth, before clutching him firmly with one hand and sliding her lips down over him again. While he filled her mouth, she used her tongue to massage him, swallowing his taste. She retreated again, giving him the opportunity to enjoy the sensuous sight of her lips, teeth and tongue as she devoted her full attention to pleasing him.

He grew even thicker and more rigid, and she detected the occasional tremble from the muscles in his thighs. She began moving more quickly and forcefully, reveling in the lush, swollen sensation in her lips.

His hands left her hair abruptly and grabbed her hands where they rested on his hips. "Abby, I need you. Now."

She sat back on her heels and licked the moisture from her lips. "No more lingering?"

He let out a laugh that was almost a cough. "Lingering might have been the worst fucking idea I've ever had."

She nibbled her lower lip, testing it for tenderness, as she stood. She peeled down her jeans and pink lace bikinis and climbed on the couch to straddle him. She knew she was soaking wet and ready, and an exploratory caress from his fingers confirmed it. She draped her arms across his shoulders, bent to kiss him, and eased herself down on him until he filled her completely. She was still for a moment, then began rocking against him, not withdrawing, but creating friction and pressure of a different kind. His hands found her breasts and teased the already-erect nipples to even tighter, nearly painful peaks before he took one, then the other, into his mouth. He worked magic similar to what she had just performed between his legs, and she thought she might shatter into her individual molecules from sheer pleasure.

Seth pulled her tightly against his chest and buried his face in her hair. "Darlin', I'm voting we move to your room. I have this image of you under me, your hair across the pillow, and if I don't see it in the next fifteen seconds I'll lose my mind."

She started to rise up on her knees in preparation for separating herself from him, but he stopped her. One arm around her back and one under her bottom, he hoisted them both from the couch without breaking their intimate contact, and carried her into the bedroom.

Seth placed a knee on the bed and eased them down, still buried inside her. She settled on the pile of pillows with him above her and lifted her face to receive his kisses. She lost herself in their rhythm. She twined her legs tightly around his, but soon shifted them higher, around his waist, as high as she could so he could plunge even deeper. As the thrusts intensified, she imagined it would be somewhat painful if it didn't feel so incredible.

The tension at her core built until it could no longer be contained. Bursting, fragmenting, a bright prism of sensation engulfed her. Her hands clutched at his shoulders as she pulled him to her, burying her face in the curve of his neck.

The intensity of her climax took him over the edge as well. The feeling of him so deeply inside her, straining and pulsing, as he whispered her name extended her own pleasure beyond anything she'd ever believed possible.

They lay on top of the comforter instead of in the tangled, sweaty sheets they'd envisioned earlier, but Abby didn't mind. First priority at the moment was to get her breathing and heartbeat steady. They collapsed on their sides, facing each other, still joined.

"I… You…" Seth had not yet completely regained control over his breathing.

"Real poetic in the afterglow department, are we?" Abby teased, licking the dragon tattoo on his shoulder.

"I think you destroyed my power of speech."

"Maybe it'll come back."

"I sure as hell hope so, because I have a lot of things to say to you."

They rearranged themselves into positions more conducive to recovery, though the caresses they shared suggested recovery would soon lead to further exertion. Abby listened to the rain on the roof, and thought she had never been more content than she was at that moment.

After a while, Abby pulled back the comforter and they slid beneath it. Their combined moisture rushed between her legs, and decided she didn't care one bit about the condition of the sheets or the comforter.

Seth's touch became bolder, and Abby pressed her body against his.

"Just so you know, there's going to be more lingering," Seth said, one hand gently parting her thighs.

"I thought you were done with lingering."

"This time I'm going to be the one doing it."

By the time they were both spent, she was starting to think perhaps she should have objected. At this rate, it would take a week before she could sit up, let alone stand. She was a sweaty, exhausted, limp puddle of utter satisfaction. Then again, looking at Seth, she could easily imagine rewinding to around the time she took off her bra, and enjoying the entire experience all over again. Soon.

Chapter Thirteen

Seth replayed the evening's activities in his mind and began devising variations to be acted upon as soon as he could manage. "I think I'm dehydrated."

"I'm not apologizing," Abby said, running her hand across his chest.

"Not complaining. Just making an observation."

"Your coffee's probably cold by now, but the pot's still on if you want some." Her hand migrated from his chest to his stomach, and if she went any lower his dehydration would rapidly reach clinical levels. And he wouldn't mind a bit.

"I was thinking maybe some IV fluids."

"I'm fresh out, but there's plenty of Coke in the fridge, thanks to Mom."

"It would require getting out of bed. And walking."

Abby laughed. "Yeah, it would." She withdrew her hand, something about which he had extremely mixed feelings, and rolled over. "But I'm going to have to get up anyway, at least for a while."

"As long as it's only for a while. What do you have to do?" He raised himself on one elbow as Abby swung her legs over the side of the bed and stood. He immediately had impulses to nibble her right in the perfect curve where her thigh met her ass, and to grab her by the waist and pull her back into bed. Since he couldn't make a decision, he did neither and just watched her walk across the room and pull a pair of shorts and a top out of the dresser.

"I remembered I was supposed to send my editor the revised synopsis for the third book. Yesterday. I probably have a dozen e-mails from her, threatening to come out here with a cattle prod if I don't stick to my deadlines. I haven't even turned on the computer since yesterday morning."

He gave himself a mental head slap. "Guess I forgot just because I'm on hiatus doesn't mean other people don't have work to do."

"It won't take long. I just have to read over it and send it. I might get some writing in tomorrow. Or the next day."

"Now that you mention it, I should send some sort of announcement to our website manager. He's probably getting tons of messages from people who heard about what happened." In fact, if he didn't take care of it pretty soon, Victor would most likely join Abby's editor in the cattle prod brigade.

Abby flipped her hair out of the neckline of her shirt. "If you want to grab something to drink, I'll go fire up the computer and the laptop so we can get everything taken care of at the same time."

He was in favor of anything that took care of obligations so he could verify the amazing things she'd recently done with her tongue weren't just wishful thinking. He rose and walked to the dresser where he took a pair of navy boxers from the pile of freshly folded laundry. This was all the clothing he intended to put on, in order to make its later removal as simple as possible.

He followed Abby to the kitchen, where she selected a diet root beer from the refrigerator. He grabbed a Coke because he figured the sugar and caffeine would come in handy. Abby started up the stairs to the loft, and he detoured to the living room to turn off the television and make sure the doors were locked. They were. It was now full dark, and though the rain had slackened, it was still coming down steadily.

"Oh, holy hell!"

Abby's shout sent a bolt of fear straight through him, and he ran for the stairs. He stumbled into the loft and found Abby staring around the room with wide, disbelieving eyes. Not a single deranged killer in a hockey mask was to be found.

"Jesus, Abby, you almost gave me a fucking heart attack! What's the matter?"

"Look!" Damned if she wasn't hot even when she was screeching and waving her arms around.

Seth looked. The loft was perfectly tidy, and he couldn't see what the problem... Oh, wait. It was tidy. When he was up here yesterday, it looked like someone had turned it upside down and shaken it.

"My. Mother." It sounded like it took a great deal of effort to get those two words past her clenched teeth.

"OK, she cleaned. Isn't that a good thing?"

Abby swung around and stared at him incredulously. "She touched. My stuff. My. Stuff. She not only touched it, she moved it, and I'm willing to bet she threw some of it away!"

Realizing he was not qualified to judge the enormity of Marilyn's transgression, Seth retreated to the armchair and took a huge swallow of Coke.

"My stacks are...stackier. The debris field has been cleared, and she even washed my ashtray. How am I supposed to work like this?" She whirled to face the whiteboard. "At least she didn't erase the murder board. So I don't have to put her name on it."

"Didn't you have e-mail to check?" He hoped to get her back on task. The caffeine was kicking in, and he wanted her distraction-free.

She took a deep breath and let it out with an exasperated growl. "Yes. Let me plug in the laptop for you." She reached for the computer on the shelf by the printer, yanked a power cord from a desk drawer, and plugged it into an outlet near Seth's chair. In moments it was chiming a welcome, and she logged in and brought up a web browser. "Do whatever you need to do. I shouldn't be more than ten minutes or so."

Seth pulled up his e-mail, deleted a bunch of spam, and noticed at least three dozen e-mails from people with subject lines like "Are you OK?" and "What's going on?" He ignored those for the time being. He sent a message to his webmaster briefly detailing the situation and giving him the standard press release to post to the band's website. When he was finished, he sat back and enjoyed simply watching Abby at her desk. She kept grumbling about how it would take her weeks to get everything back the way she liked it, and he had to smile when she methodically elbowed a pile of file folders until it gave in to the forces of gravity and spilled across the desk.

"Is she out of her mind?" Abby's shocked tone gave Seth another scare. Had she received some sort of e-mail threat?

"Is who out of her mind? Your mom?"

"No, my editor. And it appears she's in cahoots with my agent. What are they thinking?" She picked up a pen and began tapping it rapidly against the edge of the desk.

"About what?"

"They've scheduled a book tour."

"And it's a problem?"

Abby shook her head. "Not as such. I mean, I did a tour for the first book. Sort of. I did signings at five or six bookstores in Minnesota. And one in Wisconsin."

"Don't you need to do promotional stuff?"

"Well, yeah, but look at this." Seth approached and peered over her shoulder at the monitor. "Twelve cities? Twelve cities in eighteen days. And they're actual cities. New York, Atlanta, Dallas, Seattle, Phoenix, Pittsburgh, some other places, plus a couple in Minnesota." She flung the pen down beside the keyboard. "I have readers in Pittsburgh?"

"If you don't yet, I guess you will soon."

"This is all too much. I can't do it."

"Sure you can. Could you take Monique or your mom with you?"

"Mom would drive me crazy, and Monique wouldn't leave her kids for that long. Probably just be me. Business as usual."

Seth studied the proposed dates. They were in late August and early September. "If I'm remembering our schedule, I bet I could make about half of these with you. If you want."

She spun her chair around and looked up at him. "Really?"

"Sure. What's a few more frequent flier miles?" Plus, since she hadn't yet said if she'd travel with him, this would guarantee him at least a half dozen more opportunities to see her.

"I still think it's too much. I'll tell them to cut it down." She reached for the keyboard.

"Stop it. You have to promote the book if you want it to sell. At the most, see if you can adjust a few dates so I can make it to even more of them."

Abby stood, wrapped her arms around his neck, and gave him a huge kiss. "You're incredible, you know. And possibly nuts."

"Yeah, I know. I'm also selfish, because it'll give me time with you I wouldn't have otherwise."

"I don't care about the motives. I'm just glad you'll be there." She sat back down and turned to face the screen. "Two minutes. I have to send the synopsis and tell her we'll finalize the dates later." She poked another mound of papers, and a small, fabric-covered book slipped to the floor.

Seth bent to pick it up. It had fallen open, and he noticed it was handwritten. "What's this, Abby-Kat?"

She gave him a squinty look for calling her Abby-Kat, and glanced at the book in his hands. "Oh, that. Sometimes I write poetry. For some reason, I always do poetry by hand. Then when it's done—or as done as it'll ever be, because I can always edit anything I've written—I copy it in there. Most of it's pretty awful."

Seth flipped through the pages, hesitated and looked at Abby. "Is it OK for me to look at this?"

"Sure, if you like terrible poetry."

He continued, skimming the verses as he went. "Darlin', this isn't terrible at all. And these aren't poems."

"I'm fairly certain they're poems. They were when I wrote them."

"These are songs. Well, with a few adjustments, but all the elements are here."

She shrugged. "I don't know anything about writing songs. That's your field."

"Then you should listen to me." He couldn't believe how good some of these were. "Songs are basically poems. But you simplify them, which is fine because you have the music to support it. You repeat lines or similar beats or sounds, but giving it meaning has to start from the beginning. You've done that here, from what I can see."

"If you say so." She looked back at the computer.

"I'm serious. I think we could do something with this." He closed the volume to put it back on the desk, but he wanted to read those poems—songs—more carefully. "Would you mind if I took this downstairs? I'd really like to look at it some more."

"I think you're deranged, but if you want to, sure." She shrugged again, never taking her eyes off the computer.

Seth held onto the book and finished the Coke. He was about to toss the can in the trash can by the desk when Abby said, "Stop."

"Stop what?"

"Give me the can."

Seth gave her the empty can, and she placed it with hers on the desk. She appeared to give great consideration to their precise arrangement, recreating the level of organized chaos she required for her writing environment. Kind of odd, but cute.

Abby rose from the desk, and they headed to the kitchen. She nodded in the direction of the well-stocked fridge. "Go ahead and get what you want. I need to make sure Butch's repair job didn't leak."

Seth detoured to drop the book on the table on his side of the bed. He smiled a little at the thought he had a "his side of the bed." He snagged a plate and dished up some chicken and potato salad, settled at the breakfast bar, and listened to the rain while he ate.

Abby joined him a few minutes later and reported the guest room remained dry.

"Getting tired?" she asked.

"It has been a long day."

"We should definitely go back to bed, then." The smile appearing on her face, however, was definitely more salacious than somnolent. Seth wholeheartedly approved.

As they passed the couch, Abby collected their discarded clothes and dropped them in the hamper in the bedroom, muttering about not making things too easy for her mother.

When she turned, he was waiting for her. Without a word, he gently removed the clothes she had put on for her trip upstairs. He slipped out of his own and joined her in the welcoming embrace of the bed.

He pulled the blanket over them and they curled together, their bodies creating a cozy, warm nest. He lay there, contemplating how fortunate he was to be holding this woman in his arms. She was already as vital to him as his next breath, and he wondered how it happened. If he'd met her five years ago, would it have been the same way? Or did it work only because he was ready—and maybe even destined—for her at this precise point in his life?

He decided he didn't care why. It just was, and nothing else mattered. For the first time in too long Seth felt music gathering in his head. He had to write a song for her. Songs. Probably a whole CD. A double set. She was beautiful and brilliant. She was creative and quirky and sexy as hell. He needed to take care of her, but he also felt like he'd found his own sanctuary when he was with her. She could be sweet and agreeable, but when push came to shove, she was definitely not someone to cross. He still couldn't believe how she'd gone to bat for him when Trent was giving him a hard time for not showing appropriate grief over the news about Stacy. Abby could take down a vandal, plot to kick in her ex-husband's head, and then make him laugh and completely forget the turmoil of the day. And he couldn't get enough of her.

He realized, based on the significant discomfort in the vicinity of his groin, he'd gotten his second wind. Or was it the third? Didn't matter. He definitely knew what to do about it.

He brought Abby's back against his chest, and ran his hands over her full, responsive breasts. A strangled purr escaped her throat, and she arched, pressing her hips against him. He buried his face in her hair, breathing in her fragrance as he lowered one hand to her waist. Sweeping to her back and over the swell of her bottom, he delved further until his fingers were exploring her wet, lush depths. She bent one knee to give him greater access. His other arm was under her, just beneath her shoulders, and that hand enjoyed the silky skin of her breasts and belly.

She reached behind her and wrapped her fingers around him. She adjusted his angle until he was able to press inside her, and shifted her hips until he was completely sheathed in her intoxicating heat.

He trailed his fingers back over the slope of her hip until he was able to reach the slick bud, which was tangible evidence of her arousal. Gliding, caressing, and breathing her in, his own rising tide drove him to become more insistent until she shuddered around him. Her inner muscles clenched, pulling him deeper, and a loose, rumbling sound of satisfaction rose from her chest. Her response was the trigger, sending him spiraling beyond control, and he pulled her firmly against his chest, murmuring his own satisfied sounds into her ear until their bodies stilled.

When he thought he could bear it, he withdrew, but only so she could turn in his arms to face him. Her face was flushed, her lips moist, and he once again thanked whatever forces responsible for allowing their paths to cross.

He floated his hand down her arm until he could grasp her fingers. He tucked their joined hands to his chest and kissed her. "Know what I was just thinking?"

"I might be too worn out to hear it for a few minutes," she said.

"Funny. No, what I was thinking was it's highly likely everybody else in the entire world who ever had sex was doing it wrong, but we have it figured out."

Abby laughed softly. "You're cute when you're being corny."

"I was kind of serious. I mean…the way you feel around me when you come…"

"It's the way you make me feel."

Though he'd like to make her feel that way again, he settled for kissing her until they both had to come up for air.

Abby wiggled into a sitting position and leaned back on a mound of pillows. Seth settled in beside her. She angled toward him, one hand on his chest. "I think maybe we should talk about…about what David brought up."

While he'd wanted to have this conversation earlier, he was suddenly apprehensive. Everything right now felt so perfect. But could any conversation taking place in bed, naked, with her scent still all over him turn out badly? "Only if you're ready," he said.

"I am."

It wasn't exactly "I do," but it was a start. "OK. Go ahead."

"It might be a deal breaker."

He couldn't imagine anything she could say that would change his mind about wanting to be with her, but his stomach still knotted as he waited for her to continue.

Her hand fidgeted on his chest, and he covered it with his own. She glanced down at their hands, then met his eyes again. "A couple of weeks after David left, I thought I had food poisoning. Really awful abdominal pain. But I started bleeding. It turned out I'd been pregnant, maybe four or five weeks. I hadn't even known. My whole system was messed up with all the stress and it never occurred to me."

He slid one arm under her shoulders and hugged her a little more closely to him. "Were you planning on kids? You know, before?"

She shrugged. "We never discussed it. We should have. I guess on some level I assumed we would, but I was only twenty-eight. I figured I had plenty of time. Anyway, when it happened, I was a mess. It was one more loss, you know? On top of my marriage, my dad, and even Duffy, I'd lost a baby, too. I was also royally pissed, because I felt like the world had made the decision for me, before I even knew there was a decision to make."

His heart was wrenched by the raw emotion in her voice and the anger-tinted grief in her eyes. She'd had everything taken from her at once and she lost something else, something with the potential to be as important as all the rest put together. "I'm sorry, darlin'. Nothing like being kicked when you're down."

"Exactly. But what if I hadn't lost the baby? What would life have been like? I didn't know. So I thought about it a lot, and I came to a conclusion." She leaned toward him and brushed her lips along his jaw and sat back. "I don't plan to have kids, Seth. I don't want the responsibility of raising another human being." She glanced away. "Maybe it's selfish. I'll understand if you can't accept it. You probably want kids, a family. So I thought you should know, before we talk about anything else."

Seth knew the way he reacted to this was crucial. It was her decision, and he had no right to try to influence her. "Well, even if two people agree on whether or not to have kids, one or both of them could end up changing their minds."

"I can't promise you I'll ever change my mind, Seth." There was sorrow, and maybe a little fear in her voice.

"No, no, that's not what I meant." He'd have to be honest, but explain it in a way that wouldn't make her feel cornered. "I guess I always assumed I'd be a father someday, but I never gave it a lot of thought. I haven't exactly been in any relationships where the topic would come up."

Abby shifted at his side and tucked the corner of the blanket against her hip. "It's why we're talking about it now, so soon. I mean, you're asking me to leave here with you, and it's not fair to either of us to let this keep going if we know it has to end eventually because we don't want the same things. It's not like you can compromise and 'sort of' have kids."

She was right. "Another reason I haven't spent a lot of time thinking about it is I imagined it would be later, when I'm a little older, maybe not on the road as much." He'd seen a lot of musicians who barely knew their own children. If he had a family, he wanted to really be a part of it.

"You also have to remember I'm already thirty-four. Assuming I did change my mind, I sure wouldn't plan on having my first baby in my midforties."

Seth propped himself up on one elbow and leaned toward Abby. She'd been slowly inching away, and he didn't like it. "I know I want to be with you. I can't imagine ever not being with you. And I can honestly say any thoughts I've had about being a dad were more abstract. Somebody. Someday. I do need to think it through now, though, but in the context of the two of us." He rubbed her shoulder and felt some of her tension release. "I love seeing my nieces and nephews, and Pete's amazing with his daughter. But it's them, their lives. It's not me and you, which makes a big difference." Was the desire to be a parent strong enough to merit a future without Abby? This kind of responsible life planning was a whole new thing for him. He'd fallen hard for her, and he knew she'd sense it if he tried to evade the question to keep her by his side a while longer.

Abby curled against him, and he thought he might not have screwed up the conversation too badly. "That's fair," she said. "You asked me to make a big decision, and this one's yours. We have to be really sure, because there's not a lot of middle ground."

"As long as we're both honest, with each other and ourselves, we can't be wrong. Whatever decisions we make will be the right ones."

He knew he'd said the right thing when Abby hugged him until her arms trembled. He understood on some level why he'd never asked himself this important question. As he'd told her, he'd never found himself at a point in his life where it was relevant. Just like she had done in her relationship with The Asshole, he'd assumed someday his life would involve kids. But would it? Did he really want the responsibility or was he only interested in the idea of being a parent? It was an important distinction, and he owed it to himself — and to Abby — to make sure he came up with an honest answer.

He surprised himself with the discovery he hadn't quite exhausted his stamina for the evening. He moved all thoughts of decision making to the back burner and made love to Abby again, with infinite attention to detail. He was so grateful regardless of the foolish things he might have done in the past, nothing kept him from bringing Abby into his life. They fell asleep as the rain fell and the wind rattled the eaves.

They slept soundly until the barking started.

Chapter Fourteen

Abby blinked in the darkness and tried to determine what woke her. She sat up and strained to identify the sound. The rain had stopped, and only the faintest whisper of breeze in the trees could still be detected.

Beside her, Seth stirred. "What is it?"

"I don't know. Something woke me up." She heard a several sharp, insistent barks. The tension left her in a rush. "Dilbert. He must have gotten off the Nygaards' porch and decided to come here." She pushed back the comforter and started to get out of bed.

"I can go," Seth offered.

His fuzzy voice indicated he was still 75 percent asleep, so she leaned over and kissed his cheek. "No, it's fine. I'll be back in a second."

She grabbed her robe from the back of the door and made her way through the living room. Dilbert stood on the deck, peering monocularly into the darkened house. When he saw her, his tail waved, and Abby hurried to unlock the door so he could enter.

While she relocked the door, Dilbert dashed straight for the bedroom. When she caught up with him, she found the damp black dog curled on her side of the bed, his head on her pillow.

"Dilbert, off." It was hard to be stern when whispering, she discovered. She pulled a large dog pillow from underneath the bed and took Dilbert by the collar and guided him onto it. "Normally I wouldn't mind, but you're not exactly dry and fluffy at the moment." She rubbed his silky ears and smiled as he gave her a disgruntled huff before curling into a ball and settling in for what remained of the night.

Seth barely moved when she slid back into bed. The pale moonlight washed across his sleeping form, and she felt awestruck all over again. Seth had chosen to be here. With her. True, their future was far from certain. They had major life-altering decisions to make, not to mention the threat hanging over Seth's head, and possibly hers. Her feelings for him had blasted through her emotional defenses as surely as the bomb had blown a hole in the wall of her house. If she lost him because she couldn't give him what he wanted, she would have to accept it. But no maniac had the right to take Seth's life, and she'd be damned if she let it happen.

So there.

Her next conscious thought was if she wanted to escape from all the sunlight streaming into her room, she'd have to stick her head under the pillows. One cautiously opened eye revealed Seth sitting on the bed beside her, leaning back against the headboard. His hair was damp, telling her he must have been awake long enough for a shower. He was paging through her poetry journal.

She shifted in preparation for an early morning stretch, and he looked at her. A smile immediately lit his face. "Morning, sunshine."

"Morning. You been up long?" She snuggled closer to him, cursing the fact she was still enveloped beneath the blankets, while he was on top.

"Long enough to make coffee, feed Dilbert, and hit the shower." He put her book on the bed table. "I didn't want to disturb you. You're a really sound sleeper."

"I wasn't asleep. That was an orgasm-induced coma."

"And I thought those were just an urban legend."

"Not anymore." Turning her head, she peered over the side of the bed. "Where's Dilbert?"

"He wanted out after breakfast."

"I can't believe he decided to escape Trudy's porch and wake me in the middle of the night. I always thought he had the sense to stay out of the rain, but maybe not." She wiggled even closer to Seth and put her head on his chest. There were still way too many covers between her body and his, but she formulated a plan unhindered by bedding.

She brushed her lips across his chest and felt his arm wrap around her shoulders. She made her way downward, her mouth never breaking contact with his skin. He wisely didn't make a move to interrupt her progress, though his hand swept delicious circles across her upper back. She was so sensitized to his touch she swore she could feel every ridge and whorl of his fingertips.

Her only brief interruption was to free him from his boxers, and she spent a delightful interlude confirming all her observations from the night before. Yes, she remembered exactly what he liked, and she thoroughly enjoyed recreating them all, adding a few new things as they occurred to her.

She felt fabulously wicked when her feathery touches and bold strokes left him gasping. When his breathing finally slowed and he eased his grip on her shoulder, he said, "Well, that's good to know."

"What's good to know?"

"I didn't imagine how incredible last night was."

"Yeah? I don't know. I think I need more practice."

He groaned, but he was smiling. "I'm not sure I'll survive, but I'm willing to take the risk."

"Brave." She tugged his boxers back into place and kissed his chest. He reached for her, but she intercepted his hand before he could pull back the covers. "Uh-uh. You may have showered, but I am far from springtime fresh."

"Don't care."

"I do. Go drink some orange juice or something. I won't be long." She slid out of bed and took her robe but didn't put it on. She knew he was watching, and put a little extra sway in her walk.

When she came out of the bathroom, she noticed he'd relocated to the living room and was, as instructed, drinking a large glass of orange juice.

"Hey," he called as she started across the hall to her room, "Do you have an extra notebook around here somewhere?"

"Sure, up in the loft. Hang on a second." She went upstairs, observing once again her writing area was far too orderly for her liking, and took a legal pad from the desk. She went to the railing overlooking the living room and called, "Heads up!" When Seth looked up and grinned, she dropped the pad and he caught it.

Back in her room, she pondered what to wear. She'd noticed Seth was wearing jeans, but no shirt yet. Could go either way. She opted for worn low-rise jeans and a purple V-neck shirt that didn't quite cover her tummy. She felt a trifle feisty.

She returned to the bathroom to dry her hair, because she could imagine the tangled mess it would be if she ended up back in bed with Seth while it was still wet. Which was a distinct and not unwelcome possibility. She decided a touch of mascara and lip tint were called for, so she sorted through her makeup case.

When she went back to the living room, she saw Seth with his guitar beside him on the couch. He was writing furiously. After swinging by the kitchen for a cup of coffee and starting the dishwasher, she sat next to him. She noticed several pages of the legal pad were already filled with writing and musical notations.

So, Seth had broken through his block and was writing again. The knowledge lightened her heart.

He picked up his guitar and strummed a few notes, making small adjustments to several of the tuning keys before he spoke. "You've got to listen to these."

"These, as in more than one?"

"Yeah. Well, none of 'em are finished yet, but I have basic lyrics and some good ideas about the music for at least three so far. They were all in my head when I woke up this morning. And that's before we talk about what you wrote." There was a high-energy vibe to his voice she hadn't heard before. He seemed really excited to be thinking like a songwriter again. As much as he loved performing, she knew the writing was the core of who he was.

She tilted her head. "Gee, I don't know. Seth Caldwell, sitting in my living room, asking me if I'll let him play for me. And he's not wearing a shirt. I'll have to think about it." She leaned in and pecked him on the cheek.

He chuckled and moved the neck of the guitar out of the way so he could give her a proper kiss. Or an improper one. The way it made her feel, she decided it was definitely the latter. "OK, this one is kind of upbeat. It starts light, but picks up as it goes along." He sat forward on the couch, his back not touching the cushions, the Gibson across his knee, and began to play. He had about a dozen lines and a chorus, and Abby let herself drift with the song.

There was no doubt it was about them. He sang of years wasted for a reason, because you can't find happiness until you're wise enough to recognize it. As he'd described, the song started out wistful but built to a hopeful tone, and finally a celebration. And it wasn't even done. Her throat tightened and she felt her eyes brim.

Seth played a final chord, lowered the guitar, and looked at her. He reached for her hand. "What's wrong? Don't you like it? I can change the second verse..."

"No, no, that's not it. It's wonderful. I'm just a little overwhelmed." She dabbed at the corners of her eyes with a knuckle.

He blew out a relieved breath. "Good. I mean, I was afraid you hated it. I have so many spinning around in my head right now, and I wanted to get some ideas on paper so I can make room for more."

"I know how it feels." She curled into the corner of the couch to watch him run through the other songs-in-progress. "It's great when the ideas come so fast."

"I'd almost forgotten. Remember the other day when I told you it felt like maybe I'd said everything I had to say?" His voice was hesitant, as if he feared saying the words would somehow make them true.

"Yes. I didn't believe it, and now we have proof."

"I think maybe it was true. But it's not anymore."

"So, you have a theory grinding a classic guitar to sawdust resurrects creativity?" She still hadn't recovered from the impact of the song and wanted to soften the emotional edges.

He wasn't going to let her get away with dodging him. He sat the guitar on the coffee table and reached for her. She slid into his arms and tried to steady her breathing. He pressed his lips to her forehead before lifting her face to look at him. "Don't hide from me, Abby-Kat. Not ever. If you're going to make me feel things I didn't think I ever could, you're going to have to hear about them. I'm not good at keeping things inside."

"I know, Seth. But I've been alone a long time. I haven't had a lot of practice dealing with my own feelings, let alone anybody else's."

"You have been dealing with them. You've been writing. You're just not used to sharing them with somebody."

It was a rather astute observation, and she had to admit the truth of it.

He took her hand and stroked the backs of her fingers with his thumb. When he spoke, his voice was soft, but pulsed with emotion. "I haven't shared any of myself with anyone, either. Maybe I never have." His eyes met hers, his expression so intense she had to resist her instinctive reaction to avert her gaze. "But now…now I have to. I love you, Abby, and I need for you to know it, to believe it."

Too much. She had to look away. "How can you believe it? How could it happen so fast?" But, oh, she wanted it to be true.

"I think I knew as soon as I found you again outside Monique's shop. Joey called me on it the first time I said your name. Since then, it just keeps getting bigger, and if I didn't tell you, it felt like I'd burn up inside."

She realized she had a death grip on his hand, and willed herself to relax. "You don't even know me."

He slid an arm around her shoulders. "Don't I? I think I do. The important things, anyway. I feel like I've always known you. I just hadn't met you yet."

Wow. Wasn't that how she'd felt about him, too? Maybe from the first time she heard him sing? She felt the promise of his kiss at her temple and tilted her head, welcoming his mouth with hers. As soon as she regained her breath, she said, "I can't say this doesn't scare me to death."

"I wish it didn't."

"I know." *Don't hide from me, Abby-Kat*, he'd said. *No more running*, Monique had told her. Heart pounding, she said the only thing she absolutely knew to be true. "I love you, too, Seth."

A long breath escaped his chest, and she realized he'd been frozen for a few moments as he'd waited for her reaction. His gentle smile and the radiance in his eyes almost undid her. "Then everything will work itself out."

"This doesn't solve all our problems," she cautioned.

"No, but it's a start."

Seth seemed to sense she needed some space to process the deluge of emotions they'd unleashed. He let her retreat a short distance and retrieved his guitar from the table.

Abby listened to him experiment with a few variations on a song he had not yet shared, took a bottle of water and a cigarette and went out on the deck to visit with Dilbert. She thought about her mother's story of how her father had told her the night they met she would marry him. This wasn't marriage, but it was still pretty damned major, as far as life events went.

She did love him. Whether she put a label on it or said it out loud didn't matter. Even if neither of them put it into words, it was true. Her head was still spinning, but she guessed she should get used to it. Life with Seth was likely to always contain a strong whirlwind element.

When she felt more composed, she went back inside. Dropping onto the couch, she kissed Seth on the cheek and smiled.

"OK?" he asked, tracing her lower lip with his thumb.

"OK," she said, her heart melting at the slow smile spreading across his face.

"Ready to listen to some more new stuff?"

"You bet. Let's see what we can do."

Before she knew it, they were in creative overdrive. The volume of work he'd created in a single morning was astonishing. He had a rollicking song about Cujo's demise, which made her laugh. There was a romantic ballad, and he took one of her poems and tweaked it into a darkly beautiful song about betrayal.

She was pleasantly surprised to find she did, in fact, have something to contribute to the songwriting process. She saw how he crafted the music to support and enhance her poems, and soon found ways to make minor changes to her "lyrics" to make it fit the melody Seth provided. Some of his lyrics, too, benefited from her skill, when she suggested words or phrases to improve the flow or bring out the underlying emotion in a more powerful way.

Seth finally put the Gibson back in its case and went to the refrigerator for a drink. "You do realize you've just cowritten three or four songs, right?"

"I have not." While she hadn't felt totally useless, she couldn't wrap her head around the idea of writing a song, or even part of one.

"You sure did. You wrote every word of one of them, over half of another, and you made enough changes to the ones I started I'd give anybody cowriter status for the same work. You'd better get used to it, because these are going to be recorded." He popped open a can of Coke.

She reached around him for a diet root beer, and made her way to the French doors. The previous day's clouds had cleared, and the midmorning sun sparkled on the lake. She opened the door and took a deep breath. "About what I thought. Cooler than the last few days." She had to admit it felt refreshing.

"Let me get a shirt and some shoes, and we can sit outside a while." He disappeared into the bedroom, emerging a moment later wearing a vintage Lynyrd Skynyrd shirt. He put on his shoes, and they went out to the deck chairs.

As Seth leaned back and propped his feet on the railing, Abby watched him. She realized she knew next to nothing of the ordinary details of his life. She didn't know the name of his third grade teacher, if he liked Hawaiian pizza, or if he'd ever had a broken bone. But she had time to learn those things. The extreme circumstances of their meeting and the subsequent events had shown her things about his true character that would have otherwise taken her months or years to discover. Not ideal, she knew, what with all the threats to life and limb, but since they were both still in one piece she decided it was a fair enough trade.

Abby picked up her phone and spent a few minutes talking with her mother. She reported the clean-up job was impressive, and the temporary repairs had held up well in the rain. "But if you ever clean my loft again, I'm putting myself up for adoption retroactively."

"Abigail, there's a difference between comfortable clutter and places that attract the notice of the health department. Besides, Grace did most of the cleaning. I merely neglected to tell her to stay out of your loft."

"Same thing, then."

"Were you able to put everything out of your mind so you and Seth could have a nice evening?"

Danger—mother fishing for information of a highly personal nature. "Yes, we were."

"And...?"

"And I'm really grateful you somehow restrained the impulse to iron his underwear and wrap them up with mine in handy little coed bundles in the drawer."

Marilyn laughed. "Don't be silly, sweetie. Now you tell that wonderful boy I heard he gave David something to think about, and it made my day. David didn't want to tell Joyce's mother what he did to provoke him, but I can imagine."

Abby smiled. It had been one of the highlights of her day, too. Seth was able, in a few sentences, to show all David's petty attacks for the nonsense they were. It was a bonus he'd also taught David playing word games was all well and good, but might result in swift and painful consequences.

"I'll tell him." They ended the call, and she turned to Seth and grinned. "You're my mother's hero."

Without missing a beat, he said, "Yeah, I know."

"Don't you want to know why?"

"I'm figuring she heard about the orgasm-induced coma."

Abby paused for a few seconds' consideration. "She probably guesses." She relocated from her chair to Seth's lap and kissed him on the nose. "No, it was because of David."

"She heard about him, huh?"

Abby nodded. "I wouldn't be surprised if the whole town has. He probably has a pretty awesome bruise, but you can bet he's not telling anybody he had it coming."

"You don't think he's going to try to cause trouble, do you?"

Abby thought. "No. He's a bully, and he knows he can't tear me down now, so it's no fun for him. Since he made it clear he thinks we're so far beneath him, he's not going to try to stir up any charges for your hitting him. He won't want people thinking about how you got the best of him."

"Good. I was worried he'd find a way to turn it into more trouble for you."

"No worries." Abby rose from his lap and walked over to the railing. "Wonder where Dilbert is. He looked OK last night, but if he was running around in the dark, I want to check him over. He doesn't have very good depth perception with only one eye, and sometimes he runs into things."

"He looked fine this morning. Ate breakfast in eleven seconds flat."

"He'd do that if he had two broken legs and a collapsed lung."

Seth laughed. "He took off toward the lake, so I'd check with the ducks if I were you."

She took a few steps toward the stairs leading down to the yard and stopped. There was a large, muddy shoe print on the lowest step, and it gave her a sudden tingle of "something ain't right." "Seth, did you go down in the yard this morning?"

"No, I just opened the door and let Dilbert out. Why?"

She motioned him over and pointed at the print. "Somebody's been here."

Seth reached for her hand. "Do you think it was the cop who was supposed to keep an eye on things?"

"I doubt it," she said, shaking her head. "They were supposed to drive by. Nobody said anything about coming around the house. I don't think they'd get out of the cruisers unless they saw something suspicious. And they sure would've called me. But you can bet I'll be calling Bob and clarifying the point." This was one instance when having a cop who wasn't clear on procedure would actually be welcome. The alternative made her sick to her stomach.

She went inside and grabbed a pair of flip-flops, and in a minute they were circling the house. They immediately saw more footprints in the fresh mud.

Seth pointed out one particularly obvious area at the edge of the pit Dilbert had dug near the deck. "I don't like this. Look, somebody didn't see the hole in the dark and almost wiped out."

Abby stopped short. "This is what Dilbert was barking about. It's probably why he came over here last night. I bet he heard something." What would have happened if she had been a little faster getting to the door when the dog woke her?

"You think he chased whoever it was away?"

"I think he blew their cover, so they didn't stick around." She had to believe the prowler had been in full retreat by the time she opened the door. Otherwise, she might never sleep again.

They completed their circuit of the house, careful not to disturb any footprints they found. It appeared they emerged from the woods on the far side of the garage, passed along the kitchen windows to the deck, concluding with the near fall in Dilbert's den. Only one print seemed to lead away from there, and it pointed back toward the woods.

"OK, that's it. I'm calling the police." Abby retrieved her phone from where she'd left it on the deck rail. She got through to dispatch right away, and they put her on hold while they transferred her directly to Chief LeFevre. She put her hand over the receiver and spoke to Seth. "They said Bob told them to put me through to him if we had any more problems." Seth nodded in approval.

Chief LeFevre came on the line, and Abby explained what they'd discovered. "Would your officer have gotten out of the cruiser and walked around the house?"

"Shouldn't have. I'll call Decker on the way out to your place and ask. He was on duty last night, but he knows not to leave the vehicle unless he has cause. Plus, it was raining, and I don't see him getting his feet wet if he could avoid it."

After determining the chief would arrive in about fifteen minutes, Abby called her neighbors. "Trudy, it's Abby."

"Honey, how are you? Is everything OK over there?" As always, Trudy's voice was about 20 percent louder than it needed to be. This came from years of living with a husband with a hearing impairment and a stubborn refusal to get a hearing aid.

"I think so, except we just found some fresh footprints in the mud around the house."

"Oh, for goodness sake! Walt, they found footprints around the house. Footprints!" The last word jumped several dozen decibels, and Abby held the phone away from her ear until she was sure her neighbor was finished relaying information to Walt.

"Trudy, when did Dilbert leave there last night? Do you know?"

"As a matter-of-fact, I do. He made a racket scratching at the door on the screen porch. I got up to go see what had him stirred up, and he popped the latch just before I got to him. It was about ten till three this morning."

It made sense. It was a few minutes after three when Dilbert's barking woke her. "Did you hear anything else?"

"No, I don't think so. Something woke me up, and I heard Dilbert scratching, so I imagine that's what it was. Did he come over there?"

"Yes. He showed up right after three. We let him in."

"Oh, good. I didn't like to think of him outside in the rain."

"He spent the rest of the night on a big cushy pillow by the bed."

"I knew you'd let him in if he came over there." Abby held the phone out again as Trudy relayed the rest of the conversation to her husband. "Now, we want to meet that new man of yours. You'll bring him by, won't you?"

Abby agreed she would, ended the call and returned to Seth. He was sitting in a deck chair, and Abby plopped down beside him, placing the phone on the table in between. "Trudy said Dilbert woke her up scratching at the door. I might be nuts, but I believe he heard something."

"You're probably right. And I'm getting pissed all over again."

"It's not your fault."

"Yes it is!" He stood and paced along the rail. "None of this would have happened if it weren't for me. You wouldn't have sheets stapled up over holes in your walls, you wouldn't have some psycho sneaking around your house in the middle of the night, none of it!"

"Stop it." She stepped in front of him to halt his furious pacing. "If you hadn't been here, it would have been you blown up instead of a stupid wall." She grabbed his arms above the elbows and made him look at her. "Am I freaked out somebody was walking around here last night while we were asleep? Oh, yeah. But they didn't get any farther than one foot on the first step, and they were scared off by a forty-five-pound dog. Maybe we'll stay somewhere else tonight or Bob can park somebody out at the fork to the lake."

Seth's entire body was tense with agitation. "What if Dilbert hadn't gotten off the porch? Whoever sent the text all but came right out and said they were going to punish me by hurting you. They could have killed us in bed or burned the house down around us. It's the last thing in the world I want to do, but maybe it would be best if I left till all this is over."

Abby let go of him and smacked him sharply on the chest. "You did not just say that! Don't you dare even think it!" She turned her back on him and folded her arms, a sick feeling settling in the pit of her stomach. He'd told her he loved her just this morning. And she'd taken the dizzying leap of acknowledging her feelings, too. If those things were true, how could the idea of leaving—for any reason—even cross his mind?

"How can I not think it?" His voice was sad, as if the choice had already been made. "If anything happened to you…darlin', I couldn't stand it. Without me here, you might be safe."

She turned toward him, but kept her gaze directed downward. "Might be. Are you sure if you take off I'll be any less of a target? Don't you think we're both safer if we stick together?" She felt really worked up now. He might talk about distancing himself to protect her, but leaving was the same as abandoning, in her mind. Maybe those were her old issues rearing their ugly heads again, but she'd be damned if she'd stand for it. Still, she wouldn't beg him, either, which was why she wasn't meeting his eyes. If he'd even consider walking away now, when he said he didn't want to, when it wasn't his fault and they had a whole town full of people working to solve the mystery and keep them safe, what would happen if someday he did want to? Even a little bit, just for a minute? Would she wake up in a hotel room, not sure which town it was, and find him gone?

He put his hands on her shoulders, and after a moment she raised her head. He looked as confused as she felt. "You know I don't want to leave, but I've brought this whole mess to someplace that's always been safe for you. I've taken your sense of security from you, even if I didn't mean to." Dropping his hands, he turned away, now not meeting her eyes. His shoulders hitched, and when he spoke, his voice was only a few notches above a whisper. "I have to wonder, and you should, too, if I'm any good for you. Sometimes, no matter how you feel about someone, you have to back away to protect them. Or yourself."

Abby wasn't sure if what she felt was fury or panic. She stepped in front of him and made him look at her. "Somebody was after you before you arrived in Emporia. You were in danger either way. This way, though, we have each other, and we'll get through it." She was absolutely determined this would prove true. If he left her now, for whatever reason, he would just have to stay gone.

He enfolded her in his arms, and her turmoil subsided a fraction. "All right, darlin'." He sighed, and she felt the trembling of his hands on her back. "We'll get through it. I'll make sure of it." Abby relaxed further, but couldn't completely forget what he'd been contemplating.

Their embrace was cut short by the sound of a car approaching and turning into the driveway. Chief LeFevre stepped out of the cruiser, and Abby dug deep for some composure. Seth took her hand, and they went to meet him.

The chief was slightly less disheveled than he was the previous morning, but he looked twice as troubled. "If this keeps up I'm going to put a satellite precinct in your garage."

"Ha ha, Bob. I guess if we can find out who's behind this, we'll all be spared a lot of headaches." Abby kept her tone light, but his comment annoyed her.

They showed him the footprints, and he concurred with their interpretation. Personally, she felt the only comforting part of the whole situation was there were no prints anywhere near her bedroom window.

"I'll call in an extra man for tonight," the chief said, "and put him right before the fork in your road. Unless somebody wants to cover a lot of rough, wooded territory, there's no other way for them to get close. And if this all started before you even got to town, Seth, we're probably not talking about a local."

It made sense to Abby, and she was about to say so, but Bob had another bit of information.

"There's a place by the road, about forty yards down the other side of the fork, where it looks like somebody pulled a car off into the weeds," he said, pointing in the general direction. "It was muddy, so they sunk in real good, and tore some pretty deep ruts getting out. I'm going to go look around, see if I can tell anything. I'm pretty sure your prowler parked there."

Chief LeFevre left to continue his investigation, and Abby turned to Seth.

"This is good, though, right?" She was struggling to find the positive aspects wherever possible. "The more evidence we find, the easier it'll be to stop this."

"I hope so, darlin'."

"Now what?" Her vote was for more alone time, but she suspected it wasn't going to happen for a while.

"As much as I'd like to go back inside and lock the doors, I think we have to go to town again."

"Damn. I knew you were going to say that." It would be so nice to be able to indulge in a healthy sulk right now.

"Dash was sure Kevin would show up to work today, and we need to talk to him." He sat on the top step and scratched Dilbert behind one ear. "Anything he can tell the investigators could go a long way to helping solve this."

Abby sat beside him and put her head on his shoulder. "I know. You're right, especially if Kevin saw anything in the parking lot Friday night. But I really, really don't want to go."

He stroked her cheek with the back of his hand, stood and leaned on the railing. "Me, either. But I'm going to keep asking questions till something makes some fucking sense."

She hated he had to continue dealing with the unanswered questions and looming threats. Then it occurred to her she had something that might make another suspicion-filled drive into town a little less depressing. She joined him by the railing. "Of course we'll go. And I thought maybe we'd take my motorcycle."

"A bike? I didn't know you had a bike." Yep, she guessed right. Her old Honda was a good distraction.

"It's nothing fancy. I had my cousin get it ready for the summer a couple of weeks ago. I haven't had a chance to take it out yet, and it needs a good run."

"You're going to let me drive this time, right?" His teasing tone was a good sign. If he could crack even a small joke, the bike was already doing its job.

"Sure. Otherwise I wouldn't get to sit in back with my arms around you."

He smiled, and this time it actually reached his eyes. "This keeps getting better and better."

Seth went to the garage, and Abby went inside. She tucked her hair in a quick single braid, and added a gray sweatshirt in preparation for a breezy ride. She transferred the contents of her purse to a small backpack, and went to check Seth's progress. He had the bike out, and was already heading back to the house.

He ran his fingers through his shoulder-length hair. "Do you have a hat? Otherwise visibility could be a problem."

Abby went to the laundry room and pulled a plain black cap from the top of a cabinet.

"Perfect," he replied, and put it backward on his head, effectively pushing his hair back from his face.

As soon as Seth familiarized himself with the bike, he climbed on and started it up. Abby settled behind him. As she wrapped her arms around his lean waist, she couldn't resist giving him an extra squeeze. She felt his hand stroke her thigh for a moment, and they were off, racing toward town and more potentially disturbing questions.

She hoped they could live with the answers.

Chapter Fifteen

Seth loved the freedom of flying down the road on a motorcycle. He wasn't surprised to discover the sensation of Abby behind him, her breasts warm against his back, her thighs on either side of his, and her arms around his waist made him love it even more. He knew she offered the bike to distract him from the lingering suspicion surrounding his friends, but it touched him to know it mattered so much to her. And it did help. A little.

He wished they could keep riding until they were far away from all the turmoil, but he knew it would be nothing more than an illusion. This trouble would keep finding him until it was resolved, one way or another.

When they pulled into the parking lot behind Dash's—again—he decided he was getting seriously sick of the place. There were more cars in the lot than he'd expected, and he hoped one of them belonged to Kevin Merinar. In addition to Dash's huge black pickup truck, he saw a surprising number of official vehicles. He'd thought the investigation at the club had already been wrapped up. A group of people milled about, all wearing Dash's blue-and-gold softball uniforms and organizing coolers and equipment. Must be game day. They went in through the back door, and Abby greeted several of the softball players by name. Seth tucked his sunglasses in his pocket. "Well, where first?"

Abby slid her sunglasses up on top of her head and pulled her braid from the back of her sweatshirt. He decided he preferred her hair down, but the braid was nice, too. The sweatshirt, however, had to go.

As if reading his mind, Abby swept the sweatshirt off and stuffed it in her backpack, once again revealing the brief purple shirt and partially bare midriff. He was still trying to get his tongue unstuck from the roof of his mouth when she replied to his all-but-forgotten question. "I guess Dash's office would be the logical place to start."

They passed several Emporia police officers on the way to the office, which they found unoccupied. It didn't take long to discover the hub of activity was the small banquet room hosting a retirement party in a few hours. Seth saw Dash and Special Agent Kincaid conversing near the room's tiny kitchenette while several staff members bustled about setting up tables and hanging streamers. Seth thought the room could be any one of countless VFW or Kiwanis Club halls he and the band had played back in Montana. It had the same hallmarks: fake pine paneling, fluorescent lights in a dropped ceiling, and industrial-quality carpet with a number of stains that probably had interesting stories behind them. The whole space exuded a faint scent reminiscent of burned cookies.

"Hey, Dash," Seth said as they approached the men. "Any sign of Kevin this morning?" He nodded at Kincaid.

Dash looked toward the door as if expecting to see someone and shook his head. "No, and I'm worried, that's for sure. It's not like Kevin to miss a shift. If he's gonna be late, he always calls."

"No sign he's been back to his apartment since Friday night, either," Kincaid said. "At this point, I'd say he's hiding because he's involved somehow or he's in trouble."

"Well, he ain't too late yet. Could be he got the time wrong, and he'll show up here shortly," Dash said. Seth could tell he was truly concerned. Twenty seconds and not one rude remark or barnyard laugh. Definitely out of character.

"I'm worried too, Dash," Abby said, turning to Kincaid. "What's with all the officers? I thought you were pretty much done here."

Kincaid's mouth tightened in a grim line. "In the debriefing last night, we found out some of the guys didn't exactly follow the correct search procedures."

Seth thought the small-town force probably didn't have a lot of experience with searches of this magnitude. "What do you mean?"

"A few of them cut corners, missed some places." Kincaid shook his head. "I guess they figured any bomb evidence would be in the bus or at the house, but with Kevin Merinar still unaccounted for, I ordered a new search this morning."

Seth understood Kincaid's frustration. There were so many places to hide things — or hide out — in the old nightclub, and he hoped something helpful would finally be found. "If it's OK with you, we're going to hang around a while, see if he shows up. We had someone sneaking around Abby's place last night, and we'd like to talk to Kevin when you're done. He might've seen something Friday that could shake something loose in my head."

Dash said for them to stay as long as they liked, then Seth heard Trent's booming voice. "Hey, guys! Everybody's in here." Seth looked toward the door and saw his road manager, as well as Mouse and Marshall.

Dash put a meaty paw on Seth's arm. "If you want to sit in the restaurant, I'll have them set you up with some coffee, rolls, maybe a sandwich or a beer if it ain't too early."

"Thanks. When Kevin shows up, let us know, OK?" He placed his hand on the tempting bare strip low on Abby's back, and they headed toward the door.

"So, what's the word, man?" Trent asked.

"No word. We'll hang in the restaurant for now, see if Kevin shows up." Seth glanced past the assembled group and noticed Roberto hurrying down the hall to join them.

They were soon ensconced in a large booth in the restaurant. Trent remained standing, explaining he had to hit the road in the next few minutes if he wanted to make his flight. He had a long drive to the airport.

"I needed to find out if Kevin showed up, though," Trent said. "I might've been the last one of us to talk to him, when he said he had to go see somebody."

"Yeah, he poofed," said Roberto. "I was looking for him right before we wrapped so he could help get the equipment ready to load, but nobody knew where he was."

"That's what I've been thinking. I have a hunch what his 'meeting' might've been about." Trent shifted uneasily on his feet. "When we were booking the gig, Dash said there was something he should tell us before we agreed to the crew he was assigning. Seems last year Kevin was into some trouble."

Marshall's eyes narrowed, but he withheld comment while one of the club employees brought over a pot of coffee and some sweet rolls. When she went back to the kitchen, Marshall spoke. "OK, Trent, out with it. What kind of trouble?"

"He was busted last year on some drug charges. Nothing big, just some weed. Dash said charges were mostly dismissed, and he got a few hours of community service. Cops knew he wasn't a serious dealer, more like he bought his own in the Cities and some extra for his friends."

Marshall seemed relieved, judging by his more relaxed posture and amused snort. "Hell, if we didn't work with anybody who was ever in trouble with the law, 'specially over a little possession, we wouldn't have anybody left to hire."

"I told him the same thing. Didn't bother me, as long as he wasn't using while he was working with us," Trent said. "But I started wondering. What if he had some deal going? It could get a guy in trouble that didn't have anything to do with us."

Seth thought about it. "Yeah, but it's still weird he hasn't turned up somewhere."

"Guess all we can do is wait and see," said Mouse, always the philosophical one.

His statement seemed to close the topic, and after a brief silence Abby spoke up. "Did everybody else get on the road?" She stirred sweetener into her coffee and took a sip.

Trent nodded. "Danny and Jake left a couple of hours ago. Kincaid will call them when the van is released."

Roberto chewed the wad of sweet roll he'd bitten off and washed it down with some coffee. "Andy left late last night. Or early this morning. He decided if he rented a car from the used car place a couple of blocks over, he could grab a nap and head out early enough to take his Aunt Ana to brunch after Mass. I told him he was nuts, but he said it'd make her happy. He was gone when I got back to the room around one thirty."

That accounted for everybody, and didn't tell Seth one more damned thing than he knew before. Trent had no sooner departed than Seth saw Kincaid walking purposefully toward their table. He hoped the man was coming to tell them Kevin had arrived, but apparently it wasn't his lucky day, despite its promising start.

"I'm going to head over to the police department, talk to the chief. I need to hear about what happened out by the lake last night first, though."

Seth hadn't yet had a chance to tell everyone what had happened, but Abby jumped in and took care of it. Marshall looked at the table and shook his head. "Man, we gotta find a way to end this. It doesn't look like it's going to stop until we catch somebody or they get lucky and pull off one of their plans. And I'm definitely voting for door number one."

"There are a couple of things you need to know, too," Kincaid said.

"Information's good."

"The girl who vandalized the Jeep was supposed to be back in Iowa by now." The twitching at one corner of Kincaid's eye indicated he wasn't pleased to have to relay whatever was coming next.

"Supposed to be?" Abby's shoulders straightened, as if she were ready to hunt down Pam and make sure she arrived back wherever she belonged, possibly in numerous small, damaged pieces.

"She got on the bus, but never showed up in Des Moines. We think it's likely she left the bus in Minneapolis." He sighed and looked somewhat embarrassed. "So, we don't know where she is right now. We don't think she had anything to do with the bomb, but it's another loose end, which I do not like one bit."

"You're not the only one," Abby grumbled.

"The other news I have is about Drew Purcell, and we think it might be significant."

"Well, he was in Cincinnati," Seth said. "We knew that. But he also lives right across the river from there."

"True, but we found some photos and had the club in Chicago pull their security video. Turns out he was there on Thursday night, too."

Marshall dropped his roll onto his plate. "What did he do? Trent never mentioned he was there."

"No reason for the club security to bother him with it, I guess. Tapes showed him in the lobby. They have to let the public in the lobby once the doors open, because that's where the ticket office is. There was a slight scuffle when the club security tried to take the sign he was carrying, and finally he gave up and left."

Abby began drumming her fingers on the table. Seth recognized this as a sign her thought process had kicked into high gear. "So what we need to know is if he was here Friday night. Dash doesn't have cameras, though."

"There aren't any inside the club," Kincaid said, "but there are a few on this block. Two near the bank, and one in front of a little art gallery. We have somebody pulling those tapes. If we find any sign he was here, we'll let you know. So far, we haven't been able to track down his present location."

Seth felt a surge of hope. This felt like progress. Better yet, it was evidence — even if only circumstantial — which didn't point to any of his friends. "You know how to reach us. We'd like to hear as soon as you know anything."

"Absolutely. I'll let you folks…"

Kincaid's reply was cut short when shouts erupted in the hallway. The special agent was instantly in full response mode and racing for the door. Seth, Abby, Roberto, Marshall, and Mouse scrambled from the booth and hurried after him.

They found several Emporia police officers running for the open door leading to the basement. Close on Kincaid's heels, they followed him down the dimly lit stairs. Everyone seemed to be converging on a remote corner, which Seth knew from his many visits to Dash's held an area known as the "junkyard," where assorted bits of old or broken equipment ended up.

Karl Briggs, the blond Emporia cop who'd arrived at Abby's with Sammy Paulsen the day before, stood near the junkyard, facing the approaching crowd. Even in the poor lighting, Seth saw the shocked expression on the man's pale face. Kincaid reached him first. Karl spoke in a low voice, pointing to a pile of old amps and floor mats. Seth edged as near as he dared, and saw an athletic shoe-clad foot sticking out of the jumble.

Oh shit.

Kincaid pointed at two of the nearby cops and barked, "You, and you. Come over here and help move some of this stuff. But just enough so we can get a look. Watch where you're stepping." The men hurried to comply, and Kincaid's gaze moved to the rear of the crowd, landing on Sammy Paulsen, whose face was completely devoid of expression. "Paulsen, call your chief and get a medical team over here." Sammy darted up the stairs, already keying his radio.

Seth positioned himself directly behind Kincaid and could see the equipment pile — and the foot — over his shoulder. When a badly cracked Peavey amplifier was moved, he saw what they'd all feared. Kevin Merinar's body lay on the filthy cement floor, still wearing the club's security T-shirt. His face was recognizable despite its macabre discoloration, and a dark stain surrounded his head. Abby tried to maneuver around him to get a look, but he held her back. "You don't want to see this."

"Don't tell me what I don't want to see. It's Kevin, isn't it?" She shouldered him to one side. "Damn. I didn't want to see that." She sagged against him, and Seth put his arm around her.

Kincaid noticed them behind him, and lifted a single annoyed eyebrow. "Mr. Caldwell, I'm going to have to ask you and Miss Delaney to step back, please." As they hastily complied, Dash huffed down the stairs, and Kincaid motioned him over. "Dash, I believe we all know what we've found, but I'd like you to confirm for me, please."

Dash's face took on a distinctly greenish cast, but he did as Kincaid asked. "Yeah. It's Kevin." He hung his head and stepped back. "Damn. I reckon I need to sit down. I'll be in my office if you need me." He glanced at Kincaid, and the special agent nodded his consent.

After sending two officers to guard the top of the stairs and another to find some portable lights, he turned to Seth, Abby, and their friends, "This is a disaster we most definitely did not need." Frustration clouded his rugged face.

"Yeah, especially not Kevin," Marshall muttered.

Kincaid shot him a scathing look. "Nobody's trying to be insensitive, here. But the folks who will take care of Kevin will be here in a minute. My job is to find out who tried to blow up your buddy, and this development is going to make it harder for me to accomplish."

Marshall dropped his eyes and apologized.

Seth looked to where Roberto and Mouse were leaning on the wall and thought Mouse looked like he should probably be sitting down. He was dizzy if a crew member suffered so much as a scratch, and this was a whole lot worse. "Do you think we could go back up to the restaurant?"

Kincaid nodded. "I'd prefer it. We need all civilians out of the area. Someone will be up to talk to you as soon as we get the scene secured." Even as he spoke, the sound of approaching sirens could be heard.

Back at their booth in the restaurant, Abby reached for her abandoned coffee cup. Her hand was shaking. Seth gently took the cup from her and set it aside, threading his arm under hers and held their clasped hands against his thigh. He looked around the table, but no one seemed to know what to say, so he decided to break the ice.

"I guess up till now we could say everything was a mess, but nobody'd been killed." He took a deep breath. "But I won't be surprised to find out Kevin's been dead since Friday night." Because, honestly, he'd looked way past recently deceased based on the glimpse he'd gotten.

Abby squeezed his hand. "Which leaves us with two really important questions to answer. One, who was Kevin going to talk to when Trent saw him leave? And two, who stole his phone?"

As usual, she was absolutely right. "Yeah. The answer to either of those would go a long way toward finding out who killed Kevin. And it's a good bet whoever it was is behind what's been going on with me."

"Wait, wait, wait," Abby said, rubbing her forehead. "I have to think. Let me walk through this, and tell me if I get off track." She stared at the ceiling for a moment, then focused on Seth. "Last Wednesday night, somebody put a drug in the bottle of Jack Daniel's you bought. They either did it themselves or convinced someone else to do it."

"Right," Seth replied. He caught Marshall's eye, and made sure he held his attention as he continued. "And Marsh probably saved my life that night, staying with me. Otherwise, somebody could've finished me off, and I couldn't have done a damned thing about it." His voice almost caught at the end, because he realized if he'd died that night, he'd have never made it to Emporia for Abby to run over his guitar.

"Aw, man, I just figured somebody had to hold the bucket, save the poor housekeepers from havin' to deal with a mess in the morning." Marshall's tone was light, but the slight tremor in his voice said he knew how close he'd come to losing a brother.

"OK, moving right along," Abby interrupted. She was on a mission. "We know Drew Purcell was in Cincinnati, in Chicago on Thursday, and he's still furious about losing the copyright lawsuit last year." She took her hand from Seth's and warmed up her coffee. Judging by the fact her hand was no longer trembling, he knew analyzing the facts was helping her settle down, even if the subject matter was disturbing. "We also know Pam—remind me to ask Sammy or Kincaid what her last name is, by the way—was in Cincinnati and Chicago, as well as here in Emporia, and she has a rather strong attachment to Seth. We don't know, however, if either of them knows enough about GHB to be able to poison the bottle, or if they know anything about bombs."

"Or if they know people who do know about those things," Roberto said.

"Correct. OK, about the bomb. It doesn't sound very sophisticated, based on Kincaid's report, but I sure wouldn't know how to make one. We think someone was on the bus during the show and put it in Seth's bag, believing it would be under his bunk when it was set to go off in the morning."

"Which is where Kevin came into the picture," Seth said. "It's possible he was paid to place it there, in which case his death could be to keep him from talking."

"Or maybe he saw something, and was killed so he didn't tell anybody," Roberto said.

Seth knew he, Marshall, Joey, and Pete had been onstage during the entire show, and Mouse had never left the soundboard. Unless someone had gone out to the bus in the very brief time between when he and Abby left it and when the show started, it put all of them in the clear. He appreciated Abby hadn't pointed out Roberto, Trent, Danny, and Andy couldn't account for their whereabouts during the whole time period.

"The bomb goes off at my house, and later Seth gets a text from Kevin's phone. It informs him the bomber knows he wasn't on the bus and survived the explosion. It also hints the next time would be a third attempt, which is what clued us in to the whole drugged-bottle situation."

Mouse, who was starting to get a little color back in his face, jumped into the conversation. "And we don't think Kevin sent it, because it'd be beyond stupid to send an incriminating text from your own phone."

"And it looks like he was dead before we even wrapped the show," Marshall added. Seth winced at the blunt declaration, but knew his friend had a filter problem almost as severe as Abby's.

"We'll have to wait for someone to tell us for sure," Abby said. "But let's go with that for now. Next, Pam vandalized my Jeep, Sammy told us she is not exactly psychologically sound, and Stacy is in the clear because she's been dead since November. Come to think of it, Sammy mentioned booze and pills, but I wonder if GHB was in any way involved in Stacy's death." She took a huge swallow of coffee. "Holy shit, my head hurts."

"To top it all off," Seth said, "somebody was sneaking around Abby's house during the night."

Marshall pushed the coffee decanter aside and leaned across the table. "But Seth, there's one big thing we don't know. Why? Why is somebody so determined to get you? Because I have no fucking clue."

"I don't know, man. I wish I did. Do I piss people off sometimes? Hell, yeah. Purcell hates me enough. Stacy might've been vindictive enough. Beyond that, I can't come up with anything." If he could dig through the skeletons in his closet, assuming he still had any, and find a reason for somebody to hate him this much, they'd have their answers.

Bob LeFevre entered the restaurant. The middle-aged chief had a "deer in the headlights" look, and Seth wondered if he'd ever had to investigate a murder before.

"Well, folks, we're seeing a lot of each other lately." He pulled a napkin from a dispenser on the next table and mopped his forehead.

Seth looked at Abby and saw her jaw tense. If the chief was implying something, she didn't like it. "Not a picnic for us, either, Bob," she said. "What can you tell us about Kevin?"

"Not a lot at this point without compromising the investigation, but it's probably what you've been wondering. Looks like someone lured him to the basement and nailed him in the head with a microphone stand." He looked away briefly, and Seth imagined he was more upset than he was willing to show. In a town this small, he'd probably known Kevin. "Going by the statements everybody gave yesterday, and the condition of the body, I'd pretty near bet my badge he's been dead since before the end of Friday night's show."

"What about his phone?" Abby asked.

"No sign of it."

"Well, no, there wouldn't be, would there? It's not like somebody's going to kill a guy, use his phone, and return it." She was rubbing her temples, as if encouraging her brain to hang in there with her a while longer.

"The only other thing I can tell you right now, and I probably shouldn't, is he had a couple of packages of marijuana on him. They were small quantities, like maybe he was still doing some dealing. One of the bags was found under him, so it could be whoever killed him pulled him down there by asking to buy something."

"Trent thought so too," Seth said. He also realized this lessened any lingering suspicion of his road manager. Trent was opposed to any sort of drug use, no matter how minor or infrequent. Buying a bag of weed was the last way he'd use to lure someone to a remote location. "Hey, you might want to call Trent, see if he can think of anything else. He left right before they found Kevin, and he's on the way to the airport. You can still catch him for the next couple of hours, though."

"Thanks, Seth, I'll do that. We'll have a team of county guys here soon. We're going to need help with this." The chief looked overwhelmed and exhausted. "What about the rest of you? You going to be in town a while?"

"Mouse and I are leaving as soon as you're done with us," Roberto said. "Rented a car with a long drive ahead of us."

"Yeah, that'll be fine. But you will make yourselves available at any time if we need to talk to you." the chief said.

"Seth and Marshall are staying, though," Abby said. "Marsh will drive the bus back when it's released." She hesitated, and Seth wondered if she'd be including herself in the recitation of travel plans. "Seth isn't sure yet when he's going back to Austin."

Seth tried not to be disappointed. If she was coming with him, he supposed this isn't the way he'd want to be notified of such a significant fact.

The chief, if possible, managed to look even wearier. "OK, just keep me posted." He ran the crumpled napkin over his brow again. "I swear, keeping track of you people is like shoveling fog," he muttered as he walked away.

Seth had often thought the same thing.

They sat there in silence for a few minutes. Marshall reached over and slapped a hand down over Seth's on the tabletop. He realized his fingers were strumming, as more of the morning's songs ran through his head.

"Hey, man. You're writing again, aren't you?" Marshall's face broke into a huge grin.

Seth nodded. "Yeah. Yeah, I am."

"'Bout fuckin' time. I thought I was going to have to buy one of those refrigerator magnet poetry sets and see what I could come up with." Marshall looked at Abby. "See, I knew you'd be a good influence on him."

Abby blushed. "Oh, I don't think it's because of me."

"Don't kid yourself. He's been a lazy, brain-dead bum for I can't even remember how long." Marsh nodded and one eyebrow lifted. "Yep, it's you."

Seth slid his hand behind Abby's back and pulled her more closely against his side. Leaning over to kiss her cheek, he whispered, "He's right. It's you."

She nudged him playfully with her shoulder. "Hey. How about it's 'us'?"

Seth smiled at her and around the table at his friends. "I'd say that's right."

"Then you better not screw this up, Caldwell," Mouse declared.

"Doin' my best here, bro." In fact, it was becoming increasingly clear to him "us" was the only thing nonnegotiable.

He needed her. Whether they were a family of two or eight didn't matter, as long as he was with Abby. As soon as they were home, he'd find the right time to tell her.

Roberto looked at the clock near the bar and said, "Hey, Mouse, we better get on the road."

"Damn, you're right." Mouse slid out of the booth.

In the parking lot, they bid good-bye to Mouse and Roberto, who went to claim their luggage and rental car from the motel across the street. Seth was about to ask Marshall what his plans were for the rest of the day when Sammy Paulsen came outside and approached them. He looked shell-shocked, and more than a little nauseous.

"Damn shame," Sammy said. "Kevin had some problems, but I can't figure how he was caught up in this."

"I know, Sammy," Abby said. "I can't imagine Kevin being involved on purpose. I think he just saw something he wasn't supposed to see."

"That's what I think, too," Sammy said.

Abby looked back toward the club, and then at Sammy. "I can't believe he's been down in the basement all this time."

If possible, Sammy's face paled even further. He swallowed and looked at his feet. "It's my fault, Abby."

"What do you mean? You didn't put him there." She reached for his arm, but pulled back. Seth wondered what Sammy meant, too.

"That part of the basement was in my search area yesterday. I blew it." His voice sounded flat and strangled.

Seth, knowing how it felt to blame yourself, spoke up. "Sammy, he was under a pile of equipment in a dark basement. Anybody could've missed it."

The young cop didn't respond to Seth, and continued to direct his words at Abby. "I didn't do a good job. I was pissed because the chief stuck me with the basement, and I rushed when I heard there were some updates and they needed somebody to go down to the Shamrock and check in with you guys. I wanted to do it so I could check on you, Abby."

Well, that answered her question.

This time Abby did reach out, her hand resting briefly on Sammy's arm. "You're a good friend, Sam, but you have to stop worrying about me so much." Seth knew she was deliberately readjusting the other man's motivations. "Sure, it would've been nice to know about Kevin yesterday, especially for his family, but he was already dead. You couldn't have saved him."

"I know." Sammy heaved a morose sigh. "I just feel like a giant fuck-up. The chief isn't happy."

"Bob will get over it. You're a good cop, Sammy." Abby stepped back and repositioned her backpack on her shoulder. "Be sure and let me know whatever you hear, OK? And when Kevin's mom figures out all the arrangements and stuff."

Sammy said he would, and scurried back inside to do whatever he could to assuage his guilt.

Seth turned back to Marshall. "So, bud, what's the plan?"

"The plan, such as it is, is to visit my new friends at the Shamrock and have some lunch, and possibly a few drinks. How 'bout you?"

Seth looked at Abby. He'd expected they'd have some new clue to track down after they talked to Kevin. With the possibility eliminated, he didn't know what Abby planned.

She, however, was ready to take the ball and run with it. "I think we're just going to go home, Marsh. Stuff keeps dragging us into town, and when we get here, it gets even crazier. I want to hide out for the rest of the day."

"Can't say I blame you," Marsh replied. Seth noticed the gleam in his eye, which threatened to lead to a comment about exactly what he suspected they'd be doing while hiding out, but at the last minute he seemed to think better of it. Wow. Was his perpetually sixteen-year-old friend actually maturing?

"We should get together tomorrow, though, out at my place," Abby said. This was news to Seth. "I'll see if Molly's back yet, and maybe call Monique. I have a ton of leftovers from Mom's home invasion—I mean, repair—and need some hungry people to help me out with them."

While Seth initially found himself inclined to protest anything cutting into his time with Abby, he quickly warmed to the idea. "Yeah, and if they call Danny about the van, we could invite him, too."

"Great," Marsh said. "Now, there's a beer with my name on it, and I don't want it to get warm." Seth said he'd call him in the morning, and they headed for Abby's motorcycle.

"That was a good idea," Seth said.

"Well, your friends are starting to feel like my friends, too." She swung one leg over the bike, and Seth was glad to notice she hadn't taken the sweatshirt out of her backpack for the ride home. "Plus, I don't want company today, so setting something up for tomorrow felt like a good compromise."

"And why, exactly, don't you want company today?" He climbed on the bike in front of her and put his sunglasses on.

"Haven't you noticed all this trouble only strikes when we get out of bed?"

"Since you mention it."

She scooted her hips tightly up against him. "I think to avoid further trouble, and maybe even save lives, we should go back there and stay for as long as possible. And it's not very polite when you have company."

Certain it was the most brilliant theory he'd heard in a long time, Seth reached back, guided Abby's arms around his waist, kicked the bike to life, and roared off toward home.

Chapter Sixteen

When the motorcycle was safely parked in the garage, Abby went into the house and collapsed on the couch. She pulled off her shoes and socks and wiggled her toes, promising not to subject them to anything more confining than a pair of flip-flops for the rest of the day. Seth was in the kitchen, and she called out to him. "I need wine. I have to call Mom to tell her about Kevin, if she hasn't heard already, and let her know we're fine."

"And this requires alcohol?"

"You have to ask?"

A minute later Seth placed a glass of wine in her hand and settled on the couch beside her. He put his feet on the coffee table, twisted the cap off a bottle of beer, and began flipping channels on the television until he located a NASCAR race. Abby took a fortifying swallow of wine and stared at her phone. Finally, she opted to call Molly before tackling her mother.

The instant she heard her friend's shaky voice, she knew something was wrong. "You sound terrible, Molly. What's going on?"

"Gee, thanks," Molly said.

"You're worrying me. Talk."

"I will in a minute. Tell me what's going on with you first."

Abby filled her in on the unsettling and tragic developments as briefly as possible. To end her story on a happier note, she told her about Seth punching David. That actually elicited a laugh, but there was no doubt her friend was having some trouble of her own. "Now it's your turn. Tell me why you sound like you've been crying."

"Craig and I are fighting." The statement was accompanied by a noisy sniffle.

Abby had suspected as much, and wondered how many times she needed to kick the jerk in the balls for making Molly cry.

"You can't kick him at all, because I don't know where he is right now," Molly said. Her comment, and the look of amused concern she got from Seth, made Abby realize she had once again failed to censor her thoughts. Funny how it was always her most hostile impulses that leaked past the filter.

"What do you mean, you don't know where he is?"

"We've been arguing all weekend. It started Friday night, when he didn't approve of the dress I wore to dinner." Molly's voice was getting thick, and Abby thought she was about to start crying again.

"Molly, he's a jealous, controlling asshole. And, what? He left you stranded there?"

"No, he said he was going out to cool down, but I'm done. It's over, and there's no point in putting up with his bullshit. So I told him not to bother coming back, and I left all his stuff with the concierge at the front desk." She squeezed out a giggle, the sound easing Abby's worry significantly. "And I had my key reprogrammed, so he can't come storming up here and harass me."

"Fantastic! But are you OK?"

"I wasn't at first. I cried for a while, then I got it together. I put on the dress he gave me so much grief about, went down to the bar, let several very pretty boys buy me drinks, and now I'm back here."

"Alone?" Because a semidrunken, impulsive, revenge hookup would be a very bad idea.

"Yes, alone. But also without a ride home. Can you come get me tomorrow?"

"Of course I can!" She was so thrilled her friend had finally cut a dumbass boyfriend loose before he totally wrecked her heart she'd drive to Mexico. "Listen, how about if I bring you here when I pick you up? We're doing kind of a cookout thing. Marshall will be here, and maybe another guy from the crew. I'm going to ask Monique, and I know Mom will make an appearance, because I have to call her next and she can smell a social gathering right through the phone." At that thought, she took another drink of wine. Since it was a foregone conclusion she'd invite her mother, she might as well ask her to bring some of her summer pasta salad.

Molly said she'd love to come, and she was dying to meet Seth. Abby made her promise to call again later if she needed to talk, finishing her wine before dialing her mother.

Without even asking, Seth took her glass, refilled it, and returned it. She gave him a grateful smile as her mother answered.

Marilyn had heard about Kevin. "That poor boy! His mother must be out of her mind. I was going to make up a sandwich tray and take over there, but your cousin has my car right now, changing the oil. I guess I'll run it by tomorrow."

"Yeah, about tomorrow…" Abby told her mother about the plans for the next day, and was assured she would be there with a supersized bowl of pasta salad.

"I can't stay long, though, because I'm teaching a knitting class at the craft shop in the afternoon." Perfect, Abby thought.

She tossed her phone on the coffee table, tucked up her feet, and leaned against Seth's side. It was amazing how all the horrors of the last couple of days seemed so far away when it was just the two of them here, alone. She spent a while watching the race and not thinking of anything more distressing than what to heat up for dinner.

When the race entered a rain delay, Seth stood and stretched. "I hate when that happens. Mind if I check my e-mail?"

"Sure, go ahead. Use the desktop. You don't need a password."

Seth disappeared upstairs, and Abby heard a soft woof and turned to find Dilbert on the deck. She let him in and performed the head-to-tail examination she'd planned to do earlier. Other than a few burrs, which she picked out and threw away, he didn't seem any the worse for wear. She decided there was a bath in his immediate future, though.

Seth came back downstairs and dropped onto the couch. Dilbert jumped up and draped himself across his lap. Seth scratched him behind the ear, and Dilbert let out a blissful groan. Yeah, I know how you feel, Abby thought. The man definitely has great hands.

"Looks like your guest list is getting longer," Seth said.

"Longer? Did you hear from Danny? Is he going to be back tomorrow for the van?"

"No. But I had an e-mail from Joey. He sent it from the airport. He's on his way here." Dilbert twisted onto his back, and Seth complied with a tummy rub.

"You're kidding! Why would he do that?"

"He said he couldn't stand hearing everything going on and not being able to do anything, and he's driving Caroline crazy. So he's coming back, and he'll wait with Marsh for the bus and help him drive it back."

"Not that I won't be glad to see him, but what does he think he can do? We don't even have any good leads now, after what happened to Kevin." Her chest tightened at the memory of Kevin's body in the dark, cluttered basement.

"I don't know. But we've always been a team, and he feels like he's not doing his part or something." He shrugged. "Maybe it'll help. Sometimes when we have a problem, just talking and bouncing ideas around does a lot of good."

"When will he get here?"

"He has a layover in Dallas, then a commuter flight from Minneapolis to Brainerd. Marsh is picking him up tonight around nine."

She looked at Seth petting Dilbert. It was already impossible to imagine her life without him, and she was determined to help him solve this mystery. She thought up murderous plots on a regular basis, and she should be able to unravel this one. But right now she was formulating a different sort of plot.

The race came back on, and while Seth watched it, she went out on the deck for a cigarette. While she was there, she determined the day had warmed considerably, and called for a wardrobe change. She went to her room and found a pair of blue stretch cotton shorts and a sleeveless top. After she changed, she found a blanket in the hall closet and returned to the living room.

Seth looked up and took in her change of clothes and the blanket. "Going somewhere?"

"Yes, and so are you. Come on." She headed for the door. Seth left Dilbert snoozing on the couch and followed her. As they went down the steps into the yard, she made a mental note to hose the awful footprint into oblivion. She needed to erase all evidence of the intrusion from her property.

When they reached the hammock, Abby tossed the blanket inside, creating a foundation more comfortable and less likely to allow various bits of her body to smush out between the rope weave. Within moments they were nestled in the hammock, side by side, facing each other.

"You've been quiet since we got back," she said.

"Yeah. I've been thinking."

"About…?"

"Are you sure you want to hear this now?" He slid an arm under her and shifted her more tightly against him.

"I'm pretty sure I don't, but tell me anyway. I can help you think about it."

Seth's mouth tightened, and he hesitated. She wasn't sure if he was deciding whether to tell her at all or searching for the best way to say it. "It's my fault Kevin's dead."

Her response was immediate and firm. "It most certainly is not."

"Yes it is. Somebody wants to punish me, and they want it bad enough they killed him when he got in the way."

"You are not responsible for what some psycho did."

"Not directly, no, but it's because of me. I brought all this trouble here, to you, to Kevin, and to the club. If I'd been on the bus, Marshall and Trent would've been hurt, too, maybe killed. And it's driving me crazy, because I flat-out have no fucking idea why somebody wants me dead." He held her hand, and as he talked he tightened his grip until she had to squeeze back to remind him to relax.

"It's not your fault," she insisted. "None of it. And we will find out who's behind this and make sure they're caught and put away. Joey will be here tomorrow, and with three of you putting your heads together, you'll come up with something." It broke her heart to think of Seth blaming himself, and she knew the toll it was taking on him.

"I hope you're right, darlin'. I can't stand knowing the people I care about could be in danger because of me. If anything happened to you…" His words choked off, and he hugged her fiercely.

They lay there a while beside the glittering lake. The cry of a loon trilled, somehow enhancing the silence rather than disrupting it. From time to time, Seth exhaled a long, slow breath, a mannerism Abby had learned meant he was deep in thought. She wondered which weighty topic had him so preoccupied, but gave him time to work it through.

Finally, he focused on her with a hesitant smile. "I know we're supposed to be relaxing, but a light bulb went on in my head today, and I'm not going to be able to think about much else until I tell you about it," he said, his hand tracing a circuit from her waist to her hip and back again.

With the long list of dilemmas they faced, Abby couldn't imagine which one he wanted to discuss. They all felt slithery and dangerous. She tried to cover her apprehension. "Oh, really? Fluorescent or incandescent?"

"Funny, funny girl." Seth said, once again refusing to be sidetracked. "It was in the club, when we were talking about how I was writing again. The guys said it was you, and you said it was 'us.'" The shadow of hesitation left his smile, and as he brushed a kiss across her forehead, Abby's sense of foreboding diminished somewhat. "I used to have a business manager who was into all those corporate training techniques, and he called a moment like that a Blinding Flash of the Obvious, or BFO. He'd go, 'BFO,' and I'd go, 'BFD.'"

Abby could imagine exactly that sort of exchange. "Because you're so mature, huh?"

Seth chuckled. "Yeah, exactly. But anyway, when you said it was us, I remembered the first night, on your couch in front of the fire, when you said just that morning there hadn't even been an us. And that's when the light came on. I knew it's what mattered, the two of us. Whether we don't have any kids or a whole bus full, it's OK. Any family I'd ever have wouldn't really be a family if it didn't include you."

Abby found herself feeling somewhat skeptical. "You're sure you'll be able to be happy — with me — if we never have a baby?"

"As sure as anybody can be in this world, darlin'. If I'm not with you, my life's going to be empty, and that's not a good quality for a parent to have," he said with a slow shake of his head. "How could I be with somebody who wasn't you, just so I could have kids? It seems way more selfish to me than making the decision to simply be happy together."

Abby allowed herself a sigh of relief. He understood. He really, really understood her position, and accepted it. Even respected it. Maybe she'd change her mind in a few years, but even if she didn't, now she knew they'd still be OK. Which was wonderful, but now he'd kept his end of the bargain and arrived at a decision on the family issue, she heard the clock ticking and knew she would need to do the same regarding the question of leaving Emporia.

She wanted to go with him. She knew that. But she couldn't quite subdue the fear stabbing like a shard of ice behind her eyes, because she was unsure of its source. Was she afraid of change? Of leaving dull but comfortable routine for uncharted territory? Was she still a little worried Seth would, for reasons making sense to him but not to her, leave her? Or did she think she would someday, somehow disappoint him? Maybe she was afraid of losing her sense of identity. After all, Emporia Abby was the only one she knew. Until she answered those questions, she couldn't answer him.

"I'm not avoiding the question," she said, sure he'd know to which question she was referring.

His fingertips stroked her jaw beneath her ear. "I know that, darlin'. And I'm not pushing. Even if you don't come with me right away, you can make the call any time. I'll always be there with open arms." He reached behind her head and slipped the band from the end of her braid and began separating the strands.

His response was so genuine she felt both comforted and compelled to explain. "I know I love you." She looked deeply into his clear blue eyes and saw no reproach. "The thing I have to work out is why something so simple, so obvious, still scares me."

"I know that, too." He kissed her shoulder, his lips an ember warming her blood. "Let it go for now, darlin'. You can't force it. When you know, you'll know."

If only it were that easy. But he was right in a way. They were here, now, and it had to be enough. She let the weight of unmade decisions fall away, and cuddled closer to him, ready to shift into a playful, tender mood. The twinkle in his eyes indicated he had similar thoughts. She kissed him, then said, "You did notice, didn't you, I followed your instructions regarding no jeans in the hammock."

"I did, and I totally approve." Judging by the way his hand found its way under her shirt, she guessed he approved of that choice as well.

"At least now we don't have my mom and members of every branch of the law-enforcement community wandering around." She set about relieving him of his shirt. She figured he didn't have to get completely undressed, and it'd be a shame if a swarm of mosquitoes decided to fly up from the lakeshore and bite him on that spectacular ass of his. But the shirt had to go. She dropped her own shirt with his on the ground and groaned at the sensation of her flesh against his.

Seth eased himself up on one elbow and gazed down at her. He touched her hair, brushing it away from her shoulder. He moved on to her breasts for a moment, and stopped, his hand at her waist. "You're so beautiful I can hardly stand it."

When his lips met hers again, she couldn't hold back a low, hungry groan. Holy hell, he made her melt by simply looking at her, but when he touched her she completely came apart.

"Now we find out if my balance skills are any good," he murmured, taking hold of the waistband of her shorts.

She carefully nudged her hips from the blanket, allowing him to slide her shorts down her legs without spilling them both onto the ground. Yes, this was exactly what she'd envisioned ever since they were here yesterday morning. His hand moved between her thighs, parting her and distributing her creamy moisture over the delicate inner folds. She moved to meet his touch and felt herself opening, ready for him.

She unbuttoned his jeans and worked the zipper down. She pulled him free and tugged the jeans and boxers down and to the side, leaving him bare where he needed to be, without the necessity of wrestling his way out of confining denim and landing them in a heap beneath the hammock. His erection grew deliciously hard in her hand. She moved from whisper-soft touches to bolder, firmer strokes as he slipped a finger inside her. She couldn't help but lie back and part her legs further and watch his hand as he touched her.

Slowly, carefully, he brought his body over hers. She bent her knees and he entered her in one smooth, full motion. Once he was as deep as it was possible to go, he lay against her, holding her, their legs entwined. She kissed his neck and slid her hands down the back of his jeans. He rocked with her, the movement gentle and measured. Long, slow strokes filled her over and over, and the friction of their bodies turned her into one glorious, quivering erogenous zone from her lips to her ankles.

Nothing, nothing in the world could feel better than this. Wrapped up in Seth, around Seth, the sun filtering through the leaves to warm her face, the glitter of the same light dancing on the lake... She ran her hands over his back, delighting in the play of the muscles of his shoulders. She nipped lightly at his jaw, the bristles there teasing her lips while she breathed in his scent.

The pressure built at her core, an aching glow refusing to be contained. With a gasp, she let it free, a glorious burst of energy leaving her trembling, simultaneously drained and renewed.

Her legs tensed around his as he ground against her and found his own release.

She looked up into Seth's face, and neither of them made any attempt to move. Here and now was all that mattered. The two of them. The world consisted of the hammock swaying gently beneath them, the soft rippling of the water against the shore, the fresh scent of the air after the rain, and the hauntingly beautiful calls of a loon. Whispers of love, both given and received, making their world complete.

He moved beside her, cradling her, and gathered the trailing edges of the blanket over them. "Am I crazy?"

She blinked and tried to work out if this was a serious or playful question. "I don't think so. Maybe. Depends what you mean by 'crazy.'"

He twined his fingers through her hair, teasing out a few remaining tangles. "With everything happening, here I am, and I absolutely don't care about anything else. It's so easy to put it all aside when I'm with you."

She kissed his neck and said, "Then I'm crazy, too."

"The way I love you, hell, I didn't even know I could feel this way. Never came close. And it doesn't exactly make the trouble go away, but it pushes it back. I can get through it, and I don't think I could if you weren't with me."

"Fancy words, music-boy. One would think you were trying to get in my pants—if I were wearing any."

Seth chuckled. "I'm serious."

"I know you are. And I get it, because it's exactly what I was thinking a few minutes ago." She felt his lips against her temple. Draping an arm across his chest, she closed her eyes.

The next thing she knew, she was looking at the sun through the treetops and guessed at least an hour had passed. Raising her head, she saw Seth was still dozing. The afternoon sun and their combined body heat had made their blanket cocoon slightly uncomfortable, so she folded the edges back. Either her movement or the touch of the lake breeze woke him, and he smiled lazily when he saw her leaning over him.

"You weren't kidding when you said this was a good place to relax," he said.

"I know. It's almost like magic."

He stretched, his movements restrained so as not to tip them out of the hammock. "Think we should go back to the house?" She couldn't tell from his tone if he thought it was a good idea or not.

"We probably should. Dilbert might be anxious to get outside by now." She glanced at the ground beneath the hammock. "Plus, my clothes are probably full of bugs, and getting buggier by the minute."

He helped her to her feet, and she stood there for a moment, feeling deliciously scandalous. Once they were dressed, they went back up the trail to the house. As predicted, Dilbert darted out the door the second Abby opened it, and galloped into the woods. She checked her phone for messages, and was glad to find there weren't any. She probably wouldn't have returned the calls, anyway. The next day would be busy, with Joey's arrival and the planned get-together. She would worry about hostessing tomorrow, and let Seth and his friends brainstorm to see if they could get any closer to eliminating the threat against him. Tonight, no. Just…no.

They settled on the couch for a movie, but Abby found she couldn't watch it. Too many explosions. She wasn't interested in anything that made her think about explosions. She raided the fridge for an early dinner, and they ate on the deck.

They were just finishing when Dilbert appeared. It was immediately clear he'd found a delightful bog created by the previous night's rain, because he was dripping rancid mud on the deck. Abby's mood was so mellow, though, she couldn't be angry. "OK, Mr. Bog Dog, you just bought yourself a bath." Dilbert, not detecting the threat in her pleasant tone, wagged his tail, slinging mud on the side of the house. "Seth, would you go in and get Dilbert's shampoo? It's on the second shelf in the hall closet. And grab an old towel, too, one of the ones in the basket."

Seth returned a few minutes later with the requested items. "You're aware Dilbert, who is not your dog, has an entire shelf in your hall closet, right?"

"Dogs need stuff." Abby attached the hose to the faucet beside the deck. Dilbert's eye narrowed in suspicion. She snagged him by the collar as he was about to slip away.

"OK, I was just checking. Do you need any help?"

"No. Once I capture him, he doesn't fight a bath too much."

Seth settled in a chair on the deck and Abby began the process of wetting, lathering, and rinsing the filthy black dog. She also made a point of hosing the muddy footprint from the deck step while she was at it. By the time she was finished, Dilbert looked much better. She, however, was soaked. It was soon evident Seth found the way her top was molded to her body, nipples at full attention, of intense interest. He took her inside, peeled her out of her soggy clothes, rubbed her thoroughly from head to toe with a soft, blue bath towel, and warmed her all over again in the most satisfying way possible.

Abby decided then and there Dilbert was going to get a lot more baths.

Later, she watched Seth make two circuits through the house, checking the locks on the doors and windows. He brought Dilbert in and left the light burning over the side door. She understood and appreciated his vigilance, but felt a bitter twinge it was necessary. As she lay with Seth in her bed — their bed — with Dilbert curled at their feet, she vowed tomorrow would bring some answers.

Chapter Seventeen

"I'm not usually this lazy," Seth said as he rolled out of bed and reached for a pair of boxers.

Abby raised her head to squint at the clock, and dropped back onto her pillow. "It's eight o'clock. That's not exactly the middle of the day."

"That's not what I mean."

Abby stretched, pulling the blanket back up to her chin and rolling over. "Well, you've been doing a fabulous job of saving the world by staying in bed with me. That was our plan."

"And it's been working out great. For a whole lot of reasons. But isn't there some horrible property-maintenance thing you don't want to do? Lift something heavy? Kill some bugs?"

"Oh, I see. Man chores."

Seth grinned. "Exactly."

"Careful what you wish for. Unlike you, my laziness knows no bounds. I can find plenty for you to do, but not today. You're going to have your hands full being my cohost."

"What time do you need to leave?" Seth sat on the edge of the bed and started peeling back the blanket.

Abby tugged it back up. "About nine."

"Better start moving then," he said, once again grasping the blanket.

She pulled, but Seth held firm. "Fine, fine. Go make coffee." She tossed the blanket back and rose, naked and grumbling. Seth chuckled and went to the kitchen to get the caffeine flowing.

By the time Abby came out of the bathroom wearing her robe and wrapping a towel around her wet hair, he had a mug filled and waiting for her. He'd also found the last of the bagels and made a mental note to get more when he was in Emporia.

He checked his phone, but—as usual—had no signal outside town. "Can I use your phone? I want to make sure the guys are up."

"Sure. It's still on the coffee table, I think." She gulped half the hot coffee standing in the kitchen and topped it off before sitting at the breakfast bar.

Seth found the phone and dialed Marshall. After several rings, a very groggy voice answered.

"Marsh, get your ass out of bed. I'll be there in about an hour."

"Which means I can sleep for fifty-seven more minutes." A noisy yawn punctuated the remark.

"Give the phone to Joey."

Marshall complied, and Joey said, "I'm up, I'm up."

"I figured you would be. Just don't let Marsh fade on you. Haul him to the diner and start pouring coffee in him. I need full brain function from both of you today. We have to figure out who's after me, and we have new songs to go over."

"New songs? You're writing again?" The excitement in Joey's voice blasted through the phone. "Fuckin' awesome!" There was a muffled thud. "Marsh, you dumbass, why didn't you tell me Seth was writing?"

Seth snickered. "Yeah, I have some stuff coming together. Tell Marsh to bring his guitar, OK?"

"Will do. Wish I had my drums, but they're still in the trailer. I should be able to get some ideas, though."

"Counting on it. See you at the diner in a while."

After putting the phone back on the coffee table, he stepped behind Abby, slipped his arms around her waist, and started untying the belt of her robe.

Laughing, she slapped his hands away. "Stop it. If we start, we'll never make it out of here on time."

"I'll be quick," Seth said, making another grab for her belt.

"You're never quick. It's one of your most endearing qualities."

He kissed the top of her head and admitted defeat. "If you change your mind, I'll be in the shower."

A half hour later, Dilbert was fed and loped off in the direction of the Nygaards' house, probably in search of a second breakfast, and Seth and Abby were in the Jeep. He hadn't even suggested he drive this time. Besides, if he didn't have to watch the road, he could watch Abby.

When she pulled to the curb in front of the diner, he leaned over and kissed her. "Do you realize this will be the longest we've been apart since you came to the show on Friday?"

"Yeah, but it won't be too long. Just a couple of hours."

"It'll be fun having the guys out at your place, though. Did you call Monique?"

"Last night. She can't make it. Crazy woman volunteered to be one of the moms taking her kid's preschool class on a nature walk this morning."

Seth grinned. "I'll make sure Marsh is fully caffeinated, and we'll head out to the house. Do you need me to get anything before I go back?"

"No. Just be there."

He went into the diner, paying scant attention to the blue plastic tablecloths and 50s-retro decor. He found Joey and Marshall at a table along the right wall. Marsh's guitar case leaned on the chair beside him.

"I see you managed to keep him vertical," he said to Joey. He sat down and poured a cup of coffee from the full pot on the table.

"The trick is to shove him out the door before he's completely awake. Less resistance that way," Joey said, biting into a piece of bacon.

"The trick is not to drink Jœegerbombs till closing time at the Shamrock," Marshall said, dumping several packets of sugar into his coffee.

Seth snorted. "I thought you learned that lesson at the dive in Biloxi."

"Thought maybe it'd be different in Minnesota."

"Marsh, for the record, Jäegermeister is toxic in all fifty states, plus Canada and Mexico," Seth told him. "Now put your brain in gear, because we need to hash out what we know."

"Marsh made sure I was up to speed last night before the Jäeger kicked in." Joey said. "Seems to me we need to know for sure if Drew Purcell was here Friday night."

"If he was, then he's most likely still here, since it was late Saturday night or early yesterday morning when somebody snuck around Abby's house." Seth had looked before they left and he hadn't seen any signs they'd had any more visits.

Joey tapped a finger on the table, thinking. "But if he's here, you'd think somebody saw him. I mean, the guy stands out, and this is a small town."

Seth considered Joey's theory. Drew Purcell was tall and broad, his hair dyed a bright yellow not found in nature. He also had a year-round bottled tan, which would attract notice in a town full of Minnesotans just coming off a long winter. "You're probably right, but it's the start of tourist season here, so people don't notice strangers the way they might otherwise."

"I think you need to call Kincaid again, see if there's any news. Shake him up a little bit if there's not," Marshall said.

Seth helped himself to a piece of toast. "I plan to. I was hoping I'd have something else to tell him, though."

"Let's see what we've got, then," said Joey. "What about the girl who keyed Abby's car?"

"Pam? She's seriously out of whack, but I don't think she's has anything to do with it."

"Don't cross her off the list, though," Marshall said. "She did go AWOL on the way back to Iowa." His voice was gaining strength, and his eyes were less red, or at least less puffy.

"True. Another popular suspect is the 'random insane fan.' And in a weird way I hope that's not it, because there's no way for us to look into it. It could be anybody, for any reason."

Joey dropped his fork on his empty plate and pushed it away. "If that's the case, we don't have any choice but to sit back and let the cops do their thing."

"It's making me nuts, man, waiting and wondering what's going to happen next." He'd sacrifice anything to keep Abby safe, but he had to know where the danger was.

Marshall picked a bit of bacon off the front of his black T-shirt. Popping it in his mouth, he said, "Which brings us to the part we don't want to talk about. Our guys."

Seth drew a resigned breath. "Unless I see some earth-shaking evidence, I'm not even considering Roberto. There's no way."

"I'm with you," Joey said. "There'd have to be some deep, dark secret there, and 'Berto's never kept a secret in his life."

"Pete and Mouse were never out of sight during the show. But Trent was," Marshall said.

"Yeah, I know," Seth said. "My gut says 'no,' but if you think about it, Trent has parts of his life we don't know much about. He doesn't hang out with us between road trips, and I've seen him pretty out of control a few times, over stupid things."

"So have I," Joey said. "But he would've been on the bus, too, if the bomb had gone off where it was supposed to."

"If he knew when it was going to happen, he could've been in the back lounge. He usually sleeps there, anyway. It would've gone a long way to make him look like a victim." Seth hated the thought, but he didn't have a lot of names on the list to work with. "That leaves Danny and Andy."

"We haven't known them long. But what the hell could you have done to make one of them want to kill you?" Joey asked.

"I'm sure I've pissed off a lot of people a lot faster," Seth said. "But what if one of them has a mad-on for something from before they worked for us?" Marshall disagreed. "What are you sayin', man? Danny or Andy hired onto the crew so they could take you out? Wouldn't it be simpler just to walk up to you in the street and shoot you?" He was a straightforward thinking kind of guy.

"It would, but trying to kill somebody in the first place isn't real rational," Seth pointed out.

Joey weighed in. "I think it's a reach. But they are the newest guys on the crew, and loyalty like we have takes time. What if somebody came to one of them, offered them a bunch of money to be their guy on the inside? You know, feed them information, maybe do some of the dirty work?"

Seth had to admit he hadn't thought of that. He was more grateful than ever for Joey's steady, focused presence. "I think I'll talk to Mouse, see what he knows about Andy's background. He spends more time with him than the rest of us do." He gave Joey an affectionate rap on the shoulder. "Hey, I hate I wrecked your vacation, but I knew you'd help keep my head on straight."

Joey rapped him back. "That's what brothers do."

Marshall drained his coffee cup. He was definitely starting to look human again. He might shut down the bars, but he recovered quickly. "So, what's the plan? We going straight to Abby's?"

"Pretty soon. I want to go across the street and get some supplies. Stale bagels for breakfast ain't cutting it, and it turns out Abby's allergic to shopping."

"Breakfast in bed, maybe?" Joey teased. "Ain't that sweet? And how fun is it to have a front row seat to see you turn all tamed and domestic?"

"Nothing tame about it, that's for damned sure," Seth said. He didn't see the need to mention he made her coffee and fed the "not her dog." "If y'all want to go throw your stuff in the car, I'll meet you there. I'm going across the street to the bakery."

The plan met with approval, and they parted ways on the sidewalk. When he arrived at the bakery, he paused at the window display, debating the merits of bagels versus croissants. Hadn't Abby said something about liking croissants? He'd just decided to get some of each and was reaching for the door handle when he felt a hand on his shoulder. He turned and took an instinctive step back when he recognized Pam, the girl who'd managed to piss Abby off so thoroughly.

"Seth, thank goodness! I have to talk to you!" She had her hair in a ponytail strung through the back of a baseball cap, and wore a Historic Downtown Emporia T-shirt. He surmised evading law enforcement required wardrobe replenishment in any way possible.

"I'm not sure it's a good idea. Aren't you supposed to be back in Iowa right now?"

Pam seemed nervous and her eyes were slightly unfocused. Seth wondered if it was a case of medication in serious need of a dosage adjustment. "Yes, but I couldn't go. When I found out someone was trying to kill you, I had to stay." She reached out and fingered one of the silver charms around his neck, which he didn't like one bit. He eased back another half step. She brought the finger that had touched the charm to her lips, looking back to Seth. "I care about you, and you needed me here. I found out something you need to know."

There was no doubt in his mind Pam was off her rocker, and talking to her might encourage her inappropriate and disturbing behavior. But if there was even the slightest chance she had information that could help him determine why he was the target of someone's homicidal urges, he had to take it. "OK, fine." He pointed to the pair of small café-style tables. "Have a seat."

Pam sat and plucked a napkin from the chrome dispenser on the table and began twisting it in her fingers. "I hoped I'd see you in town today. I don't have a car, so I couldn't come find you. And I know she wouldn't let me talk to you."

Seth pulled out a chair and sat across from her. "There's the first thing we need to discuss. You have to back off Abby."

Pam looked down at the mangled napkin in her hands. "Maybe. But you're so special, you know? She's nobody."

"She's who I want. So you're going to have to deal with it." He hoped it wasn't a mistake to be so direct with someone who didn't have both oars in the water, but he wasn't going to spend all day with this girl.

"You mean, like, you're with her permanently?"

"Yeah. Permanently." If he had anything to say about it.

"Oh." She made the word sound almost like a question, as if she weren't sure she believed him. "Um, tell her I'm sorry about her car."

"I'll do that." He propped his elbows on the table and folded his arms. "Now, what did you need to tell me?"

She abandoned the first tattered napkin and pulled a fresh victim from the dispenser. "I saw somebody yesterday. He's not supposed to still be here. He's around all the time, but he shouldn't be here now. I thought you should know."

She wasn't making a lot of sense. Maybe he should've let her tell him what was on her mind first, before telling her about Abby. Either she was getting farther and farther away from her last dose, or hearing him spell out he and Abby were together —

and staying that way — had scattered her thoughts even more. "Who's still here, Pam?" He congratulated himself for managing to sound so patient.

"You know. Drew." Her head bobbed, as if she were confirming to herself she'd relayed the information correctly.

"Drew?" So, the son of a bitch was in town.

"Uh-huh. Stacy's brother."

The blood ran cold in Seth's veins. "Stacy's brother? Drew?" Sure, he knew she had a brother, but she hadn't seen him in years. Had he even known the guy's name? He couldn't remember if Stacy had ever told him. Anything that happened before her parents died in a car accident when she was eighteen had been almost totally off-limits.

"You didn't know he was Stacy's brother? Funny." Her voice was distant, and even though she was looking right at him, it felt like she was talking to someone in her own head. Maybe she was.

"No, I didn't. How did you know?"

Pam sat up straighter and seemed to make an effort to organize her thoughts. "After Stacy went away, I kept track of her. I was glad she was gone, and if she was busy somewhere else, I knew she wasn't coming back."

"How did you keep track of her?" And why hadn't it ever crossed any of their minds to check on her?

"Oh, it was easy. I'd Google her. Sometimes she'd turn up in a story or blog about the guy she was with. The one in Darknoise."

"You know she's dead, right?"

Pam nodded, not altogether sadly. "Yeah. I found out a few weeks after it happened. I saw a story about it online and there was a picture from a memorial service. There was this guy in the picture, and it said it was her brother, Drew."

Unbelievable. His fan/stalker had come up with the grand prize. His ex-girlfriend's estranged brother was a frustrated songwriter, and perhaps because he knew his sister was traveling with Dead End Road he noticed the band and became fixated. This led to the copyright lawsuit. When he lost the lawsuit and his sister in the same year, he evidently went off the deep end.

"OK, Pam. Great information, and it really helps a lot."

She smiled brightly. "I'm glad. After I saw the picture, I noticed that guy whenever I came to a concert. Maybe he was there before, but I didn't pay attention. I, um…mostly at the shows I'm looking at you."

He'd been almost pleased with Pam a few seconds ago, but her last comment had creeped him out all over again. Too bad the conversation wasn't quite over. "Where have you seen Drew? When?"

"I saw him early yesterday morning. He was putting gas in a car, and he was all wet, like he'd slept outside or something. But if he had a car, he could sleep there, right? I don't know why he was wet." Her head tilted as she tried to puzzle out this inconsistency.

"Was it the only time you saw him?" If he was gassing up a car, maybe he'd been on his way out of town.

"No, I saw him again last night. I couldn't sleep, so I went over to the park. I saw him cross the street over on the other side. I was going to follow him, but he jumped in his car and drove off before I could get close." Seth noticed in addition to being glazed and unfocused, her eyes were terribly bloodshot. In light of her comment about not sleeping, he wondered if she'd been roaming around Emporia every night like some sort of ghoul. As his dad would say, crazy as a shithouse mouse.

Seth stood up. He had to call Kincaid. "I'm glad you told me. It's a huge help."

"That's all I wanted to do. Help you."

"You did. We know who we need to look for, so the police can take over."

Pam looked up at him from under her lashes. "When are you leaving?"

"Soon." Shit. He couldn't decide if Pam should get free tickets to all their shows for life or a restraining order.

"Maybe I'll go home, then."

Seth nodded in what he hoped was an encouraging manner. "I'll tell the guy in charge of the investigation what you told me. But you should go by the police station and tell them in person. That would be really great." He pointed up the street. "It's about three blocks over there." He hoped her desire to "help" would last long enough to reach the station, but he'd damned sure tell Kincaid where she was so they could track her down if she didn't appear as promised.

"I'll go. If you're sure you'll be OK."

"I'll be fine."

He managed to keep Pam from following him into the bakery, nudging her in the direction of the police station. When he came out with his bagels and croissants, she was nowhere to be seen. He hurried over to the motel parking lot and found Joey and Marshall leaning on their rental car. Marsh turned to open the back door, while Joey walked toward Seth, dragging his fingers through his mop of blond curls.

"What took you so long?" Joey asked, taking one of the bakery boxes.

"I ran into our friend Pam outside the bakery."

"No way. So she did come back here."

"She did." He thought he could still smell a bit of residual psychosis in the air. "At first, she had the hair standing up on the back of my neck, but it turned out she had something really interesting to tell me." He put the box on the backseat and told them what Pam said. By the time he was finished, their mouths were hanging open in shock.

"Un-fucking-believable," Marshall said succinctly.

"No doubt. So the first thing I have to do is call Kincaid. If Drew Purcell is still around, they should be able to find him." He couldn't wait to tell Abby.

Seth pulled out his phone and dug the agent's card from his wallet. He was put through immediately, and told him Pam was still in Emporia, as well as someone else who wasn't supposed to be.

"Pam Gresak figured out Purcell was the dead girl's brother. Amazing," was Kincaid's gruff reply. "I'll get Chief LeFevre to check around town, see if we can figure out where he's staying. You still need to be on your guard, though. If he's hiding out somewhere, maybe holed up in a vacant cabin, we might not get our hands on him right away. After failing twice he's probably rattled. Might do anything."

"I know, and we will. Can you e-mail me one of those pictures of Purcell? I want Abby to know what he looks like."

Kincaid said he'd do that, thanked Seth, and hung up abruptly. Seth thought the man wasn't thrilled an unstable vandal and the intended victim had been the source of valuable information.

Seth turned to his friends and grinned. "All right, guys, let's hit the road. We have some music to play."

Chapter Eighteen

Abby parked the Jeep beside the white rental car in her driveway. She was relieved her friend was taking the relationship implosion so well. There was no sign of last night's tears, and she wore a cheerful floral print top and hot pink Capri pants. She'd chattered nonstop during the whole drive, and hadn't mentioned Craig once.

Before they got to the side door, Abby heard the sound of guitars. These guys didn't waste any time, did they?

"I'm so glad you decided to do this today," Molly said.

Abby pushed the door open. "Everything's been so crazy lately. This felt like a nice, normal thing to do."

They entered the living room and found the three musicians spread out on the couch. Seth and Marshall had their guitars, and Joey leaned forward on his elbows, listening intently. When Seth saw her he put down the Gibson and stood. "Take five, guys," he said, crossing the room to enfold Abby in his arms. "Missed you," he murmured.

"You too," she said. When they parted, she stepped over to Molly and put an arm around her shoulder. "Everybody, this is my best friend, Molly Lanier. Molly, you can probably figure out who's who, but the big guy with the guitar is Marshall Rogerson, and the one looking like he'd kick somebody in the head for a pair of drumsticks is Joey Garvin. Seth, you probably already know too much about."

Joey and Marshall both rose and came over, making all the polite nice-to-meet-you greetings, though Abby noticed Marsh held Molly's hand a bit longer than was customary when he said hello. Should she be concerned? Probably not. Who was she, after all, to be suspicious of sudden chemistry?

Introductions complete, Joey bounded toward Abby and planted a noisy kiss on her cheek. "You, sweetheart, are a goddess!"

Laughing, Abby patted him on the chest. "Nice to hear, but hardly true."

"It's a fact. I absolutely do not want any details, but whatever you did to get Seth to start pulling songs out of his head again is a miracle."

Abby started to object, but Seth interrupted her. "She doesn't want to take any credit, but she's just being bashful. We're going to have all the material written for the new CD before we go back out on the road."

Joey went back to the couch. "See, what did I tell you? Miracle."

"We might even be able to get a few tracks down over the summer, if we can get the studio in between gigs," Seth said.

Abby tossed her purse on the end table. "I hope Caroline's not mad at me. I never did get around to calling her."

"She knows you've been busy," Joey said.

She promised herself she'd call Caroline tomorrow. "Before you guys get back to work, how about you get the beer out of the car?"

Joey and Marshall went out to the Jeep, and Seth took Abby aside. "I have some things to tell you, but I want to wait until I get an e-mail I'm expecting. I'll check again in a few minutes, and if it's not there, we'll talk anyway."

Abby nodded. While the beer was retrieved and placed in the refrigerator, she and Molly settled on the floor by the coffee table with bottles of hard lemonade. It was fascinating to watch these guys flesh out a new song. She jumped in from time to time with suggestions for the lyrics, but she mainly enjoyed listening to their thought process. They were going over the song about Cujo's demise, and Marshall said, "Pete's going to want a heavy bass line in this part."

"He can have it," Seth said, nodding. "But it's going to have to trail off before the tempo change in the bridge."

"I should come in with some kick for the transition to the chorus," Joey added.

Seth wrote something in his notebook. "Do it, but take it easy on the cymbal. I want a deep, solid beat there."

"No problem. Damn, I can't wait to get my hands on my drums." Apparently there was nothing worse than a frustrated drummer.

Their lemonades empty, Abby and Molly went to the kitchen for more. "Oh, wow, he is gorgeous," Molly said.

Abby peered through the serving window at Seth. "He sure is. And you should've seen him on my motorcycle yesterday. I think my brain short-circuited for a few minutes."

"What? No," Molly said, shaking her head and setting her long, blonde ringlets swaying. "Well, yes, Seth is gorgeous. But I was talking about Marshall."

Oh. Of course she was. Abby smiled. "If you like the shaved-headed, goateed, tall, dark, tattooed musician type who really needs a shirt with sleeves."

"I didn't think I did, but all of a sudden it's my new favorite thing."

"Just be careful, OK? Your head's probably still spinning."

Molly's perfectly shaped eyebrows rose. "Mine? What about yours, Miss Whirlwind Romance?"

Abby ducked her head sheepishly, chuckling. "Guess I don't have much room to talk, huh?"

"No, you don't," Molly said, twisting the cap off her lemonade. "But, Abs, I'm not saying it's a bad thing. I know there's not some universal flowchart for how long it takes to fall for somebody." She put the cap in the trash under the sink, and sipped at the frosty bottle. "But I wouldn't be your friend if I didn't ask...are you sure? Do you really think he's the one?"

Abby took a long pull from her own bottle before answering. "Is it ever possible to be sure about something like this?"

Her friend made a thoughtful humming sound. "Probably not. I suppose the question is whether this is about Seth or the musician you've been crushing on for, like, five years now."

Abby tilted her head, seeing Molly in a different light than the girl with the habit of always choosing the worst possible guys. "You know, you're one of the few people who realizes how different those two men are." She noticed condensation was trickling up her wrist, and grabbed a tea towel to wipe her hand and the bottle. "One thing I do know for sure is this is all about Seth Caldwell. I don't think I've really seen Seth the Musician, the one I thought I knew, other than at the concert Friday night."

Molly's lips lifted in an approving smile. "Right answer. Look, I admit I was a little worried, but look at you. Your whole world has changed in the last few days, and I've never seen you this happy."

Abby thought. "I don't think I ever have been. I don't even think I knew I could be. Which is insane, considering all the chaos coming with the package."

"See? If there's hope for you, there's hope for me." She clinked her bottle against Abby's in an informal toast.

They entered the living room as Seth stood, stretching. "I'm going to go check for that e-mail now," he said.

"Just a second," Abby said, holding up a hand. "I told you I had to know something, and now is when I find out." She turned to Joey. "What's Seth's middle name?"

Joey's gaze flew to Seth, who had his hand over his face. "You wouldn't tell her? Why the hell...?" Marshall leaned over to whisper in Joey's ear, and his eyes widened. "Ooh, now I see. Well, she's going to find out sooner or later." He looked back at Abby, his eyes twinkling. "Seth's full name is Seth *David* Caldwell."

Abby sank to the couch and groaned. "Crap. I think I'd have preferred Euripides."

Seth uncovered his eyes. Abby could see he was trying not to smile. "I would've, too. And I'm changing it. Tomorrow."

"Courthouse opens at nine." She burst into laughter. What else could she do?

Shaking his head, and with a teasing "I told you so" tossed over his shoulder, Seth went up to the loft.

While he was upstairs, Abby heard the side door open. Her mother came around the corner by the kitchen carrying a huge covered bowl. Abby estimated there was enough pasta salad there to feed at least two-dozen people. She took the bowl and put it on the kitchen counter. "Thanks for making this, Mom. But I think you're going to end up taking most of it home."

"Don't be silly. You and Seth will eat it."

"Not before it grows legs and crawls into the lake."

"I'm sure it won't come to that." Her mother began pulling food from the refrigerator and assembling it on the stovetop and counter. She informed Abby she'd run into her contractor in town earlier, and he had an emergency and wouldn't be out until tomorrow. She shot Abby a sidelong glance. "I did have a long talk with Rebecca yesterday."

"Rebecca?"

"Seth's mother."

"Oh." Did she really want to hear this?

"She's very nice. She's worried sick, of course, but she has faith the police will take care of things." She rummaged in a drawer for serving utensils. "She said she's always hoped Seth would find the right person, but she never pushed. She gave him his space and didn't interfere, because he never made any promises he wasn't ready to stand behind." A package of paper napkins was pulled from a cabinet above the stove. "His life might have looked reckless and irresponsible to people who didn't know him, but he always held up his own kind of honor, and she supported it."

"She sounds like someone I'd like to meet."

"She's already planning it. Seth can expect a call."

Now the mothers had joined forces, Abby knew it was out of their hands. They only had to show up as instructed. "Let me introduce you to Marshall and Joey. And keep an eye on Molly. She and Marsh are already picturing each other naked."

Her mother's warm smile led them into the living room. Abby introduced Seth's friends, who responded with lots of Texas-boy manners, full of ma'ams and Mrs. Delaneys until Marilyn set them straight, just as she had with Seth. Abby noticed she sat on the couch in a position allowing her to keep Marsh and Molly in her sights, and to run an intercept pattern if necessary.

Seth came back downstairs with a sheet of paper in his hand. "Marilyn, I'm glad you're here. You need to hear this, too."

He handed the page to Abby. She looked at the image of a big man with yellow hair and tan-in-a-can, then at Seth. "Who's this?"

"Drew Purcell." He sat beside her. "I ran into your favorite fan in town this morning."

Abby sat back. Huh. "Pam?"

"Yeah. Her last name's Gresak, by the way. Kincaid mentioned it when I called him."

"She did sneak back here instead of going home." She felt a growl threatening to form in her throat.

"Yep. She wanted to 'help.'" Seth took the printed photo and passed it to Marilyn. "But it turned out it was a good thing Pam was around, because she said she'd noticed someone in town who wasn't supposed to be here. She recognized him from a picture she saw online. And she said Drew is Stacy's brother."

Abby had to run the last part through her head a few times before it sank in. "You have got to be fucking kidding me." She shot an apologetic look at her mother to neutralize the coming reprimand for her language.

"I knew she had a brother, but they hadn't been in touch for years, since not long after their parents died. But that's all I knew about him." Seth turned his attention to Marilyn. "You know everybody, and we need to know if anybody's seen this guy around town. Pam saw him early yesterday and again last night, and there's a damned good chance he's still here."

"Print me a copy. If he's here, I'll find out where." Abby's mother spoke with the firm conviction of a military general facing certain victory. You didn't mess with her family, her town. Drew Purcell was toast. He just didn't know it yet.

Seth explained the theory he and the guys had formulated. Drew was interested in music, and Stacy, his estranged sister, was interested in musicians. While she was with Seth, her brother had kept an eye on things, and became fixated on the band in general and Seth in particular. After the failed lawsuit and Stacy's death, his animosity had grown into something much more dangerous. It made sense.

And Pam was the one who brought this to their attention. Wasn't that a kick in the head? "This is good," Abby said. "I mean, we know who it is now. With the whole town and every cop in the county looking for him, they'll catch him."

Seth sat next to her on the couch and pulled her onto his lap. She'd gotten so used to touching him, holding him, over the past few days this semipublic display of affection failed to make her the least bit self-conscious. "Yes, darlin', it's a good thing." His eyes swept the room. "But it's not over yet. Molly, get a good look at the guy, because anybody who's close to us could be a target. You, too, Marilyn."

Marshall sat up straight and looked at Molly as if he were planning to initiate his own version of bodyguard duty. Abby thought it might not be a half-bad idea. She looked at her mother, who gave a slight nod. So far, Marsh was passing muster, but the evaluation was ongoing.

The more Abby thought about it, the greater her relief became. She knew the part tearing at Seth most was having to look at his own crew with suspicion. It was also disturbing to know someone wished you harm when you had absolutely no idea what you'd done to drive another person to such an extreme. Knowing that, he'd get through it. All they had to do was keep their heads down until Drew Purcell was caught.

Seth went back up to the loft to print copies of the picture for her mother and Molly. Joey and Marshall started talking about one of the songs they'd been working on earlier, debating if it needed strong harmony vocals or if it would be better to feature only Seth's voice.

"C'mon, Mom," Abby said, rising. "Let's set the food out. I've seen these guys eat, and it's best to be prepared."

Marilyn looked at Joey and Marshall. "Would you go out to my car? There's a cooler with some hamburger patties and a propane tank for the grill." They went off to retrieve the food and fuel, and Marilyn turned to Abby. "I'll help you get things running, but then I have to go. My class starts in about forty-five minutes. I'm glad I had a chance to meet Seth's friends, though."

Before long, Seth was back with the additional copies, and burgers were sizzling on the grill.

When her mother was ready to leave, Abby walked with her to the car. "Be careful, Mom."

"Don't worry about me, sweetie," she said, patting her daughter on the arm. "I'll be in town all day, and if I feel like anything's wrong tonight, I'll go stay with Grace."

"Good." She cleared her throat. "I don't know what I'd do if anything happened to you." Though she and her mother weren't usually very demonstrative, she couldn't stop herself from wrapping her in a hug.

"Nothing's going to happen to me."

"You're the only real family I have, so nothing had better," Abby said, releasing her mother.

"Nonsense. You have a wonderful family."

"Mom, you know Eileen and I have never been close." What an understatement. Her sister was five years older, and they'd never had a single thing in common.

Her mother shook her head and nudged Abby several steps in front of the car. She pointed at the people gathered on the deck. "Abigail, tell me what you see."

She felt her brows knit in confusion. "I don't know what you mean. Seth trying to keep Dilbert from burning himself on the grill. Molly, Seth's friends."

"No, look again. That, sweetie, is a family. Molly's been a sister to you since you were ten, and those are Seth's brothers." She returned to her car, and Abby followed behind. "Now, nothing is going to happen to me, but you do have a family."

"Maybe," Abby admitted, struggling to incorporate the notion. "But if I can't bring myself to go with Seth, it probably doesn't matter." Suddenly, she understood if she failed to conquer her fear, she'd not only lose Seth, but the extended Dead End Road family as well. The prospect of that loss wasn't as bad as losing a couple of semivital internal organs, but she thought it would be close.

Marilyn took her daughter's hand. "No one can see the future, but I'm as sure as I can be if you do decide to go you'll never regret it, no matter how things turn out. And I'm absolutely positive if you don't go, you'll always wish you had."

Before Abby could formulate a reply, Marilyn was gone in a whirl of BeDazzled T-shirt and red Volkswagen. Abby went back to the deck and settled in with her...family. Wow. When was the last time she truly felt she had one of those? She blinked unexpected tears from her eyes as she watched them. Joey and Seth drank beer and discussed whether they needed to book additional hours in the studio. Dilbert leaned hopefully against Seth's leg every time he rose to tend to the grill. Molly sat by Marshall, finding excuses to touch him as they spoke. Mom was right. Again. As far as families went, this was a great one.

When the burgers were done, everyone milled about, drifting into the house to fill their plates. Fresh drinks were taken from the refrigerator, and they returned to the deck to eat. Seth put a Reckless Kelly CD in the player and left the door open so the music could be heard outside.

After it became clear he wasn't going to score any more handouts, Dilbert trotted off in the direction of his favorite trail.

Abby felt warm contentment as she and Seth sat with Joey. Marshall and Molly strolled down the path toward the lake.

Noticing an increasing number of flies buzzing around the discarded plates, Abby collected them along with some empty bottles, and took them to the kitchen. As she loaded the dishwasher, she heard the side door open. A moment later, a familiar face surrounded by brown curls peeked around the corner from the hallway.

"Monique, hi!" Abby said, pleased her friend made it after all, if a little late. "Come on in."

"Oh, no, no, I can't stay," Monique said, her fingers fluttering. "I just need to talk to you for a minute. Can you come outside?"

"Sure," Abby replied, closing the dishwasher with a click. Something was off. This sort of covert behavior wasn't typical for the normally forthright shop owner.

She followed Monique to the back of the house, walking till they were near the road. Exactly how much privacy did they need? The back of her neck gave a warning tingle. She noticed her friend looked a bit disheveled. She had some scratches on her arms, and Abby was sure it was a twig she saw tangled in her hair. "Nature walk not go well?" she asked, preferring banter to whatever was on Monique's mind.

Monique gave a wry smile. "We cut it a bit short," she said. "Cory saw a bunny, which ran into the bushes, and before you knew it, there was a swarm of preschoolers charging into the bushes in pursuit." She looked down at the fresh scratches on her arms and frowned. "Some of them had thorns."

Despite Abby's growing apprehension, she had to laugh at the mental image.

"Abby, I only have a few minutes. I have to get back to the shop." Her gaze darted around, betraying her discomfort. "Your mom stopped in on the way to her class. She told me she thinks you're going to go with Seth when he leaves."

Abby drew a blank regarding why that would require such a serious visit. Wouldn't it be considered good news? "She did?" Abby dragged out the words, still trying to make sense of it.

Monique looked at her, her lips in an uncharacteristic firm line. "Honey, you know I love you…"

Oh, rackenfrazzle. No good conversation ever started this way. Abby waited for the other woman to get to the point.

Monique chewed her bottom lip for a moment and blurted, "I think you're making a mistake."

It took Abby some time to absorb Mo's statement. She crossed her arms, knowing even as they settled at her waist it was a defensive posture. "A mistake?" she repeated. "First of all, no matter what Mom thinks, I have not made up my mind about anything. And second, I thought you — of all people — would be happy for me if I did. After all, you're the one who pointed out life was passing me by, and I needed to stop hiding and start living."

Monique's head snapped up, her chin at a slightly higher elevation than normal. "It is not what I meant, and you know it."

Abby's lips pursed, and she inhaled deeply through her nose. "Well, excuse me, Mo, but I didn't see that spelled out in your disclaimer."

"I also seem to recall telling you not to get carried away."

Abby snorted. "Maybe there should've been a glossary along with the disclaimer, then, because I have no idea what that means." She couldn't remember the last time she had an argument with Monique, but this was sure starting to feel like one.

Monique ran a hand through her hair, encountered the twig, and plucked it out. "It means to put yourself out there, meet people, date, maybe bring a nice guy home occasionally. It means to come out from under your goddamned rock once in a while."

Abby opened her mouth to retaliate, but her friend was on a roll. "It does not include walking out my front door, practically straight into the arms of a perfect stranger, taking him home the same night, and rearranging your whole life in a few days so you can run off with him."

When Monique had to pause for breath, Abby jumped right in. "Wow, Mo, you sure have a lot of rules for living my own life. But let me remind you I have not made any such decision. And if I did, it would not qualify as 'running off.'"

"I'm not saying this to hurt you, you idiot. I'm saying it to save you from being hurt. You don't know anything about him." Her head was angled forward, neck extended, as if her hackles were raised. "You've known him for three days!"

Well, they had been three pretty eventful days. Abby gave a noisy sigh. "I don't know what to tell you, Mo. Sometimes it happens like that. It did for my parents."

"Maybe so," Monique said, hackles lowering slightly. "But your mom didn't change her whole life overnight and take off with him, going where she didn't have anyone to watch out for her."

Abby did more than roll her eyes. She rolled her entire head. Apparently Monique was not going to believe she didn't already have her bags packed in the back of her Jeep. "Who says I need anybody to watch out for me? In case you didn't notice, I'm not an eighteen-year-old fresh off the farm. And furthermore..." She heard herself and mentally cringed. Who said *furthermore*? "And furthermore, knowing someone for a long time is no guarantee, either. Hell, I knew David for two years before we were married, and look how it turned out. A fucking disaster, that's how it turned out!" Now it was Abby's turn to be on a roll. She paced in front of her friend, making pointed gestures with one arm. "Right out of college, I did what all the nice, sensible girls my age were doing. I met a guy who wasn't bad to look at, knew how to lay on the charm, and had a good job. Everybody told me what a catch he was. Even you."

Monique's face flushed, and she averted her eyes. "I guess he had a lot of people fooled."

"Yes!" Abby almost shouted, and forced herself to ratchet it down a notch. "A lot of people present the side they want you to see. I dated him for a proper amount of time, then we were married. It was only later I realized his charm was pretension, his jokes were always at someone else's expense, and I only mattered to him because I fit the image he wanted to build." She stepped around Monique, until her friend once again met her eyes. "He never supported or encouraged me, and he never respected me. I could vomit right now, thinking how hard I tried to get him to approve of one single fucking thing I did. Seth already has him beat by about seventy light-years."

"But honey, look at everything happening! I think he's bad for you, whether you go with him or not." A pleading note crept into Monique's voice, and she pointed at the plywood making up a large chunk of the wall of Abby's house. "A bomb went off in your house, and someone is still trying to kill him. What if he's killed? What if you're killed?"

"What if you're hit by a logging truck on the way back to town?" Abby countered. "We know who it is now, and it's not one of his friends. It's a guy with a grudge, and everybody's looking for him. He's not going to have a chance to hurt us."

Monique was momentarily derailed. "You know who?" She blinked and gave her head a shake. "Marilyn said she had something to show me, a picture of someone to keep an eye out for, but she left it in the car. She's bringing it by later."

Abby nodded. "His name is Drew Purcell."

Catching her equilibrium, Monique squared his shoulders. "It's only part of the picture. Dash says Seth's never had a committed relationship. What makes you think he'll start now? How are you going to feel if he leaves you? You didn't handle it too well the last time."

Abby drew back as if she'd been slapped. "That was a low fucking blow, Monique."

Monique dropped her eyes. "Maybe. I'm sorry."

"Look, we've discussed his leaving, believe it or not. He thought he was no good for me, with the nomadic lifestyle, not to mention someone trying to kill him recently, and probably killing Kevin in the process. Pretty much all the things you just said. But we concluded we'll make decisions together, and he won't leave me, not in the way you mean. I believe that."

"You can't be sure."

"Nobody knows anything absolutely, Mo." Abby's voice was wilting. She was about done with this conversation. "But I trust him. You might be trying to take back the advice you gave me the other day, but it's still valid. Life's not worth the space you take up if you don't live it."

"I just don't want you to get hurt, Abby." Monique's shoulders slumped.

"I know you don't, and I appreciate it. You wouldn't come clear out here to yell at me if you didn't care." She approached her friend and put a hand on her arm. "But it's my life, and I have to decide what to do with it. I need you to respect that."

Monique put her hand over Abby's. "OK, fair enough. It doesn't change how I feel, not yet, but I promise to think about it." She glanced toward her car. "I guess I should be going now. Just don't you forget, no matter what happens, good or bad, I'm here for you."

Abby managed a small smile. "I know it, Mo. I'd better go back inside before everybody wonders where I am."

Monique turned to leave, and Abby felt strangely as if arguing about her as-yet-unmade decision had brought her that much closer to making one.

Inside, Abby headed to the bathroom to splash some cool water on her face and gather her composure. Monique's unexpected disapproval had confused and angered her. She knew her friend cared and only wanted what was best for her, but dammit, it was nobody's job but her own to decide what that was.

She picked up a bottle of water in the kitchen, and returned to the deck. Molly and Marshall were still gone. They'd better not be in her hammock. She settled in the chair next to Seth and leaned over to give him a kiss on the cheek.

"Where've you been?" Seth asked, taking her hand.

"Monique stopped by to talk to me about something." They wouldn't be discussing this in front of Joey.

"Yeah, what was it?"

"I'll tell you later," Abby said, giving a tiny nod in Joey's direction. Seth nodded in return, indicating he got the message.

The three of them sat for a while, talking about inconsequential things. What kind of fish were in the lake, what the club district was like in Austin, when the new Randy Rogers Band album would be out, and some amusing stories from life on the road.

Despite her argument with Monique, Abby relaxed and was thinking about letting her eyes drift shut when she saw Dilbert come out of the woods with something in his mouth. Oh, shit, she thought. What now? She stepped out in the yard to meet the dog. "What do you have, Dilbert? Let me see."

Dilbert stopped in front of her and she saw the object was a chunk of meat. It was about the size of a softball and solid, not the ground meat they cooked earlier. This struck her as strange. The Nygaards weren't home, which was why they hadn't come over this afternoon, so it wasn't something they gave him. Other things Dilbert brought home tended to be fur covered and occasionally still alive. A feeling of deep unease snaked up her spine.

With a little encouragement, he dropped the meat and sat. Abby poked it with a finger, revealing a deep slice on one side. Unease turned to alarm. "Seth! Come here!"

Seth hurried over. He crouched beside her and looked at the chunk of meat. "What the hell is that?"

"Nothing we've given him." She pointed at the cut. "I think it's been tampered with or baited or something."

Seth picked up the meat, which Abby thought looked too fresh and bug-free to have been outside for long. Maybe early this morning. He pulled at the edges of the cut and revealed a cavity full of small, white pills.

Abby gasped. She knew she was going to be furious in a few minutes, but right now panic was in charge. Molly was a veterinary technician. "Molly! Come here! Hurry!" She heard her friend and Marshall charging up the path, and she began looking at Dilbert for signs he'd been poisoned.

Molly and Marshall ran up, looking confused and out of breath. "What's wrong?" Molly asked.

Abby's hand trembled as she pointed to the lump of meat and pills in Seth's hand. "Dilbert just came out of the woods with that. Look at all those pills in there. What the hell are they?"

Molly picked up a stick and poked at the pills. "It's Valium. I recognize it because what we use for animals is the exact same thing prescribed for people." She put down the stick. "But that's a lot of it. Did he eat any?"

Grabbing Dilbert's face and looking at the dog as if he could answer the question, Abby choked out, "I don't know!"

Seth said, "It looks like this piece was intact, but how do we know if there were more?"

Abby's heart pounded as she looked at Molly. "What do we do?"

"Hydrogen peroxide. Do you have any? And a squirt bottle or a flexible plastic cup?"

"Yes, peroxide's in the hall closet, and empty plastic bottles under the bathroom sink. Seth, can you get them?" She was not letting go of this dog.

Seth ran toward the house.

Molly checked Dilbert over. She looked in his mouth and opened his remaining eye to study the pupil. The dog seemed concerned about all the attention, but didn't struggle. Abby wondered if it was just his sweet, mellow disposition or due to a rising level of Valium in his system. Marshall and Joey stood frozen to one side, faces tight with concern.

Seth returned with the peroxide and a small bottle intended to hold shampoo or dish soap. Molly quickly filled the bottle and squirted some down Dilbert's throat. He struggled, shaking his head, but most of the peroxide went down.

"Now what?" Marshall asked.

"We wait," Molly replied. "He should start throwing up any minute. If he ate any pills, they need to come up. If there was another piece out there with this many pills in it, he's in trouble."

Abby hugged Dilbert as tears streamed down her face. "That filthy son of a bitch! Trying to kill Seth, blowing up my house, sneaking around here in the middle of the night, and now he's poisoning my dog! An innocent dog!"

Seth had one arm around Abby and one on Dilbert's side. "Your dog?"

It was part of their repertoire of running jokes, and she knew he said it reflexively. But right now it wasn't funny. "Yeah, I know, I keep saying he's not my dog. But a few days ago I didn't have a boyfriend or whatever the heck you are, either. So now I have a dog. You have a problem with that?"

"Nope."

Which was, of course, the only acceptable answer.

She might have said more, but Dilbert began making the rhythmic heaving sounds telling them the peroxide was about to produce results. Abby positioned herself with her hand across Dilbert's shoulder as he brought up the contents of his stomach. By the time he finished, he'd thrown up several large chunks of hamburger and bun, some pasta salad, an entire graham cracker—how had he managed that?—and part of what might or might not have been a chipmunk. But no sign of any pills.

Molly, who was used to dealing with what came out of one end or another of dogs, used the stick to poke through the piles. "Nope, no Valium. I think we're safe."

Drawing a deep, shuddering breath, Abby hugged Dilbert, careful not to kneel in the recently evacuated stomach contents.

Marshall walked over to Molly and casually put an arm around her. "But, Abby," he said, "why didn't he eat the meat when he found it? I mean, most dogs I know would've practically inhaled it."

Abby sat back and leaned against Seth. "Dilbert's funny that way. When I found him, his eye was infected and I had to give him antibiotics. I had a terrible time." She stroked Dilbert's head. "I tried putting them in cheese, peanut butter bread, hot dogs, you name it. But he could always tell the pills were there, and he either wouldn't touch it, or he'd eat the food and leave the medicine completely untouched. Bugged the shit out of me."

"Turned out to be a good thing today," Molly said.

Dilbert gagged again but only succeeded in producing a small puddle of foamy yellow bile. He stood up and ambled over to lie in the hole he'd dug by the deck.

Molly went to Dilbert and lifted his lip, checking the color of his gums. "He looks OK. But let his stomach rest an hour or so, and then you can try giving him some water. If he keeps it down, he can have a little food tonight."

"Thanks, Molly," Abby said, wiping her eyes. "I don't know what I'd have done if you hadn't been here."

"Well, he didn't eat any of it, so he would've been fine."

"But I might have had a fatal panic attack."

"You're tougher than you think," Molly said with a smile.

Seth went to the garage, emerging a minute later with a shovel and small bucket. He proceeded to clean up the peroxide's results and take it to the trash bin. He never said a word, but came to kneel by Dilbert after he was finished, scratching him under the chin.

Abby looked at the chunk of meat still lying where they'd dropped it. "What should we do with that?"

Molly stood, put her hands on her hips, and leaned back, stretching. Marshall seemed to find this fascinating. "If you have a container, I could take it home and put it in the clinic freezer tomorrow. You know, in case you end up needing it for evidence."

"Thanks, Molly. I can't stand to be anywhere near it. I have some empty butter tubs under the kitchen sink. I'll go get one in a minute." She didn't think she could move right now if she had to. After the argument with Monique and this rush of adrenaline, she felt drained.

A short while later, everyone gathered in the living room. Joey sprawled on the floor, idly stroking Dilbert's ears under the table. Abby went to Seth's side, and Molly sat with Marsh. The party, however, was definitely over. It wasn't long before Molly started making "gee, isn't it time to be going?" noises, and Marshall agreed. It was decided they would take Molly home on the way back to the motel. Seth walked out to the car with them, and took his time coming back.

He'd been awfully quiet ever since she'd called him off the deck to see what Dilbert found in the woods. He answered questions briefly, his voice even softer than usual. Abby knew he was extremely fond of Dilbert and blamed himself for this latest violation, just as he did the others.

She gave Dilbert some water. He lapped it eagerly, and it stayed down, much to her relief. She puttered around the house, working off the remnants of her nervous energy on mundane tasks. From time to time Seth came to her and offered a gentle kiss or touch, as if he wanted to comfort her but wasn't sure how. That wasn't like him. He was usually very direct when dealing with things of an emotional nature. Oh, well, she thought. We've all had a very upsetting afternoon. He'll be better in a little while.

He told her he was going upstairs to forward the photo of Drew Purcell to Pete and Jackie, just to be safe. He must have found a lot of other mail waiting for him, because he was gone a long time. When he came back down, he didn't join her in the living room. He went in the bedroom, and when he didn't come out, Abby went to see what was keeping him. She found him stuffing his clothes in a canvas bag he must have found in the laundry room. She froze just inside the door. "Seth, what are you doing?"

He sat the bag on the bed. It took him forever to lift his head to look at her. "I have to leave."

"Leave? What do you mean? You can't leave." She felt as if she were hearing her own voice from the far end of a long tunnel.

"Abby, I don't have a choice anymore. He was here. Again. He tried to get Dilbert out of the way so he'd have a free shot at us. At you. I went up to check mail, and I found this!" He pointed at a crumpled sheet of paper on the floor by the bed.

As Abby bent to retrieve it, Seth said, "The website has been backed up from all the traffic, and Victor just received a bunch of messages sent earlier today. It came to my website e-mail, not my personal one."

The plain white printer paper in her hand, Abby leaned against the dresser to read it. What she saw almost took her legs from beneath her. The address was an anonymous remailing service, and the words were chilling:

Clock's ticking, Caldwell. Hey, is she a screamer? No, don't tell me. If she's around when I catch up to you, I'll just find out for myself. I think I'll even let you watch. And listen.

"You see, Abby? He came right out and said it. I have to go so he won't hurt you." His voice was thick and his eyes were red-rimmed, the way blue-eyed people look when they're trying very hard not to cry.

"You...can't...leave," she repeated. Because when people left, when people made you cry and left, they never came back, did they? She put her hand on the wall to steady herself, as the whole room seemed to sway.

Seth came to her, took her hand, and led her to the bed. He sat with her on the edge and held her. "It's me he wants. This all started a long time before I met you. If he can make it worse by hurting you, he will. But we have to be together, or it won't give him what he wants, which is to torture me and watch me suffer." Her head was bowed, and he kissed her forehead softly. "If I go and he knows I'm not with you, he'll leave you alone. I'll come back when they catch him, when this is all over."

"Will you?" Her voice was harsh and bitter. Nobody ever came back.

"I will, I swear."

He swore? Swearing was like a vow, and people broke those all the time. "And what am I supposed to do until then? Tell me that." Her voice was so raw it was almost strangled. "I'm supposed to watch the news and wonder for days, weeks, months, if that's the day he's going to find you?" She was less afraid of what might happen if Drew Purcell found them together than she was of how she'd handle a world where Seth left her. She told Monique just a few hours ago Seth would never do this. Maybe her certainty had been viewed as arrogance by the Fates, and this was her punishment.

His hand trembled as it clung to hers. After a long moment, he touched her cheek and turned her face until she met his eyes. "I want you to go to your mom's place. Now, before it gets dark. Will you do that for me?"

"I won't leave my house."

"Please. I need to know you're safe."

"Then stay."

"If I thought it was the best way to keep him away from you, don't you think I'd do it? But no, if I'm here, I'm inviting him right to your door." He stood up, crossed to the closet, and began cramming shirts in the bag, the hangers rattling on the rod. "Don't you think this is killing me? It's ripping my fucking guts out! Goddammit, I knew I wasn't good for you. You'd be better off if I never came back."

Suddenly she couldn't breathe, couldn't move. Was her heart still beating? She couldn't tell. This was too much. In that instant, she almost wished she'd never met Seth Caldwell. Those people who spouted the "it's better to have loved and lost" cliché were a bunch of fucking morons. It wasn't better.

It was as if a switch flipped at the base of her brain. She stopped thinking. She stopped feeling. If she stopped, this couldn't hurt anymore. As far as she was concerned, he was already gone. She dropped the tattered message to the floor, stood, and walked out the bedroom door.

He caught up to her in the living room. "Abby, please. I have to..."

She cut him off and looked at him with eyes hot and dry. "No. Just go."

"I love you, Abby-Kat." He tried to grab her hand, but she turned away.

"Don't say it. If you're leaving, you don't get to say it. And don't ever call me that name again." Her hands clenched at her side. "Do you want to know why Monique was here?" She didn't wait for an answer. "She came to tell me being with you was a mistake. That it all happened too fast, and I didn't know you. She said you'd leave me. I guess she was right, but I bet she never thought it would be tonight." She choked on a single, bitter laugh. "I sure didn't."

He took a step and extended his hand, reaching for her again, but she ignored it and walked into the kitchen. She poured a big glass of water and stood over the sink sipping it. She heard him on the phone.

"Joey, where are you, man? I need you to come get me. Right now. Just do it. I'll talk to you when you get here. Hurry, OK? Thanks. See you in a few." He hung up and returned to the bedroom.

While he was in there, Abby went out on the deck. She didn't want to see him leave. She stood, staring at the lake and smoking a cigarette, until she heard the door ease open behind her. She knew he was watching her and if she turned, he'd come to her. But letting go of him would be too hard, so she kept her back to him. After a minute, the door closed. She heard the side door open and close, but she stayed where she was. Eventually she heard a car pull into the gravel driveway. The door slammed, and the car drove away.

She went back inside and dumped the nearly full bowl of pasta salad in the trash. She turned off her phone, poured a glass of wine, and sat on the couch petting her dog.

Chapter Nineteen

Seth put the bag and his guitar in the back of Joey's car, then slumped in the passenger seat. He thought he might be sick, and breathed deeply until the feeling subsided.

"Man, what the..."

"Not now, Joey. I'll talk about it when we get to your room, but not yet." He was still so raw he knew he'd break down if he tried to explain. It wasn't as if he couldn't let Joey see this side of him. But he felt like if he fell apart now he would shatter so completely he'd never get himself together again.

Joey drove, casting frequent, troubled looks his way, but he respected Seth's request and didn't say anything.

They pulled into the motel parking lot, and Seth grabbed the bag and guitar from the car and carried them upstairs while Joey unlocked the room. Once inside, Seth carefully placed his things on the floor by the closet and headed straight for the half-full bottle of Wild Turkey he spied on the dresser. He unwrapped a cup from a small molded plastic tray, sloshed a generous serving into it, and drank. It burned like hell, but he didn't care. He stood by the window, staring out at nothing.

Joey came up behind him and put a hand on his shoulder. "OK, man, I can't wait it out anymore. Tell me what happened."

"I left."

"I figured that out, Einstein. But the only reason you better be here is because she kicked you out. In which case you need to give her time to cool down. Then I'm taking you back so you can throw yourself on the ground and beg her to forgive you for whatever dumbass thing you did. After that, you start kissing her feet, then move north and don't stop till you get to her earrings." He crossed the room and flopped on his bed and leaned back against the headboard.

Seth drained the cup and poured a refill before sitting on the other bed, facing Joey. "You saw what happened today. That son of a bitch was there again. He tried to poison Abby's dog, which tells me he was planning to come back." He took another deep swallow of Wild Turkey. It didn't burn as much going down this time. He hoped he could get numb enough to get through tonight.

"Yeah, and now Abby's there alone. Brilliant fucking move."

"No, Joey, there's more." He pulled the crumpled sheet of paper from his pocket and flung it at his friend and waited as he read it. Joey's face paled, and he put the message on the table between the beds. "It's me he wants. Sure, if Abby's around when he finally catches up to me, he'd hurt her to make it worse. But he's not going to go after her unless she's with me." He closed his eyes for a few seconds and waited for a wave of nausea to pass. "You remember how he was during the trial. He loves the spotlight. He was always talking to anybody with a microphone. He wants the drama, and if I'm not there to be the audience, he'll leave her alone."

Joey reached for a bottle of water on the bed table, opened it, and handed it to Seth. "Slow down on the booze, man. You need to think."

"I don't want to think. Thinking sucks."

"You have no choice. You fucked up royally, and you're going to have to be sober to fix it."

"What is there to fix? I had to leave! If I stay and something happens to her, Purcell not only wins, he gets the bonus prize, too. If I can hurt a little now and know she's still alive because I found a way to do it, that's how it's gotta be."

"You don't get it, do you? It's not only about you anymore. It hasn't been about you since Abby ran over Cujo." Joey faced Seth across the space between the beds. "You've been part of a band all your life. When does one of us make decisions for everybody else?"

Seth shrugged. "Never."

"And you, my friend, are no longer a solo act. You're part of a duo, and you just made one fucking whopper of a decision all on your own and dropped it right in Abby's lap. How do you think it made her feel?"

Sometimes Joey made too damned much sense. Seth started to worry about what would happen if he was wrong, but he forced the possibility from his mind. "I don't believe Purcell will go after her if I'm not there. The farther away I am, the safer she is. In case he isn't watching the road to Abby's house, or however he's kept track of me, we should go over to the Shamrock. Let people see I'm there and not at the lake." Plus, they probably had more Wild Turkey.

"That is not the fucking point!"

"What could be more important than keeping her from getting hurt?" He flung the half-empty bottle of water at the dresser. It impacted the edge with a heavy, dull sound and ricocheted across the room, splashing water in all directions.

"You don't think she's hurt now? Look, Drew Purcell might or might not take it in his head to go after her even if you're not there. Based on the note, he probably won't, but he might. But it's a one hundred percent certainty Abby is hurting like hell right now."

Seth stood and began pacing. "I'd rather have her upset now than dead later."

"You think she's upset? You're upset if Taco Bell is out of guacamole. I know how things are between you two. I've known you forever and I can read you like a book. But right now I'm wondering if I've been wrong, and you're actually the biggest fucking idiot I've ever met." He stood and grabbed Seth's arm, forcing him to turn to look at him. "You. Left. Her."

"I know it," Seth snapped. "I told her I was coming back as soon as they caught Purcell."

"And how does that help her? What if Purcell shows up here tonight and blows your brains out? She'll never see you again, and she'll always wonder if it would've turned out differently if you'd stayed there with her. If she'd been strong enough to make you stay. You say you left so she'd be safe and you wouldn't have to deal with it if she died because you were there. But hey, ass jack, what if you get killed because you left? Because that's how she'll see it. And she has to live with it."

"Nothing will happen, and they'll catch Purcell. Then I can go back."

"You think it'd be simple? Think about what Abby's been through. Look what happened when people left her. Her ex-husband, her dad. All that shit when what she thought, what she wanted, didn't fucking matter. And everybody knows how musicians are. They blow into town, break a bunch of hearts, and blow back out again. She doesn't believe it now, but she might start to. As far as she's concerned, gone is gone, and people don't come back."

Seth sat on the bed again, his knees suddenly weak. Was that really what he'd done? Had he made Abby think he didn't respect her courage and strength? Had he just become one more person who'd left her? He put his head in his hands. "Joey, she'd be better off if I don't go back. I never should've thought she could be happy with somebody like me." He threaded his fingers through his hair and gripped tightly, trying to pull the right answer out by the roots. "Oh, holy fucking hell. I have to figure out what to do."

"Well don't think too long, because by my calculations if you're going to fix this, which I strongly advise, I have to get you back out there in about the next fifty-one minutes. Then we have to hope she lets you in."

Seth stretched out on the bed and stared at the ceiling, paying unnecessary attention to a badly patched water stain in the corner. "Joey, I'm fucked. Whatever I do, I'm going to lose her."

"Wrong. You're both at risk from Purcell. You might be the main target, but it's better if you're together, watching each other's backs. Or fronts. Whatever. And don't give me a song and dance about not being good enough for her. She loves you. At the moment I'm not sure why, but it's her decision." Joey picked up the now-empty water bottle from the floor, filled it in the bathroom, and handed it to Seth. "Drink this, man, all of it." Joey watched until Seth drained half the bottle. "Now the way I see it, you have one chance to pull this out of the fire."

"I don't want to hurt her. And I can't let her get hurt because of me, either."

"Shut your mouth and listen. Let's say this plays out the way you tried to set it up. You leave, Purcell comes after you, gets caught, and you go back to Abby. You're thinking it's happily ever after, but your head is up your ass. First of all, I'd be real surprised if she let you anywhere near her, because you took the trust she put in you and threw it in her face. Even if she took you back, it wouldn't be the same. She'd never trust you the way she did before."

"This isn't sounding too good so far, Joe."

"I'm not done. That was the way you were trying to play it. And you're right, it's not good. But it was the best you could've hoped for, because you didn't think it through." He sat on the edge of his bed and leaned forward, his elbows on his knees, and stared until Seth gave him his full attention. "You have to go back to her, and you have to do it as quick as I can haul your sorry ass out there. Right now she's still working this through. I bet she's a total wreck, but it's not real to her yet. If you let her get to the point where it's real, it's too late. You have to tell her you made a gigantic mistake, you're sorry you panicked and went all caveman, and whatever happens till they catch this guy, you'll get through it together. Then you hope like you never hoped before in your life she loves you enough to forgive you for what you did to her."

Seth scrubbed his hands over his face. "What if she's not there? I told her to go to her mom's."

"She's there." Joey sounded certain.

"What if her mom's with her, or Molly?"

"Molly's with Marsh. I dropped him off at her house when we took her home. She's bringing him back later or tomorrow or whenever they can pry themselves apart. And Abby isn't going to call Marilyn. Eventually, but not tonight." Joey shook his head. "No, she's alone, and she's doing a lot of thinking."

Seth lay there, stunned. The thought of Abby sitting alone, probably hating him, tore something loose deep inside. Had he really screwed everything up so badly, when all he'd wanted to do was protect her? And was Joey right, and there was still some hope of undoing the damage? "How'd you get so smart?"

Joey cracked his first smile since Seth had gotten in the car. He held up his left hand and pointed to his wedding ring. "Caroline."

Seth dragged his fingers through his hair and tried to organize his thoughts. Maybe the Wild Turkey hadn't been such a great idea after all, though it sure had seemed like it at the time. He chugged the rest of the water and swung his legs over the side of the bed. He needed to get the blood flowing and burn off the alcohol. He stalked back and forth across the room for a while, drinking another bottle of water, and ran the whole range of scenarios through his mind.

He was glad Joey waited quietly by the window, letting him work things out. His friend had seen him deal with problems plenty of times, though none as critical as this, and he knew when to stop talking and let Seth think.

There were no guarantees he'd still have Abby in his life, no matter what he did. She could refuse to take him back, whether it was tonight or months from now, whenever the threat of Drew Purcell was behind them. Or there was still the sickening thought Purcell could kill her to completely destroy Seth before ending his life. He felt the risk was elevated the closer she was to him, but he also recognized the need to make decisions and face uncertainty together.

The only absolutely sure thing was if he left Abby, even if it was to keep her safe, he'd lose her forever.

"Joey, take me back to her."

* * *

The late afternoon sun shifted toward early evening. Abby hadn't looked at the clock when Seth left, so she wasn't sure how long he'd been gone. Was it an hour? Two? She knew it was a mistake to try to answer that question. If she started counting hours, what would happen when those hours turned to days? She wouldn't even think about longer increments of time.

The bottle of wine she'd brought with her to the living room was empty. It had started out half-full. There was another bottle in the kitchen, but she didn't have the energy to uncork it. Sitting still was the way to go. Dilbert had gotten up a few times to drink more water and he hadn't vomited again, so she'd give him some food soon. But not just yet.

She had asked Seth not to leave, and he left anyway. She'd stopped just short of begging, or maybe she did beg. She guessed it depended on your definition. Now she might never see him again. He could be killed before they caught the man who had targeted him or he could change his mind about being with her. He might find, once he'd spent some time away, he had merely been caught up in the heightened emotion of a crazy situation, and coming back to her no longer felt important.

He was still all around her. She breathed in his scent on the cushions behind her, and she knew what would happen if she went to lie on his side of the bed. She would be wrapped in his memory, but alone. She couldn't sleep there tonight. Tomorrow, well, she'd have to see. There were probably strands of his hair on the pillow, and she wondered if he'd forgotten any of his clothes in her hamper.

He was here, yet he wasn't. He might never be here again, and she had no way to know. There wasn't a calendar she could mark, like families who sent their loved ones off for military deployment. They didn't know if their people were ever coming back, either, but at least they had a date by which to expect them home, if they were coming at all.

She hadn't done anything wrong, but perhaps she should have done something differently. Seth had asked her to let go of the safety line to which she'd clung for years, and she had been too frightened. Should she have pushed aside her fears and said yes right away? Or should she have refused outright? Had the way she'd handled it made her seem uncertain or weak? Was that why he didn't trust her to stand by him while he faced the most serious crisis of his life?

She didn't feel rage. She didn't think she had it in her anymore. There had been plenty of rage before, when David left. She'd also cursed the Fates when her father died, and when she'd lost the baby she hadn't known existed. She'd burned out the rage while working on her house. She helped Clancy and Butch, and every nail she pounded into place released some of the gnawing anger and took her that much closer to building her new life.

When all the rage was gone, she never bothered to fill it with anything else. The emptiness was peaceful in its own way. So that was what she'd do now. When she was able to think about getting off the couch, she'd go back to what worked before. She would write, sometimes she would see her mother and her friends, and she'd write some more. Some people said writing was a lonely profession, but she didn't think so. She was comfortable in the world she created.

Dilbert removed his head from her lap and climbed down to get another drink. She sat forward to follow his progress around the end of the couch, and something on the floor caught her eye. Against the leg of the coffee table, almost lost in the pattern of the rug, was a guitar pick. The Dead End Road logo was clearly visible on the side she could see. The side hidden from her view would have the imprinted signature of the pick's owner, and she hoped it was Marshall's.

She shouldn't look, but she wouldn't be able to stop staring at it until she did. She reached down with chilled fingers and lifted the guitar pick from the floor. She held it for a moment, unable to breathe. At last, she opened her hand and turned the pick over. Seth's signature. It was his. This very afternoon he'd probably used this pick to play one of the songs they'd written together, and the irony of the thought threatened to destroy her.

She sat back on the couch and drew up her legs. Wrapping her arms around her knees, she clutched the pick so tightly it bit into her fingers as she let hot, silent tears bathe her face. Dilbert jumped back onto the couch and nudged her elbow. She draped her arm around the dog, the pick still in her other hand. She stayed there until the tears stopped, but she made no move to get up.

Abby continued to sit there, forcing herself back into the empty place where things didn't hurt so much. She knew how to do this. She'd done it before.

Dilbert abruptly jumped off the couch and began pacing from the hallway, to the French doors, and back again, whining softly. Fear prickled her spine. What had attracted the dog's attention? Had she locked the doors? Probably not. She'd planned to check them when she fed Dilbert. Eventually. Besides, what difference did it make? If someone wanted in badly enough, all they had to do was knock out a panel in the French doors and open the latch.

She was about to go lock both doors when she heard a car pull into the driveway. It didn't have the distinctive sound of her mother's Volkswagen. Maybe it was the Nygaards stopping by on their way home. She didn't imagine someone coming to kill her would park right in her driveway, but perhaps she should be more concerned than she was.

The slam of a door was followed by the sound of the car pulling out of the driveway and heading back the way it came. Abby felt a flutter of hope in her chest, but smothered it. Hope only led to disappointment, and she couldn't bear any more.

Dilbert whirled in circles at the entrance to the hallway then stood, his tail wagging and his front feet prancing with excitement. Abby heard the door open, and ordered her mind to be still. Don't jump to conclusions. Don't hope.

At the sound of footsteps she lowered her eyes because, dammit, she did have some hope after all. By turning away, she could delay the disappointment for a few more precious instants. The footsteps stopped, and she steeled herself and looked.

Seth stood at the end of the hall, holding the canvas bag and his guitar case. She almost had to turn away from the intensity of his gaze. The lines of his face were harsh, and the rims of his eyes were red and swollen. He looked as rough as she felt.

He put down the bag and guitar case, never taking his eyes from hers. He approached cautiously, as if he expected her to bolt. He sank to his knees in front of her, his hands hovering uncertainly. She lowered her legs from their drawn-up position, placing her feet on the floor, and he put his hands on the couch on either side of her and bowed his head. His hair brushed her legs, but he didn't quite touch her himself. It seemed like he wasn't sure whether she would permit it. Should she?

Abby's hand trembled as she let her fingers rest on the back of his head. He breathed in, and his forehead came to rest on her thighs. She put her hands on his shoulders, still clutching the guitar pick, then bent forward and let her lips brush his hair. They were still, until he brought his hands to her sides and raised his head. His face was wet, and she realized hers was, too.

Still on his knees, he said, "I didn't know."

She blinked, confused. "What didn't you know?"

"I didn't know what I was doing, what it would do to you. I thought it was the right thing, but I blew it."

"You were leaving me."

He swallowed. "I was. I wanted to keep you safe, but I didn't think it through. I only knew if I wasn't here, he wouldn't come after you. But I shouldn't have made the decision on my own. It wasn't fair, and I can't tell you how sorry I am. You deserve more from me."

The ghost of her banished rage flickered around the edges of her consciousness. Hell, yes, he was wrong. How dare he make life-changing decisions for her and tell her it was for her own good? How could he hurt her so badly she tried to retreat into that numb, empty place again? She wanted to say these things, and maybe at some point she would. But for now she soothed the anger back to its resting place. After all, he'd done the one thing nobody else had ever done, and the only thing she needed. He came back.

"We were supposed to face this together," she said.

"I know." He almost choked on the words. "I thought I'd go crazy trying to figure out what to do. All I wanted was to do the right thing. I would have come back."

"Maybe. But I can't live with 'maybe,' Seth. I trusted you, and you left anyway."

"I was wrong. Is it too late?" The grief in his eyes felt like a dagger through her heart.

His question required a yes or no answer, but she couldn't give him one. The answer was there, but some vestige of battered pride kept her from telling him what it was. The best she could say was, "You're here now." An acknowledgment he had returned, he was here with her, and she wasn't ordering him to leave.

Seth rose to his feet and took her hands to bring her to stand in front of him. He hesitated when he found her left hand clutched into a fist, until he gently uncurled her fingers and saw what she was holding. His breath caught and he closed his eyes, a flash of pain shooting across his face. He took the pick from her hand, placed it on the table, and enfolded her in his arms.

She sagged against him and felt the warmth where their bodies met. His heart pounded against her chest, and she lifted her face to his. Lips she'd thought she might never feel again met hers, and the pieces of her world moved back into alignment.

His arms tightened around her, and his kisses deepened. She tasted whiskey blended with his own smoky-sweet flavor. She wrapped her arms around his neck, fingers twisting through his hair, and kissed him back.

She thought she must be dreaming, asleep on the couch, until he drew back from her and looked into her eyes. "Abby, please tell me I can stay. Tell me I didn't ruin everything."

"If you stay, nothing's ruined." She had to believe it. She did believe it.

"I'll make it up to you. I swear."

"You already have."

His next kiss was soft and full of promise. "What happens now?"

Abby felt a ghost of a smile rise through the receding fog of numbness. "I think first we take care of Dilbert and get your things out of the hall."

"Then?"

"If I have to tell you, you haven't been paying attention."

He drew an unsteady breath and brushed her hair away from her face. With his lips against her forehead, he murmured, "I love you, Abby-Kat."

"I know. I love you, too." Dilbert bumped against her leg, and she looked down. "I'm going to give him a little food, and take him out for a minute. Go put your stuff away, OK?"

Seth moved off to take his things from the hallway and back where they belonged. Abby scooped a small amount of leftover rice and cottage cheese into Dilbert's bowl and watched him eat it. When he licked the last speck from his whiskers, she surprised him by attaching a leash to his collar. He could protest if he wanted, but she was keeping both her boys very close to her tonight.

After a quick trip around the yard, she returned to find Seth standing on the deck watching her. She'd felt perfectly safe with Dilbert by her side. He would know if anyone lurked nearby. But it was nice to know Seth was watching out for them, too. That's how it was supposed to be. Looking after each other.

Back inside, Dilbert settled on the couch, and Seth took Abby's hand and led her to their room. She saw all his clothes neatly folded and placed exactly where they'd been earlier in the day. His guitar leaned against the dresser where her mother had put it on Saturday. She could almost imagine the last few hours hadn't happened. Almost. But she would work on it.

He undressed her quickly, with no ritual or finesse. When he joined her in their bed, his urgency stole the breath from her lungs. She responded with equal fervor, desperate to wash away the earlier anguish with pure, raw passion. As his hands and mouth swept over her body, she watched his every move. She told herself it wasn't so if one day he were gone again she'd always have these memories, and it was mostly true.

She touched and tasted every inch of him in turn, thinking how terrible it would have been to have never loved him like this again. She pushed the thought away, because she believed him. He would stay. And so would she.

He entered her with a crushing need that didn't lend itself to subtlety. She welcomed it, because she needed to be claimed as much as she needed to claim him. He drove into her over and over, the headboard protesting, but the sound was soon overwhelmed by the hoarse cry coming from her own throat. Her hands clawed at his back. She knew she must be marking him, but she didn't stop. Her body shuddered with each thrust as he took her closer and closer to completion. At last, the storm broke, surging through her and setting every nerve aflame. She felt him come with her, wildly, with a shout, almost a sob. She clung to him, wanting this moment to last, and wanting to share every last instant of it with him as fully as it was possible to share.

Finally still, they sprawled in a tangle of relaxed limbs and sweat-dampened hair. He whispered to her countless times he loved her, and he was sorry. She returned each declaration with a kiss, and told him it was OK, they were OK.

Sometime later, she smiled. "Caldwell, if it's going to be like this every time, I'm going to need a hip replacement."

He laughed, and just like that, the ease was back between them, and she knew she hadn't been lying when she said they were OK.

He took her at her word, and the next time was gentler. There was lots of teasing and playing and laughing and absolutely no doubt this was where they were both meant to be. Eventually they did sleep, but they woke each other often throughout the night for a kiss or touch meant to reassure themselves and each other.

After one such interlude, Abby lay with her head on his chest. She prepared to tell him what had become crystal clear to her the second he'd crossed the living room and knelt at her feet. "Seth, I know what to do now."

He looked at her, and apprehension drifted across his expression. "About what?"

"Wait," she said. "First I need to tell you what I figured out. You need to know the reasoning behind it, or I don't think you'll understand." She sat up, leaning into the pillows against the headboard, and Seth did the same. He looked like he expected the world to end at any moment, and she gave him a slight smile to ease his worry. "When you walked in the door tonight, I saw something that should have been obvious before. When you left, I thought you were making decisions for me, maybe even being controlling, or at the very least not respecting what I wanted. What I needed." He opened his mouth to correct her, but she put a hand on his chest to tell him to be patient. "But that wasn't it at all. You were terrified. Probably even more than I was. That's why you left."

He nodded and put his hand over hers. "I was never more scared in my life."

Abby lifted his hand and kissed it, then returned their clasped hands to his chest. "But you thought it through and worked past the fear. No matter how frightening it was to come back here, because I know you believe it puts me at risk, you got past it and did the right thing."

"Maybe I'm being selfish, but I realized I couldn't stay away. Not if you'd let me come back."

"It's not selfish to let me decide if you're worth the risk. It's not selfish to trust me." He still looked worried, but she felt strangely calm. "I figured if you could work around that huge, terrifying roadblock, I could, too. I wasn't even sure exactly what I was afraid of. Being hurt, losing myself, not knowing every day was going to be just like the one before. It was easier not to do anything, but it couldn't go on if I really love you. And I do." He smiled. "So, I'm not going to let a bunch of unidentifiable, irrational fears keep me from doing what I want more than anything."

She felt the hitch of his breath under their hands. "And what's that?"

"Do you even listen to me when I speak?" she teased. "I'm going with you, of course."

His eyes shone, and he squeezed her hand. "People will tell you it's not a good idea."

"Probably. But if you aren't allowed to make my decisions, I'm very sure nobody else is, either." She put her head on his shoulder, her lips not far from his ear. "Nothing in this world is for sure. The only thing I am sure of is I want to be with you, wherever it is. And I won't be so afraid I don't try."

Seth reached up to stroke her hair. "I'll spend every day making sure you don't regret it."

"No regrets, Seth. Not ever. The only regret is letting fear take away a chance at happiness."

He kissed her, and before long he was making sure she was very, very happy in more ways than she could count.

As he held her, sweat still cooling on their skin, he said, "Knowing you'll come with me is the best news I've ever had, but right now I don't want to leave this exact spot."

"We'll have to, eventually." She snuggled closer to his side, reveling in the feel of him. "The contractor is coming to start work on the other room tomorrow." She glanced at the clock. "I mean today. It's almost morning already."

"Damn. I don't suppose we could just keep the door shut?"

"Only if we can also convince him to wear earplugs. Besides, I think we should go see Joey and let him know we worked things out. I want to thank him for talking some sense into you before things went too far."

"How do you know that's what happened?"

"When you make up your mind, it's made up, but you're always willing to listen to Joey. And I think he's smart enough to know what would happen if he tried to pull something similar with Caroline."

Seth nodded. "I can't say you're wrong. So, yeah, we'll go see him in the morning. Marsh, too, if he's back from Molly's."

"He went to Molly's? I wondered if he would."

"Yeah, but don't worry. I'll talk to him, make sure he's not playing games."

"I'm not worried. Not really. But after we check in with them, I have an idea where we can go while the house is put back together."

"Where would that be?"

"Somewhere quiet and beautiful. But I'm not saying any more. I want you to be surprised."

"I'm not sure I can stand any more surprises," he said, his hand gliding over her hip.

"You'll like this one. Trust me."

"I do." His arms tightened around her. The heavy emotion in his voice told her he meant he trusted her with far more than the next day's destination. As she drifted back to sleep, her heart felt so full she couldn't imagine tomorrow could hold anything other than more of this utter contentment.

Chapter Twenty

Abby sat on the couch with the laptop balanced on her knees while Seth leaned against her, his chin on her shoulder. She'd brought the computer downstairs to check her e-mail, but he convinced her to help him look at real estate listings in Austin. Speechless at first, she understood when he pointed out his apartment was more like a dorm room. Seth wanted her to have someplace that felt like home when they were in Texas. Her brief hesitation before she started typing key words into the search engine had almost stopped his heart. Again. He might never stop kicking himself for jeopardizing their future. He'd dodged a bullet, and he knew it.

"A lot of these houses have pools," Abby said. "Do we want a pool?"

"Mmmm. Probably not. As much as we'll be away, we'd have to hire somebody to take care of it." Though the thought of late night swimsuit-free rendezvous with her did have a very strong appeal.

"You mean we'd need a pool boy? I could live with that. Twenty-four, tanned, no shirt…"

He poked her in the ribs. "I was having second thoughts because I just remembered pool sex, but now you can forget it. No pool."

"Rats. I need to learn to keep my mouth shut." She was still smiling as she continued scrolling through properties.

With his chin on her shoulder, he couldn't resist nuzzling her neck. Her hair brushed his cheek and he breathed in its fresh scent. He remembered how much he'd enjoyed rinsing the shampoo from her hair earlier, watching the suds sluice over her wet skin. This prompted him to suggest another important feature to consider in their house hunting. "Find one with a really big master bath."

"I already entered it in the search criteria."

How lucky was he?

They bookmarked several possibilities, and Abby e-mailed the agents to make appointments to view the properties next week. "I liked the one with the big, arched window in the upstairs bedroom. That'd be a nice office."

Seth heard the rumble and clatter of a large vehicle approaching the house. "Either it's your contractor or we're being invaded."

"Sounds like Clancy." She put the computer on the coffee table and went out to meet him.

Seth continued to look at houses and marked a few he wanted to show Abby. They were close to where Joey and Caroline lived, and he thought she'd enjoy being near the other couple.

Abby returned, accompanied by a middle-aged man wearing jeans, a heavily laden tool belt, and a Grateful Dead T-shirt. His shaggy, graying hair was caught back in a ponytail, and his beard was long and unruly. Was Jerry Garcia really dead or had he simply run away to northern Minnesota to be a contractor?

"Seth, this is Clancy Soderstrom. He built this place, so if anybody can put it back together, he's the man."

Clancy offered his hand to Seth. "I hear you're tryin' to take our girl here away from us."

Shaking the man's hand, Seth replied, "Nobody takes Abby anywhere she doesn't want to go. We might be on the road a lot, though."

"Don't worry about me, Clancy," Abby said, nudging the burly man in the shoulder. "I'm a big girl."

"I know it, Abby. Don't get your panties in a twist. I'm just playin' with you." He headed toward the spare room. Abby and Seth followed. The contractor spent several minutes taking a look around and describing the repairs he would make.

"Thanks, Clancy. Is Butch coming to help you?"

"Yeah, he should be here shortly. He did a nice job with the temporary repair." He pulled back the edge of the pleated sheet to better inspect Butch's handiwork.

"Not a drop came through when it rained," Abby said. "If you have things under control, we're going to head to town. We thought we'd find something to do to keep us out of your hair while you're working."

"You go ahead. If I run into any trouble, I'll call you or Marilyn."

Seth accompanied Abby to the kitchen, doing nothing other than watch her. He liked the way her snug red shirt set off her dark hair, and how she leaned against the sink with one foot propped on her knee. She packed some things, including two of the chocolate croissants left over from their breakfast, into a small cooler.

"Somebody going on a picnic?" he asked. It was definitely a nice day for it. This time of the year could still be chilly in Minnesota, but other than the rain on Saturday night, the weather had been beautiful.

She closed the lid and sat the cooler on the floor. "I'm not confirming or denying. But there's something I want you to do before we leave."

"I thought you said we couldn't do that while Clancy was here."

"Oh, stop it," Abby said with a laugh. "No, would you go out and check the trail where Dilbert found the meat and make sure there isn't any more? I've been afraid to let him outside without a leash until we look."

He hated being reminded of the dog's near disaster and how much it had distressed Abby. "Sure. If there's anything still there, I could probably find it by the smell by now."

He followed the path from the side yard all the way to the Nygaards', casting his eyes well into the weeds and underbrush on both sides. Other than a small, bare patch that seemed to have an unusual number of flies buzzing around, he didn't see anything suspicious. He returned to the house, as satisfied as he could expect to be there were no more nasty surprises lying in wait for the happy-go-lucky dog. Abby visibly relaxed when he told her.

"I need to pack some things for Dilbert," Abby said. "I wasn't going to bring him, but I'm not ready to leave him yet."

"I don't want to leave him, either. What does he need?"

"There's a canteen in the hall closet, and a folding nylon bowl. If you find those and fill the canteen, I'll put some of his treats in a bag." She was already crouched, rummaging in a cabinet for Dilbert's goodies.

Seth found the canteen, and they were soon in the Jeep and headed toward town. She even let him drive, saying she wanted to keep an eye on Dilbert. He hadn't ridden in a car often, and she wanted to be sure he didn't try to drive.

They were on Buchanan Street approaching the center of town when Abby asked him to park along the curb near the park. "We can walk Dilbert a little before we go to the motel."

"Probably a good idea. I should call and make sure Marsh's up and decent. No telling when he rolled in." He turned on his phone and waited for it to pick up service.

"I was going to call Molly, but figured if she hadn't called me she was either at work or…busy."

Seth imagined he'd get the full report soon, whether he wanted it or not. Marshall never had a problem with kissing and telling. He hoped if things heated up last night, Marsh'd have the discretion not to shoot his mouth off in front of Abby.

He called Joey's phone and learned they were both up, but Marshall was still trying to get his eyelids above half-mast, having rolled in at 5:00 a.m. "Just make sure he has clothes on. Abby doesn't need to see that."

"She's with you?"

"Yeah, man. We'll talk in a few." He disconnected and watched Abby lead Dilbert past a handy row of bushes, and they started down the sidewalk toward the motel.

When Joey opened the door, Dilbert bounded into the room. He made straight for Marshall, who was sprawled on his rumpled bed, wearing the same clothes he'd had on yesterday. He walked across Marsh's chest and sat at his shoulder, waiting for a welcoming chin scratch. As soon as he got his breath back after a paw to the diaphragm, Marshall complied.

Joey leaned on the dresser. "So, crisis averted?"

Seth stepped forward and gripped his friend's hand. "Yeah, once you pointed out what a fucking moron I am."

Joey pulled him into a backslapping hug. "No, all you needed was a reality check." He turned to Abby. "Sometimes he has a head like a brick, but he means well."

She went up to Joey and gave him a warm hug and a kiss on the cheek. "Thank you," Seth heard her whisper. Apparently their tried and true tactic of joking to avoid the gravity of tough situations didn't work with Abby. It must be a guy thing.

Seth looked at his friends and grinned. "We have some more news, too."

"Am I gonna be an uncle?" Marshall joked, winking at Seth.

"No, butt-munch. You'll have to channel your uncle-related fantasies elsewhere." He took Abby's hand. "We did a lot of talking last night…"

"Among other things, I'm sure," Marshall chuckled.

Seth sighed theatrically. "Again with the crackin' wise. Do you want to hear this or not?"

"If he doesn't shut up, I'm flushing all his bandannas," Joey said. "Ignore him. Tell me."

Seth almost couldn't speak around his huge smile. "Long story short, Abby's going to come with us when we head out."

This resulted in another round of hugs and backslaps, and more kisses to Abby's cheek.

Finally, congratulations out of the way, Marshall looked at the clock. "If we're going to go eat lunch or breakfast or whatever the hell it's time for, I'm going to take a quick shower." He grabbed jeans and a T-shirt from an open suitcase on the floor and disappeared into the bathroom.

Abby shook her head. "Does he own any shirts with sleeves?"

"Not many," Seth said. "He says he paid good money for his tattoos, and he ought to be able to show 'em off."

"Guess it's a good thing he doesn't have them on his ass," Abby said.

"Oh, he does," Joey said, nodding. "And there have been incidents."

Seth laughed, remembering. "I think the last time was at the bar in Biloxi, where he failed to learn about Jäegermeister."

Joey sat on the bed and started rubbing Dilbert's side. "Yeah, I always told him the two things were related, but he won't believe me."

Seth wasn't sure if he should ask his next question with Abby present, but he reasoned Joey would be tactful if the news was less than ideal. "Did he say how things went with Molly?" He tried to sound casual, but Abby's direct look and raised eyebrow left no doubt she expected a straight answer.

"Hey, no worries," Joey said, as Dilbert rolled onto his back and offered his tummy for scratching. "Our boy was on his best behavior."

"You're going to have to be more specific," Seth said. "Because I don't think I have a frame of reference for Marsh's best behavior when it comes to women."

"Whole new territory, man. He said they sat up all night, talking."

"You've gotta be shitting me." Seth wasn't saying it wasn't true, but if so, it was definitely out of character for Marsh to admit it.

"Nope. I'm sure there was something, but I don't think it got out of hand, and he was not willing to spill the particulars." He rolled his eyes and looked at Seth. "I don't know how I'll deal with it if both of you grow some sense in the same week. Might be a sign of the apocalypse."

"Get used to it," Seth said. "Because here's another one. I'm gonna need the name of the realtor you used when you and Caroline bought your house."

Joey patted himself on the cheeks with both hands. "Huh. Nope. Seem to be awake. I wasn't sure there for a minute." His smile radiated genuine warmth, and Seth knew he was lucky to have Joey as his best friend. "You know there will be the housewarming party to end all housewarming parties, right?"

"Wouldn't have it any other way," Seth replied, already looking forward to it.

He heard the shower shut off, and a few minutes later the possibly reformed horn dog emerged, rubbing a towel briskly over the stubble shadowing his head. He tossed the towel on the dresser, stuck a baseball cap on backward, and said, "Let's roll."

Before they could get out the door, however, Seth's phone rang. A glance at the display told him it was Special Agent Kincaid. He was anxious as he answered, hoping they'd finally catch a break.

"I have some news for you about our suspect, Drew Purcell," the agent said.

Seth thought the clipped, gruff voice did not sound like it was going to tell him anything he wanted to hear. "Did you find him?"

"We found him."

Then it was good news.

Kincaid cleared his throat. "But he's not involved. He's in the clear."

All the oxygen seemed to have been sucked from the room. "What? How?"

"He finally turned up at home in Owensboro late last night. He admits to being in Cincinnati and Chicago, but it's only what we already knew. He showed up, security kept him out, and all he could do was badger people out on the street."

"But where was he all weekend?" Surely he could have been in Emporia, if he hadn't gotten home until last night.

"He met a couple of buddies in Indianapolis. It was a qualifying weekend at the Speedway, and he has a camera full of pictures and about a dozen people who can confirm he was there from late Friday afternoon until yesterday."

"Shit." Seth felt sick.

"Plus, Drew Purcell has one sister. Her name's Karen, and she's a twenty-one-year-old student at Ohio State. He's not related to Stacy Ballantyne, as Pam Gresak thought." He sounded like he was reading from a report.

"I shouldn't be surprised, but I am." Surprised, and sick.

"Yeah. Anyway, I wanted to let you know, because we're back to square one." Kincaid took a deep breath and blew it out. "Look, the van is going to be released this morning, and Danny Dawkins and his friend in St. Cloud are on their way to the county garage to pick it up. If we learn anything else, somebody will give you a call. How much longer are you planning to be in Emporia?"

"We haven't really discussed it, but I was thinking maybe till Saturday."

"Until you go, Chief LeFevre will keep increased patrols around town and out at the lake." He paused, and Seth felt he was trying to think of something else he could say to help. He failed. "We're looking at the bomb components, but I'm afraid it's the best we can do, until we get more information."

The conversation ended and Seth hung up, unsure what to say to the three people staring at him, concerned looks on their faces. He went to Abby and put his arms around her, his head slumped against hers. "Purcell's been at the Speedway in Indianapolis since late Friday afternoon. Pam was wrong. It's not him."

Abby started to gasp, but cut it off barely short of a whimper. "We're right back where we started." Her fingers curled into the back of Seth's shirt.

And that was what was really tearing at him. Unless they went with the idea of a nameless, faceless fan who went off the deep end, he was back to considering someone close to them was responsible. It was completely unacceptable. How were they supposed to stay safe when the danger could come from anyone, at any time, and be disguised as someone they considered a friend?

"Pam was so sure," he said hoarsely. "She saw the picture, and saw the same guy in town."

"Yeah, except she's nuts, and she'd say anything if she thought it was what you wanted to hear." Abby's voice was pure, flat anger. Seth knew she saw Pam's lucky acquisition of what they'd thought was the key bit of information as nothing but a ploy to get close to him. He didn't know if it was deliberate or if the girl was so out of it she saw something and reshaped it to fit what her fragile psyche wanted it to be.

"He's not even Stacy's brother," Seth said. "He has one sister, but she's a college kid. Karen."

Joey leaned an arm on the wall by the bathroom. He looked toward the ceiling, thinking. "If Pam really did see a picture from the memorial service, maybe we should look and see if we can find it, too. There could be something there."

Seth thought it was a long shot. "Sure, give it a try if you have time. It's not like we have anything else to go on."

Marshall sat on the bed, his head slumped in his hands. He rubbed at his face and looked at the clock. "The Shamrock should be open by now. I know it's on the early side, but I need a very large drink." He shot a look at Seth. "You're buying. After the damage you did to my bottle last night, you owe me a couple."

Seth looked at Abby, who nodded. "Yeah, OK, let's go. Can Dilbert wait here till we get back?" she asked Joey.

"Sure."

They moved toward the door, Dilbert burrowed into the nest he was making of Marsh's blankets, and Seth put his hand on Abby's arm. When she stopped and focused on him, he said, "Try not to worry, darlin'. I don't care who's guilty. They're not going to win. We just have to back up a step or two."

She blinked in an attempt to clear the sheen from her green eyes. "As long as they're caught before something happens to you."

"Nobody's taking me away from you. That's the only way it's going to be." He didn't have any guarantee other than his fierce determination.

He hoped he wasn't lying.

* * *

They entered the Pickled Shamrock, and Abby's eyes scanned the sparse lunchtime crowd. Was there anybody there who didn't belong? Would she recognize veiled hostility if she saw it?

The group was seated at a booth, and Chanda appeared to take their order. Joey and Marshall ordered drinks and lunch, Seth wanted a beer, and Abby requested a root beer. She mentioned she'd want some sandwiches to go, and Chanda said she'd place the order when she brought the lunches.

When Chanda bustled off to the kitchen, Seth looked around the table. "What do we do now?" He tried to sound positive, but Abby heard the undercurrent of uncertainty he attempted to hide.

"We keep digging," Joey said.

A few minutes later, Chanda placed their drinks on the table. When she was gone, Abby unwrapped her straw and stuck it in the frosted mug. "The most likely motive is revenge. But revenge for what?"

Seth drummed his fingers on the table. "I'm tripped up there every time. I've been wracking my brain trying to think of who I crossed up bad enough they'd want revenge. I was so sure Purcell was it."

Abby sighed. This was depressing. Now they'd have to go back to wondering which friend was responsible for this.

Joey chewed on his thumbnail. "I was just wondering if any of us have talked to the rest of the crew since they left."

None of them had.

"I think we should make a point to talk to all of them. Today. Trent, Andy, Danny, Roberto, even Mouse." Joey didn't look any happier about the idea than the rest of them did.

"Why Mouse?" Marshall asked. "He was at the sound board the whole night."

"I know, but he's been with Andy more than anybody else, and he's supposed to be with Roberto right now. I want to be sure everybody's where we think they are, and with who we think they're with." Joey looked at Seth. "If you and Abby have plans, Marsh and I will touch base with everybody after lunch."

Seth's eyes lowered to the tabletop. "I hate it, man, but go ahead. I don't know what else to do."

Abby rubbed her eyes in frustration. "It was easier to understand when we thought we were dealing with Drew being Stacy's brother. At least that made some sense."

"Maybe something will come up in the investigation of Kevin's murder," Seth said. "It's damned near certain it was the same person, so maybe they made a mistake, left a clue pointing us in the right direction." He didn't sound like he believed it. Abby hoped he wasn't still feeling responsible for Kevin's death, but she suspected he was.

The lunch orders arrived, and Abby told Chanda which sandwiches she wanted for her take-out order. They weren't accomplishing a damned thing here, and she thought the best thing would be for her and Seth to proceed with their afternoon plans. They could check in with the guys later and see if they'd come up with anything.

Seth seemed to be reading her mind. "If you guys will make the calls and see if you can find that picture, we'll talk to you later. We're going to head out."

Marshall dug his room key out of his pocket. "Here. When you get Dilbert, just leave the key at the desk."

Abby couldn't stop herself from asking, "Are you seeing Molly today?"

Marshall smiled. He didn't leer or smirk. It was a perfectly normal, somewhat shy smile. "Yeah. She had to work at nine, but she's coming over when she gets done."

Interesting, Abby thought.

They rose, and Abby stopped by the bar to pick up their sandwiches. She perched on a bar stool to wait, and Seth said, "Hey, I forgot to tell Joey something. And I wanted to give Mom a quick call while we're in town. I'll meet you out front."

Abby nodded, pulling out her wallet. She turned back to the bar, and Sammy Paulsen slid onto the stool beside her. He wore jeans and a baseball jersey, suggesting he was not on duty.

"Hi, Abby," he said, clutching a nearly empty beer. "Heard they cleared your prime suspect. Chief ran us half to death yesterday, looking everywhere for the guy."

"We're back to not knowing which way to look," Abby said.

Sammy finished his beer and signaled for another. He looked nervous, but she couldn't imagine why. He peered into the bottom of his empty glass and sat it on the counter. "Look, Abby, I know this is none of my business…"

It was never good when someone started out with such a statement, in Abby's experience. "If it's none of your business, Sammy, maybe you should keep whatever you're about to say to yourself." She had a hunch what the subject matter would be, given the young officer's long-time crush on her.

"I can't help it. I've known you too long, and I have to get this off my chest."

She closed her eyes and wished she had a bottle of wine in front of her. "Fine, but be quick. I'm on my way somewhere."

"With Seth."

"Yes, with Seth." It would always be with Seth.

Sammy's fresh beer arrived, and he took a deep drink. "So, are you going to do it? Go to Texas with him?"

Abby gathered her thoughts, trying to determine the best way to have this conversation without hurting Sammy's feelings. Nice guy, but he always reminded Abby of those ducklings who imprinted on the first thing they saw and followed it everywhere, unaware it wasn't a duck. "Yes, I'm going to Texas with him. And Santa Barbara and Denver and Phoenix and everywhere else they play. We'll be coming here when we can, and spending time at the house we're buying in Austin."

Sammy blinked. "But I'm worried about you! Look at all the trouble you've had since he showed up. Wouldn't it be better to

stay here, where you have people to look out for you? At least
until they catch whoever's after him?" He seemed to add the last
part grudgingly.

"No, Sammy, it wouldn't be better." Her temper started to
heat up, and she told herself to calm down. He didn't mean
anything by it. He just had the protector thing going on, along
with the crush. "Seth and I are looking out for each other. And
we have Marshall, Pete, Joey, and their wives, too."

"It's not the same as being home."

"Try telling my mom that. She'll call your mom and you'll
be grounded retroactively back to the age of twelve." Sammy's
expression didn't change, and she knew jokes weren't going to
cut it. She decided to be straight with him. The whole town
would know most of it, anyway, before long, and would guess
or make up the rest. Might as well go on the record with a
reliable source. "I love him, Sammy, and 'home' is wherever
we're together."

Sammy looked like someone had kneed him in the crotch.
"Does he love you?"

"Yes, he does." She leaned toward Sammy and waited until
he met her eyes. "He almost left me last night. He did it because
he thought it was the only way to keep me safe. But he came
back, because whatever we have to face, we're better off if we do
it together."

His eyes dropped, and he cleared his throat. He understood
protection. "I get it. I'm happy for you, Abby. You deserve
somebody who'll always put you first. If he can, then I read him
wrong. I'm sorry."

The bartender put the bag containing her order on the bar.
She placed her hand over Sammy's and gave it a pat. "It's OK.
Just don't make the mistake of believing the musician stereotype.
I'm finding out it's not true nearly as often as you might think,
and Seth is a whole lot more than a stereotype." She picked up

the bag and went outside, leaving Sammy to finish his beer alone.

She found Seth waiting on the sidewalk in front of the Shamrock. He walked up close to her, until their bodies were almost touching, and brushed her lips with his. "Ready to go liberate Dilbert before he chews any remaining sleeves off Marsh's shirts?"

"Are there any?"

"Probably not. Dilbert's too well behaved to do that, anyway. Maybe we can use him to help train Marsh."

Abby thought it was a decent idea.

A few minutes later they were once again walking through the park, the black dog prancing along beside them. Dilbert jumped in the Jeep and Abby made sure the lid to the cooler was securely fastened. It wouldn't do to prepare for lunch, only to discover it was covered in dog slobber. Or missing altogether.

"You drive, I'll direct," Abby said, settling in the passenger seat and fastening her seatbelt.

"Driving the Bitchmobile twice in one day. I must've been promoted."

"Don't count on it."

Seth chuckled. "Hey, did I see you talking to Sammy before we left? Did he have more news?"

"No. He was doing the mandatory 'make sure Abby knows what she's doing' thing. At least he won't be issuing a kidnapping warrant for you the second we cross the state line."

"Are we crossing any state lines today?"

"Nope. In fact, it's closer than you'd think, but somewhere we're sure not to be disturbed."

Chapter Twenty-One

"Turn here," Abby said, pointing to the right. Seth slowed and guided the Jeep onto a narrow dirt road he hadn't noticed on any of their previous trips. They'd driven only a few miles outside town, both of them casting frequent glances in the rearview mirrors, but trying to pretend they weren't. They only passed two cars, and Abby had waved at the drivers of both.

The road wound through thick trees, the branches brushing the sides of the vehicle. He drove cautiously over the rocks and ruts in an effort to keep the jostling to a minimum. A few minutes later the foliage thinned, and the road ended in a wide spot showing signs other vehicles also parked there from time to time.

Abby took the cooler and a faded green blanket from the backseat while Dilbert zigzagged happily, sniffing everything in the vicinity. Seth looked around speculatively. "Um, are we there yet?"

Abby handed him the cooler, draping the blanket over her arm. "Almost. We just have to do a little walking." She led the way to a path, calling to Dilbert not to wander too far ahead.

The path didn't look like it was used often. A few lingering puddles showed the last signs of Saturday night's rain. They followed the path until it crested an incline and brought them to a wide clearing.

Seth put down the cooler. It was strangely like stepping out of a tornado-tossed Kansas farmhouse and into Oz. After the deep shadows and unbroken canopy of the forest, a bright, inviting space spread before them. "So, where are we?"

"Bainbridge Farm," Abby said. She stood beside him, watching him to gauge his reaction. "It used to be an orchard, and there were some fields where they grew pumpkins or corn. Back in the '50s or '60s, the owner died, and his wife moved in with one of their daughters."

"They just abandoned it?"

"More or less. The kids had all moved away, and I guess nobody was interested in running the place. It's close to town, but hard to get to. Nobody who hasn't lived here forever would even know it's here." She began walking across the clearing toward the remains of a brick chimney. "I'm not sure who owns it now. Someone must pay the taxes, but nobody's ever done anything with it."

"What happened to the house?"

"Burned down years ago."

Seth took in the flat area and patches of concrete adjacent to the crumbling chimney. When he looked more closely at the ground cover and creeping vines, he could see evidence of well-weathered wood and brick, all remaining of the farmhouse. Previously tamed flowers appeared in clusters on every side, having long ago escaped their untended beds. The grass was lush and green after the weekend's rain. He imagined it would be much less inviting later in the season with no one to keep it trimmed.

They stopped by the broken cement steps. "Leave the cooler here for now," Abby said. "I want to show you around. I used to spend a lot of time here growing up. I'd load a backpack with books and snacks and ride my bike out."

Seth put the cooler down and sat on the most stable-looking part of the crumbling steps. Pulling Abby onto his lap, he pictured her as a shy preteen. He envisioned long, dark hair, freckles, and bare feet. Her legs were tanned and possibly bore skinned knees from bicycle-related mishaps. She sat for hours under one of these very trees reading her favorite books. He smiled as he savored the dual images of the quiet little girl she had been and the gorgeous, intelligent woman he held now.

"I don't blame you. It is beautiful here." Seth studied the trees surrounding the remains of the farmhouse. He saw how the forest had slowly marched forward into the clearing, shrinking it. In a few more decades, it would be completely reclaimed, and visitors would have to search to find signs it had once been a family's home. "Show me."

Abby led him to the far side of the clearing. Past a small cluster of trees, they came to another open space and an old barn. Its roof and part of the hayloft had collapsed and the walls canted at unstable angles, but it was mostly intact. The rusted-out shell of a 1950s-era tractor stood to one side under a tangle of vines.

"I used to poke around in there," Abby said, nodding toward the barn. Sometimes it was cooler in there, and I liked how it smelled," she said. "The orchard is over there."

They went around the barn and down a narrow path through another area where the trees had almost completely reclaimed the property. The path ended abruptly, and Seth found himself standing in an orchard straight out of a dark fairy tale. The trees had gone without care for so long they were overgrown and unruly, their branches gnarled together over the spaces once separating them into orderly rows. It could have felt like another Oz moment, reminiscent of the scene where the apple trees come to life and hurl fruit at Dorothy and her friends, but it didn't. These apple trees were in full bloom, their white-

and-pale pink blossoms covering every twig and saturating the air with their fragrance. Seth looked around him in amazement.

Beside him, Abby smiled. "I used to sit up in these trees and read when I was a kid, but I haven't been here in the spring for a long time. I'd forgotten about the apple blossoms. This is great."

He stepped behind her and wrapped his arms around her waist. With his chin on her shoulder, he said, "Maybe we should have lunch here."

"Let me show you the rest, and then we can decide."

They made their way through the orchard, only slightly impeded by the saplings and underbrush uncleared since the property's caretakers had moved on. The fresh, sweet scent of apple blossoms surrounded them, and the breeze sent an occasional petal wafting toward the ground. Bees buzzed, still doing their work for the trees, even if the people no longer did. Dilbert trotted along with them, sniffing and marking those trees to which he felt some particular canine attachment.

At the far side of the orchard they came to a small creek. It meandered along and emerged in what Seth guessed was the abandoned farm fields. The creek curved to bisect the space, and the skeleton of a decaying split-rail fence paralleled its course.

Leaning against him, Abby said, "This is pretty much it, except for one more spot."

"What is it?"

"You'll have to wait and see. I hope it's the way I remember it." She moved back through the orchard and toward the barn, veering off to the left before they reached it.

The trees gave way again to an open area. To the right was another outbuilding, perhaps a shed or chicken house, and sunlight filtered through the surrounding forest. At their feet, the grass blended with a profusion of blooming violets. From one side to the other, the whole place was carpeted in them.

Abby clapped her hands. "Oh, wow! I hoped this was the right time. It's only like this for a week or two every spring." She crouched and swept her hand through the grass, touching the individual violet blossoms.

Her recollection added another dimension to his image of the little girl who'd grown up here. "We'll pick some before we leave and take them home. They remind me of the top you wore to the concert Friday night. I think I'm going to have a soft spot in my heart for violets from now on."

"It's why Monique knew I'd like the halter so much. She knows I used to come out here a lot."

Seth had visions of lying with her in the violets, but couldn't decide if it was a romantic or corny notion.

Standing, Abby said, "I was thinking maybe we'd have lunch and come back here."

Romantic, then. Excellent. Sometimes it was a fine line. "How about if we just have lunch here?"

She agreed it was a fabulous idea, and they quickly transferred the cooler and blanket to the violet-filled clearing. She spread the blanket under a large maple tree, while he opened the cooler. Dilbert appeared from the woods, following the canine instinct signaling when there was food to be mooched. Seth opened the wine and a beer. Abby unwrapped a sandwich and handed him half. Dilbert focused his lone eye on them, tracking every bite they took, until Abby tossed several doggie treats into the grass in various locations around the clearing. Seth chuckled as the dog bounded off in search of crunchy snacks.

Seth leaned back against the tree and positioned Abby to sit between his legs, her back to his chest. She let her head fall against the front of his shoulder and sipped her wine from the plastic cup. He knew his growing arousal had to be evident to her, and he wondered if he'd ever stop wanting her so fiercely. He couldn't believe it was possible.

He'd never experienced desolation as complete as he had last night when he was sure he lost her. The prospect of living his life without her left him with a hopelessness he wished never to feel again. If only he could rid them of the threat hanging over their heads everything would be perfect.

As if reading his mind, Abby said, "Do you think we should've stayed in town and helped Joey and Marshall?"

"It doesn't take four people to make a few phone calls and do some web surfing." Though he admitted to himself he did feel somewhat guilty for running off on a picnic while they did the work.

"I know. It's why I didn't say anything earlier." She twisted around enough to be able to kiss the underside of his jaw. "Now I'm sitting here with you, and I started wondering if I was being selfish."

"We'll see them again in a little while."

Abby murmured her agreement. "One thing is bothering me, though."

"What's that?"

"If Pam really did see a picture—and I'm not totally convinced she did—it means Stacy's brother is still out there. And whether they made up before she died or not, he cared enough to show up at her memorial service."

This thought troubled him, too. "I knew she had a brother, but that's about it. She wouldn't talk about him, and it wasn't a big enough deal for me to push her on it."

"Pam said his name was Drew, though, and it's what has me confused."

"She was the one who was confused. You should've seen her. She wasn't tracking at all. She'd most likely seen Drew Purcell outside some of the shows, and followed the trial in the news. She just combined everything into one mixed-up thought."

Abby sighed. "You're probably right. But it still doesn't tell us who she saw in town she said wasn't supposed to be there. If anybody."

"True. We'll have to put our heads together with Marsh and Joey when we get back. See if we can come up with some ideas." He really didn't want to think about this now.

Luckily, it appeared she didn't, either. She took his beer bottle and her wine cup and placed them a safe distance away. She returned to where she'd been sitting between his knees, only sideways. He slid his left arm behind her, and she leaned back onto the light support of his arm and bent knee. He'd noticed she'd applied a touch of sheer coral lipstick earlier, and he had an almost overwhelming urge to lick it off. Unable to think of a single good reason to resist, he bent and traced his tongue around the edges of her sinfully shaped lips. She allowed this for a minute, and he followed the changing shape of her mouth as it spread into a smile.

Apparently wanting more, she stretched her arm upward and placed a hand on the back of his neck. She pulled him more tightly to her and kissed him. Heat coiled in his stomach. He shifted on his hip until they lay side by side on the green blanket. What was wrong with them, wearing so many clothes? Something had to be done about that. Moments later their shirts were on the grass and he was slipping her bra from her shoulders. Better. But not good enough. He needed to touch every bit of her. He set about remedying the situation, and breathed a sigh when they finally lay together amidst a scattering of discarded clothing.

He remembered what Joey had said about how he should kiss his way up her body and not stop until he reached her earrings. Joey Garvin was a damned genius. He started at the peacock quill tattoo on her calf, but had to admit he didn't distribute his time equally. He did some lingering when he reached the juncture of her thighs, lost in her delicious and vocal responses to his touch.

When he finally made it to her earrings, he wasted barely a thought on the splendor of their surroundings. Why bother? The most breathtaking thing he'd ever seen was lying beneath him. She was every song he'd ever written—hell, every song he'd ever heard—all wrapped up into one.

She skimmed her hand over his stomach, and he felt a nearly electric surge as her fingers closed around him. She shifted until she was positioned properly to guide him where she wanted him to go. He didn't need any clues. He already knew how wet she was, how ready for him. He was glad she wasn't shy about letting him know what she wanted, though. Especially now, since he was nearly frantic with the need to be inside her.

Gliding in until he was fully sheathed, he paused as her legs wrapped around him. He gathered her in his arms and rolled until she was on top, and edged himself into a sitting position, leaning against the tree. He decided he was quite fond of this position in spite of the prickly bark. They were free to kiss and touch, and the tight, dusky peaks of her breasts were conveniently within range of his mouth. She tightened around him, and his hips lifted to match her rhythm. When her pace increased and she leaned her upper body against him, he knew it was because she craved even more contact. Her skin practically blazed when she pressed against him. He brought his hands up and down her back in bold, full strokes as she began to tremble. Her thighs stiffened, and he hugged her to him as she came, riding the wave with her until he, too, was swept away.

When he was able to think again, he edged his back away from the tree. Frankly, he wasn't as open to the potential for splinters as he'd been earlier. Abby reached behind him and brushed the chunks of bark from his back.

"Maybe next time one of us should keep his shirt on," she said, her lips by his ear.

"I'll see if I can remember that."

"What time do you think it is?"

"Don't know. Don't care."

"I haven't seen Dilbert in a while," she said, her eyes scanning the perimeter of the clearing.

"If you open the cooler, he'll show up in no time." Plus, another sandwich sounded like a good idea.

Abby refilled her cup with wine, and took both a sandwich and another beer from the cooler. They lay on the blanket for a while, snacking, sipping, and talking about some of the houses they'd seen online. Someone eventually said they should get dressed. Seth was pretty sure it wasn't him. After he put his gray T-shirt back on, she stepped up to him and smoothed his hair out from beneath the collar.

Seth put the leftovers away in case Dilbert came back for a snack while they weren't paying attention. He noticed they hadn't eaten the croissants yet. Maybe they'd go for another walk, come back here and try the leave-the-shirt-on thing, then have the croissants. Abby's purse strap was looped through the cooler handle, and he considered checking her cell phone for the time, but decided it didn't matter.

Abby went over by the old outbuilding where there was an especially thick cluster of violets, as well as some other wildflower Seth didn't recognize. "If I lay them in the cooler, they might stay nice till we get home. They won't be in good enough shape to put in a vase, but I want to press a few."

Seth thought that sounded sweet. He liked her having mementos of their day together. He wandered across the clearing, thinking he'd take another look around the barn, though he might rather just watch Abby gather violets. He paused before he entered the trees, suddenly feeling he should stay close. Had he heard Dilbert barking? He strained his ears, but decided if he'd heard a dog bark, it had been very far away.

He heard a short, strangled cry and spun around. The world as he knew it came apart in an instant when he saw Abby being held from behind by a man, one arm around her waist, and his other hand pressing a gun under her jaw. A flood of useless information assaulted his brain. The only thought that mattered was to get to Abby. Get her away from that man.

Away from Andy Hicks. A member of his crew. A friend. A kid.

With a fucking gun jammed against Abby's neck.

He took several lunging steps before Andy barked, "Stop! Any closer and it's over, man."

Seth froze. Every instinct he had screamed at him to move, get to her, keep her safe. But moving even a single muscle could cause Andy to make good on his threat. Abby was about twenty-five feet away from him. Fright was evident in her eyes, but there was a calculating look, too. She was evaluating the situation and looking for a way out. There wasn't one. He gave his head a minute shake. She shouldn't move. He had to think. Andy?

"You gave me a real run, Seth. Seeing you die alone in a hotel room seemed like a great plan at first, but I think I like this way better."

Seth's brain was experiencing a huge disconnect between the apprentice lighting technician with the long, sandy bangs always falling in his face and the dead-eyed stare of the bastard holding Abby's life in his hands.

His mouth was desert dry, and he swallowed several times until he could trust his voice. "So it was you who messed with the Jack Daniel's bottle in Cincinnati." Why he did it was another question, and one Seth hoped he had time to ask.

"Yeah, I thought it'd be appropriate. I wanted you to die the same way she did, but I must've mixed it wrong." Abby winced as Andy ground the gun against her neck. "Don't move," he ordered. Turning his attention back to Seth, he said, "I still could've finished you if Marsh hadn't decided to play nursemaid."

Seth struggled to sort through all the information. He'd been right about Marshall saving his life. And Andy always acted as bartender, so it would've been easy for him to tamper with the liquor bottle. That left him with one major thing he couldn't work out. "You wanted me to die the same way who died?"

Abby jerked and started to say something, but Andy struck her across the cheekbone with the barrel of the gun. Seth started to move, but Andy quickly fastened his gaze on him. "Not one inch. I swear, man."

Seth had never been angrier or more terrified in his life. He didn't know human emotion stretched this far. It appeared the blow to Abby's face had been more to make a point than to inflict damage. There was a welt, but she wasn't bleeding. It had, however, pissed her off, if the glitter in her eyes was any indication. Hold it together, Abby-Kat, he silently begged. We'll get out of this. Somehow.

She cleared her throat. When it didn't bring about any further violence, she said, "The same way Stacy died, right Andy?"

"Yes! The way Stacy died! Alone and full of drugs and booze." He glared at Seth. "I wanted everybody to spend the next ten years debating whether you were a stupid drunk who liked to mess with drugs or a basket case who killed himself. Like they're saying about her."

Something clicked in Seth's mind. Andy. Drew. He couldn't believe he hadn't figured it out before, or at least as soon as he saw Andy in the clearing. "You're Stacy's brother. Andrew. But she called you Drew." He'd condemn himself later for being so fucking slow, assuming he made it to later. Right now he had to figure out how to get Abby away from the gun.

Andy sneered. "Yeah, genius. I about shit myself laughing yesterday when every cop in town was running around looking for Drew Purcell. That blonde bitch did me a huge favor. I thought she'd seen me, and maybe I was going to have to get her out of the picture, but she didn't have it together enough to even get the story straight."

Seth's eyes darted around the clearing, checking the vicinity for anything he could use as a weapon. Icy sweat ran down his spine. But as long as Andy was talking, he wasn't shooting. "Like you got Kevin Merinar out of the way? What did he do?"

"Stupid shit came out to the bus while I was putting a little surprise in your duffel bag." He laughed harshly. "I told him it was a smoke bomb, a prank. Everybody knows guys on the road always pull stuff like that. But I knew once it blew, he'd go straight to the cops. I'd heard Kevin had been in some trouble for dealing, so when we went back in the club I told him I wanted to buy some weed. Dumbass followed me right into the basement. The mic stand was right there and did the job."

Seth didn't see anything within his reach he could use to help Abby. He felt sick.

"And you used his phone to send Seth a text," Abby said. Seth couldn't believe how steady her voice was for a woman with a gun pressing into her flesh.

"Yeah, just for extra kicks. I ditched it on Sunday when I went to the Cities for supplies."

"Supplies?" Abby asked.

"After my visit to your place on Saturday night, when that fucking mutt showed up and started barking, I needed a new plan. Picked up this cool toy," he said, nodding at the gun, "and a treat for the mutt. Plus I bought the tracker I put on the car Monday morning when she stopped to get beer. I left the present for the dog earlier, but couldn't get back out to finish things with the cops crawling around. I decided I might not be able to get close to your house again before you left town, so I wanted to be sure I had a way to find you. I knew if I kept my head down and hid out, I'd get a chance." A macabre smirk twisted his face. "Then I made a stop at the library to send you a friendly e-mail."

He shifted his eyes from Seth and looked at the side of Abby's face where he'd hit her. She stiffened, and Seth watched in horror as Andy lowered his face toward hers. He didn't touch her, but he breathed in and his expression darkened. "It was nice of him to bring you here for me. I've been imagining your scream for days." His nose grazed her hair and he inhaled again. "You smell like him. Guess I missed all the fun. Hope you had a good time, because it's the last one you're going to have."

Abby uttered a short, sharp laugh. "Oh, give me a fucking break. I can't believe you just said that. Where'd you get that line? The Psycho Killer Manual?" She laughed again. Clearly, she'd had enough, and the writer in her hated cheap dialogue. Of all the times for her internal editor to take a break.

"Um, darlin', this might not be a good time to criticize." He wanted nothing more than to dive across the intervening space and tear Andy's shaggy, sandy head from his shoulders, but he and Abby both needed to stay alive in the process.

"Oh, come on," Abby said. "I might as well say what's on my mind. But Andy, here's what I don't get. Why would you think Seth needs to be punished for Stacy's death? She'd been gone a year before she died."

"He threw her away, and she never got over him. She came home to Aunt Ana in Chicago, and she was a mess." His voice shook, but the hand holding the gun never wavered. "I hadn't seen her in years. After our parents died, Aunt Ana tried to take care of her like she took care of me, but Stacy was eighteen and wouldn't let her. Next thing I knew, she was back in Atlanta and married to a drummer. Lasted about five minutes. But then his band broke up, and she left."

None of that clarified the issue for Seth. "I'm not buyin' it, Andy. She forgot about me five minutes after our bus pulled out of town."

"You didn't see her, man. She was wrecked. All she could talk about was you. Lived in a bottle till she was so messed up she took off with another band. And when they found her dead in the hotel in Vancouver, it was exactly a year since you threw her out. But you didn't catch that, did you?"

"I didn't even know she was dead till Saturday."

"Exactly!" Andy's eyes flashed dangerously. "You never fucking cared enough to even find out if she was OK! As soon as I heard she was dead, I knew it was all your fault. So I went to Austin. Stacy told me you liked to hang out at Stoney's Tavern when you weren't on the road. I met Danny there, and I heard you needed some new hands. I'm the one who convinced Danny we should try to get hired on. I knew sooner or later I'd figure out the best way to nail you."

Seth was stalling. He knew he was. He tried to remember everything he knew about guns, which took about three seconds. Despite living in Texas, he didn't own one. He didn't know what kind of gun Andy held or how many bullets it might contain. The only potentially useful information he could recall was that handguns didn't tend to be accurate from any sort of distance.

He had to get Abby away from the gun. For now, he had to keep him talking. "So you tried to poison me, and when it didn't work, you got your hands on a pipe bomb."

"Yeah. When you were still alive Thursday morning, I called a connection of mine in Chicago. I met him and set it up, and he brought it to me Friday night."

"But you left too much to chance, didn't you, Andy?" Abby was still pushing his buttons, and Seth wished she'd stop. "The bomb blew up my house instead. What about Trent and Marshall, though? Didn't you care if your plan had worked, they would've been hurt, too?"

Andy shook his head and snorted. "Hell, no. I don't care one way or another about Trent. And after Marsh babysat Seth all night and complicated everything, I wasn't going to shed any tears over him."

With every word out of Andy's mouth Seth's burning desire to abandon caution and go after him increased. But he had to hold it together, just for a few more minutes. He'd think of something by then. He had to. He'd managed to take several small steps in Abby's direction during Andy's delusional rants, inching his way every time she drew attention away from him. He knew what she was doing, but he didn't like it. Anything could set this guy off, causing him to squeeze the trigger.

Andy was looking at Abby again, and Seth cautiously edged one foot forward. The killer's eyes suddenly snapped back to him, and Seth froze. In that instant, Abby shifted her weight and tried to elbow Andy in the ribs. He jerked her back against him and gave her arm a cruel twist. Abby cried out, and Seth almost lost it. If he could be sure he'd be the only one to die, he'd rush Andy in a heartbeat. His legs ached with the tension of constantly forcing them not to move.

Seeing Seth's momentary indecision, Andy shouted, "I mean it, man. I'm telling you how it's going to be, and you ain't moving. You do, and I'll blow her head off."

"If you were going to do it, you'd have done it by now," Abby snarled. She was pushing too hard. Was she trying to rattle Andy enough for Seth to get a good run at him? The only problem was he couldn't run faster than a bullet as it blasted from the gun to her head.

She began struggling in Andy's arms, and the gun moved away from her neck as he tried to restrain her.

Seth made it two steps before Andy's head whipped up. He swung the gun in Seth's direction, and Abby screamed.

Andy shot him.

Chapter Twenty-Two

A bby froze, horrified, as Seth clutched his right side. Bright blood flowed between his fingers, quickly soaking his shirt. He was still on his feet, though, so maybe it wasn't a life-threatening wound. Please don't let it be serious, she silently pleaded.

Andy pressed the gun to her neck again. It reeked of burnt gunpowder and was hot against her skin. He laughed, the sound ugly in this beautiful place. "Damn. Wish I'd had time to test fire this a few times. But no big deal. I like seeing you bleed."

Seth wiped his bloody hand on the leg of his jeans and straightened, placing the hand back over the wound. "Just do it, motherfucker, but let Abby go."

"You're not running the show anymore, Caldwell," Andy rasped. "It's all over for you, but I decide when. Turns out I'm glad I had to do it this way. Dying in a drunken stupor was too good for you. The bomb would've been messier, but too quick. This way you know why, and you get to watch her go first."

Abby's mind raced as she tried to think of a way out. Just one chance, that's all they needed. If she could elbow Andy in the face or knock the gun out of his hand, they could run for the trees. If they got that far, they'd have a chance, however slim, of making it. But if she made the wrong move, he'd shoot her.

Probably in the messiest, most painful way possible. And then he'd shoot Seth while he watched her bleed to death.

Not an option.

The entire right side of Seth's shirt was now dark with blood. Even the top of his jeans was soaked. The pain had to be excruciating, but he never took his eyes from her. They were running out of questions to ask, which meant they were running out of time. A thought occurred to her. "What did you do with our dog?" He hadn't appeared for the sandwiches, which was strange enough, but her scream and the gunshot should've brought him running.

Andy looked at her as if he couldn't believe she'd ask such a useless question. "He's alive. For now. He must've heard my car and came running out of the woods. I opened the door, he jumped in, and I got out the other side and shut him in there. I'll decide what to do with him later."

There was a burst of sound, and everybody's eyes swung to its source. Abby's purse, tied to the cooler. Her cell phone was ringing. "Make or Break."

She suddenly realized this was the distraction they needed. She heard underbrush rustling. The low-lying foliage erupted and Dilbert raced straight at her. Andy turned and pointed the gun at the dog. Abby shoved him with all her might. "Run!" she shouted.

She and Seth sprinted toward the orchard. Abby's heart pounded as they frantically tried to reach the trees and any safety they might provide. Objects on the ground tore at her bare feet, but she didn't slow her pace. She caught up to Seth, and Dilbert ran alongside them. Andy shouted, pounding behind them in pursuit.

Seth grabbed her arm and pushed her ahead of him. He was trying to stay between her and Andy. She would've yelled at him for it if she'd had any breath to spare. They crashed their way through the orchard, the glorious apple blossoms now appearing to be a cruel joke.

The most dangerous part was just ahead. When they broke out of the orchard, they had to cross the open area that had once been the Bainbridges' cornfield. They would have to jump the creek and run like hell for the trees on the other side. If they made it there, they had a decent chance of escaping. There were at least two houses located a short distance beyond. If someone was home to help them, or if they could get inside, lock themselves in and call for help before Andy caught them, they might be safe.

As they broke from the orchard, Dilbert cut in front of her and she nearly stumbled. She regained her momentum and kept running. A glance over her shoulder showed Seth was falling farther behind. How badly was he hurt? She kept looking back, despite the toll it took on her speed. Andy's shirt caught on a branch for a second or two before ripping free. Seth widened the distance between them.

The creek was only about six feet wide, but filled with slippery, treacherous rocks. She'd have to clear it in one leap. Approaching the bank, her lungs burning, she gathered all her remaining strength and jumped. A silent cheer rang in her head when she landed safely on the other side. The cheer hadn't quite faded away ten yards later when she stepped in a hole and fell.

Clutching her ankle, she saw Seth had almost reached the creek. Behind him, Andy raised the gun. Abby shrieked a warning. Not breaking stride, Seth hurdled the creek just as Andy fired. He rolled when he landed on the other side. When he got to his feet blood was streaming down his left arm.

In seconds, Andy would also make it to the creek. If they weren't running in the next few seconds, they were finished. She tried to rise, but her ankle gave way beneath her.

Andy gathered himself for the jump, only to have Dilbert dart in front of him, barking madly. The hitch in his momentum caused Andy to fall short of the opposite bank. He crashed to the ground, his lower legs in the water.

At the sound of the impact, Seth halted his attempt to reach her and turned. Seeing Andy on the ground, he reversed course and went straight for him. Abby couldn't see the gun. Did Andy have it in his hand? Was it in the creek?

Andy tried to struggle to his feet, and Abby screamed, "Seth! He still has the gun!"

Seth reached him and kicked him viciously in the chest. Andy flew backward. The gun arched through the air and landed in the rocks, out of reach.

Dilbert reached Abby, and stood between her and the fight, growling like a rabid wolf. Andy rolled to his hands and knees. Seth looked about wildly, reaching for a large rock in the creek bank. When it didn't come free, he quickly abandoned it and lunged for another weapon. He grabbed one of the fallen posts from the split rail fence running along the creek and swung it at Andy. The blood coursing down his arm flew from his fingertips with the impact, and Andy went down. He started to make another attempt to get to his feet, but Seth swung again and nailed him on the side of the head. This time he lay still, but Seth stood over him with the post.

For a moment she thought Seth would continue to bludgeon Andy until his head was reduced to paste, but he somehow restrained what must have been a powerful urge. Andy was still breathing, and that was something for which he should be extremely grateful. When he woke up.

Shouts carried across the field from the orchard, and Joey and Marshall ran out of the trees. As their friends raced toward them, Abby climbed painfully to her feet and limped to Seth. When she reached him, he lowered the post to the ground and pulled her to him. She worried the fierce embrace was hurting him, but he didn't let her go.

"Your ankle. Your feet. Are you OK?" He touched the welt on her face.

"Forget me. I'm fine. You're the one who's been shot. Twice." She pulled frantically at his shirt, trying to see the extent of his injuries.

He grabbed her hands and stopped her exploration. "It's OK. If it was bad, I'd never have made it this far." He winced. "I think he cracked a rib, though."

"What about your arm?"

Seth peeled up the bloody sleeve and grimaced. "The bastard shot my tattoo. It's totaled."

The absurdity of the situation struck her, and Abby laughed. "It's a horse skeleton with flaming wings. Believe me, a scar is only going to improve it."

"It's a post-apocalyptic Pegasus. It's cool. Or it was."

Abby sagged against him, not caring about the blood staining her skin and clothes. Dilbert pranced around them, shooting furtive glances at Andy's prone body. "Pam was right after all. It was Stacy's brother, Drew. She just wasn't specific enough." You couldn't trust mentally unbalanced groupies to get the details right, Abby thought. Go figure.

Seth swiped his sweat-soaked hair behind his ears and bent to kiss her. The kiss was salty, but whether it was the sweat or the tears pouring down her face Abby couldn't be sure.

Marshall and Joey scrambled across the creek. Marsh picked up the fence post and approached Andy.

"If the fucker so much as twitches, take his head off," Seth said.

"Count on it," Marshall growled, tightening his grip on the post. "Excellent work, by the way. It's not a bar stool, but at least you didn't use your fist. You wouldn't be able to hold a pick for a month if you had."

"The police are coming," Joey said, dragging Seth into a hug, despite the blood. "We called them as soon as we knew where we were headed."

"Be careful," Abby said. "He might have a cracked rib."

"We tried to call you, too, when we got here and saw Dilbert inside a strange car."

"The timing was perfect. The ring was part of the distraction giving us a chance to run. The other part was Dilbert." She scratched the one-eyed dog's chest. Turning, she saw several figures coming out of the orchard. She recognized Bob LeFevre and Karl Briggs, and the uniforms of two other Emporia police officers. Sammy was there, too, still in the jeans and jersey he'd been wearing earlier at the Shamrock. With a rush, all the energy left her, and she sank to the ground and put her head between her knees.

Seth sat beside her and wrapped his arm around her. He looked up at Joey. "How'd you know what was happening? How'd you find us?"

Joey remained standing. Abby thought it looked like he was positioning himself to help Marshall if Andy showed any signs of regaining consciousness. "We started making those calls, and we couldn't track down Andy. That was the first clue."

"He never went to his aunt's," Abby said, resting her head on Seth's shoulder. The not-bloody one.

"Nope, he's been here all along. We dug around online looking for the picture. Took a while, and we'd never have found it if we hadn't known when Stacy died, and where she was from. It was in the *Atlanta Journal-Constitution* the second week in November. Made the paper because one of the guys in the band she was hanging with was from there, too." Joey's face was flushed, and he looked like he should sit down for a minute, too.

Marshall looked up from Andy's prone form. "Jackpot, man. There was a picture all right, but it was Andy, not Drew Purcell.

Took us a minute to make the Andy-Andrew connection, but once we did everything fell into place."

Joey finally sat on a rock beside the creek. "The problem was we didn't know where the hell you were or where Andy was."

"There's a GPS tracker somewhere on Abby's Jeep," Seth said. "He followed us here."

"Son of a bitch." Joey shook his head. "Since we had no idea how to find you, Marsh called Molly. He figured if anybody knew where Abby would go, she would."

Marshall nodded, pulling the bandanna from his head to wipe his face. "She said it was either here or another place down on the river, but she was almost sure you'd be here."

Abby silently resolved to do something very, very special for Molly. After all, she'd saved Seth's life twice. The first time was when she backed out on the concert, which indirectly led to his not being in his bunk on the bus. And today she'd sent the cavalry. If Joey and Marshall hadn't arrived and let sweet, goofy Dilbert out of Andy's car, they might never have gotten the distraction they needed to escape. Come to think of it, Dilbert had just earned himself a lifetime of big, juicy bones and duck chasing. She'd build a duck pond if she had to. It wasn't like he'd ever catch them.

The chief and the rest of the officers forded the creek, full of questions. Once Andy had been checked over, pronounced unconscious rather than dead, and secured, they radioed for a medical team to assess and transport him.

While they waited for the paramedics, the chief inspected Seth's injuries. "I expect you have a cracked rib, and it probably hurts like blue blazes, but we'll get you patched up. You'll be good as new in a few weeks."

Seth was itching to get out of there. He made a very determined case with the chief, until it was agreed they could go into town and get medical treatment at the clinic. They were better equipped to deal with the injuries than the team soon trekking across the fallow cornfield. The chief's only stipulation was they had to go directly there. Though Seth wasn't showing signs of shock, it could set in at any time, and taking chances was not an option.

Marshall reluctantly gave up the fence post, but only after making Karl promise to shoot Andy if he tried to get up. Karl agreed, and Sammy looked like he'd do it if his partner had any second thoughts.

They gave their statements to Chief LeFevre, while an officer went back to the Jeep to locate and remove the tracking device. The four of them made their way back across the farm and down the trail to the cars, Seth and Joey helping to support Abby when her ankle started to throb again.

When they reached the parking spot, they decided Joey would drive Abby's Jeep. He asserted she and Seth were both too traumatized to drive. They climbed into the backseat, and Dilbert hopped onto the passenger seat beside Joey.

Abby was quiet as Joey drove them to the clinic. She needed time for her mind to settle, and she needed to hold Seth. His arm wasn't bleeding much anymore, and she thought the more serious wound in his side was only seeping. The awful image of blood drenching his shirt and dripping from his hands onto the ground was something she knew she'd never be able to erase from her memory.

The temptation to close her eyes and drift away from the entire ordeal was powerful, but staying fully present with Seth was more important. The tight lines around his mouth told her he was in pain, but his arm around her was so real and warm. His lips, as they repeatedly brushed her forehead, cheek and mouth were soft and reassuring.

She couldn't stop looking at him. There were few people who would dispute the fact he was attractive. He'd always been more to her, though, even before she met him. Now that she knew him, he was even more beautiful. Objectively, she could see his nose might be a shade too long and sharp. One bottom tooth was turned at an odd angle. The vivid, clear blue eyes under the heavy brows several shades darker than his golden-brown hair presented an impression too intense for conventional good looks. But never for her. There wasn't one single thing she'd change about him, inside or out.

Except he should stop getting shot. Because that was definitely problematic.

Joey pulled up to the emergency entrance at the clinic. Abby noticed a figure pacing the sidewalk and groaned.

Seth interrupted his neck-nuzzling to look around. "What's wrong? Is it your ankle?"

"I wish it was my ankle." She nodded at the person hurrying toward the Jeep. "It's my mother. I can't imagine why I'm surprised." But the comment was automatic. The truth was she was almost painfully glad to see her mother.

Seth and Abby got out of the car. She found a slip leash in the glove compartment and looped it around Dilbert's neck. He'd helped save their lives. She had no intention of making him sit in a hot car while they were treated.

Her mother stopped a few feet away, her eyes wide. "Look at the two of you!" She brought her hands to her face and breathed deeply, as if she were about to burst into tears.

Abby went to her side and put a hand on her back, careful to avoid getting blood on her shirt. "Mom, it's OK. We're fine. Just need a little patching up."

Her mother's gaze shifted back and forth between them, evaluating the truth of her daughter's claim. "I heard something happened, and someone was shot. I've been out of my mind." She stepped away from Abby and started toward Seth.

"Don't grab him, Mom. He probably has a cracked rib, and he's kind of a mess."

Her mother stopped in front of Seth, stretched up, and kissed him gently on the cheek. "Let's get you inside, sweetie."

They gave her mother the condensed version of what happened, knowing they'd be able to fill in the details — probably over and over — later. Marilyn shook her head and uttered soft exclamations of shock.

The transformation once they reached the admissions area, though, was remarkable. Her mother went from semihysterical parent to drill sergeant. When the medical staff tried to banish Dilbert, Marilyn was not about to permit it. "This dog is a hero, and you're not taking him away from the people he helped save. Not for one second." Her folded arms and steely expression, not to mention her reputation as a force to be reckoned with, resulted in her being allowed to keep Dilbert in the waiting area while Seth and Abby were treated. Someone even brought him a bowl of water.

After Abby's feet were disinfected and declared "superficial injuries," and her ankle diagnosed as "twisted," she went to the room where Seth was being evaluated. The bullet struck him in the right side and dug a deep furrow, glancing off a rib. The other shot had left a gouge through the outside of his left arm, and while it was bloody, the main victim of that bullet had been post-apocalyptic Pegasus. Seth was given a clean scrub top to put on over his bandages. Abby didn't know what had become of his T-shirt, and didn't care. If he said anything about wanting a bullet-ridden shirt as some kind of stupid male badge of honor, she'd be forced to jab him in his cracked rib.

When they returned to the waiting area, Abby saw her mother and Dilbert had been joined by Marshall and Joey.

"You look a ton better than the last time I saw you," Marshall said.

Seth grinned. "Fuckin' awesome pain meds."

Marshall elbowed Joey. "Hey, man, next time I want to be the one who gets shot."

"Yeah, I don't think it'll be a problem," Joey replied, thumping Marsh on the back of the head.

Abby smiled. Things were getting back to normal. She decided now would be a good time to share their other news with her mother. It was sure to cheer her up and get her mind off her earlier worries. "Mom, by the way, you were right."

"Of course I was, sweetie. But about what, specifically?" Her mother blinked innocently, and Seth laughed.

"About fears and regrets, all the stuff paralyzing me." She smiled at Seth before continuing. "Which means if you're inclined to shower me with gifts any time soon, a suitcase would be handy. You know, since I'm going to be traveling a lot."

Marilyn's face lit up. She was nearly vibrating with excitement. "Oh, sweetie! That's wonderful. You can't look back, only forward."

"I know that now," Abby said.

Her mother returned Dilbert to her custody. "I want you to call me tomorrow morning, Abigail." Her tone left no room for argument. "And if you're both feeling up to it, you should plan to come over for dinner. Joey and Marshall, too."

"We will, Mom," she said, taking Dilbert's leash. "And thanks for…well, just thanks."

Now that Seth was no longer quite so blood covered, he couldn't escape one of her mother's hugs. He didn't look like he minded, though. She gave him another kiss and patted his cheek, and made him promise to call his mother right away. Team Mom always worked in tandem.

In the parking lot, Joey and Marshall agreed to come to Abby's the next afternoon, and go to Marilyn's for dinner from there. Marsh would see if Molly wanted to join them. Since Seth was beginning to feel the effects of his medication, Abby drove, and he called his mother from her phone. She listened to him reassure her it really was over, and he was going to be fine.

After he hung up, Seth said, "Would it be all right with you if we went to Montana?"

"Sure. When?"

"Mom wants us to come for a couple of days right before we go back out on the road."

"Fine with me." She figured getting along with his mother would be a snap, since she was reportedly so much like her own. Plus, Seth had been subjected to her mom from the beginning, and fair was fair.

When they arrived home, the first thing Abby did was feed Dilbert. She'd put a pound of ground beef out to thaw before they left, intending to grill hamburgers later. It was one of the few things she could cook consistently. Instead, she gave the whole thing to Dilbert, reasoning he hadn't gotten to eat much the day before. The little guy had earned a reward.

It all seemed so normal. Seth was on the couch flipping channels on the television, and she was feeding their dog. But there was a lot going on beneath the placid surface. They were both still processing the awful events of the past several days.

She went to the couch and curled against him, careful not to hurt him. They stayed like that for a while, just breathing, heartbeats, and warmth. Comfort. Love.

He stroked her hair. When he spoke, his voice was soft, with equal measures of anguish and relief. "Standing there, watching Andy with the gun pointed at you..." He shuddered. "I've never been as terrified or as furious in my life. And I felt so goddamned helpless. You were right there, and I couldn't even move or he'd kill you."

Abby sensed he wasn't quite done with what he wanted to say. Instead of replying, she brushed her lips against his neck and waited.

"If he had, if I'd let it happen, he would've had to kill me fast, because there's nothing in the world that could've stopped me from ripping him apart with my bare hands. I never thought I could feel that way, but I did. I do." He seemed awed and saddened by this realization.

"Don't you think I felt the same way? He had the gun, but I was right beside him. I wanted to be able to do something to give us a chance." She knew they were both going to have a hard time coming to terms with another human being driving them to such wildly diverse emotions as rage and helplessness.

"But I…"

"But nothing." She stroked his cheek. "We faced him together, as a team. And we won." She looked at the black dog dozing on the floor by the fireplace. "With a little help from our secret weapon."

Seth cast a fond look in Dilbert's direction. "He was pretty amazing."

"Not too shabby for a one-eyed stray. I wouldn't trade him for any dog in the world."

"But, darlin', you know it's not exactly over. There'll probably be a trial. We'll have to be there, relive it."

She brought his hand to her lips and kissed his strong, graceful fingers. "And we'll get through all of it together."

That night, they held each other in the dark. They loved each other as gently as they could and still express the life-affirming passion sustaining them. They had healing to do, physically and emotionally. But if crazy fans, drugs, explosives, and bullets couldn't come between them, nothing in the world ever would.

Epilogue

There was no way the suitcase was going to close. Abby forced the zipper past where it was stuck on one of the excessive number of garments stuffed inside. She removed a St. Cloud State University sweatshirt, two sweaters, and a light jacket. What was she thinking? It was probably ninety-five degrees in Austin. She didn't have to take everything she owned with her, anyway. She and Seth planned to come back here several times over the summer. This time the suitcase closed without undue effort.

Looking up, she saw Seth standing in the doorway smiling at her. "Almost ready, Abby-Kat?" It had been four days since their confrontation with Andy, and the first day Seth hadn't replaced the bandage on his arm. The wound was scabbed over and ugly, but healing. She knew he still had the bandage beneath his Nirvana T-shirt. The injury was better, but having it wrapped kept him more comfortable while the cracked rib mended.

She swung the suitcase off the bed and wheeled it across the floor. "I think so. Did Dilbert come back from his run yet?" They'd decided they should let him chase ducks as long as he liked this morning, since he would spend so much time over the next couple of days in the back of the Jeep.

"He's in his trench by the deck."

"Did you talk to Joey this morning?"

"Yeah. He and Marsh were on the road early. Would've been nice if they'd found out the bus was going to be released yesterday afternoon before they came out here and drank all your beer. Then they could've left last night."

Abby chuckled. "Well, somebody had to help you drink it."

They went into the living room, and Seth looked out the French doors while Abby checked to make sure everything was turned off. "It was good getting everybody out here before we left, too," he said.

It had been. Abby had a chance to say good-bye to her mother, Monique, and several other friends. And despite Abby's earlier apprehension, the relationship between Molly and Marshall seemed to be developing into something more than a brief flirtation.

Seth slipped his arms around her waist and smiled down at her. "How about if we go for a walk down by the lake before we take off?"

"Sure, let's do that."

They walked hand in hand down the path to the shore and settled on the Adirondack bench. Dilbert checked for ducks, but they were on the other side of the lake near the Nygaards'. She tilted her head against Seth's shoulder and tried not to fall into the trap of thinking about leaving. It was a small sacrifice in order to be with him. Instead, she thought about how much her life had changed—for the better—since she met him. "Can you believe it's only been a week since your duffel bag blew up my guest room?"

"Seems like a long time ago, doesn't it?" Seth concurred, draping an arm around her shoulders.

"It's been a pretty full week." After everything happened at Bainbridge Farm, they hadn't been able to dodge the media with a simple press release. A substantial part of Wednesday was spent in the banquet room at Dash's, answering questions and making statements about Andy's vendetta and its connection to

Kevin's murder. It might have been completely overwhelming if they hadn't taken Dilbert along. A "hero dog" story always received a lot of attention, and his charming, one-eyed face had been on television more than they had. Which was fine with them.

Seth's hand drifted lazily back and forth over her shoulder. "When I came to Emporia, I didn't know somebody was after me. Maybe I should've picked up a clue somewhere, but I was closed off, kind of going through the motions. I had the guys and the music, but I wasn't going anywhere or doing anything to make my life matter." He kissed her gently on the cheek. "Then I met you, and I won a whole new life."

"And almost lost it the next day," she reminded him with a nudge.

"It was about Andy, not about us. But it sure made us face a lot of tough situations right from the start, and we made the right decisions and ended up where we are now."

That was true. They'd figured out the depth of their feelings and the extent of their trust while most couples were still trying to decide if they should go on a second date. Abby shook her head. "You know, there might be something to be said for relationships where you can take it slow."

Seth chuckled. "Probably, but that's not how we do things."

"No, apparently not."

He shifted on the bench until he was facing her. "When you spend as much time onstage as I do, a lot of people think they know you. But they're just seeing the work, the performance. They know that piece of me, but nothing more. You saw who I really am, though, right from the beginning."

Abby couldn't resist the urge to tease him a little. "You always yell at people in the middle of the street?"

"No, you sort of caught me by surprise," he said with a smile. "But I might've gotten out of the way a little faster if I didn't catch a glimpse of you through the windshield. Slowed down my reaction time."

"You're such a bullshitter."

"I shit you not. I needed more than a split second to believe my eyes, and Cujo paid the price. But you're worth it."

If she was more precious to him than a 1997 Taylor Cujo, she was one lucky girl. She had to smile at the notion. "I like you better than the antique table that used to be in my guest room, too, so I guess we're even."

"No, not yet." Despite the joking, he had a thoughtful look in his eyes. "You did a tough thing, making changes to your life so we could be together. You really had to trust me, and believe I meant everything I said, even after I almost ruined everything."

She put her hand to the side of his face and rubbed her thumb over the stubble-covered dimple she loved so much. "It wasn't as hard as you think."

"It was, and I'm still amazed you'd do it for me." He drew a slow, deep breath and looked into her eyes. "I want you to know, without a doubt, you're not wrong to trust me. I'll always be here, and I love you more than I ever thought I could love anybody."

Abby was about to reply when he reached into his pocket. When he withdrew his hand, he kept it closed and rested his loose fist on his thigh.

"I don't want to pressure you to make another big decision, but I do want to show you how much you mean to me." He opened his hand to reveal a ring, its round diamond nestled in a bezel setting. Small emeralds decorated the band on either side of the central stone.

Abby's heart stopped beating for a few seconds, and then began racing. She looked up from the ring to find him watching her anxiously. "Seth, it's beautiful. But when did you have time to even think of a ring?"

"Tuesday, while you were talking to Sammy at the Shamrock, before we went to the farm. When I went back to talk to Joey, I asked him if I could have something shipped to his room at the motel. I called Mom to see if we could have the ring." He ran his thumb over the ring's gleaming white gold band. "It was my grandmother's."

An invisible fist squeezed the breath from her lungs. He was giving her his grandmother's ring. "You don't have to give me a ring for me to know I can trust you to be here."

"I know. It's not just that. This is what I want, too, more than I've ever wanted anything. It might be wrong to ask you to take another huge step with me so soon, but you already know time isn't a factor for me when I know something's right. If it's too much..." He began to close his fingers around the ring.

She put her hand over his. "It's not too much. And it's not a hard decision. It's the easiest thing in the world."

A smile spread across Seth's face. "You think being married to me will be easy?"

Married. Wow. "Probably not easy, but it'll always be an adventure."

He slipped the ring on her finger and held her hand open on his palm. She looked at it in wonder. It even fit.

"Adventure? Yeah, I'm pretty sure you can count on that."

His kiss was achingly tender, yet it still managed to warm her in all the right places. "I guess this means your mom and Joey approve, at least."

"Of course they do. Marsh knew, too, and I was sweating all week he'd let something slip. Especially after he drank his weight in beer last night." He lifted her hand to take another look at the ring. "You probably don't have any ideas yet, but we'll have to talk about when and where. It won't be a surprise I'm not a long engagement kind of guy, though."

"My thoughts exactly. As long as I can have Mom, Molly, and a few other people there, I don't care about the rest." She'd marry him right now if she could.

More post-engagement kissing followed. Abby was considering dragging her husband-to-be into the hammock when Dilbert nudged Seth's arm. He didn't want to be left out of this family moment.

Abby had something to give Seth, too. She was supposed to wait, but now the timing seemed ideal. "Come back up to the house. I have something for you."

Inside, she went to the suitcase still sitting by the side door and withdrew a blue package a little larger than a hardback book. She directed Seth to the couch and handed it to him.

"When did you have time to go shopping?" he asked. "I don't think you've been out of my sight for more than ten minutes at a time, and I know you didn't go to town without me." He picked at the tape. It was wrapped in several layers, in order to protect it in her suitcase.

"It's not really from me. It's from Marshall and Joey, and it was supposed to be a housewarming gift, whenever we decide on a house. But I don't think they'll mind."

The last of the paper fell away, and Seth held a wooden plaque in his hands. Mounted on the plaque was a six-inch section of the beautifully inlaid neck of the guitar formerly known as Cujo. The piece had the image of a dog, the character from Stephen King's book and movie. The top and bottom edges were irregular, but had been smoothed. Seth looked at it, his smile spreading to a grin, and finally he couldn't hold back the laughter. "How the hell did they manage this?"

Abby snuggled up to his side, one hand on his shoulder. "Do you think Marsh could just toss Cujo in the Dumpster? He worships guitars. He saved this piece, figuring he'd do something with it someday." Knowing Marshall, he'd probably planned to leave it on Seth's pillow some night, a la *The*

Godfather. "But after everything started happening, he had an idea and took it to the craft store in town. They made it for him."

Seth turned his attention from the symbolic piece of his beloved guitar to the rectangular brass plate below it. Abby watched him as he read. "In memory of Cujo, who gave his life for Seth and Abby." It even had the dates of the guitar's manufacture and destruction. "I can't believe those guys. It's just like them. Sincere, meaningful, hilarious, and kind of in the plastic vomit category, all at the same time."

Abby laughed. Exactly. She rewrapped the plaque and returned it to the suitcase.

After a final tour through the house, during which Abby admired the newly repaired guest room and thought she liked the light blue walls better, they loaded the suitcase into the Jeep.

Soon they were driving through Emporia, the town she loved. She looked at the ring on her hand, the man beside her and the dog with his silky black ears flapping in the breeze. She rested her hand on Seth's thigh, marveling again he was hers, and was nearly overwhelmed by a feeling of profound peace. This wasn't good-bye to Emporia. It was only see you later. She now knew adventure, danger — and even love — would find you when the time was right, no matter where you were. With that knowledge, she was ready to let her life extend beyond her previous boundaries, because home was where you made it. And their home was wherever the road took them.

"Make or Break"
(Seth & Abby's Song)

The blank page bleeds, the words won't come
You've been left high and dry by your muse
Time to burn it all down and throw it away
Tell yourself you've got nothing to lose

Better stay true to your vision
Ignore how they tell you to roll
'Cause if you don't listen to your own voice
It's the hook that will rip out your soul

Chorus:

Sometime life you're gonna make or break
And which one is all up to you
But if you should find you can't make it alone
Darlin', I'll always be there for you

You can't be scared to go against the grain
To blaze a new path, destination unknown
Then you'll find, when it's all said and done
The only voice in your head is your own

Repeat Chorus

~ About the Author ~

Lori spent her early years reading books in a tree in northern West Virginia. The 1980s and '90s found her and her husband moving around the Midwest, mainly because it was easier to move than clean the apartment. She currently lives in a northwestern suburb of the Twin Cities for reasons that escape her, but were probably good ones at the time.

Since arriving in Minnesota in 1996, she has worked in public libraries, written advertising copy for wastewater treatment equipment, and managed a holistic veterinary clinic. Her dogs are a big part of her life, and she has served or held offices in Golden Retriever and Great Pyrenees rescues, a humane society, a county kennel club, and her own chapter of Therapy Dogs International.

Parents of a grown son, Lori and her husband were high school sweethearts, and he manages to love her in spite of herself. Some of his duties include making sure she always has fresh coffee and safe tires, trying to teach her to use coupons, and convincing the state police to spring her from house arrest in her hotel room in time for a very important concert. That last one only happened once — so far — but she still really, really appreciates it.

Please visit her website at www.loriwhitwam.com, and check out the links for her blogs. Lori loves hearing from readers, and can be reached at ripleygold@gmail.com.

Find Lori here:

Facebook author page: http://www.facebook.com/loriauthor
Humor blog: http://www.fermentedfur.com
Writing blog: http://writecrastination.blogspot.com
Twitter: http://twitter.com/#!/ripleygold

~ Available Now from Etopia Press ~

Loose Cannon
© 2010 Kendal Flynn

This time, the op was different. This time, they had her son...

When Raeanne Springfield's son is kidnapped by Dmitryi Petrov, a ruthless enemy from the past, Raeanne finds herself thrown back into the dark world of covert operations she thought she left behind. But she's backed into a corner when Alex Dante, her former superior at the Counterintelligence Defense Agency, shows up to take her into protective custody. Should she obey orders from an agency that already betrayed her once, or slip back into the covert life and do whatever it takes to bring her boy home safely—even if it means endangering her heart?

Harder still—how to tell Alex Dante that Ryan's his son.

Between Petrov's demands, the agency's evasiveness, and Alex's whirlwind reentry into her life, Raeanne can trust no one but herself. Only after she gets Ryan back will she worry about fixing past mistakes. If she lives long enough to fix anything...

Available now in print and digital format.

~ Available Now from Etopia Press ~

Haunted Heart
© 2011 Carolyn Rosewood

All Rowena Sommers wants is a quite life away from Hollywood gossip and her vicious Oscar-winning ex-boyfriend Brett Fontaine. Her career and reputation in a shambles, thanks to Brett, Rowena returns home to restore her ancestral home and soak up some familiar, hometown sympathy. But having won a twenty-million-dollar defamation suit against Brett hasn't endeared her to the hometown fans, and the man she's hired to restore the old home is none other than the ex-jock who used her cruelly in high school to win a bet. And now a paranormal investigator is telling her the place may be haunted.

Van Whitney is no stranger to gossip. He's been struggling to keep his family's restoration business afloat, and when he agrees to restore Rowena's home, he vows to keep their relationship professional. His childhood friend has become a beautiful, sexy woman, but she attracts gossip like flies to honey. When strange things start happening at the house, Van discovers secrets upon secrets, and a plot that may be other than it seems. But his attraction to Rowena might be more dangerous than anything from the past…

Available now in digital format. Coming to print 2012

~ Available Now from Etopia Press ~

Full Throttle
© 2012 T. C. Archer

Fast cars and a smokin' hot passion...

Rex intends to own and drive his own car, but that will cost him millions up front. Last season was a disaster, thanks to a nasty break up, but it taught him a lesson and helped sharpen his focus on what he needed to do: Win every race. And stay away from pretty girls. The last thing he needed was to learn that his new head mechanic, Jimmy James, was the gorgeous redhead pin-up walking around his pit like it was some kind of dance floor.

Gail "Jimmy" James is the first female NASCAR mechanic. As if competing in a man's world isn't tough enough, her bombshell figure bellies her genius IQ, and the pit is no place for either. Nothing Jimmy knew about Rex Henderson the driver prepared her for Rex Henderson the man. But Jimmy has no time to dwell on her feelings as strange mechanical problems curse Rex's car. Whether sabotage or her own mistakes, Jimmy must stay one step ahead of trouble if she's going to keep her job, and keep her driver alive...

Available now in digital format. Coming to print 2012

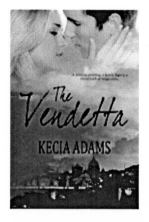

The Vendetta
© 2011 Kecia Adams

A missing painting, a family legacy, a blood oath of vengeance...

Italian businessman Nick Carnavale has spent his life seeking revenge for his father's murder. So when an old woman—with an agenda of her own and access to a rare painting—contacts him with a proposal, he jumps at the chance to launch his plans for vengeance, no matter the cost.

Ski-town barista Lisa Schumacher meets sexy Nick when she serves him espresso in the small art gallery-café where she works. Intrigued by her unusual customer, and ignorant of Nick's connection with her grandmother, Lisa shares dinner and a heart-stopping kiss with him.

Spurred by temptation and an unexpected invitation, Lisa takes up Nick's challenge to follow him to Rome and reunite with her one remaining family member. But when Lisa's grandmother unexpectedly dies, and her will dictates a marriage-of-convenience to Nick, Lisa must weigh her family's legacy against her dreams for her future. And as Nick draws ever closer to his revenge, they both must decide if love is stronger than the blood oath of vengeance—*la vendetta.*

Available now in digital format. Coming to print 2012

CPSIA information can be obtained at www.ICGtesting.com
Printed in the USA
BVOW05s1424070414

349965BV00002B/333/P